Praise for the novels of WIL McCARTHY

THE COLLAPSIUM

"The future as McCarthy sees it is a wondrous place. While there are amusing attributes and quirks to McCarthy's characters, the greater pleasures of this novel lie in its hard science extrapolations. McCarthy plays up his technical strengths by providing a useful appendix and glossary for the mathematically inclined reader."
—*Publishers Weekly*

"Ingenious and witty . . . as if Terry Pratchett at his zaniest and Larry Niven at his best had collaborated." —*Booklist*

"The author of *Bloom* once again demonstrates his talent for mind-expanding SF. Vibrant with humor, drama, and quirky ideas. Highly recommended." —*Library Journal*

"A fairy tale [with] . . . the most delicious superscience since Larry Niven's *Ringworld*. Stylistic diversity and hard scientific rigor blended with panache and striking imagination. McCarthy works hard to draw out pathos and character development. Genuinely exciting—a wonderful hoot."
—*The New York Review of Science Fiction*

"Fresh and imaginative. From a plausible yet startling invention, McCarthy follows the logical lines of sight, building in parallel the technological and societal innovations. 'Our Pick.' I wanted to visit this Queendom and meet these people." —*Science Fiction Weekly*

"[A] comedy of manners about High Physics, immortality, mad scientists, and murder. Great fun [with a] Wodehouse-meets-Doc-Smith aesthetic. As ingenious as the physics and special effects are, it is their juxtaposition to the wit and comedy that gives the novel its particular flavor. [A] playful, thoughtful book." —*Locus*

"Top notch. Terribly good fun. This very funny book has something for everyone." —*Entertainment Tomorrow*

"McCarthy knows his physics, and makes it extremely easy to suspend in disbelief. He creates a world that is both foreign and amazing . . . but in McCarthy's hands it appears all but inevitable." —*Mindjack Magazine*

"Wil McCarthy is a certified science fiction treasure, a real-life rocket scientist with a gorgeous writing style and rapier wit to boot. [While his] high-concept physics ideas . . . are deft and fascinating, it's his characters and story that make *The Collapsium* a book to savor, a complex and layered story in the grand tradition of science fiction's masters."
—Therese Littleton, Amazon.com

"Quite entertaining. The science is larger-than-life, and so are the characters." —*SF Site*

"I don't recall the last time a book made me laugh out loud. I did so here on page 146, and at the book's end I did so again . . . though my eyes were moist as well. McCarthy has created a story here that is distinctly Asimovian in flavor, though his voice is very much his own."
—*SF Revu*

"Prepare to use your grey matter. [McCarthy] fills his pages with lovingly rendered descriptions . . . but it is the strength of his scientific imagination that really shines through."
—*SFX Magazine* (UK)

"A most dazzling future. What follows is a mind-spinning struggle that recalls a Henry Fielding novel of manners, Michael Moorcock's epic sagas and the cosmic free-for-alls of Doc Smith. There's fascinating science aplenty, mad scientists, robots running amok. . . . What more could you want?"
—*The Weekly Australian*

"A decidedly odd but enjoyable mix of mannered, decadent comedy and far-out physics. I liked and was even prepared to believe in [it]." —*Ansible* (UK)

BLOOM

"*Bloom* is tense, dynamic, intelligent, offering a terrifyingly vivid view of how technology can rocket out of our control." —David Brin

"What clever and compelling science fiction! The *Bloom* future is all too believable." —James Gleick, author of *Chaos: Making a New Science*

"Wil McCarthy makes ideas jump. *Bloom* grabs you from the very first scene and doesn't let go till the last page. It's irresistible." —Walter Jon Williams

"Ultimately [humanity] must learn to ask new questions. The book's message is [that] in a universe stranger than we know, ignorance may be inevitable, but it's definitely not bliss." —*The New York Times*

"Swiftly paced, consistently inventive and tightly written. This is a novel that knows its business." —*The Washington Post*

"McCarthy has worked out a bleakly dramatic future. This is the kind of broad view of mankind's future and the universe reminiscent of Arthur C. Clarke." —*The Denver Post*

"The science is consistent and integral to the story, and the characters are much more plausibly drawn than are so many folks in [other speculative] fiction. In nearly every passage, we get another slice of the science of McCarthy's construction, and a deeper sense of danger and foreboding." —*The San Diego Union-Tribune*

By Wil McCarthy

THE
COLLAPSIUM

WIL McCARTHY

BANTAM BOOKS

THE COLLAPSIUM
A Bantam Book

PUBLISHING HISTORY
Ballantine/DelRey hardcover edition / August 2000
Bantam paperback edition / December 2002

ISBN 0-553-58443-X

Published simultaneously in the United States and Canada

Bantam Books are published by Bantam Books, a division of Random
House, Inc. Its trademark, consisting of the words "Bantam Books" and the
portrayal of a rooster, is Registered in U.S. Patent and Trademark Office
and in other countries. Marca Registrada. Bantam Books, 1540 Broadway,
New York, New York 10036.

PRINTED IN THE UNITED STATES OF AMERICA
OPM   10   9   8   7   6   5   4   3   2   1

for Quentin and Casey,

because I said so

acknowledgments

I'd like to extend my heartfelt thanks to Chris Schluep, Shelly Shapiro, Scott Edelman, and Simon Spanton for understanding and believing in this project. Wouldn't trade you guys for diamonds. Also, for their help in nailing down the basic ideas on which the novel rests, I'm indebted to Gary Snyder, Richard Powers, and especially Shawna McCarthy for being so difficult to please. The many people who helped with technical details are listed separately in Appendix C, but I'll extend special thanks here to Bernhard Haisch for inspiration and for serving as a brilliant sounding board, and to Sid Gluckman for making a place where imagination matters.

For assistance on matters of Tongan language and culture, I'm grateful to Lonely Planet's Errol H., and Vincenc Riullop and Periques des Palottes for information about Catalonia.

Also many thanks and apologies to those who faced the early drafts of this story, including Geoffrey A. Landis, Stanley Schmidt, Richard Powers, Maureen F. McHugh, and Cathy, my long-suffering copilot.

book one

once upon a
matter crushed

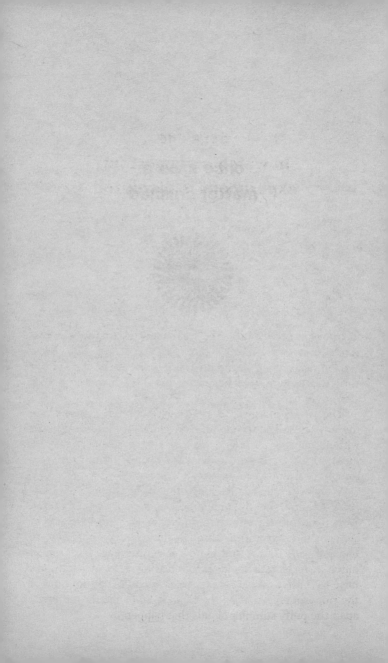

chapter one

in which an important experiment is disrupted

In the eighth decade of the Queendom of Sol, on a minia-ture planet in the middle depths of the Kuiper Belt, there lived a man named Bruno de Towaji who, at the time of our earliest attention, was beginning his 3088th morning walk around the world.

The word "morning" is used advisedly here, since along the way he walked through the day and night and back again without pausing to rest. It was a *very* small planet, barely six hundred meters across, circled by an even tinier "sun" and "moon" of Bruno's own design.

Walk with him: see his footpath cutting through the blossomy meadow, feel the itch of pollens in your eyes and nose. Now pass through into the midday forest, with its shafts of sunlight filtering warmly through the canopy. The trees are low and wide, citrus and honeysuckle and dogwood, not so much a shady, mushroom-haunted wilderness as a compromise with physical law—taller trees would reach right out of the troposphere. As it is, the highest limbs brush and break apart the puffy summer clouds that happen by.

Pass the Northern Hills; watch the stream trickle out between them; see the forest give way to willows at its bank. The bridge is a quaint little arch of native wood; on the far side lie the grasslands of afternoon, the vegetable gardens tended by stoop-backed robots, the fields of wild barley and maize tended by no one, lit by slantwise rays. Behind you, the sun dips low, then slips behind the planet's sharply curved horizon. Despite the refraction of atmospheric hazes, darkness is sudden, and with it the terrain grows rocky—not jagged but hard and flat and boulder-strewn, dotted with hardy Mediterranean weeds. But here the stream winds back again, and as evening fades to night the channel of it widens out into cattail marshland and feeds, finally, into a little freshwater sea. Sometimes the moon is out, drawing long white reflections across the silent water, but tonight it's only the stars and the Milky Way haze and the distant, pinpoint gleam of Sol. All of history is down there; if you like, you can cover the human race with your hand.

It grows colder; realize the planet shields you from the little sun—the only local heat source—with the deadly chill of outer space so close you could literally throw a rock into it. But the beach leads around to twilight meadows, and the horizon ruddies up with scattered light, and then suddenly it's morning again, the sun breaking warmly above the planet's round edge. And there is Bruno's house: low, flat, gleaming marble-white and morning-yellow. You've walked a little over two kilometers.

Such was Bruno's morning constitutional, very much like all his others. Sometimes he'd fetch a coat and take the other route, over the hills, over the poles, through cold and dark and cold and hot, but that was mainly a masochism thing; the polar route was actually shorter, and a good deal less scenic.

He'd already eaten breakfast; the walk was to aid his digestion, to invigorate his mind for the needs of the day: his experiments. The front door opened for him. Inside, robot servants stepped gracefully out of his way, providing a clear path to the study, bowing as he passed, though he'd told them a thousand times not to. He grumbled at them wordlessly as he passed. They didn't reply, of course, though their bronze and tin-gray manikin bodies hummed and clicked with faint life. Mechanical, unburdened by imagination or want, they were utterly dedicated to his comfort, his satisfaction.

Another door opened for him, closed behind him, vanished. He waved a hand, and the windows became walls. Waved another, and the ceiling lights vanished, the floor lights vanished, the desk and chairs and other furnishings became optical superconductors: invisible. Projective holography created the illusion of his day's apparatus: fifty collapsons, tiny perfect cubes visible as pinpoints of Cerenkov light, powder-blue and pulsing faintly, circling the holographic planet in a complex dance of swapping orbits.

He'd spent the past week assembling these, after his last batch had gone sour.

Assembling them? Certainly.

Imagine a sphere of di-clad neutronium, shiny with Compton-scattered light. It's a sort of very large atomic nucleus; a billion tons of normal matter crushed down to a diameter of three centimeters so that the protons and electrons that comprise it are bonded together into a thick neutron paste. Left to itself it would, within nanoseconds, explode back into a billion tons of protons and electrons, this time with considerable outward momentum. Hence the cladding: crystalline diamond and fibrediamond and then crystalline again, with a bound layer of wellstone on top. Tough stuff indeed; breaking the neutrons free of their little jail was difficult enough that Bruno had never heard of its happening by accident.

These "neubles" were the seeds of seeds—it took eight of them, crushed unimaginably farther, to build a collapson—and the little "moon" was actually just Bruno's storage bin: ten thousand neubles held together by their own considerable gravity. Another fifteen hundred formed the core of the tiny planet, a sphere about half a meter across, with a skeleton of wellstone built on top of it, fleshed out with a few hundred meters of dirt and rock and an upper layer neatly sculpted by robots and artisans.

Bruno was very wealthy, you see.

But instead of moons and planets, one could also make black holes of these things, black holes held rigidly into stable lattices, a phase of matter known as "collapsium."[1]

Bruno had been the first to do this, and was still doing it these seventy years later. He'd traded his soul for it, in some sense. Traded a whole phase of his life, anyway: his love, his adopted home on Tongatapu. But what a thing to swap them for: the bending and twisting of spacetime to his personal whims. The *potential* of it . . .

That was the exciting part, and in truth, he'd be happy enough to direct the enterprise, leaving the gruntwork to a horde of employees or devoted grad students or something. The biggest problem was that almost no one was patient enough to work the equations, even to deduce which structures were stable and which were not, much less to derive the properties of the stable ones from first principles. The work was *hard*, and there were very few graduates to be had for it. That was the biggest problem. The second biggest was the sort of accidents you got when collapsium experiments went awry, and the third biggest problem was the twenty billion people who got understandably upset when this occurred.

So of the handful of people competent to perform the research, most stuck contentedly to the safer paths, the trodden paths, the paths on which accidents were far rarer than fame and fortune. Plodders, he sometimes called them.

He settled down in his invisible chair, feeling it subtly reshape itself beneath him. Not soft but *smart*, a solid thing that yielded only for him. He cracked his knuckles, flexed his shoulders, jiggled his wrists like an old-fashioned strongman

1. See Appendix A: Collapsium, page 361

preparing to lift something heavy. He did these things slowly; an observer might almost have said *grimly*. It didn't matter that the actual lifting was done by electromagnetic grapples; he would submerge himself in that same mental space where athletes go, where the body obeys the mind, where stiffness and pain and time are reluctant to penetrate. On your marks . . .

Bruno had tried to be one of the plodders, he really had. He'd spent years making his telecom collapsiters faster and better and cheaper, building the Iscog, building his fortune. But all that was *boring* compared to what he really wanted, which was to build an *arc de fin* capable of snatching photons from the end of time itself. Time *had* an end—the state equations made that clear enough—but what *sort* of end was the subject of endless noise and conjecture. And why grumble and theorize when you could just open up a window and see the whole business with your own two eyes?

Hence these fifty collapsons, with their prancing orbits and their ghostly Hawking/Cerenkov glow. Not to *build* the arc—what a laugh!—but to build a tool that might build a tool that might build a *piece* of the arc, or at least point to a method by which it might be built. Bruno expected the project to last many thousands of years.

He was all but immortal, by the way, and like everyone else he was still struggling to come to terms with it. It wasn't so unequivocally wonderful a thing, really, a society in which death was always by suicide or freak accident or carefully concocted murder, in which the rare childhood death deprived its victim not of years or decades of life, but millennia. Such disparity, the very opposite of fairness. But again, the *potential* . . .

Was it strange to be excited, even after all these years? The eternal question, worn smooth with age: Was obsession a gift? He breathed deeply, preparing to submerge.

Bruno's fifty collapsons weren't stable in their orbits and couldn't remain there forever without some sort of collision or ejection event messing the trajectories up and making a ruin of all his hard work. So he compared them against the blueprint in his mind, pressed his fingers against the invisible desk to bring up an interface, and triggered the gravity induction mechanisms.

With them he grabbed a collapson, watched it jerk and flutter on his display. The forces he could apply here were weak, nothing compared to the gravity of the collapsons themselves, but of course the collapsons were in free fall. Weak forces, adding up over time, were just as effective as strong ones applied suddenly. And Bruno had learned to be a very patient man indeed. Slowly, he took hold of a second collapson, nudged it toward the first, then nudged it again a few seconds later to reduce the closing velocity. With ponderous momentum they drifted together, and finally touched. Their binding produced a flash of green; they continued on as a single joined piece. He grabbed a third collapson and carefully added it to the structure, grabbed a fourth and fifth.

The other collapsons seemed almost alarmed, their orbital square dance taking place now as if on a gigantic quilt being ponderously dragged and folded around them. Bruno's movements were careful, practiced; he'd done this hundreds of times, made enough mistakes to feel out the limits and breakpoints and failure modes, to know what he could and couldn't get away with. Before his network gate had gone down and stopped the endless questions and exhortations of his fellow man, he'd often been asked why he did this part by hand, why he didn't devise some software to handle these exacting manipulations. If the question came from a scientist or technician he'd generally ignored it, but for the craftsmen and artisans and landscape designers he'd had a ready reply: Why don't *you*? The truth was, if he could automate this creative process he'd do it, and become the Queendom's richest human all over again.

He found himself singing, quietly, under his breath. Muttering, really; he had no real gift for song, nor any strong passion, but it bubbled up sometimes, unbidden, while he worked.

Malgrant ens feia anar a església
era un món petit . . . i meravellós
un món de . . . guixos de colors
que pintàveu vós . . .

An old lullaby, he supposed. Catalan words, extinct in the absence of Catalan notes to carry them along. It didn't bother
him that he was probably mangling it, though he briefly imagined his parents wincing and rolling in their graves. Such
thoughts were fleeting, quickly crushed beneath the jugger-
naut of the business at hand.

Slowly, his design took shape: something like a bucket, a
fan, a lens. The shape wasn't useful in and of itself; most collapsium structures weren't. But to get to the shape you
wanted, you had to pass through stable intermediate designs,
adding bricks one by one without upsetting the system's precarious equilibrium. Often, this meant building complex
shapes that "fell" into simpler ones when completed, as a key
and a lock might fuse to extrude a single, solid doorknob. Or
in this case, a kind of spacetime crowbar able to "pry" bits of
vacuum apart to see what lay beneath. Or so he hoped!

Before the assembly was half complete, though, an alarm
bell chimed. This was a sound he'd chosen carefully, one that
penetrated, demanding attention. The gravity wave alarm.
Grunting, he thumbed a lighted yellow circle, increasing
magnification, leaning forward to scrutinize the display, to
isolate the source of the anomaly.

He didn't find it. Everything was right where it should be,
his little Cerenkov pinpoints all well within spatial and vibrational tolerances. The warning chimed again, though, louder,
the perturbation stronger, and Bruno cursed, because the
crowbar-to-be was in a very delicate stage right now, its collapsium lattice supported by little more than good intentions.
He grabbed the ends of the structure, hoping to steady it, but
through the desk's sensory pads he felt a mild shudder, then
another, stronger one. The warning chimed a third time, and
this perturbation *had* to be external, because soon his project

was waving like a seaweed, the collapsons growing uncertain as their holes' gravitic interactions wandered in and out of phase.

"Excuse me, sir," the house announced through a softly lit speaker that appeared in the wall. "A ship is approaching."

The collapsium slipped from his fingers and fell in on itself, an origami structure folding and wrinkling into a spitwad of glowing dots.

"Blast," Bruno said. Then the dots winked out one by one, and a few seconds later it was finished and gone.

"ETA, seven minutes," the house said, providing a flat schematic wallplate that showed the spaceship's approach vector in relation to planet, sun, and moon.

Bruno sighed. The newer, much larger black hole he'd just created was difficult to detect, lacking the clear emissions of a collapson, but he found it by feel, charged it with a stream of protons and then, with a grunt of disgust, hurled it off toward his *other* storage bin, the "wastebasket" hypermass orbiting his world a thousand kilometers out. The trajectory was fine, nowhere near that of the approaching ship. Maybe he should have arranged to graze them with it; a warning shot, a demand for apology. But no, such horseplay could too easily go wrong, else he wouldn't be stuck out here in the first place.

He sighed again, already trying to convince himself that seven days' lost labor meant nothing, that he had plenty more time—infinitely more—where that came from. The dollar expenditure was actually harder to accept: two hundred neubles down the drain, literally, along with the twenty he'd wasted last week, and the eight last month, and the twenty more he'd thrown—at one time or another—into the wastebasket for this or that reason. The moon grew smaller, ever smaller, in his sky, and while he certainly had the money to buy more substance for it, the logistical difficulty of getting it *delivered* was daunting. His last shipment had required the efforts of tens of thousands of people, whole corporations commandeered for the purpose, and altogether the enterprise had cost even more than the planet itself. Insanely selfish extravagances—the leading vice of the wealthy. But he couldn't postpone the next purchase forever.

Cursing once more, Bruno waved the floor and ceiling lights back up. Glass windows appeared in the walls, admitting the morning sun once again. His furniture reverted to wood—wellwood, anyway—its colored controls and displays vanishing, leaving smooth surfaces behind. A couple of murals appeared beneath the stenciled images of telescopes and rocketships on the walls. This was a plain room—small, uncluttered and maybe a little old-fashioned—exactly as Bruno felt a study should be.

"I apologize for not detecting the vessel sooner," the house said with quiet, reflexive contrition.

"It's all right," Bruno grumbled, and surprised himself by meaning it. Nothing genuinely new had happened around here for a very long time. There'd been no reason to expect . . . anything, really.

"The vessel is approaching much faster than a neutronium barge would do," the house went on, as if feeling the need to explain itself. "Anticipating nothing of the kind, I'd set the detection radii much too close. The failure of your experiment was likely a direct result."

Bruno waved himself a door and exited into the living room, a mess of models and food containers and discarded clothing, which was exactly as *that* should be, but seeing it now he nodded, pursed his lips and said, "Stop apologizing and clean this up. If we're to have company, we must be presentable, yes? What's the ID on the ship?"

"None available, sir. Our network gate is nonfunctional. For four years now."

"Oh. Right."

The robot servants were neither wholly autonomous nor wholly appendages of the house software, neither self-aware nor rigidly programmed. Creatures of silent intuition, they danced through their chores like dreams, like puppets in some tightly choreographed ballet. They knew just what paths to take, what joints to swivel or extend, their economy of motion perfect. They knew just where to put everything, too; most of the clutter was faxware and went back into the fax for recycling, but some objects were original or natural or otherwise sentimental, and each found a place on a shelf or table, or in his bedroom closet around the corner. Speaking of which . . .

"Seal that," he said, gesturing at the bedroom door. It slid closed at once, merged with the wall, sprouted bright mural paints—nonrepresentational.

He grunted his approval, then asked, "ETA?"

"Five minutes, twenty seconds."

He grunted again, less approving this time. The house had standing orders never to mark time in seconds—there were just too many of them, a whole eternity's worth. But under the circumstances, he supposed it had little choice.

Visitors.

Visitors! Suddenly alarmed, he sniffed himself. "Damn, I probably stink. These clothes are probably ugly. Bathe and dress me, please. Quickly!"

The robots were there so fast they might well have anticipated the request. Cap and vest and tunic and breeches were torn from Bruno's body and hurled into the fax orifice for recycling. He forced himself to relax, to let his arms be lifted, his torso turned. The robots, with their faceless expressions of infinite gentleness, would rather die than cause him the slightest injury or discomfort, and any resistance on his part would only slow them down, make them gentler still. He let them work, and in another moment their metal hands were buffing him with sponges and damp, scented cloths. A wellstone grease magnet was stroked seven times through his hair, becoming a heated styling comb on the eighth stroke. The fax produced fresh clothing—suitable for company— that smoothed and buttoned itself around him as the robots fussed.

He refused an application of blush.

"Is it landing here? Nearby?" he asked.

"Its course indicates a touchdown in the meadow, forty

meters to the east. It is recommended that you remain indoors until this procedure is complete."

"Hmm? Yes, well. Full transparency on the roof and east
wall, please."

Obligingly, a third of the house turned to glass. To actual
glass, yes—wellstone was an early form of programmable
matter[2]—and if danger threatened it could just as easily turn
to impervium or Bunkerlite, or some other durable superreflector.

"There's a good house," he murmured approvingly, his eyes
scanning the now-visible sky.

Despite the interruption, despite the loss of his collapsium and the rudeness of this too-swift approach, Bruno
found himself almost anticipating the landing, the arrival of
visitors. Almost. It was a long time since he'd last had company, and that had just been the men from the neutronium
barge, eager for a breath of fresh air before turning their ship
around and faxing themselves back home.

One of them, newly rich and bursting with gratitude, had
given Bruno a gift: a neuble-sized diamond ball filled with
water instead of neutronium. There'd been algae and bacteria
and near-microscopic brine shrimp inside, a whole ecology
that needed only light to function, perhaps eternally. "In case
you get lonely, sir," the man had said. Indoors, though, Bruno's
light-dark cycles were irregular, and the thing had died on his
shelf in a matter of weeks. His last human interaction. A
lesson?

The morning sky shone brightly through the glass. Bruno
asked for a reticle to indicate the ship's position, and the
house obligingly cast up a circle of green light the size of a
dinner plate, which barely moved and inside which he could
see nothing. Soon there were glints of yellow-white at the
center, though, sunlight reflecting from bright metal, and in
another minute he could see an actual dot beyond the shallow

2. See Appendix A: Wellstone, page 363

blue-white haze of his atmosphere. The dot resolved into a little toy ship, then a big toy ship drifting high above the sky—a wingless metal teardrop spilling outside the boundaries of the green reticle—and finally, with alarming swiftness, it swelled to something the size of his house and burst though the feathery cirrus layer and the haze beneath it. Clouds rolled off its bright burnished skin, seeming to wrinkle and snap in the blur of a gravity deflection field. Jets fired, little blasts of yellow-hot plasma that scorched his meadow grass white, then black, in tight bull's-eye circles. A shadow raced from the horizon to throw itself beneath the vehicle as the space between it and terra firma shrank to meters, centimeters, nothing.

There was no thump of impact, no solid confirmation of landing until the maneuvering jets darkened and the shimmer of the deflection field snapped away into clear focus. The sounds of reentry and landing had been no louder than a breeze through the treetops. Skillfully done.

What fixed Bruno's attention, though, was the seal imprinted on the side of that gleaming hull: a blue, white, and green Earth shaded by twin palms, with three more planets hovering in the background. And hanging above them all, a crown of monocrystalline diamond.

"Door," he said, standing in front of a row of shelves, looking past them at the landing site. The house seemed to hesitate for a moment, as if wondering whether to open the wall right there—carefully, of course, so as not to drop or break anything—or to make him go a few steps around. Which choice would minimize his inconvenience and displeasure? But the decision itself, teetering precariously at a balance point, took long enough that Bruno became annoyed anyway.

"Door!" he snapped, when almost two seconds had expired. The wall before him opened instantly, robots rushing quietly forward to steady the shelved vases and picture frames, to whisk the little drink table out of his way. He stepped through the opening, out into dewy, meadow-fragrant air.

The side of the ship was marred by a rectangular seam, ringed all around with rivets. No wellstone, that, but honest metal, a passive device for containing air, for holding out vacuum. A hatch. Presently, light fanned from its upper edge, and the hatch swung downward, revealing a carpeted staircase affixed to its inner surface. This made contact with the ground, forming a perfect little exitway.

On the other side stood a pair of dainty robots, delicate-looking things with frilled tutus ringing their waists and feathered caps slanted *just so* on their heads, their metal hands bearing ceremonial halberds that looked as if they might be twisted out of true by a strong breeze or a harsh word. In perfect synchrony, the pair descended the staircase and came straight forward, straight toward Bruno. The ship had been set down with even greater care than he'd first realized, set down by entities obsessed as much with decorum and pomp as with aero- and astrodynamics.

Ten meters away, they stopped, clicked their metal heels, and bowed.

"Declarant-Philander Bruno de Towaji," one of them said— or maybe both, in too-perfect synchrony to distinguish. "We bring you the greetings of Her Majesty, and a request for your immediate audience. You are to come with us."

It was always strange to see robots speak, because they did it so rarely and because they had no mouths. By royal decree, it was Uncouth to build machines with faces, or hair, or genitalia, except for the express purpose of sexual perversion, which was itself Uncouth and needed no further encouragement.

"Excuse me?" Bruno said.

"You are to come with us," the robots repeated, their joined voices fluid, elegant, courtly in a mechanical, clockwork-ballerina sort of way.

"Really. Am I to know why?"

"It is a matter of utmost importance, Declarant. The explanation of it is beyond our tasking."

"Beyond your tasking. I see." Bruno nodded sagely, thinking to wonder whether his image was being recorded or transmitted, and if so, whether he looked dignified and wise or simply hermitty, possessed of too much hair and beard. "Her Majesty isn't with you, then, all the way out here. And why should she be?"

Why indeed, when she could simply order him around by proxy? Feeling a sudden, petty anger, he whisked off his cap and threw it at their golden feet. "Pick that up. Deliver it. It's my reply. If Her Majesty wishes an audience, she is cordially invited to enjoy it here. My work, alas, does not permit me to travel at this time."

The robots considered that.

"Her Majesty requests your immediate presence," they finally said. "Groundless refusal is both Uncouth and inconvenient. There is no reason to be rude."

"Rude? Not at all. Not a bit of it. Tell Her Majesty that it pleases me, as always, to answer her every request. The requests of robot messengers, however, will hardly obligate me. You've interrupted important work, *expensive* work, without explanation or apology. Her Majesty is ill served by such tools as you, and is invited to petition me by the much more reliable method of face-to-face communication. Unfortunately, my network gate is down. I'm afraid you'll have to go back and fetch her in the flesh."

He drew a breath, ready to say more, but stopped himself. Baiting robots was a fool's hobby—they had no feelings to hurt, only needs and obligations to fulfill. They could be frustrated, in the same way that a deaf man could be shouted at: They saw you doing it, knew what it was, but would never be affected in the desired way. But by the same token, this made them ideal absorbers of displaced anger. Killing the messenger was fine and dandy, when the messenger was never alive in the first place, when any fax machine could recycle its smashed components back into the original robot. Not "good as new," but actually, literally new. So he supposed a little baiting was harmless enough.

Wordlessly, the robots turned and went back up their staircase, which lifted and closed behind them with a faint clunk and hiss.

Bruno would regret this, or course. He would add it to his collection of regrets. But it did feel good.

He retreated a bit, waiting for some indication of impending liftoff before hiding himself back in the house again. But the ship sat, and sat, and sat some more, and finally he understood: There was a fax gate in there, a fax machine coupled to a high-bandwidth network gate linked to the Inner-System Collapsiter Grid, the Iscog. The robots were faxing themselves back to Her Majesty's throneroom to deliver his "invitation," and clearly, since the ship remained, they expected her to take him up on it.

His heart quickened a little. So much for his clever manners.

Bruno had his own, fully functional fax machine, of course. For years he'd been getting his clothing and equipment that way, built up atom by atom from stored patterns and extruded whole through orifices inside and outside the house. It produced much of his food as well, supplementing the fruits of his stubbornly anachronistic garden.

The gate could even reproduce a person; he'd done the old parlor trick a time or two, spending the afternoon with a perfect copy of himself. Well, *two* copies spending time together, actually, with the original Bruno having been destroyed in the reading process. But this amounted to much the same thing in the end.

With copies, you were supposed to hit it off at first and then quickly get on your nerves, but Bruno had found his own company alarmingly dull; what did he have to teach himself that he didn't already know? He could send a copy off to learn new things, he supposed, but he wouldn't want to *be* that copy, sent away from the work that really mattered to him, and of course one of him would have to do just that. Invariably, he reconverged the copies within the hour, faxing them back into himself, concluding that maintaining one

Bruno de Towaji was quite trouble enough. Hence the disinterest in repairing his failed network gate.

The silence of network abstinence had been nice, too. He'd better enjoy the last of it while he still could, before the robots came back with company, or else hauled him through their gate by main force.

He was just turning to reenter the house when, to his utter surprise, the hatch opened once more on the side of the metal teardrop, swinging its staircase out and down, framing in its doorway the figure of none other than Her Majesty herself. The robots followed at a respectful distance as she descended the steps.

Staring stupidly, Bruno computed: Earth, regardless of season, was always at least seven light-hours away. For the robots to return there and come back with Her Majesty in tow should have taken fourteen hours. Even if she'd been on *Jupiter* for some reason, it would have taken more than twelve, possibly a lot more, depending on where the planet was in its orbit. Ergo, she must have sent her pattern ahead, timing it to arrive when the ship landed. Had she anticipated his refusal? She might simply have broadcast her image into the void, instructing the robots to capture and instantiate it if the need arose. There was something cold-bloodedly logical about that sort of reasoning, and that was how he knew it was true. *Quod erat demonstrandum.*

The spaceship's stairs were carpeted in red, and their metal base extruded still more carpet, its end snaking out ahead of the Queen across scorched grass and flowers until finally it stopped, seemed to gather itself for a moment, and then extruded a low platform, a little marble pedestal rising up as if exposed by receding tidewaters. Her Majesty mounted this platform, and the robots assumed stations on either side of her, ceremonial halberds at the ready. Ceremonial, hell; she was here, and they carried no other obvious weaponry. Those blades could probably cleave the planet in two.

The robots spoke more haughtily than before. "Declarant-Philander Bruno de Towaji, you may present yourself before

Her Majesty Tamra-Tamatra Lutui, the Virgin Queen of All Things. You are encouraged to kneel."

Clad in the shade of purple forbidden to all others, with the diamond crown atop her head and the Scepter of Earth in her left hand and the Rings of Mars, Jupiter, and Saturn on the fingers of her right, she was black haired and walnut skinned and scowling deeply. She was beautiful and terrible and in a bad mood, and could destroy him with a word.

"Hi, Tam," he said lamely, then sighed and threw himself to his knees.

in which an urgent
plea is heard

.

She was a figurehead, by the way. She couldn't *literally* de-stroy him, have him killed, have his pattern erased and his name stricken from every stone and pillar, but she could make his personal and professional life difficult enough that he might wish she had.

"Don't 'Hi' me," she snapped as he knelt there before her. "Rise. Approach."

Ground moisture had soaked through the knees of Bruno's trousers. Rising, he wiped them absently with his hand, then caught himself and wiped the hand on his vest, in case she demanded to shake it or something. Approaching gingerly, he spread his arms.

"My world, Your Majesty. Welcome."

She nodded regally. "Yes. Your world." Then she cocked her head, looked at him strangely. "Are you all right? Why are you leaning like that?"

He blinked. "Leaning? Ah, it's the curvature. The planet being so small, local vertical swings a full degree every six meters. Your 'up' is not the same as mine. The trees—" He pointed. "—seem to tilt away from you as well, more so the farther away they are. You see how they're angled?"

The Queen of Sol surveyed the horizon, nodding absently. "I wondered about that. The way the ground slopes away, I feel as if I'm standing on a mountaintop. Is that your house down there?"

"Er, yes," Bruno replied, following her gaze. "It isn't 'down,' though; the ground's quite level here. Shall we go inside?"

She nodded. "Somewhere we can sit, yes. There's much to discuss."

"I'd gathered."

He led her back across the meadow, dainty robots trailing behind. Her velvet skirts smoothed a trail in the grass as she walked, the sunlight full in her round face. Even her long shadow was more regal than lanky, a Queen among its kind. Bruno couldn't keep his eyes forward. Didn't try.

"It's closer than I thought," the queen remarked as they approached the house. "Smaller. You've dwelt in a shack all these years? A hovel?"

Bruno shrugged. "The planet size again. If the house were any broader, the curvature of the floor would become apparent. You couldn't roll a ball bearing on my floor—it's gravitationally flat—but indoors I find the eye prefers straight lines and right angles."

"Add another level, perhaps?"

He shook his head. "The upper story would feel less gravity, and a lot less air pressure. Thirty percent less. The gradients are steep on a planet this small." He pointed to the snow-capped Northern Hills. "The air's thin up there. And cold."

She smiled. "Those little things?"

"My Himalayas. I'm quite comfortable, Tamra, really, and I don't think you've come here to remodel the planet."

Bruno waved for a door as they approached. It opened, and they stepped through. The house had remodeled itself in his absence, throwing down trails of red carpet joining furniture more elegant than he'd normally employ. Chandeliers of gold and diamond hung from a ceiling striped with stained-glass murals of green and tan and blue, stylized scenes from Her Majesty's native Tonga. They moved and changed, almost too slowly to see.

Presently, a ring of speakers formed along the walls at chest level, and began playing "Thank God for the Revival of Monarchy," which was the Queendom of Sol's quite popular unofficial anthem; the official one was the dreary "Praise upon Her," which was almost never played. Or hadn't been, anyway, when Bruno's network gate last functioned. He supposed fashion had probably overtaken such musical preferences by now, along with all the clothing and furnishing styles he knew best. Fashion was always doing things like that, making the most ordinary things seem ridiculous and the most ridiculous seem ordinary. Immortality had yet to bestow any higher aesthetic upon the Queendom, although he supposed that, too, could have changed in his absence.

It was nineteen years since he'd quit Tamra's court, eleven since he'd quit civilization altogether, trading it for this silence, this peace and solitude. Out here, he *wasn't* peerless or depended on. Just alone.

He realized he should speak, behave as a host. "Uh, refreshment? Food, drink? I have vegetables fresh from the soil."

She wrinkled her nose. "Still doing that, are you? Thank you, no. A glass of water, perhaps. Shall we sit?"

"Oh. Yes. Forgive me." He indicated a chair beside a low table, waited until she'd seated herself, waited until she'd nodded permission for him to join her, and finally sat in the chair across. A gently clicking robot appeared, whisked a pair of glasses of ice water onto the table between them, and was gone. "You look well, Tamra. I mean that."

"You look good yourself," she said, her voice betraying a hint of pique. "You always look good."

Shrug. "Everyone does. But I've dressed up!"

She studied him for a few moments before replying, "Yes.

Actually, you look like you're playing yourself in a melodrama. The gray hair is new. It suits you, I suppose."

Her tone, while sharp, was not unkind. Like her expression and her too-correct posture, it bespoke a mingling of amusement and ire and haste, as well as a kind of bruised dignity. He'd left her court without permission, after all. Without even a proper good-bye, for he'd feared his resolve would crumble. It had been a cowardly, disrespectful, unkind thing to do, and whatever business drew her here now . . . Well, he'd made her jump through hoops for it, hadn't he? What urgency would permit a queen to beggar herself before such a determined expatriate?

"Something's happened," he prompted. "Something awful."

She shook her head, but her eyes looked nervous, uncertain. "Not awful, no. Inconvenient. A . . . project of ours has gone somewhat awry. No one's been hurt, but there's a . . . cleanup effort that isn't progressing well. I thought perhaps you'd have some advice for us."

Bruno wasn't sure he understood, and said so. "My so-called expertise is in collapsium engineering, Highness. Industrial accidents are hardly . . ." He caught her expression. "Oh, I see. It *is* a collapsium accident."

She nodded, pursing her lips, and for a moment Bruno felt paralyzed by her beauty, unable to think, unworthy to speak. The human brain was said to be *wired* for monarchy, for hierarchy, for the elevation and admiration of single individuals, and now the truth of this hit Bruno like a heavy gilded pillow. There wasn't any one thing about Tamra Lutui—not her long black hair or the tilt of her head or the gentle swell of her hips and thighs and bosom—that should affect him so. He knew her very well indeed, well enough that her pout shouldn't fill him with this boyish, trembling awe. But she was Queen, and that made all the difference in the worlds.

Her Majesty, being well familiar with this reaction, this social allergy, waited politely for it to subside.

"Yes," she said finally. "A collapsium accident. You should

be proud of us, Bruno; we've finally attempted something big. Too big, evidently."

Bruno clucked and shook his head. "Ambition has to imply some willingness to fail, Tam. It isn't a stretch, otherwise. You mustn't regret your mistakes."

"This one I regret, Declarant," she said coolly. "That we can hope for a favorable outcome is immaterial. Some errors are inexcusable." With these words she fixed a mild glare on him: Had *he* no regrets?

"Fair enough," he said, raising his palms in immediate surrender lest he be forced, in some way, to explain or apologize for himself. He had good reasons for all of it. Didn't he? "Er, perhaps you should tell me what you've been doing. With the collapsium, I mean."

Her Majesty rapped the tabletop. "Sketch pad, please." Obligingly, the table darkened, and where her finger traced, colored lines and dots and circles appeared. "This is the sun, all right? I can't draw well, but these here are the orbits of Venus, Earth, and Mars."

In fact, for hasty finger paintings her renditions were fairly accurate.

"Sol is *big* in the inner system, and if two planets are aligned with the sun between them—opposition, they call it?—then network signals have to be sent around via satellite. There's a time delay associated with the extra distance, and this implies a cost."

"Yes," Bruno agreed in a knowing tone. He'd laid the foundations for the collapsiter grid himself—besting previous network bandwidths by six orders of magnitude—and he understood a thing or two about how the system worked.

Tamra looked up at him but declined to glare. "Some of our people have worked out a fix, Declarant, by putting an annulus of collapsium around the sun. The 'Ring Collapsiter,' as Declarant Sykes has named it."

"Ah!" Bruno said, grasping the idea at once. The speed of light was much higher in the Casimir supervacuum of a collapsium lattice than in the half-filled energy states of normal space. A *ring* of collapsium encircling the sun could admit signals at one side, expel them at the other, and reduce the time not only of the trip around, but of the trip *through* as well. Like a highway bypass where the speed limit was a trillion times higher than in the crowded streets of downtown. Why crawl through when you could blaze the long way around in half an instant, cutting light-minutes off your journey? "Very elegant, very impressive. Very enormously *expensive*, I'd imagine."

Tamra shrugged. "The cost ladies say it'll pay for itself in a century, through increased efficiency. It's actually just the first piece of a whole new kind of network our componeers envision: a spiderweb of collapsium threads stretching to every corner of the Queendom."

That metaphor had been stretched a few times too many, Bruno judged. A "spiderweb" would twist apart in hours, each rung of it orbiting the sun at different levels, different velocities. Unless . . .

"Good Lord. This ring of yours. It's static?"

Tamra quirked her head, not understanding.

"It's stationary?" he tried. "Does it orbit the sun, or is it suspended above by some other means?"

"Oh," she said, nodding. "Static, yes. I'm told it needs to be, to function properly. You'd have to ask Declarant Sykes' people for the details."

Bruno marveled. A static ring completely encircling the sun? The mother of all collapsiters, not orbiting but *hanging* above its parent star like a gossamer suspension bridge? Unthinkable! Life in the Queendom certainly *had* changed in his absence. He found his mouth overflowing with questions.

"What holds it up? Good Lord, what holds it *together*? You'd have standing waves at multiples of the gravitic frequency. Around the ring, that's fine, but *across* it I don't see how the phases would match. You'd get shearing forces that would tend to pull the collapsium out of—"

He caught himself; Her Majesty's expression showed nothing more than polite incomprehension. Sol was fortunate to have a queen so sharp, so quick, but it had trained her in more superficial pursuits, made a kind of glorified video star of her. No scientist, she.

"Forgive me," he said, bowing his head, exposing his hair's grayed roots to her inspection. "I'll stop interrupting. What problem brings you here? To me, of all people?"

She frowned, the troubled creases deepening across her face. "Bruno, I need you to come back with me. Really, I'm not kidding. Fax yourself downsystem; have a look at this thing; tell us what we can do. I wouldn't have come all the way out here if it weren't important."

"The ring needs stiffening?" he guessed.

She shook her head. "Every analysis tells us the design is sound. Even the environmentalists agree it's more than strong enough, even now, when it's only a third complete, still held up by electromagnetic grapple stations."

"Hmm. So what's the problem?"

Her Majesty sighed, looking almost as if she might begin to fidget, embarrassed by some personal inadequacy. Finally, she said, "We had a solar flare last month. A big one, that hit the collapsiter dead center and burned out half the grapples that were holding it up. We're moving new ones into place, but . . ."

"But meanwhile the structure is slipping," he said.

She nodded, then picked up her glass and drank deeply from it, as if the ice water were something stronger to soothe her nerves. It was a gesture Bruno hadn't seen—or made—in a long time. Afterward she held onto the glass, kept it close to her lips, until Bruno realized she was using it as an excuse to keep from speaking further. When he'd waited long enough for her next words, she took another sip, then another, until finally the silence had dragged on long enough and Bruno was obliged to fill it himself.

It was uncharacteristically clumsy of her; another indication of her alarmingly unQueenly distress.

"It's accelerating," he suggested. "You can't get enough grappling force in place fast enough."

Again, she nodded.

"When a boulder first starts rolling downhill," he said, reaching for the sort of analogy she preferred, "you can stop it with a well-placed pebble, but if you're late on the scene it takes more, a stone, an iron chock. And if the boulder rolls over those . . ."

She set down her glass. "You have the essence of it, yes. As the ring falls closer, the sun's gravity increases, and we simply can't build new grapples fast enough to stop it. I'm told we've got six months."

It was Bruno's turn to frown. "Six months before what? Before this 'Ring Collapsiter' falls into the sun?"

Tamra nodded yet again.

Bruno felt the blood draining from his face. "Good Lord. Good *Lord*. An accident indeed!"

"You'll help us," Tamra said. It wasn't a command; her tone hovered right at the edge of *asking*. As if he had some right to refuse her. As if he had even the *ability* to refuse her, else why would he ever have left her side in the first place?

His glance took in her copper eyes, her almond skin, the elegance of her purple dress, cinched at the waist with a chain of diamond-studded gold. With a start, he realized it was precisely the outfit he'd last seen her in. Precisely the haircut, precisely the cosmetic palette. Had she worn it deliberately, in some coarse attempt to influence him? The idea was unsettling.

"Glass ceiling," he said to the house. Light flooded in. Looking left and squinting, he pointed. "My sun warms exactly one subject, Tamra. Yours warms billions. Even assuming a solar collapse were somehow survivable to those nearby, which I doubt very much, the idea of there being no Sol to have a Queendom of . . . Tamra, do you think I'd refuse you? We've squabbled, all right, but do you think so little of me? Why are you here? Your robots should have *dragged* me to you."

"They nearly did," she said, her voice hinting at sadness. "And no, I didn't think you'd refuse me. But you do insist on being difficult. One has to approach Bruno de Towaji in very particular ways, I'm afraid. Even if one is Queen of all humanity."

He hoped his scowl was impressive. "I'm your servant, Tam. As always. Lead me to your fax machine, and think no more of it. We leave at once!"

chapter three

in which an impressive structure is examined

They stepped through the ship's fax gate to a worker's platform: a flat, domed-over plate of di-clad neutronium large enough to host a volleyball match.

Bruno's breath caught in his throat. "Good Lord," he said.

"Yes," Her Majesty agreed coolly.

Diamond—the crystalline form of carbon—is beautiful because its high index of refraction causes the light passing through it to be trapped and split. The stone itself is clear to the eye, but the light that enters is forced—very much against its will—to slow down, to bend, to bounce from shallow edges as though they were mirrors. Upon striking a diamond, a ray of white light may find its red and yellow and green components shunted onto wildly different paths, a phenomenon commonly known as "sparkle."

When diamond surrounds a core of degenerate matter, the effect is heightened further by the Compton scattering of photons off the neutron surface. The usual trite description—that neutronium looks like white fog inside a gem—misses the point entirely: it looks like nothing else in existence, more like a *dream* of fog made solid. Very solid. But that was merely the view beneath Bruno's and Tamra's feet. Above their heads, well . . .

Even di-clad neutronium is dull as cut glass next to the haunting light of collapsium, inside which a sundered light beam can circle for days or weeks, or until the end of time. Just as the speed of light is higher in air than in diamond, and higher still in the "vacuum" of empty space, so too is the speed of light higher—a trillion times higher—in the Casimir supervacuum of the collapsium lattice. "Cerenkov blue" is the radiation given off by swift particles that find themselves slamming into a denser material and briefly exceeding its speed of light, and it is *this* unearthly glow for which collapsium is best known.

So imagine an arch of it filling the sky. Imagine a universe of stars reaching up to infinity above you, pinpoint splashes of light filtering through and around the collapsium. Imagine Sol beneath your feet, swollen and huge but eclipsed by a disc of di-clad, invisible but for the effect of its light echoing through the arch rising high above you.

Like choir music through the rafters of heaven, Bruno de Towaji would later write, to be quoted out of context for tens of thousands of years. In truth the passage continues, *It was grand, enormous, an absurdity of unprecedented scale and scope. A glimpse of heaven, yes, but as we dream it, beach monkeys fond of glitter. If it's God we hope to impress, I daresay a tower of socks would serve as well.*

This by itself is significant: that even Bruno de Towaji, upon seeing the Ring Collapsiter for the first time, reacted to it not as a work of engineering, but of art.

"Astonishing," he conceded.

"Yes," Her Majesty could only agree. Her two robots stepped through, assuming positions on either side of the fax gate.

After them came a man—short haired, short statured, neatly shaved and groomed and dressed—whom the robots examined only briefly. They seemed to know him, and he in turn carried himself as one accustomed to their dainty-hard robotic scrutiny, and to the dainty-hard company of the Queen herself. He seemed properly respectful without appearing awed or worshipful or afraid, and for this Bruno approved of him instantly, although he also sensed, almost as quickly, something cool and detached back behind the eyes somewhere. Mathematical, one might say.

Bruno's people skills were a bit out of practice, though, and we may suspect he put little credence in his first impressions, pending further analysis.

"Majesty," the man said, doffing his cap and bowing low, so that his hands nearly brushed the slick surface of the platform.

"Marlon," the Queen acknowledged, inclining her head slightly. "Thank you for coming so quickly. I take it you loaded your pattern here ahead of time?"

The man bowed again, less deeply, then offered a courtly smile. "I stow copies of myself where they're likely to be of use, Majesty. This one is a few days old, though I'll happily send for a fresh one if you prefer."

She shook her head. "Not necessary." To Bruno she said, "Marlon Sykes is the father of the Ring Collapsiter project. Without his prolonged and dogged efforts, this—" She indicated the collapsium towering above them. "—would never have come about."

Did she mean the structure, or the accident? Was there reproach in her tone? Bruno couldn't tell, couldn't detect her mood through the calm mask she projected. But surely the implication was clear enough: Marlon Sykes had convinced her the ring project was safe. And he'd been wrong. Bruno felt immediate kinship with the man—it was easy to be wrong. It was always so easy to make a mistake.

"Dr. Sykes," he said, offering a greeting bow of his own.

The man smiled warmly. "*Declarant* Sykes, actually. It's nice to see you again, sir."

"Bruno," Tamra chided, "you know Marlon from your days

at court." Now there was clear warning in her tone; she was embarrassed, and he, Bruno, was the cause of it.

He thought for several seconds, trying to place the name, the face. There *had* been a Marlon Somebodyorother, but he was First Philander, more an afterimage than an actual presence at court. Ex-lover to the Queen, allegedly a gifted matter programmer of some sort . . . Marlon Sykes, yes. Gods of memory, had the details of his life faded so quickly?

"Declarant Sykes," Bruno repeated, now bowing more deeply and assuming what he hoped was a tone of proper contrition. "Declarant-*Philander* Sykes, yes, of course! I've been isolated of late, sir, but the lapse is, er—" with a glance and nod in Tamra's direction "—inexcusable. I beg your indulgence."

"Forget it," Marlon said with a dismissive wave and smile. "It's been years, and the acquaintance was never a strong one. This admirer is happy to be remembered at all."

"Hmm," Bruno said, unconvinced. "Yes, well."

He was expected to feel embarrassment at a time like this. In fact, he felt only a twinge; that he'd failed to remember Marlon Sykes was no surprise, and no real fault of his own. There'd been so many people. His childhood had been spent among tolerant adults. And at University he'd begun to encounter people who felt the same way he did about such things, enough people to persuade him that his laissez-faire attitude toward social interaction was simply a minority view, rather than a mental defect per se, a result of his having been orphaned or some repartitioning of his brain to make room for gardening or mathematics. So he'd spent several years of study in a sort of private resistance movement, asserting himself, presenting himself in precisely the forthright manner that everyone claimed to respect and admire.

It was the worst time of his life, bar none; this phantom "decorum" was no trifling matter, but actually some kind of genetically coded pecking order thing. Even *he* didn't like tactless boors, though for a while they'd become his only company. So he'd decided to approach these foolishly subtle but socially compulsory responses as a kind of language, and with less ef-fort than he would later spend learning Bad Tongan, had gone about memorizing their basic vocabulary and grammar.

The effort had proved, at best, a partial success, but it did give him some foundation to work from. And through his fa-ther's alcohol recipes, he'd found both courage and a kind of unself-conscious ease that really helped, especially if other people were drinking as well. What happy drunks they'd made! Being good at darts and shuffleboard had also proven useful.

He'd still been prone to fits of distraction, but that was at least partially a consequence of his having to impress the scholarship committee or starve. This was before all the money had started. And the fame, yes. Tamra's court had sharpened those social skills still further, in a careless, sink-or-swim kind of way. But by then, settling into life at Nuku'alofa, he'd found a kind of prison accreting around him: erst-while colleagues tarring him with labels like "tycoon" and "politician," while the media adopted him as a sort of Romeo Einstein. Increasingly, people seemed to "know" a de Towaji whom Bruno himself had never met.

Even at court—or perhaps especially there—no one seemed prepared to advise him, to take him under a friendly wing, to understand his life or his problems at all. Was he permitted to *have* problems? Even Tamra, wrestling incomprehensible demons of her own, had thrown her hands up at his grousing. That was when he'd begun to daydream—and eventually ob-sess—about the end of time, and the *arc de fin* that would someday show it to him.

And of course living alone meant not having to think about these things at all, getting lazy about them, forming a bond with the house software that gradually let the language de-volve to shorthand codes and even, sorry to say, preverbal grunting and pointing. At least he wasn't in his underwear.

So with a twinge of guilt and no decorum whatsoever, he simply strode to the edge of the platform and looked down, pressing first his hands and then his forehead against the slick, clear surface of the dome, straining for a view of the sun.

The best he could manage was an edge of the corona, the vast, diffuse, superhot solar atmosphere. As in an eclipse, magnetic field lines stood out clearly; looping threads of bright and dim against the blue-white glow, but much nearer than any eclipse he'd ever seen. Beneath this platform, the corona flared huge, as wide as ten full moons, as structured and detailed as a wreath of burning, phosphorescent ivy.

"Quite a view," he said. "We're close in. Six months until this ring falls in? Solar disturbances could begin sooner than that, as it passes through the chromopause."

He tried to picture such an event. Collapsium was a "semisafe" material in that it didn't consume matter the way a large black hole would; the component hypermasses, being precisely the size of protons, couldn't *swallow* protons, any more than a standard manhole could swallow its cover. But they could swallow smaller particles, and slowly stretch in the process.[3]

Would coronal plasma densities be sufficient to trigger such a chain reaction? The plasma nuclei would certainly cling to the collapsons as they fell past, sliding into orbit around the lattice points like planets in newly formed, rapidly growing star systems. Enough nuclei to make a difference? Enough to alter the behavior of a star?

"There've been detailed simulations," Marlon Sykes said, after an apologetic clearing of the throat. "From now, it's six months to the earliest symptoms. After that, barely a week until the photosphere is penetrated. It was the first thing we checked."

Well, now Bruno genuinely *was* embarrassed. Of course they'd check a thing like that, long before they ever thought to send for *him*. Marlon Sykes clearly was not stupid; the glittering arch above them was proof enough of that. Bruno stepped away from the dome, absently wiping at it where his forehead had rested, though no smear or smudge remained.

3. See Appendix A: Semisafe Black Holes, page 366

"Of course," he said, now with proper and unfeigned apology. "Of course you did. Forgive me, Declarant."

Sykes smiled, indulgently if not quite warmly. "Stop it, Declarant. Am I to forgive you every fifteen seconds? It seems a waste of our talents, this officiousity. Call me Marlon, please. Speak to me as a friend, loosely and without calculation, and we shall both be the happier for it."

Well, that seemed rather a courtly way of asking him not to be courtly. Was there some cunning insult here, buried in subtexts and subtleties? Bruno grunted noncommittally, then caught himself. What if there were? What did it matter? He was here to help Tamra, to help the Queendom in general and Marlon Sykes in particular. It wasn't difficult to imagine some rancor there, some resentment at imagined usurpations of authority and respect, but did that change the physics one iota? No. Here, at least, it was better simply to state his thoughts as they actually were, with social filters disengaged.

Which of course was exactly what Sykes himself—what *Marlon*—was proposing.

"Damn me," Bruno said, with forced cheer. "I've been away too long. Marlon it is, and you may call me Bruno, or 'fathead,' or anything you please. We've a sun to save, yes? And not with our manners."

Marlon's grin widened. "Well spoken, fathead."

Despite Her Majesty's sharp intake of breath at this, the two men shared a sudden laugh, and Bruno felt the easing of a mutual hostility he hadn't fully realized was there.

He looked up at the sparkling arch of the Ring Collapsiter again, this time with an eye for the details of its construction. Based on the spacing of its gently pulsing Cerenkov pinpoints, he judged the structure's zenith to be some two kilometers above the platform, its range increasing to perhaps millions of times that much as it sloped away to the sides. A ring, yes, but one so enormous that it looked flat, ruler-straight, until it had all but vanished in the distance, at which point it seemed to turn down sharply, and finally vanish beneath the platform. But for all its enormous girth, the ring was only about six meters thick. Its cross-section appeared to be circular—an observation that Marlon confirmed when asked.

So what were these other lights, these bright flarepoints of yellow-white, spaced along the lattice every half kilometer or so?

"Curved sheets of superreflector," Marlon said, with something like rue in his tone. "Placed near the ring's outer edge, they reflect Hawking radiation back in the direction of the sun. Since the radiation already headed for the sun *isn't* reflected, there's a net downward flow of mass-energy, pushing the collapsiter upward. Like a very weak rocket engine, using collapson evaporation as the energy source."

"Ah!" Bruno said, impressed. "What holds the superreflectors in place?"

Marlon pursed his lips, shook his head. Now he did look rueful. "Nothing, my friend. Nothing at all. They're perfect sails, and between light pressure, solar wind, and Hawking radiation, they start accelerating right away. Within an hour they're pushed too far to do any good, and within a few days they've exceeded solar escape velocity. Bye-bye, superreflector. We could hold them down with electromagnetic grapples, but of course that simply reverses the problem of holding the collapsium lattice *up*."

"So it's useless, then," Bruno said cautiously.

Sykes gave an emphatic nod. "Quite useless, yes. I told Her Majesty as much—" Here he raised his voice and looked glumly at Tamra. "—but she's in a mood to try . . . almost anything." And here his gaze was directed at Bruno: another idea born of royal desperation.

"Not your idea, then," Bruno said, ignoring what must certainly have been a deliberate jibe.

"No. Some functionary's."

They were silent for a while, Marlon looking at Tamra, Tamra looking at Bruno, Bruno looking at the collapsium arch, the two golden robots looking studiously at nothing.

"Tell me *your* idea," Bruno said to Marlon after a while.

The clearing of Marlon's throat held an indication of

surprise—the question was unexpected. Bruno turned in time to see the smaller man blush. "*My* idea. The, uh, grapples are my idea. Build them faster, you know. Find ways to crank them to higher frequencies, for greater pull. We have to pull the ring *up*, away from the sun. That's really the sole nature of the problem, dress it up however you may. We've got to *apply force* to the collapsium, and the grapples are our only means of doing so without tearing the lattice out of whack and creating ourselves an even bigger problem."

"Hmm," Bruno said, nodding absently, pinching his chin between thumb and forefinger.

A flicker of resentment crossed Marlon's features. "You disagree?"

"Hmm?" Bruno looked up, met Marlon's gaze. "Disagree? No, of course not. You've got the right of it, clearly."

Her Majesty cleared her throat at that, her eyes flashing angrily. "Nobody's giving up, Declarants. It's time to broaden your thinking, and *keep* broadening it until a solution emerges. That, or all your brilliance is for naught. There *is* a solution; I'm sure of that."

Marlon smoldered visibly at the rebuke, and it was several seconds before Bruno, deep in thought, realized the obligatory reply was his to make. "Um, yes," he said, looking up and nodding, because he didn't disagree with *that* statement, either.

He and Marlon were *orbiting* Tamra, he saw, striding slowly around her on the platform as if she had some dangerous gravity of her own. Which of course, she did, and his reticence clearly did not put him on the right side of it. A not-so-subtle no-no in the grammar of decorum: ignoring the Queen of All Things.

"I do need time to think," he pointed out.

She nodded once, and her gravity seemed to drop a bit. Permission granted; his orbit could slow and widen. God, how many times had scenes like this played out? Tamra impatient for answers—scientific or otherwise—and Bruno begging silence to contemplate them? He hadn't missed the feeling, exactly, but now it had a kind of déjà vu effect, reminding him of a lot of things he *had* missed. He was back in her world, yes. Nodding to himself, he pinched his chin again, and looked down to examine the reflection of the collapsium in the di-clad whiteness of the platform.

Time passed.

"Can I answer anything else for you, Bruno?" Marlon asked, with perfect politeness, when ten minutes had gone by.

"Bruno?" he prompted diplomatically, after another sixty seconds. Finally he snapped his fingers. "Hey you, fathead! Are we through here?"

Bruno looked up, blinking. "Hmm? Oh, yes, please, go on about your business. I think I have all the information I need for the time being. The problem, as you say, is an exceedingly simple one, even if its solution is not."

"You don't need anything more from me, then?" Marlon prompted.

"Er, not that I can think of," Bruno said, realizing that some more time had passed. "I can reach you, yes? If further questions occur?" Then it dawned on him that he was being rude again, perfunctory, exactly the sort of boor Marlon had probably thought him in the first place. Peerless indeed, usurping this other man's place, his project, his problems. To compensate, if belatedly, he allowed his gaze to narrow, his face to grow shrewd. "If you must go, Declarant, I implore you not to go far. This matter's been on my mind a fraction of the time it's been on yours, but once we're on a more equal footing, I'll be more ready to assist you."

Marlon Sykes was, it seemed, not impressed by such transparent flattery. Without a word he doffed his cap, bowed deeply, replaced it again, and walked to the fax gate; and if it's possible to disappear in a testy, irritable way, then be assured Marlon Sykes did just that.

"Nicely handled," Tamra chided, emphasizing the remark with a not-so-playful punch in the arm.

"Hmm?" he said, looking up. "What?"

She sighed, then removed the diamond crown and scratched

the indented band it left across her forehead. "Bruno, Bruno. I thought you'd changed. You *seemed* to have grown at first, matured, but maybe that was just the gray hair. Maybe we're just ourselves, irredeemably, until the end of time. A dreary thought. So are you going to stand there all night? If I send for a chair, will you sit?"

He looked at her, his attention divided, struggling to understand what she wanted here. Finally he just shrugged. "I'm comfortable enough, Tam. If I need to sit, I'll sit. There's a fax machine, right? So really, I've got everything I need."

He saw right away that it wasn't an optimal response. In fact, she seemed to find it funny.

"Have you? Are you dismissing *me* now, Philander? Don't be foolish: left to your own devices you'll happily starve out here."

He frowned, not liking the condescension in her tone. Was that what she thought of him? "You're the first human being I've seen in nearly a decade, Majesty. I think I've gotten on rather well without your assistance."

"I suppose you have," she said, clearly amused at his expense. "But I must attend a dinner party tonight, and I think you shall accompany me. You'll eat; you'll socialize; you'll astonish me with your ability to get on."

"Ah." Dinner parties: loud, complicated. Bruno sighed, feeling his delicate chain of thought breaking apart already. "Bother."

"Oh, bother yourself. For all your complaining, you do think best when you're distracted. Leaving you here alone is really a disservice to all." Frowning, she pinched the shoulder seam of his vest. "Bruno, where did you get this pattern? We'll need to stop by the palace, have it dress you in something suitable. And me, for that matter; we look like a couple of time travelers."

"From twenty years ago?"

She nodded. "At least."

Well humph, he'd been trying to continue his apparent funny streak. He was pretty sure there'd been a time when

Tamra had laughed at his jokes, finding them witty and apropos. So long ago? Perhaps he *should* go partying with her, freshen up the skills a bit. With six whole months until disaster struck, he could hardly begrudge himself a single evening's fellowship, could he? Particularly when the Queen herself commanded it.

He grunted suddenly, recalling that "disaster" meant, literally, "bad star." Perhaps *that* could be made into a joke later. Or perhaps not, since nothing leaped immediately to mind. Jokes you had to think about were not usually the funniest. Especially if they were in bad taste to begin with. He did smile a little at that.

"What?" Her Majesty asked, marking his shift of mood.

"Er, nothing. I'll . . . tell you later."

Accepting that answer, she smiled, took his hand, threaded her fingers through his, and began leading him toward the blank vertical slab of the fax gate. "Well. It's time, then."

"Wait," he protested, "it's not evening *now*, is it?"

"It is on Maxwell Montes."

"Maxwell Montes? *Venus?* That's where we're going?"

"Yep. And it occurs to me we've less than an hour to get ready."

"But . . ." he said, realizing the futility of the words even as they left his lips. "An hour? Bother it, I've only just eaten breakfast."

in which a legendary
mead hall is christened

Maxwell Montes is the highest point on Venus, reaching through fully a third of the planet's thick, toxic atmosphere, and as such, was the first place to become marginally habitable once terraforming began. Or so Tamra informed Bruno as her Tongan courtiers—a trio of gorgeous but nearly flat-chested ladies affecting a quite implausible adolescence—fussed with the final details of his hair and clothing.

Two of the women were vaguely familiar; he'd already feigned embarrassment over forgetting their names. He had been at court for almost three decades, so there really wasn't much excuse. The third woman, Tusité something, was one of Tamra's personal friends, and consequently treated him with chilly regard. *Are you back, Trouble?* Her conversational barbs were subtle, though, and since he had pretty well earned them, he resolved to take them with good grace.

But still, eyeing his triple reflection, he had to ask her. "You're not playing a trick on me, are you?"

"You'll be with Her Majesty, Declarant," Tusité replied coolly. He supposed that meant no, it wasn't possible to embarrass Bruno without also embarrassing Tamra. But there might be another barb here he was missing. This was typical; Tamra's courtiers were mostly kind people, but their sparring was constant, driven by hypertrophied senses of wit and honor and propriety. They were like athletes who had honed a particular set of skills to the point of bodily distortion: runners with cricket legs, or weightlifters who could no longer throw a ball. He could believe Tusité had altogether *lost* the ability to speak plainly, without layers of veiled meaning.

Bah.

Tonight, he'd balked at sequins, but had otherwise yielded judgment to the palace and its ladies, who'd promptly swathed him in green-and-black suede. Spurious zippers and snaps and buckles on the jacket were complemented by fat laces down the trousers' outer seams. The matching hat was wide brimmed and glossy, the sort of thing one expected a big ostrich feather to protrude from, although none did.

Each piece had looked absurd in isolation, and Bruno had been hard-pressed to stifle his protests. The total ensemble had a different effect, though. It did look ridiculous, in the way that unfamiliar clothes always did, but it also seemed, in a strange way, to suit him. If this was a joke, it was of the contextual variety: well dressed but out of place. A time traveler. But probably it was no joke, and people actually dressed this way these days.

The handmaids had wanted to stroke the gray out of his hair and beard as well, and now, eyeing himself in the dressing hall's triple mirror, he wondered what that might've looked like. No color was "natural" in this age of artifice, after all, and his own tastes were clearly outdated and otherwise suspect.

"Whom are you trying to emulate?" the would-be teenage Tusité had asked him earlier, her voice brusque with amusement. The question gave him pause. His post-court appearance had evolved gradually, over twenty years, without much in the way of conscious planning or assessment. And yet, as Tamra also had teased him, he seemed to have become a sort of theatrical construct, less himself than an iconification of himself. Symbolizing what, he couldn't guess, but there it was: his eyes brooding between gray-black thickets, fat eyebrows merging with overlong hair, bushy sideburns slopping down into curls of untamed beard. The handmaids had done what they could in the time allotted, but still he looked uncomfortably like a mad prophet, combed over but hardly couth. Strange that he hadn't noticed it in his own mirror this morning.

That was court life for you: self-consciousness without end. Silly clothes. Comments so veiled and obtuse that they might as well have been encrypted.

"You look . . . better," Tamra told him, gliding in, dismissing her courtiers with a look.

"Yes," he agreed grudgingly, straightening a blousy sleeve beneath the cuff of the jacket. "I'm quite the dandy. Compliments to your software and staff; you do seem to surround yourself with the tasteful."

"Usually," she said, and took his arm. "Did Tusité give you a hard time?"

"I'm not sure," he admitted. "She seems to have her doubts about me."

"She does have a good memory."

Tamra herself had adopted a blue-gray, long-sleeved evening gown that—like Bruno's jacket—suggested Venus was no longer the hot-house of ages past. Circling her brow was a simple platinum band, adequate for semiformal occasions where she was, nonetheless, on public display.

Robot guards came to life for them as they approached the fax gate, transiting ahead of them to prepare the way. Watching them disappear was interesting; the gate itself didn't look like anything, just a vertical slab of blackish material swathed in a thin layer of fog. But the robots melted into it with tiny pops and flashes, like ice cubes slipping into something carbonated and phosphorescent.

It took some conscious effort to approach the slab as though it weren't there, but stepping through it was as easy as stepping through a curtain, and provided as little in the way of sensation. On the other side lay a gallery, a vast mall of stone and glass, its windows looking down on twilit cloud tops.

The robots' heels and toes clicked against a floor of glossy stone as they danced out of the way, elegantly unobtrusive, their movements interrupted not at all by the journey between planets.

Bruno marveled again that faxing now seemed to provoke no sensation at all, though their bodies were sundered, atomized, quantum-entangled and finally recreated. Exactly as before? Indistinguishable, anyway. The soul, it was imagined, followed the entangled quantum states to the new location. Inconvenient to think it might be destroyed and duplicated along with the body, or worse, that copies of it might be piling up in an afterlife somewhere. But weighed against crowds and traffic and bad weather and all the other inconveniences of physical travel, people were surprisingly willing to take the risk.

At any rate, in the early days of faxing there'd been some pain, some discomfort, some small degree of disorientation that let you know the transfer had happened. This new way, it hardly seemed like travel at all. This might as well have been another room of Tamra's palace, or anyplace, really.

He paused at the transom, turning, eyeing their new surroundings dubiously. Venus? It looked more like Colorado, some glassine lodge clinging to the side of a mountain, looking down on someone else's rain clouds. Above, stars twinkled faintly, as if through a yellow-brown layer of smog. All around the floor were man-high juniper trees in iron pots, not in rows but scattered, a faux forest lying silent and still. Behind the fax gate lay the rock face itself, Maxwell Montes, sealed and structurally reinforced but otherwise left in its natural state, smooth basalt planes broken at jagged edges like petrified layers of pastry. The floor beneath them was opaque and solid, probably a single sheet of whiskered stone held up by metal stanchions and trusswork without a gram of wellstone anywhere in the mix. Why risk a power failure dumping one's party guests—

not to mention one's junipers—screaming into the cloud deck below?

As far as other guests went, Bruno didn't see any, but then again this was clearly a kind of hallway, a place between places, albeit a large one—forty meters across if it was an inch. In both directions, the stone and glass followed natural contours of the mountain, folding around corners and out of view. They were on a promontory of sorts, a jutting outcrop of rock; above, the mountainside sloped away rapidly from the arcade's ceiling.

A faint, light snow was falling, he saw, clinging in places to the juncture of rock wall and sloping glass roof and, when enough had accumulated, spilling down the glass to be whisked away by swirling breezes. Beyond this, splashes of lichen were clearly visible on the rock face, and there were even, he thought, some leafy plants waving up there in the gloom.

Below, the clouds somehow managed to look chilly, like Earthly rainstorms after the sun has set.

"Venus," he said quietly. A parched, poisonous world of crushing pressures and furnace temperatures, tin and lead running liquid on its surface like so much quicksilver? No longer.

Tamra quirked her head at him as if puzzled by his stopping. "Something?" she asked. The view didn't seem to faze her, to affect her at all. Perhaps too familiar, too ordinary a thing in her life: a whole planet brought to heel, another ring for her hand.

He shook his head. "No, nothing."

He felt someone crowd in through the fax gate behind him, heard a grunt of surprise. "Excuse me," a voice said testily.

Tamra sighed, pulling him away from the gate. "You needn't stand *right there*, Declarant."

"Of course," he mumbled, his eyes still flicking around hungrily, taking it all in.

"It's been a while since you've seen anyplace new," she observed, with some degree of sympathy.

"Indeed," he said, nodding absently. "One forgets the sensation. The overwhelmingness of it. Without realizing, one forgets how to *be* overwhelmed."

His gaze finally came to rest on her face, finding the expression there amused. This displeased him. "Is it intentional, Highness, to distract me from the very problem I'm summoned to solve? Changes of scene undermine one's concentration. If your desire is to frustrate me, I admit you've succeeded."

"Oh, hush."

"De Towaji?" another voice, a man's, said. Bruno turned, saw four strangers clustered at the fax gate now. Strangers, yes; he was quite sure he recognized none of them. The man who'd spoken was tall and thin, dressed head to toe in crimson, and—if Bruno dared think it—possessed of the sort of shallow, almost effeminate beauty he generally associated with actors and politicians. Two of his associates were female, swathed respectively in yellow and green velour dresses that seemed little more than long, endlessly winding scarves. The third, a portly man in indigo, was looking wide-eyed at Bruno.

"De Towaji," he echoed.

Oh, bother.

"Gentlemen," Bruno said, bowing slightly. Then, with greater conviction, "Ladies."

The ladies eyed him skeptically, this clownish figure late of the wilderness.

"My God," the indigo man exclaimed. "Her Majesty went and got you, didn't she?"

And the woman in green said, "You're here to fix the Ring Collapsiter."

And the crimson man, at a loss but apparently feeling the need to say something, added, "Er, that's quite a handsome jacket!"

"Doctors," Tamra said, placing a hand on Bruno's back, "allow me to present Declarant Bruno de Towaji."

"Pleased," the crimson man piped.

"To meet you," the woman in green finished, half apologetically, touching the crimson man lightly on the hand. He was, Bruno saw at once, her husband, whose sentences she was well accustomed to finishing. The love and shyness and exasperation between them radiated out in invisible rays, like infrared. Warming.

The indigo man simply nodded.

Well, they made Bruno feel less clownish, at any rate. Or in better company with his clownishness, perhaps. Nice to know he wasn't the only awkward chap in the worlds.

Tamra looked at him sidelong and said, "Doctors Shum and Doctors Theotakos, of Elysium province." She paused, then added, "Mars."

And here were court nuances aplenty: Her Majesty had given these people's titles and last names, but not their firsts, meaning she knew them, but not well. And she'd made a point of emphasizing Bruno's rank over theirs; the Queendom's educational system being by far the best humanity had ever known, "Doctor" was very nearly no title at all. There were more subtle levels in the exchange as well, as invisible and inevitable as the basalt pastry layers beneath Maxwell Montes' outermost surface. That Bruno couldn't parse them—and wouldn't even if he knew how—didn't mean their presence had escaped him. This much he knew: that these Martians had been smartly, artfully dressed down, acknowledged for their value but instructed in no uncertain terms to keep their distance.

It was perhaps a necessary gesture, reflexive, else Her Majesty would be mobbed at all times with admirers. Such was her job, after all: to be admired. But it was still a snotty thing to do, this enforced distance, and Bruno felt an instant sympathy for its victims.

"I am very pleased to meet you all," he said sincerely, realizing that these were, in fact, the first people he'd met in five or six years. He bowed again, and felt a friendly smile creeping onto his face. "We'll talk later, if you like."

The relief on the men's faces was palpable. Bruno wondered

what sort of doctors they were, that they so craved his attention.

"Er," the crimson man said.

"Thank you, very much," his wife said, smiling, touching his hand again to lead him away. The indigo man and yellow woman fell in behind them, strolling down a path between the junipers, past Tamra's guards. In a few moments, they were lost from sight.

"Ah, civilization," Bruno said.

Her Majesty grunted. "Wiseass."

Another figure materialized in the fax gate: a man. A smallish man in black and green, a shiny black hat cocked jauntily atop his head. It took Bruno a moment to recognize him as Marlon Sykes, prettied up for the ball, and still another moment to recognize the clothing ensemble as very nearly identical to his own. Perhaps suggested by the same piece of software?

Perhaps *this* was Tusité's joke?

Sykes, it seemed, made the connection more quickly, eyeing Bruno up and down and then glaring pointedly. Tamra, for her part, looked at the two of them and burst out laughing.

"Am I to be second in *all* things?" Sykes muttered.

Bruno, somewhat taken aback himself, could only stammer, "It . . . why, it looks much better on you, Declarant." Which was true, but it mollified Sykes not at all.

"Damn you, de Towaji," Sykes said, then stepped backward and vanished.

Another batch of people filed through the fax gate, and in another moment Bruno felt his arm clasped again, Tamra's strong fingers pulling him away from still another encounter, down the juniper path toward the party.

The robots, earlier so conspicuous in their duties, now seemed almost to sneak alongside them, quiet, holding to the walls and shadows. They remained ever vigilant, of course, their blank metal heads facing Her Majesty no matter how they moved, but now they followed a program of discretion, balancing etiquette against the need to protect—or perhaps protecting Tamra's image along with her skin.

A few turns and twists later, the glass arcade opened back into a sort of dining hall, a chamber cut back into the mountain. Or possibly a natural cavern of some sort; beneath a ceiling of white-glowing wellstone, the walls retained that same rough pastry look. At the back, a staircase rose up into rock and darkness. Five long tables filled the hall, eight seats to a side and one on each end, enough for a hundred people in all. Half these seats were filled already, and from the arcade's other side a steady stream of guests filed in. Had he and Tamra come in through some sort of VIP entrance? The crowd was certainly thicker over there, and while neither wealth nor status could be gauged from clothing, from their movements and muddled-together speech they seemed a slightly more raucous bunch. The brightly clad Martians were ahead, strolling along the nearest table, looking at place cards to find or confirm their seats.

Bruno and Tamra seemed to be right on time, at any rate. That was another thing about faxing: it left no sense of the minutes elapsed during transmission through the collapsiter grid. One could, in theory, specify longer-than-optimal packet routes, bouncing a signal to the outer planets and back as many times as desired, effectively transmitting oneself into the future. Why wait for the party, when you could—in effect— bring the party to you? But the cost was such that Bruno doubted many people had tried it; there were easier ways to skip over dull time. Sleeping, for example.

Presently, a little bald man detached himself from the crowd and strode briskly forward, arms outstretched, his attention fully on Tamra. In the corners of Bruno's vision, the robots tensed.

"Your Majesty," the man said, sounding delighted. *"Malo e lelei. Na'ake 'i heni kimu'a?"* His hands closed on hers, enfolding; he was bigger than he looked, taller in fact than the "Virgin Queen" herself. There was deception in the stoop of his shoulders and the draping, nondescript grays and browns of his clothing. Deliberate deception? It seemed unlikely in such a grandfatherly figure.

"Declarant Krogh," Tamra acknowledged pleasantly, lifting and inclining her hand for a ceremonial kiss.

Suddenly, the face clicked: Ernest Krogh, inventor of the fax morbidity filter that had all but banished death from the Queendom. The first Declarant Tamra had ever named.

"I've seated you next to myself," Krogh said, "if that's all right. Rhea is eager to speak with you about . . . something-orother. It escapes." He waved a hand absently.

"I've brought a guest," Tamra cautioned.

Krogh nodded. "Thought you might. Saved a place. Backups in case, yes, but I thought . . ." He interrupted himself and turned to Bruno. "Son, you look familiar."

Son? Son? No one had called him that in decades. But then, few people affected such advanced decrepitude, as if the mechanics of biology weren't so rigorously mapped and filtered in fax transmissions after all. Krogh had, of course, come by his decrepitude honestly, the old-fashioned way, but so had many others who'd long since abandoned it for the comfort and vitality of youth.

He supposed Krogh was probably healthy in the ways that mattered: free of diseases and mechanical degenerations, his weathered exterior a kind of uniform or honor badge. Like height or muscle or decisive skin pigmentation, it did draw a kind of knee-jerk attention to itself. A kind of respect, he grudgingly supposed, though he'd rather respect the man's record and title, his taste in buildings, his obviously quite large number of friends.

"De Towaji," he said finally, thrusting out a hand to be shaken. "Bruno."

"Declarant," Her Majesty chimed in.

"Oh! Right!" Krogh exclaimed, grabbing the hand and pumping it enthusiastically. "Collapsium, yes! Still alive, then? Outstanding." To Tamra he said, "Brought him to us, have you? Haven't heard much from this one lately. Bit of a recluse, yes?"

Bruno shrugged. "My work demands isolation."

"I daresay it does," Krogh laughed. "Crushing matter into nothingness. None for me, thanks! God's own spacetime is agreeable enough. Not that there's anything wrong, of course, with a tweak here and there. Mustn't grow complacent. Kiss of death for an immorbid society, I'd say."

"Uh," Bruno said, then realized he had no response. Bit of a recluse, yes, no longer able to hold up his end of a conversation. Blast.

"Well, do come in, Your Majesty. Declarant." Krogh urged them both, not seeming to notice Bruno's discomfiture. "Follow me, follow me. The table is right over here. Rhea, darling, I've brought visitors! Now Bruno, this thing about the Ring Collapsiter. Falling into the sun, they tell me. Not very desirable, that."

"Certainly not."

"You're on it, I hazard? Fixing it up for us?"

Bruno, feeling bothered, could only shrug again. Then he identified the source of his irritation: he felt like a child, like a bright little boy in the company of an adult. Not that he was being patronized, particularly, but Young Prodigy was clearly the role he'd be called upon to play here. What a thought! He, the gray, brooding prophet! That was the problem with putting on airs: other people were free to cut right through them.

Well, blast. So be it. Served him right, probably.

"I've looked," he said to Krogh, nodding. "I'm thinking the problem over, but really I've only just arrived. And since Her Majesty insisted I join her for dinner . . ."

Krogh smiled knowingly, reached out an arm, and for a moment Bruno feared his mad prophet's hair might be given a good-natured tousling. But no, the arm was merely gesturing, pointing out the seats marked LUTUI TAMRA and LUTUI GUEST. *So many utensils,* Bruno noted with an inward groan.

A few seats down was a place marked SYKES MARLON, which, presently, was occupied by the frowning Declarant-Philander himself, now swathed head to toe in white, a cap and smock and jacket and breeches which, if anything, suited him better than the previous ensemble had done. Pulling out his chair, he cast a smoldering glare in Bruno's direction, then softened it a little and nodded in simple acknowledgment, one peer to another.

In another moment Tamra seated herself, and with that the crowd seemed to shift, change phase, its members drawn down into their chairs over a period of seconds like kites dropping out of a suddenly windless sky. Not unusual, Bruno recalled; people tended to keep half an eye on the Queen at times like these, and to draw their cues from her. But still it was strange, a thing half forgotten in his years away.

Soon Krogh alone remained standing, whereupon he lifted a metal cup from the table, raised it to eye level, and brought a hush down over all.

Bruno found his eyes drifting toward the back of the chamber again, surveying the rough staircase there. Where did it lead? Outside? To the surface of Venus itself?

"Ladies and gentlemen," Krogh said quietly, his voice echoing from the pastry walls, "Welcome to our planet—a work in progress, I'm afraid—and thank you all for coming. There will be time to continue mingling after dinner; I'll have to ask you not to do it during. Rhea's gone to quite a bit of trouble about the seating, you understand, and she won't see her efforts undone. Now, we have some very special guests tonight, whom I'll ask you not to pester. This is a fund-raiser after all, and any pestering is to be done by Rhea exclusively." There was polite laughter all around, which seemed to surprise Krogh a little. He looked around sheepishly. "Er. If you *are* a special guest, do come and talk to her before you leave. Or an ordinary guest, for that matter; I'm sure she's dying to speak with you all."

"Pish, there are no ordinary guests here!" the woman at Krogh's side called out. Like him, she'd chosen an appearance of physical maturity, and though it was nowhere near as advanced as his, her red dress and rouge and lipstick and eyeliner did clearly emphasize the pallor of her skin. That is, if "pallor" could describe the graying and weathering of a face so darkly brown.

Again, polite laughter filled the chamber. Again, Krogh seemed good-naturedly put off by it. He looked as though he had more to say, but after pausing a moment, he finally shrugged and sat down again. A few diners clapped uncertainly.

"Oh, well done, Cyrano," the woman—Rhea—teased him, amusement winking in her eyes. "Such an orator, such an inspirer of men. How our coffers will swell tonight."

"As you say, darling."

Both faces turned politely toward Tamra then, and waited.

Smiling, Her Majesty delicately lifted a fork, at which signal plates of brightly colored salad rose up from the solid wellwood of the tables, one to a diner.

"*Kataki ha'u o' kai,*" she said in one rote breath, granting permission for the meal to begin.

Bruno, still unsure of his etiquette, waited for others to dig in before doing so himself. When he did, though, he found the salad excellent, every bit as crisp and succulent as anything he'd grown himself, and clothed in a quite zingy dressing he couldn't identify.

"Very good," he remarked around a mouthful of it, which technically was a social error but which seemed to please Rhea Krogh well enough. The beverage, too, was striking; when Bruno had last dined among the civilized, fashion had favored mood enhancers of excruciating subtlety, perfumed drugs that elicited a temporary bliss or ardor or thoughtfulness and then erased their own tracks, suppressing the users' desire for more drug until some seemly interval had passed. But this time his metal cup, when he touched it, filled with a foamy amber fluid that smelled like—and was—ordinary beer. Beer! He nearly choked on it in his surprise.

"It's only the default, son." Rhea explained, seeing his

reaction. "Whisper the name of any drink you'd prefer, and the cup will change it. Water to wine, the full menu."

"No, no," Bruno said, mastering himself. "It's quite good. A quaint, clever touch. I haven't had beer in . . . well, decades, I suppose. It's good to taste it again!"

"A little hoppier, perhaps? A touch of the bitter?"

"No," he insisted. "This is fine. Really."

Rhea Krogh beamed for a moment, then looked thoughtful for another moment, then shook a finger at him admonishingly. "You are. You're Bruno de Towaji, aren't you? Shame on you, not telling me; I suppose I've gone on like a fool."

"You've barely spoken, madam."

"Oh, you."

Her Majesty cleared her throat and smiled. "Bruno is here at my behest. Doing some work for us, some consultation."

Her words echoed a little; their end of the table had gone silent, all eyes on Bruno, all faces surprised or expectant or hopeful. Even Marlon Sykes was looking at him with some grudging cousin of admiration.

"Sir!" someone exclaimed. "Declarant, you've come to save the Ring Collapsiter?"

"To save us *from* the Ring Collapsiter?" another demanded. And *their* words echoed; the ring of silence was spreading.

Suddenly, the air around Bruno and Tamra filled with buzzing, swooping cameras.

"Your Majesty!" one of them called out in a tinny but amplified voice. "How long has de Towaji been with us?"

"Is he collecting a fee?" another asked.

And then, "Philander, have you resumed sexual relations with the Queen?"

Bruno had been drinking, hiding behind his cup really, but at this he gasped and spluttered, remembering too late the crassness of civilization, ever the counterpoint to its huge, brittle lexicon of manners. Sexual relations? With the Queen? As if the old title of Philander made this, somehow, a matter for public discussion?

"You dare," Tamra said warningly to the nearest camera, to

all the cameras. Instantly, hairlines of sharp blue light connected the buzzing faux insect to the pointing fingers of Tamra's robots, who suddenly were no longer unobtrusive, no longer standing politely among the shadows.

"Reportant Clive W. Swenger," they said together in quick robot voices. "*Luna Daily Tabloid.* Teleoperating from this building, although the camera pings, fraudulently, as an autonomous agent billing to Universal Press."

"Eighty thousand dollar fine," Tamra said, eyeing the camera coldly. Her gaze swept the other buzzing insects. "Cordon is set at two hundred meters, effective immediately."

The blue beams vanished, and as if pushed by invisible turbulence, the cameras fled wildly toward the exit; the dining chamber was barely seventy meters across, much too small for them to obey the cordon and remain inside. Her Majesty's word wasn't law, exactly, but as the strong recommendation of law it carried considerable weight and consequence. No doubt Clive W. Swenger would pay his steep noncompulsory fine, rather than explore the quite dismal consequences of challenging or—God help him—ignoring it. And the other reporters and their robotic agents would obey the cordon almost as if their lives depended on it. Almost.

"Now, the rest of you," Ernest Krogh said dryly to the many human faces still staring, "back to what you were doing, right? No bothering the other guests; that's our agreement."

Bruno, wishing he could slip through the floor, shot him a grateful look. Then, because he had to say something about something other than himself, he said, perhaps too quickly, "Tell me, Declarant: how did you come to invent immortality?"

"Eh?" Krogh turned fully toward Bruno, blinking. "Immortality? Immorbidity, you mean."

Bruno waited.

"How did I?" Krogh repeated, as if the question were a strange one. "Yes, well, there were lots of people working on it, of course. Evolutionary, not revolutionary; once you had the fax able to reproduce whole people, it was rather an obvious notion to fix them up in the process. I say obvious, but of course I wasn't in on the early stages of it. Standing on the shoulders of giants, as they say, one gets a better view than the giants themselves have got. No, it wasn't until little Ania was born that I really became concerned. She's my daughter, you see. I was in pharmaceuticals until then; waste of time, but I suppose I had it to waste, didn't I?

"Anyway yes, when Ania was born and I held her, brown and perfect in my two hands, I burst out crying because I realized something right then and there: death was going to take her someday. Really crying, I mean. Needed sedation to quiet me up. Because she'd grow old and wrinkly, you see, and fill up with pain until it extinguished her, and it just . . . seemed intolerable. Shouldn't it? I mean, even a *diamond* is forever, and a diamond can't grip your finger.

"So I switched professions, right there, and I daresay it was the proper course. Very nearly lost the race, too, not so much with my colleagues as with the Reaper himself. Got rather wrinkly before I was through."

"But you didn't lose," Tamra said.

"No. No, I didn't. Our backers were . . . very generous."

"So, what are you raising funds for this time?" Bruno asked.

Krogh's eyebrows went up. "Why, for Venus, of course. Can't change a whole planet so easily; not on what I make, at any rate."

"So much the better," a sharp, reedy voice said from farther up the table.

"Oh, do hush, Rodenbeck," Rhea admonished, not entirely unkindly.

"It's your planet I speak for, Krogh," the man called Rodenbeck complained in roughly the same tone. "I see—*we* see—the way you mistreat her."

"By bringing her to life?" Rhea waved a hand, dismissively, then said in a childlike falsetto, *"Goodness, Mang, that's a goober lot of weight you say won't loosen. Will it collapsy on us?"*

There was scattered laughter at that. Even Rodenbeck himself cracked a smile.

"Really, playwright," she said, "you *are* better off whining about the Ring Collapsiter. People listen then. But seeing that de Towaji is with Her Majesty this evening . . ."

Krogh laughed at that, and explained to Bruno. "Wenders Rodenbeck—the playwright, you know—is one of your greatest detractors. A rising star among them, one might say."

"Ah," Bruno said, remembering the Flatspace movement, which began almost immediately after the invention of collapsium. Dangerous stuff, they'd insisted. Too dangerous to be used around inhabited planets or, preferably, anywhere else. Even excluding the fate of the Ring Collapsiter, it was a difficult argument to refute. But then, electricity was dangerous, too. He examined Rodenbeck: red haired, freckled, with the sort of face that would age slowly under even the worst of conditions. He wore the uniform of his people: a black sweater over black trousers over heavy black boots, with a brown, brass-buckled belt running round his middle. Hardly a rogue—not with that face and voice together!—but not quite a poseur, either. There was something formidable about him, something easy and smug and self-assured. He was probably a savage card player.

"A detractor of mine as well," Krogh said, laughing again. "Generally, people find purity in the *cold* places. A tundra, a permafrost, an ice cap: hands off, thank you. Rodenbeck is unusual in finding scorched rock as pristine and beautiful as a new blanket of snow." He glanced at Tamra. "As Her Majesty is well aware, we've promised to leave the clouds alone, no changes, nothing you'd pick up from a distance. Venus remains the evening star, bright, featureless, all our work hidden safely beneath, but it's no use. We're to leave her altogether alone, according to this one. He's not widely agreed with."

"More do every day," Rodenbeck said, "since Maxwell Montes started protruding above the cloudtops, in spite of your promises."

"Oh, hush," Rhea repeated. "Not everyone hates progress."

"Tut," Tamra cautioned her. "This man is your guest, Mrs. Krogh."

"Indeed. As Her Majesty wishes, although no disrespect was intended."

Rodenbeck grinned at that, saying, "Majesty, our hosts have invited me to provide the *appearance* of balanced debate. I hope they'll pardon my . . . overstepping the assignment. For what it's worth, I don't hate progress. Why would I hate progress? The fax machine has been a boon for man *and* nature, freeing up billions of acres once enslaved to food production and waste disposal. Any invention that helps us leave more things alone is okay by me, and even things that *don't* aren't necessarily all bad."

"Such balance!" Someone at one of the tables jeered.

Unperturbed, Rodenbeck spoke a little louder, widening his audience. "I'm also a lawyer."

There was more laughter at that; Bruno gathered that Rodenbeck's legal maneuvering was well known, at least among this crowd.

He went on. "I didn't choose these movements. Flatspace, Leave It Alone, the Smith Club—they chose me. Reluctantly, a guy suspects, since I don't toe their full party lines by any means. I never saw 'Uncle Lisa's Neutron' as a blueprint for action—it still surprises me to see it treated that way. I mean, it's just a play. But one thing I do believe is that someone has to take the side of nature in these debates. The way I see it, that's just common sense. The air can't sue on its own behalf."

"I quite agree," Tamra said, in a tone calculated to close the subject. "It's Queendom policy to seek a devil's advocate in all endeavors."

Ouch. *Rodenbeck, you are necessary but overruled.* Bruno found himself liking this man, this greatest of his detractors. But he liked the Kroghs as well, and theirs was clearly the prevailing side here. Following their lead, Bruno returned to his meal, quickly finishing off the salad. His mug, which he thought he'd drained, stood full again at his elbow. He lifted it and took another long draught, savoring the flavors.

"How much do you need, exactly?" he asked when a minute or two had gone by.

"How much *don't* we?" Krogh laughed.

The next course arrived: meatballs with tough, bready centers. Again, Bruno drank deeply from his mug, this time watching it refill when he set it down. Pulling matter through the tabletop from a reservoir somewhere? The same place the food and dishes came from, and then went back to when the diners were through with them? Bottomless, a veritable miracle of loaves and fishes. One felt no urge to hoard, to pace or measure one's consumption.

With a start, he realized that Rhea Krogh was engaged in the old-fashioned and quite roguish practice of getting her dinner guests drunk. To soften them up for solicitation? Was he to have known this? To prepare, to steel himself? Alcohol was a crude drug, but in Enzo de Towaji's Old Girona Bistro it had flowed freely, practically a dietary staple. That was before the earthquake had killed Girona's faux retro medieval phase, of course, along with Enzo and Bernice de Towaji, and 850 other unfortunates. Afterward, as an orphaned student in a grieving community, Bruno had had little *besides* the beer and wine recipes to remember them by. He'd drunk deeply in those days.

"You're drunking me," he snapped at Rhea Krogh suddenly. "Er, well. That is, I fear I'm drinking too much. Too quickly, that is. I'm unaccustomed . . ." his voice trailed away uncertainly, a strange feeling tickling in his chest. And then a massive belch escaped him, silencing all conversation once again.

"I warned you," Rhea said to him, with perfect innocence. "Whisper the name of any beverage. Ask for the intoxicants to be removed, the carbonation, whatever your preference." Then her face took on a look of weathered, knowing sympathy. "Oh, but this is new to you. Sequestered on your little planet, so far away. When was your last dinner party? Of course, of course, the fault is entirely mine."

Beside him, Tamra sighed. "The fault is no such thing, Mrs. Krogh. I apologize for bringing him here, with so little warning to himself or to you. He *is* unaccustomed, although for that he has only himself to blame. But these disruptions are my fault."

"Stop," Bruno growled at her. The room swam a little; he felt its heat in steamy waves. The alcohol was finding its way into his bloodstream, his brain. Bother, how many decades since he'd been drunk? He'd had a fantastic tolerance for it, once, but clearly that wasn't a health trait Krogh's morbidity filters had maintained for him. "Stop it, Tamra, please. I'm not a child, or a fool. I response . . . that is, I take responsibility for myself. This woman—" He shook a finger at Rhea. "—wants money. She plies for it, cleverly, in the manner of a restaurateur. She deserves, she *earns*—"

Tamra reddened. "Bruno!"

"It's all right," Rhea insisted, her good humor fading now into genuine concern. "He's perceptive, and I fear I've treated him poorly. A mug of Prudence should help, or a trip through the fax."

"Nonsense," Bruno said, more loudly than he'd intended. "No. I've drunk it; I'll keep it down. Serve me right. I'll be sober soon enough. And I *do* have money. For your project. Just . . ." He glanced over at Wenders Rodenbeck. "Just leave the clouds alone, all right?"

He paused, scratched his ear, did some muzzy calculations in his head. "Would, ah, would a hundred trillion dollars be enough?"

A universal gasp went up, from the Kroghs, from Rodenbeck, from Marlon Sykes and Tamra Lutui and a hundred painted lords and ladies. All eyes were on him again, and he knew at once that he'd erred, that all his careful efforts to treat these people as friends or equals had just been dashed to flinders.

Peerless. That was his curse, yes, the curse of isolation, of knowing that no other human commanded even a tiny fraction of the resources at his disposal. Even Krogh, who had changed the worlds forever, reaped only a tiny royalty when someone faxed him- or herself across space and time, the morbidity filter one of many background processes running behind every collapsiter grid transaction. Whereas Bruno, who had built the grid, earned a *large* royalty, too large, more than he'd ever asked for or wanted. Tamra's lawyers had set the whole thing up, and in the end even they were stunned at what they'd wrought: a fortune dwarfing Tamra's own, growing faster than anything the worlds had ever seen or contemplated. So large that even giving the stuff away was an exercise fraught with peril.

Because he, albeit unwittingly, had *really* changed the worlds. Because he, albeit unwittingly, had won the power to break spirits with an ill-chosen word, to show people just how small and futile their life's works had been.

"Too much," he said, looking around him morosely. "I'm . . . sorry, I didn't intend any . . . offense."

And then he bent forward and vomited into the enormous metal cup, where his bile changed at once to fresh, foaming beer.

chapter five

in which a great
mountain is climbed

The worst part about the evening was that that wasn't the worst part. With taut aristocratic deference and diplomacy, no one present gave any sign of noticing his lapse, not the tiniest quivering of disgust or sympathy. It was a nonevent, shunned, disacknowledged for its impropriety. This simply wasn't a barf-in-your-mug sort of gathering, and when he'd asked to be excused on grounds of fatigue, Her Majesty had smiled thinly and suggested a hot tonic. Having no other cup to drink it from, he'd naturally demurred, and wound up sitting out the hour in queasy mortification and almost total silence, while his head grew muzzier and then began, slowly, to clear.

The astronomer Tycho Brahe, he recalled, had died of a burst bladder at a dinner like this one, that being entirely more polite than barbarically excusing himself to go pee. Perhaps Bruno should do that in his cup as well, just to see if a head would turn or an eyebrow quirk somewhere in the room, but he'd noticed the lavatory door at the back of the chamber and went there instead, not bothering to ask permission like a child but simply standing, saying he'd be right back, and lurching off.

All these people's lives hung in the balance, he realized suddenly. It was hard to believe he could help them, hard to believe they *expected* it of him. He'd been so rude, and they so patient.

On his way back he passed the gloomy staircase he'd seen earlier. He glanced up its length, curiously. The passage was steep, and curved away to the right. Reflecting from the pastry walls was the same twilight glow as the sky outside the gallery windows. A conservative sky, he thought, all but unchanging; Venus took thousands of hours to complete a rotation, its sidereal day actually slightly longer than its year. The sun followed it around like a child running alongside a merry-go-round, falling slowly behind but remaining stubbornly in view while the stars whirled beyond. This gloomy evening would probably last another four or five standard days, possibly longer, before fading to night.

"Will you be staying long?" someone asked him, a while after he'd returned to his seat. In reply, he simply shrugged and looked to Tamra, and paid little attention to her answer.

In his absence, dessert had arrived: a light berry sorbet that looked as if it might ease his stomach a bit. He tried it; it did.

"Are you reachable by network again, Declarant?"

Again, he shrugged. So long as he remained in civilization, even with no fixed address, a message directed to him would eventually find its way. But why encourage the practice? Why rub these rotted social graces against the fabric of society any more than necessary? Surely society deserved better. He mumbled some reply, then leaned in and finished his dessert.

"Declarant," Wenders Rodenbeck finally said to him, as part of some larger conversation, "how are we going to fix the Ring Collapsiter?"

He looked up. "Eh?"

Ernest Krogh clucked in distress. "No, no, Wenders. Mustn't harass. Haven't I mentioned? Leave the guests alone, all that?"

"It's all right," Bruno said, perking up. "Really." It was, in fact, the most interesting subject he could think of. A matter— regardless of whether Tamra chose to admit it—of life and death. To Rodenbeck he said, "You know something about collapsium?"

A nod. "Enough."

Bruno snorted. "Enough? Enough for what? I don't know enough, and I'm allegedly the Queen's expert. I've been trying to work out the equilibrium of the thing, never mind the dynamics. What keeps it even statically stable? The lattice points are all rigidly in phase, of course; that's what we mean when we speak of collapsium. And imagining the structure as linear, as a long rectangular prism, it's all very straightforward. But in twisting it around to a ring, a toroid, we have to worry about crosswise forces, every part of the structure exerting strange diagonal influences on every other part. It should throw the whole thing out of phase; a collapson swarm, chaotic and perilous and in no way useful as a telecom shunt.

"So what do we do? Adjust the ring size so that every node is an even wavelength away from every other? No, that wouldn't work, would it? There's no such size; the set is empty. You'd have to fiddle with the lattice rows, too, not so much circular rings as huge, frilly doilies of collapsium. Dimensionality . . . what? At least one-point-two. Would that work?"

"One-point-two-nine," Marlon Sykes said, a stunned look on his face, "and yes, it does. Declarant, did you just work that out? In your head? Just now?"

"I'm only guessing."

"Very intelligently," Sykes insisted, all trace of rancor gone from his voice. "Do you know how long it took me to work out the same scheme? With Her Majesty's finest computers at my disposal?"

Bruno grunted, unwilling to acknowledge the point. "I don't recall seeing these . . . crenellations from your work platform."

"No, you probably wouldn't, not when you're that close. And on the inside! Better, I suppose, to see the ring from afar, preferably a little out of the ecliptic plane."

"Venus is two degrees out of the ecliptic, isn't it? Can we see the ring from here?"

Sykes shrugged at that, so Bruno turned to Ernest Krogh, who said, "Expect you could, this time of year. Sun's just set and all. Parts of the ring still above the horizon, yes, another couple of weeks at least. Yes. But you're out of luck, I'm afraid; we've no fax gates on the other side of Skadi, which is where you'd see it."

"Skadi?"

"The mountain."

"I thought the mountain was Maxwell."

Krogh squinched his lips up and shook his head. "On the continent of Ishtar, Maxwell is a prominence the size of Britain. Buckled plates, you see, very nearly a continent's continent. Skadi, the Norse goddess of winter, is the highest of the peaks which crown her. It's where the house is, you understand, on the north face. A poor decision in retrospect: gets cold at night, these days especially."

Bruno, with a tingling of excitement, waved a hand at the staircase at the back of the room. "What about that? Where does it go? To the surface?"

"The rock face, you mean," Krogh corrected uncertainly. "Stairs go all the way to the summit, lad, but it's a steep climb. Over a kilometer."

"Pish," Bruno said, feeling his blood rising, feeling the strength in his limbs like a reservoir waiting to be tapped. "We're young, aren't we? Children. If we're to live forever, shall we have nothing to look back on but the hills we declined to conquer? I, at least, shall climb."

"The air is . . . unsuitable," Krogh objected. "Smoggy, smelly, impure. Carbon dioxide of course, still more than we'd prefer, and residual traces of sulfuric acid. Not to mention all the intermediate hydrocarbons . . ."

"It's breathable?"

"Well, yes, but—"

"Then I, at least, shall climb. Marlon? May I have the privilege of your company?"

Marlon nodded once. "An honor, Declarant. Try and stop me."

Krogh squirmed in his seat. "I am responsible—"

"Nonsense," Bruno said. "I am responsible. I absolve you of any liability for myself."

"But you can't—" Krogh stammered.

Her Majesty stood, eyeing Bruno and Sykes and Krogh himself in turn. "No, legally he can't absolve you. I, however, can. Pray, let de Towaji do as he pleases; the responsibility is mine. Bruno, for our hosts' sake I'll need to keep a close eye on you."

Bruno felt a wry grin creep onto his face. "In that dress, Majesty? I doubt—"

"Pants," Her Majesty whispered, apparently into her right shoulder strap. The dress pulled in around her, sliding, tucking, forming a crease between her legs that unzipped into two separate sleeves of material, one enclosing each leg. In moments, the dress had become a kind of coverall or jumpsuit. The odd thing was that the general cut and style of it had barely changed.

"Oh," Bruno said. Neat trick. He wondered what his own clothing might turn into, if he accidentally whispered the wrong word. A cloak? A dress? A settling cloud of feathers?

Ernest Krogh cleared his throat. "Yes, well. If you insist. The way is clear enough, I should hazard. No need to be shown. Do let me accompany you, though. As host."

"Let us," Rhea corrected.

At the table across from them, the four bright Martians broke a huddle and rose to their feet. "Declarant," the indigo man said, "may we accompany you as well?"

"And I?" another voice said, elsewhere in the banquet hall.

"And we?" A bishop and her husband.

"Myself? Yes?"

Soon the voices were everywhere, and Bruno realized he

was yet again the center of attention, something he had never sought to be—had in fact fought not to be. Rather than answer the many voices, Bruno stood and waved his hands dismissively: Yes, yes, do as you wish; my permission is hardly required. Sliding his chair back, he turned and made for the staircase with long, purposeful strides. Marlon Sykes fell in half a step behind him, Her Majesty and her robots half a step behind that, and behind her came the Kroghs and Wenders Rodenbeck, and behind them were sounds of a rising crowd as Bruno mounted the stairs and began to climb.

Around the passage's first lazy curve there came another, sharper one in the opposite direction, and beyond that lay a thick sheet of curved glass that was part wall, part ceiling. Behind it the mountain shot up in a fist of blunt rock, the little staircase winding up it like a varicose vein, lit with periodic circles of soft wellstone light. Not jagged on the outside, this mountain, this Skadi Peak on the crown of Maxwell Montes. No, soft metals had once frosted here right out of the atmosphere's furnace, and eons of hot, thick, corrosive wind had swept over it like ocean currents, inexorable, smoothing every contour, actually polishing in places, so that the tinned, leaded rock shone almost wetly in the twilight. What Skadi looked like, more than anything, was a cheap computer graphic, a platonic ideal of mountainness. Or perhaps a tall scoop of chocolate ice cream, just beginning to slump in summer's heat. Here and there, patches of blue and green and butterscotch lichen interrupted the smooth silver-browns of windswept basalt.

"Door," Bruno said to the glass, and obligingly, it opened for him, a rectangle of wellwood appearing in the glass and swinging upward on creaky, faux iron hinges. The wind swirled in at once, whistling, much thinner and less cold than he'd been expecting. He stepped through.

Beside him, Marlon Sykes noted, "You know, I'm not sure that actually seeing the fractal structure of the collapsiter will help you, particularly. You seem to have worked out the crucial insight already."

"Yes? Well, we shall see." He drew a deep breath, sampling, releasing it with the hint of a cough. Ernest Krogh had not exaggerated the air's impurity—it tickled the lungs, filled them without wholly satisfying them. It reeked faintly but distinctly of sulfur. It was dry and cool and seemed to suck the moisture right out of him. It was, he thought, good enough for a mere kilometer's hike.

"Can you breathe?" he asked Marlon.

Inhaling deeply, the Declarant nodded. "Adequately, yes."

"Majesty?"

Tamra sniffed, wrinkled her nose, then finally nodded. "It will do, yes."

There were others behind her, dozens of others, but he felt no need to interrogate each of them. Whatever Tamra might say, people were responsible primarily to and for themselves, and if the air displeased them they could, obviously, go back downstairs and finish their dessert.

Bruno pointed with his shoulder. "Upward, then!"

The climb commenced.

The stairs were less smooth than the rock face around them. Rough; perhaps deliberately so, though traction didn't pose much of a problem. With the latest clothing technology a sheet of smooth glass might have served nearly as well, boot soles finding and clinging to the tiniest bumps and ridges, or holding fast with suckered tentacles where no such imperfections presented. The climb was steep, though, and there was no banister, just the edges of the stairwell groove itself, wobbling up and down from ankle to shoulder height and back again as it passed through the tallowy features of the rock face. Above, the stars winked and glittered through postsunset haze and burnt-orange smog—glittered in precisely the way they never had on Bruno's tiny planet, with its too-low, too-thin atmosphere.

"Invigorating," he said, relishing the feeling of being truly outdoors, on a real planet, for the first time in years. The cool wind alone was a new, freshly real sensation as it puffed through his beard, pulled his hair aside in streamers, fluttered at the brim of his hat.

"Yeah, whatever," Marlon muttered beside him. Tamra grunted something unintelligible in a similar tone as her guards clanked along beside her.

The first hundred meters seemed trivial enough, and the second hundred, but halfway through the third he detected Tamra's voice well behind him, and turned to see her dropping wearily, setting one buttock down on the edge of a tall stair. She looked at him half plaintively, half commandingly.

"Keep climbing like that, and you're going to send someone home in a cast," she said.

He grunted, with mingled amusement and annoyance. Rolling injured limbs in foamed plastic was pure hyperbole; nobody treated fractures that way anymore. Why bother, when the injured party could simply be hurled into the nearest fax, murdered, disassembled, and replaced with a perfect—and perfectly healed—duplicate who'd thank you for the service? But as a figure of speech, Bruno grasped it implicitly: he was somehow in charge of this expedition, somehow responsible for all who followed behind him, and he was failing to take proper care. Everyone was healthy these days, well muscled and aerobically fit. Faxware saw to that. But that wasn't quite the same, he reflected, as actual exercise, which after all got one used to a certain amount of hardship and strain. He supposed all those walks around the world had done some good after all.

Beside him, Marlon appeared hale enough, if a bit flushed and pink against the white of his jacket. But he saw that Rodenbeck and the Kroghs had overtaken Tamra, and behind her along the snaking stairway were strewn what must surely be the party's entire guest list, in varying stages of fatigue. Some looked fit, eager, though reluctant to crowd past the Queen on her resting stair, or the halberd-bearing robots looming on the steps immediately above and below. Others, farther back, climbed more slowly and deliberately, and behind them lay a great many who slogged with great heaviness, as if their feet were shod with iron, as if the Earthlike gravity of Venus were far more than they were accustomed to, but also as if this climb were a matter of strange importance to them, an historic event in which they were determined to take part. The news cameras, he saw, had also returned, zipping and buzzing around the invisible, two-hundred meter cordon.

He could almost hear the voices echoing back from some distant future: "I was there on Skadi Peak, when de Towaji climbed it to examine the Ring Collapsiter. You've seen recorded images, maybe saw it live on the network, but I was actually there." The notion bothered Bruno for several reasons, first because it underscored this fame, this unseemly *significance* that dogged him always, whatever he did, and second because it presumed, axiomatically, that there was a future to look back from. That he would, in other words, fix the Ring Collapsiter, single-handedly saving the Queendom from its otherwise certain doom. What basis did they have for such an assumption? What right did they have to demand it of him, if not of themselves?

He wondered how eager and solicitous their faces would be if the blasted thing fell in. Plenty of time to worry, no doubt; the collapsium's lattice holes would widen slowly at first, gobbling solar protons only occasionally, later perhaps a few neutrons. They'd play hell with the sun in the meantime, of course, ejecting flares, wreaking massive disturbances, creating localized zones of greatly increased density as solar matter crowded in around the holes but was not immediately swallowed. Would there be pockets of neutronium kicking around inside the convection zones? Settling in toward the core and then pulling the core in after them? Eventually, no doubt. Eventually.

"Marlon," he said, "how long between chromopause penetration and total solar collapse?"

"Four months," Sykes puffed without hesitation.

"Hmm." Bruno placed his chin in his hand, thoughtfully, wishing again for a less distracting environment. He didn't want to lead his fellow humans or absorb their admiration; he just wanted another look at the Ring Collapsiter, and some quiet time to think. "We're only a quarter of the way up, you know," he said to Tamra,

"I'll make it," she replied. "But I think a lot of us need to catch our breath."

Looking down at the crowd behind her, he nearly said, "I didn't ask them to come." But he didn't like the way that might sound on later repetition, so instead he raised his voice and called out, "We'll rest for a few minutes, and then proceed more slowly."

He watched the faces react to that, all the faces and bodies spilling out below him like the followers of some wise, all-knowing Moses. A mad prophet, yes, late of the wilderness; he should have let the ladies trim and color his hair after all. Grumpily, he sat.

A snowflake lit beside him on the stone, failed to melt, and was whisked away again by the sighing wind. Strange, the rock didn't feel that cold beneath his hands; the snow should have melted. In a sheltered corner, he spied a little pile of it, gathered there like dust. He stretched a hand out to touch it, found it dry and somewhat sharp. Not quite like coarse sand or tiny glass shards, but similar in some way to each.

"This isn't snow," he said, surprised, pinching a bit between his fingers and dropping it into his palm for examination.

"Snow?" Ernest Krogh asked, eight steps below him.

"It's wellstone flake," Rodenbeck called up from two steps farther down. "Also known as terraform ash. It sprouts reactive ions to strip 'unwanted' chemicals from the air, then settles out, changes composition, and sloughs the impurities off as solids to join the lithosphere. Then the wind carries it up again, and it starts all over. There are equivalent devices freeing oxygen and nitrogen from the rocks; it's precisely the antagonist of nature: the geochemical cycle running in reverse."

"Only much quicker," Krogh added with a trace of smugness.

Bruno peered at the little crystals, so much like snow-flakes. The design made immediate sense: maximum surface area for a given mass, to increase reaction space, to maximize the chemistry a single flake could perform. How many were needed to change a whole planet? What fraction were really lifted into the sky again, after settling to earth? He imagined dunes of the stuff piling up here and there, strange geological strata for future generations to ponder. An immortal society could afford to be patient, but still it was no wonder this enterprise was short of cash. A small enterprise, yes, compared with shipping neutronium all the way up to the Kuiper Belt. But that didn't make it easy, or cheap.

"We could just love Venus on her own merits," Rodenbeck said, in weary, futile rebuttal. "Attacking her isn't compulsory. You're the worst sort of real-estate developer, you know; a sanctimonious one."

Krogh laughed. "Son, when *you* buy a planet, I promise to let you care for it as you choose. No one will dream of stopping you. But the shareholders of Venus have voted, almost unanimously, to alter it. Most of us live here after all, or plan to, and while we don't desire a second Earth, we do at least hope for homesteads that won't rust and implode the moment we erect them. You know very little of our hardships here."

"Yeah, yeah, poor baby. You knew the conditions when you moved here."

"Hush, you two," Rhea Krogh said, with a sort of long-suffering amusement.

Other conversations drifted upward, along with some coughs and wheezes.

"If you're having trouble breathing," Rhea called down, "do please go back inside. Her Majesty can't take responsibility for the way I'd feel if anything happened."

No one took her up on the offer.

"At the very least, go fax yourself an oxygen tank and some filters."

A few responded to that, turning around the way they had

come, their steps a little lighter in descent. Bruno let a few more minutes go by, giving them every chance, before rising to his feet once more and resuming the climb at a much-reduced pace and with many backward glances.

Leadership, iconhood, bah. Was it so wrong, simply wanting to do his work? Was that so grave a trespass on the rights of humanity? Humanity certainly seemed to think so. Could everyone be wrong but himself? Was that a reasonable thought to entertain? They trusted his opinion with regard to collapsium, why not with regard to himself? Perhaps, after all, they knew something he didn't. Or perhaps, as with the collapsiter grid, their need simply outweighed any cautions or caveats, outweighed Bruno's own desires. The good of the many demands the sacrifice of the able, yes?

The worst of it was that he had no role models, no historical personages from whom to draw example. Wealthy, strong, well connected to the seats of power; there'd been many like that, some of them even philosophers and inventors, the Declarant-equivalents in their respective eras. But none of them immortal, none forced to live eternally with the consequences of their actions. How paralyzing would they have found it, the eyes of history always on them, not for the sake of posterity but for on-going and literally ceaseless dissection? Knowing that their adolescent bumblings would look ridiculous even to their future selves, and worse, that such adolescence would never end?

Perhaps some could have managed it. Perhaps some would manage it in the far future, with Bruno's failed example to look back on. But that didn't help him now, didn't show him how to *be* this flawless philosopher-saint of society's expectation.

Bah. Bah! Better to worry about the collapsium, about the physics underlying it, and the universe underlying that, and the *arc de fin* that might somehow make sense of it all. *That* should be his historical role! That!

But his opinion mattered little; tonight he was a mountain guide, leading idle stargazers to their latest amusement. Well, not amusement; not that. Their lives did hinge on the fate of the Ring Collapsiter, after all. And they didn't know how to fix it, and they thought perhaps he did; they were therefore understandably eager for his answer. So perhaps there was nothing strange about any of this, no reason for his ire or discomfort. Had he been harsh, foolish? Probably, yes.

So his thoughts had come full circle, and every time someone coughed or stumbled or demanded a rest on that long, slow climb, the circle began anew, starting and ending in the same places like a stuck recording, belying the myth that Bruno's mind was extraordinary, somehow elevated above the norm. Bruno's mind was, in point of fact, messier than his living room, crowded with lusts and irrationalities and stuck recordings beyond number. It was a wonder he accomplished anything at all.

But he engaged Marlon Sykes in sporadic conversation, when certain non-useless thoughts occurred to him. He looked up and down, as the mountain slowly grew beneath them and shrank above. He tugged his beard, pinched his chin, even fretted periodically about the Ring Collapsiter's fall, and how it might be averted. $F=ma$, obviously, and by corollary, $F=ea/c^2$. Did that help? If so, it wasn't apparent.

Finally, the summit approached, the sky widening above and below them. It was unsettling, the way the sky never changed. The hazes drifted slowly in the jet stream, yes, but the post-sunset colors that lit them refused to deepen, to lose the last hints of red, to fade to blue and then darkness. The stars refused to really come out. There was no moon, and beneath the gloomy cloud deck below them, it was easy to imagine nothingness: Venus a planet of pure sky with no solid surface at all except this mountain, rising up like a pillar from the depths.

The staircase widened at the last, doubling and tripling its breadth before opening, finally, to a flattened, roughly circular depression at Skadi's summit, some thirty meters across. The rock into which it was sunk formed a waist-high wall all around, broken by sheets into rough-smooth pastry layers. To the southwest, the twilight was brighter; Bruno hurried in that direction, crowding up against the wall, looking out toward the sun, hidden by miles of cloud and miles more of rock.

And there, standing nearly vertical in the sunset glow, was the Ring Collapsiter, barely visible as a filament of blue-green Cerenkov light, not quite a line but the peak of an arch; two very fine lines rising together to join at the top. Like the stars themselves, too small and distant to see as objects; this was a sort of stretched pinpoint, a brightness without dimension, but not without structure. Marlon's promised crenellations were quite apparent, though subtle: little scallopy waves in the smoothness of the ring, and smaller waves scalloping those, placing each of the structure's millions of collapsons into one of gravity's infinitely many vibrational nodes, making it a stable, eternal structure. In theory.

Again, he was struck by the beauty of the thing, by the sheer elegance of function cast into form. Would future generations perceive its marvel, its grace? Would it slide into mundanity, one more work of engineering fading into civilization's background, like cabling and sewer pipes? The very thought made him angry.

And then it struck him: he was doing it too, presuming a future for this thing, for the people whose lives it threatened. He, too, presumed unconsciously that this problem would be solved. And that was interesting, because he'd never presumed, for example, that the Earth could be towed to a warmer orbit to thaw its frozen regions, or that wellstone iron could magically change to atomic iron, or that one fine day, people would all cease being rotten to each other. Bruno prided himself on a good sense of which problems were and weren't tractable, and this one—the fall of the Ring Collapsiter—apparently passed the test.

So what did his subconscious know that he himself did not? What had it been doing, while he was off barfing into cups and whatnot?

"There it is," Marlon Sykes said, pointing vaguely. "In all its glory. You can even see Her Majesty's superreflectors, little white dots all around."

Bruno peered, squinted, and decided Marlon was right. The pinpoints were faint, much fainter than the collapsium itself. They were yellow-white, like sunlight, and they hovered outside the ring at various distances, sunlight pushing them away as fast as they could be lowered into place. In fact, a few of the more distant dots were moving with just-barely-perceptible speed.

"Hmm," Bruno agreed. "Yes. Interesting. How big are the sheets?"

"Not large. A hundred meters."

"Hmm," Bruno said again, nodding slowly and pinching his chin. "Enough to wrap around the torus, like tape around the rim of a steering wheel. Goodness, if the ring were solid, we'd have no problem, would we?"

And then the world stopped. He drew a slow, reeking breath, filling his lungs, and then released it slowly, loudly, in an extended sigh. Because that was it. Because by God, that was bloody well *it*.

"They're wellstone sheets?" he asked excitedly. "Thin and flexible, but able to be rigidized quickly?"

"Uh, affirmative," Marlon said, noting Bruno's change of mood with less-than-complete certainty. The resentment, Bruno saw, hadn't really vanished. It was just better hidden.

"So we wrap them around!" he said, excited anyway, anxious to share the insight. "Send it home in a *cast*, letting sunlight and solar wind do the lifting for us! If the inertia is still too great, which I'm sure it is, we erect solar sails, hundreds of kilometers wide, to collect the necessary force. With perfect reflection, momentum should build fairly rapidly, at least as compared to the alternative. It should provide enough time for your additional grapples to be built and placed, to stabilize the structure. It should; I believe it will!"

"Uh, Declarant," Sykes said, hesitantly and with visible

reluctance, "the collapsiter is made of black holes. Universal superabsorbers. They'll devour the wellstone sheets; we have no way to prevent this."

"Indeed!" Bruno agreed, doffing his cap. "Indeed. But devour them how quickly? The holes are far narrower than a silicon nucleus. Semisafe, yes? Statistically, some erosion is bound to occur—*bound* to—but any resulting damage could be repaired locally, without interrupting the overall process."

He thrust his fist against the top of his hat, thinking to burst it out, to create a model with which to demonstrate. The hat proved tougher than it looked, though. He punched it harder, with no better result.

Sykes glanced down at the hat and back up again, as if doubting Bruno's sobriety. "Sir," he said tightly, "the space between the silicon atoms is enormous compared to the size of a neuble-mass black hole. At best, the collapsium will pass right through."

Bruno punched his hat again, aware that a crowd was building steadily all around, conscious of the weight of their collective gaze. "Will it, Declarant? After sucking electrons off the wellstone's surface? The nuclei, being positively charged, will be attracted directly to the collapson nodes, blocking them partially, all but plugging them." He looked at the hat, still good as new in his hands. "Blast. Look, you: I'm trying to remove your top."

At that, to his astonishment, the hat's crown separated all around, and fluttered end over end to the ground, leaving a flat ring of leather in his hands, a broad disc with a head-sized hole through its center.

Blinking, he said to it, "Er, assume a toroidal cross-section, please."

Obligingly, the hat shrank one way and fattened the other, inflating to a kind of oversized, black leather donut in his hands. Still a bit surprised, he held this up for Marlon's inspection.

"Imagine this as your Ring Collapsiter." He held up a hand

beside it, palm flat, fingers together. "This is your sheet of superreflector. When you wrap the one around the other—" He demonstrated by slowly grabbing the donut. "—and then rigidize it—" He tensed his fist. "—what you're doing, effectively, is balancing a sheet of joined marbles on a bed of . . . I don't know . . . small drains with tremendous suction behind them. Yes, each of your big marbles is really fourteen drain-sized marbles, and yes, the substance of the drains is somewhat pliable. Wait long enough, and despite the energy barriers their mouths will pull protons right off the nuclei, widen, pull some more, widen some more . . . But they won't get big enough to suck whole marbles down, not in the time frame that concerns us. So the erosion will be slow, and the collapsium's mass gain negligible. If there's damage, we'll just snip those collapsons out and replace them. It ought to work."

Did Marlon's face grow pale? In the twilight it was difficult to be sure.

"Good Lord, Bruno. I believe you're right."

"I haven't tried the math, of course. I'm guessing."

"As you guessed before? Phooey. I'll begin the computations in the morning, and then we'll know for certain. But at this point, I'd say you're well within the bounds of decorum to leap and prance and shout 'Eureka!' You've banished my doubts, and that's no mean accomplishment."

Eureka. Hmm, well. With his Greek-philosopher haircut fluttering in the breeze, Bruno had no doubts how ridiculous that would look. Should he run naked down the stairs as well, carrying the Archimedes impersonation to its logical conclusion? Conscious of the news cameras at his back, framing his silhouette against the changeless sunset, he instead cocked his hand back and snapped it forward, sailing the leather donut of his hat out into the empty air, in the general direction of the Ring Collapsiter.

"Majesty," he said quietly, "I believe we've found it."

But his words echoed from the rocks, booming, repeated and amplified by some reportant mechanism aimed at him, or perhaps by wellstone devices buried in the mountain itself and activated surreptitiously. In any case, a great cheer went up from the crowd, and suddenly everyone was thronging around him, wanting to shake his hand, and neither Tamra nor Krogh interceded this time, for they were the first two in line.

chapter six

in which an historic ceremony is conducted

A week later, Bruno sat, chairless and alone, on the smooth, di-clad surface of Marlon's work platform, gazing up at what he'd wrought. That haunting Cerenkov glow was gone, super-reflected back into the body of the Ring Collapsiter, which now arched overhead as a pinkie-thin ribbon of yellow-white light, a huge smeared reflection of the sun below. Not too bright to look at, not quite; the reflecting surface was large enough to diffuse the tremendous radiance of Sol here inside the orbit of Mercury. Spaced around the ring were great circular patches, the "sails" he'd described to Marlon, but from this vantage, none reflected anything but starlight, too dim to make out in the brightness as anything but a lighter shade of black.

Fortunately, this new structure was only temporary. The collapsiter's fall had already slowed significantly, buying time and promising to buy still more, and once the new electro-magnetic grapples were finally in place . . . Well. He supposed the superreflector "cast" had a raw, functional beauty of its own, like the skeleton of a building turned inside-out, but of course it was nothing compared to the hidden glory of the collapsium itself. He wondered if there were more aesthetic solutions, if he'd hit by chance on one of the grimmer, uglier routes to salvation. He hoped not; the eyes of the future—his own included—would have enough to criticize him for as it was. To look back and find that he was, after all, a *bad collapsium engineer* . . .

The notion troubled him for a few minutes, but finally faded until he was able to enjoy the peace here, the stillness, the absence of pressing gratitude and curiosity with which he knew no graceful way to cope. In the last seven days he'd been wined, dined, interviewed, and applauded without end. Without *purpose*, it seemed, for every demanded speech reinforced what the fax had taught him long ago: that his company was dull, that he had almost nothing witty or fascinating of his own to say, that in fact he had a penchant for offending and embarrassing the very people who offered him kindness. And yet they pressed on, offering more and greater kindness, until for their own sakes he felt compelled to withdraw. He didn't mind being distressed half as much as he minded causing it in others, and he knew no other way to prevent it.

But eventually, this thought faded as well, and it might be said that Bruno meditated there on the platform, his mind drifting among the planets, untroubled. How long he sat there is not known, but after some interval had elapsed, he became aware of another presence on the platform with him, of Marlon Sykes settling down cross-legged next to him, following his gaze upward.

"I hear you're leaving," he said.

"Indeed," Bruno agreed. "My work demands it."

"Today?"

"Probably, yes. Does that please you?"

"A bit," Marlon said, an admission for which Bruno respected him all the more. "It's difficult, being confronted with the likes of you. I didn't ask to be resentful; I don't seek it. Things would be much easier if I could count you as a friend."

"But you can't."

"No. Never. Least of all now. Go back to your brilliant *arc de fin* project, please. I've followed your work, you know, sometimes convinced myself I could have done likewise if you hadn't been there first. I hate that it isn't true. And of course there's Tamra, who no longer pines for *me,* her First Philander, if indeed she ever did. I suppose I should keep these thoughts to myself, but I can't quite manage such courtesy. For that, I apologize."

"Unnecessary," Bruno said. "I respect you, and would have you speak your heart."

"Thank you, Declarant. That means . . . something to me, at least."

They were silent for a while, looking up at their collapsium arch, each man alone in thought, until finally another voice called out behind them: Tamra's. "Marlon, blast it, I told you to get him *dressed.* The ceremony is *dress.* Formal. He can't wear *that.* Is it your goal to embarrass me?"

"Not you, Highness," Marlon said innocently. "Why should I desire such a thing?"

"Ceremony?" Bruno asked, with rising alarm. The air, he realized, had been filling slowly with the buzz of news cameras.

"It's a surprise," Tamra said, "and we haven't much time. Quickly, step over to the fax! We'll . . . erect a privacy screen or something." She was wearing the Diamond Crown, he noted, along with the Rings of Mars, Jupiter, and Saturn, and a formal gown of deepest purple. Even her perfect golden robots seemed, somehow, to have been gussied up for the occasion.

Sighing, Bruno examined himself; the clothing he'd selected this morning was casual, comfortable, no doubt long out of fashion. Would the eyes of history care about such a thing, or even notice? Did it make, really, the slightest bit of difference? He'd trimmed his foliage back a bit and combed most of the gray out of it, casting aside the ridiculous cartoon sage's facade, leaving only that measure of maturity that—in his estimation—he'd fairly earned. Surely that was enough.

Smirking uneasily, he spread his arms wide. "If you must take me, Majesty, I think it proper that you take me as I am. For this surprise of yours, which I do not seek."

"I'm not 'taking' you anywhere. We're doing this right here, in view of the collapsiter, and you *do need* to be properly dressed. Come on."

He shook his head. "No, Tamra. I won't."

Her eyes narrowed, her expression sharpening, weapon-like. She was not accustomed to refusal; the last time it had happened, Bruno had knelt in the mud to placate her. But he was, after all, the man of the hour. He was, after all, leaving once more for his true home in the wilderness, and not in any stiff contrivance of cummerbunds and ribbon silk. She seemed, finally, to sense that he felt no compulsion to obey her. And by corollary, that she had no means to force him.

The standoff ended; she sighed. "My feral sorcerer. All right, have it your way. Do at least stand up straight. We'll begin."

On that cue, the sides of the dome came alive with holie screens, three-dimensional windows looking out as if from balconies, looking down on crowds of people thronging below skies of blue, of pink, of saffron yellow, beneath mirrored domes and huge, vaulted ceilings of rock, of plaster, of ice and wellstone and steel. The bottom of the work platform's dome was soon covered; a new row started, like an igloo being constructed of video screens, until it seemed there must be at least one window open on every planet, moon, and drifting rock of the Queendom. Tens of millions of people, a goodly sampling of the Queendom's billions, all planning ahead for this, knowing where and when to show up.

"Typical," he muttered, looking from one screen to the next. "Everyone's in on the joke but me."

The responding laughter all but toppled him from his feet. Thousands of people laughing all at once, from something he'd said! Even Marlon Sykes was chuckling. Bruno could not have been more astonished. Or embarrassed—he felt his cheeks warming. And the laughter went on! The speed of light placed a moat of seconds or minutes between himself and each of these screens. But every few seconds, his remark reached another crowd, and provoked another explosion of cheer, even as the previous ones were dying out.

"I'll make this as quick as light speed permits," Tamra said tartly to the assembled millions, when the chain reaction had finally subsided. "De Towaji has business elsewhere, and doubtless we've taken enough of his time already. Declarant Sykes, do you have the medal?"

"I do," Marlon said, stepping forward, a bronze-colored disc in his outstretched hand, trailing a loop of ribbon.

Tamra lifted it, took the ribbon in both hands, and said, "Declarant-Philander Bruno de Towaji, it is my privilege as monarch of this Queendom to present you with an honor devised specifically for this occasion: the Medal of Salvation. It has no special properties, save the love and gratitude which inspire it."

Grudgingly, Bruno lowered his head and permitted her to loop the ribbon around his neck. She let the medal fall, so that when he stood up straight again it rested just over his heart.

"As the voice of all humanity, it is my privilege to say to you, 'Thanks, Bruno. We owe you one.'"

It was Bruno's turn to laugh, the Queendom's millions falling in behind him, less deafening than before. To the crowds Tamra said, "Actually, that's it. Thank you all for coming."

And then, to Bruno's relief, the holie sceens began winking out, the igloo unbuilding itself around the three of them. Half an hour later, the last of the crowds had vanished, leaving only the Ring Collapsiter itself to observe them.

"Leave us, please," Her Majesty said to Marlon Sykes.

"Gladly," he replied, walking to the fax, casting Bruno a pointed look before vanishing into it.

"So," she said.

"So," Bruno agreed.

"We've quarreled."

"Indeed."

"But we're okay now. Friends again?"

He shrugged. "We always were."

"Really," she said, seeming to find that funny. She took his arm, and led him in the direction Marlon had gone. "Will it be another decade before I see you next? Longer, perhaps?"

Bruno shrugged. "I have no way of knowing, Majesty. My work is intricate."

"Stow the formality, jerk. I've missed you."

"I've missed you, too. Did you think otherwise?"

"But you don't miss . . . this." She gestured, somehow indicating the whole of the Queendom.

Startled, he replied. "Who said I didn't miss it? Of course I do! Not all of it, but enough. I miss the smell of bread on a rainy street. I miss the laughter of children. Not court, of course. Not fortune or fame. Civilization demands things of me which I really don't know how to provide. Perhaps I'll learn someday, or people will stop asking, but for the moment I find it much simpler to be alone with my work."

"Simpler, perhaps. But are you happier?"

He stopped walking for a moment to think about that, and finally decided he didn't have an answer.

"You may kiss me good-bye," she said, stopping beside him, turning her face up toward his.

On either side of them, her robots tensed slightly.

Ignoring them, he bent and kissed her, reflecting that this, at least, he treasured from his old life. This, at least, he could always treasure. How many knew the softness of her lips? How many Philanders could a Virgin Queen declare? Precious few.

"Good-bye, Tam," he said, with unintended gruffness. And then, more softly, "I shouldn't think it's forever."

And then he stepped through the fax gate, into the little spaceship she'd parked on his lawn.

Home again.

He took a moment to admire the ship's red velvet interior, its burnished silver fittings and leather seats, superfluous since Tamra had no need to actually *ride* in this thing. But he supposed the ship would look strange without them. He drew a breath, then stepped out toward the little debarkation staircase and descended to his meadow below.

His sky was a much deeper blue than Earth's, and much clearer than Venus'. The little clouds drifting through it seemed like toys; the horizon was so very close. Behind him, the little teardrop-shaped spaceship closed its hatch and began to hum as if warning him of impending liftoff. Very well. He strode purposefully toward his tiny house. His cottage, really.

"Door," he said when he was close enough. Obligingly, the house opened up, and he entered. All was still neat and tidy and gaudily chandeliered from Tamra's too-brief visit. Robots lined up in front of him, forming a corridor, bowing in twin waves as he passed.

"Stop it," he ordered, refusing at least to put up with that sort of thing in his own home. "Unseal the bedroom," he said after another moment.

Again, the house obliged immediately, but still Bruno looked around him, frowning, dissatisfied.

Outside, Tamra's spaceship lifted silently from the ground, hurling a shadow at the horizon and then vanishing into the sky. Still, Bruno frowned.

"Is anything wrong, sir?" the house finally asked.

Bruno grunted, then threw himself down on the sofa and grudgingly shook his head. "No, it's fine; everything's fine. It just looks smaller, that's all."

Every known tradition of human folklore includes references to "ghosts," lingering traces of people and events long past, and particularly to hauntings, the infusion of certain places with ghostly happenings. Such places are usually man-made, usually built of stone, and the images captured therein are typically unpleasant in character and almost always described in frightening terms regardless of content. A ghost is, to a first approximation, a multimedia record of human terror or anguish, impressed in cut stone and released gradually over time.

In the early ages of rationalism, even through the beginnings of space flight, disbelief in such phenomena was considered a fashionable—even obligatory— rejection of primitive and outmoded superstition. This despite the almost universal dread inspired by graveyards and mausoleums and ruined castles, most particularly at night, when their thermal infrared emissions stood out most prominently. This despite the discovery of semiconductors, the invention of cameras whose silicon-oxide lenses channeled images onto arrays of silicon detectors and thence to silicon memories, from which they could be viewed through silicon-based video displays.

Any rock is 99.999% computationally inert, yes, but particularly in iron-rich basalts and granites, most particularly in those that have been shaped with metal tools—which of course tend to become magnetized with frequent use—chance doping of conveniently sized pockets or vacuoles yields electrical properties ideal for the capture and storage of patterned radiation, such as the image of a body flushed with fear or rage. That the inventors of magnetic tape and bubble memory failed to recognize this is often cited as one of history's stranger anomalies.

Granted, it often takes quite sophisticated archaeological instruments to extract the information *again, to reconstitute some recognizable echo of the image itself. It's difficult to imagine that human sensory processors can distinguish so finely, and filter so well. Unaided ghost "sightings" remain rare and difficult to confirm, leading perhaps to the conclusion that they don't really occur. But it pays to remember that ancient folklorists—the well-nourished ones, at least—were as intelligent and reliable as any modern witness, and also that they knew, one way or another, not only about hauntings but about the vanished "dragons" and "oni" and "troglodytes" of ages past.*

At any rate, modern archaeologists make a livelihood of studying ghosts virtually indistinguishable from those described by medieval scholars. It's from just such a source that we know the following:

1. That while faxing himself home that day, Bruno de Towaji was simultaneously diverted to a place of cut stone, deep inside the Uranian moon of Miranda.

2. That he looked around in puzzlement for several seconds upon arriving there.

3. That his eyes settled on a particular location, about six meters away from where he was standing.

4. That his skin temperature rose by nearly a full degree and then dropped precipitously, and that he said "God, oh God, you've got to be joking."

The ghost reveals nothing else about that particular incident, although archaeologists dutifully report a sense of dread and foreboding in the heel marks where de Towaji stood.

book two

twice upon a
star imperiled

chapter seven

in which an anomalous result is pondered

In the ninth decade of the Queendom of Sol, on a miniature planet orbiting at the middle depths of the Kuiper Belt, there lived a man named Bruno de Towaji who, at the time of our latest attention, sat brooding in his study, staring at the measurement his desk had reported for the umpteenth time. Feigenbaum's number, yes, hmm.[4]

Bruno had built an apparatus, a structure for testing the nature of true vacuum. The structure was called "the Onion," and was composed of miniature black holes held in place by carefully balanced electrogravitic forces, a state of matter known as "collapsium." Naturally, such a thing could not be kept *on* the miniature planet itself; it orbited several miles away, a faint puckering of the star field, powder-blue with escaped Hawking-Cerenkov radiation.

Distance notwithstanding, the Onion's tides disturbed the planet's tiny ocean and atmosphere, playing hell with the weather, playing hell with the orbit of the miniature moon. When there'd been one, anyway; the "moon" was really a storage

4. See Appendix A. Feigenbaum's Number, page 367

heap for inch-wide spheres of extremely dense matter: neubles. Diamond-clad balls of liquid neutronium, a billion tons apiece. Black hole food. All gone now, used up.

Presently, the floor seemed to tilt under Bruno's chair and then jerk upright, then tilt again and slowly right itself, as the Onion passed overhead. The atmosphere crackled, alive with static electricity; the ground, pulled several inches out of true and then released, rumbled in protest.

Sounds and images flitted through Bruno's mind. Bricks, dust, cries of alarm; the *ground* was *shaking*. Well, not any-more, but his heart still hammered like a wet fist at the base of his throat, and would do so for the next ten minutes at least, before it finally faded from notice. And in another two and a half hours, whether Bruno was ready or not, it would all happen again!

He felt he should have gotten used to this at some point. Sabadell-Andorra, after all, was eight decades in his past. He couldn't help but remember the bells of Girona clanging as the weary brick towers crumbled around them. He couldn't help but remember the Old Girona Bistro—his own house!—falling in on itself like a magician's box, taking his parents down with it while he bounced and surfed, more or less unscathed, on the street outside. To a fifteen-year-old, the calamity had been absolute.

But Girona's demise had been a freak, a chance synergy of tectonics and soil composition feeding precisely the resonant frequencies of the local architecture. He'd learned some new terms that week: feedback, fluidization, condemned, after-shock, pyre. There hadn't been another case like it in all the years since, and probably—given the extreme conservatism of Queendom building codes—there never would be again. So why was he still afraid of earthquakes? Even minor ones, even ones whose timing and severity were under his direct control?

His failure to acclimate made him wonder, sometimes, just what he was doing out here. Alchemy? Aversion therapy? The inane bumblings of a man who should, by now, have grown senile and sessile with age? He wasn't doing controlled science, that much was obvious.

He'd never intended—never imagined—orbiting such a massive structure so close to his little planet. He'd never imagined using the *entire moon* in the Onion's construction, but what began as a transient curiosity had become first a tinkering, then a project, and finally a heedless, sleepless obsession. A handful of collapsons in low orbit had become—seemingly overnight—a nested cage of fractured spacetimes, one within the other like wooden babushka dolls, magical ones, straining at the very underpinnings of universal law. And orbiting right overhead! A structure too massive to relocate, too delicate to risk disassembling, too dangerous and disruptive to leave where it was. What had he been thinking?

No, he knew the answer to that: he'd been after the True Vacuum. Hard to blame himself for that.[5]

The project had taken several weeks, he thought. Or months, maybe; he'd long since stopped marking the passage of time. He'd eaten and slept on a schedule not matched with the rising and setting of his miniature "sun." He remembered that much. But looking now at the wreckage of his study—the mess of socks and cups and wellstone drawing slates filled with notes and diagrams and 3-D animations that had been abandoned half finished or else crossed out with savage strokes—he marveled at how *damnably* entranced he could sometimes become.

It was like waking up underwater, at the bottom of a bathtub or something: looking up, seeing the surface rippling above you. It isn't hard to sit up and take a breath, so the initial panic fades to simple confusion and astonishment. How the fudge did *that* happen?

And the results he'd brought back with him were astonishing, too. Or confusing. Or simply—probably?—wrong. Feigenbaum's Number? This was the trouble with basic research. Expected results told you nothing, told you that you had *learned*

5. See Appendix A. True Vacuum, page 369

nothing. But unexpected results could mean anything; experimental error or flawed conception or simple insanity on the part of the experimenter. Bruno had known his share of scientific kooks, and this was exactly the sort of thing they were always going on about, in a thousand different mutual contradictions. So in the end, you still learned nothing, maybe for hundreds of years, until the rest of physics caught up and could finally tell if you were full of beans or not.

Humph.

He waved for lights, for windows. The study brightened with warm, incandescent yellows and whites, but where stone wall faded to glass window there were only reflections of those same lights against darkness. It was nighttime outside.

He realized he was famished, and wondered how long it had been since he'd eaten. A full day? He hoped not, else gas and bellyaches would follow soon after any meal.

"Good evening, sir," the house said through extruded wall speakers, as if he'd just arrived and required a greeting.

"Hmm, yes. Door, please."

Obligingly, a rectangular seam appeared in the wall plaster; the space within it darkened, turned to wood, acquired picturesque brass hinges, and swung outward.

"Sir, you have—"

He held up a hand. "Actually, I need something to eat before I hear the day's problems."

"Yes, sir," the house replied, a bit uneasily. "There's a bowl of peeled grapes ready for you. Chilled. But you have—"

"Grapes?" Bruno passed through the doorway, into the darkened living room. "Grapes? Where? No, don't turn on the lights, just tell—"

His shins collided with something knee high and solid, something that felt cool and smooth through the silk of his pajama breeches, felt in fact like the torso of a robot that was resting on its hands and knees. At least, that's how it felt for the moment it took Bruno to lose his balance and spill over sideways.

"Hugo! Blast it!" he called out.

Can a house gasp in dismay? Bruno's seemed to for a moment. Beneath him there was the crackle of programmable matter shifting substance at maximum rate; he landed on a thick, yielding carpet of foam rubber. Not real rubber, of course, but wellstone rubber, a structure of designer electron bundles alternating with superfine silicon threads. Presently, the foam grew patchy beneath him, as if dissolving; two seconds later he lay in a Bruno-shaped depression, his left side resting directly against the granite of the house's foundation. A cloud of silicon dust rose up all around him.

The foam had yielded too far, lost structural integrity, broken the fine mesh of circuits that gave it the illusion of substance. Had the floor changed to iron instead, *he'd* have been the one to yield, but as it was he'd probably been saved from a cracked elbow. Of course, in the Queendom of Sol "breaking the floor" was the very *metaphor* for foolish clumsiness. Or had been, once upon a time; he didn't get down there much anymore.

"Declarant-Philander!" the house cried out, using the longest and most formal of his titles, though he'd told it a thousand times not to. "Are you all right? Are you hurt?"

He didn't speak at first, fearful of inhaling the fine silicon dust. Instead he sat up, brushing himself off, breathing lightly—experimentally—through his nose. At once, small multilegged robots scuttled forth from the shadows, undulating, wrapping sinuously around him and racing over his skin and clothing with tiny vacuum-cleaner probosci. They raced around the edges of him as well, finding the dust where it lay. Two seconds later they were finished and gone, scuttling back into hiding like fast-motion figments of his imagination.

"Sir?" the house prompted again, anxiously. "My humblest, humblest apologies, sir. Are you all right? I tried—"

Bruno sighed. "I'm fine. Hugo?"

The robot he'd tripped over, perched there in the darkness on its hands and knees, looked up slowly at the sound of its name. Its neck joints clicked, golden bands sliding one inside the other, as it turned its blank metallic face toward him. A faint mewling sound emanated from somewhere in the vicinity of its nonexistent mouth.

"Your robot is in need of recycling," another voice, a female voice, said from deeper in the living room's darkness.

Startled, Bruno rose to his feet, spied a silhouette there on the divan. Long hair, long dress, a sparkle of diamonds at the waist.

"Lights," he said, though he knew at once who it must be.

"I tried to tell you, sir," the house complained. "You have a visitor."

The lights came up softly, illuminating the form of—who else?—Her Majesty Tamra Lutui, the Virgin Queen of All Things. Bruno had known no other visitor for years, and even *she'd* been here only the once. She'd been desperate, then, in need of his help. And in the here and now, her posture gave the impression that she'd been sitting there in the darkness for some time. Fair enough; the house had standing orders never to disturb him in his study unless his safety or his work were in immediate danger. Had it made her wait? Had she agreed to, when Royal Overrides could compel any software to her immediate bidding?

"Malo e lelei," he said, as prelude to his many questions.

She inclined her head slightly, acknowledging the greeting. No crown adorned her tonight; her black hair spilled out over bare, walnut-colored shoulders. Her dress was of crimson suede, with round black shoes sticking out underneath. Casual attire, even for a figurehead ruler of billions. *Especially* for a figurehead, he supposed. The only concession to her station was a wide bracelet of porcelain bearing the traditional plus sign and six-pointed star of Tongan heraldry, half smothered in laurels and filigree.

"You're quite welcome here, Highness," he went on, now a bit testily. "I'm at your disposal, as always, but I'm afraid I wasn't prepared for a visitor this evening." He glanced around at the floor and furnishings. "I see the house has cleaned up, at least. By choice, I wouldn't inflict my usual housekeeping on you."

"Your robot," she said, pointing, "is defective. I nearly tripped over it myself."

Beside him, Hugo had moved, slowly, to the side of the Bruno-shaped dent in the floor, and was probing the edges of it with slow, tin-gray fingers capped in gold. The faint mewling sound had never quite stopped.

"Not defective," Bruno said wearily. "Free. I wanted *one* animate object around here that wasn't simply a house appendage. Do you realize there isn't a single animal on this planet? Not a bird to sing, not a fish to poke ripples in the water's smooth surface. Did I really do that, craft an entire world, landscapes and biomes and evaporation cycles, and then forget to populate it? Someone gave me a little toy ocean once, alive with miniature creatures, and even then I didn't take the hint. I suppose I sought to correct the oversight. I have entirely too many servants as it is, so I decided to free one."

She frowned. "Free it?"

He nodded. "Yes. I severed its link to the house software."

Her Majesty looked aghast. "Robots have no volition, Declarant, no desire to do anything but *fulfill*. Nor do they possess intelligence, unless you'd count raw intuition as such. You severed the link to its processor, its ability to grasp and assess the very needs it must fulfill?"

He nodded again. "Just so."

"How . . . unkind. You leave it helpless and confused, in an environment beyond its comprehension."

Bruno shrugged. "Such is the nature of freedom, Highness. I've often said that life is nothing more than the choices thrust upon us when ability and incident collide. Which of us truly knows our course? Generally, we don't even know the landscape *beneath* our course. It's a terrible gift, in some ways, but a great one as well. Hugo is more fortunate than some."

Bruno was intrigued even as he said the words, because there'd been no one to ask him these questions before, and he hadn't really reflected on them himself. Freeing Hugo was something he'd simply *done* one day, and never reconsidered. After all, what software existed to tell *him* what to do next? None. And if it came about somehow, if some master house intelligence could plot the course of his life, or even his afternoon, would he listen? He'd never expected to wind up out here, in the Queendom's upper wilderness, with only the collapsium for company, but at least he could look back and know that for whatever inane reasons, he'd done this to himself. Such was the nature of freedom.

It *was* sort of a grim thing to inflict on a robot, he supposed.

Hugo, once again looking up at the sound of his name, mewled and fell face first into the hole in the floor.

"Ahem," Her Majesty said.

"Oh, bother it." Bruno sighed and took a seat across from her. "Where are *your* robots, Tamra? Your guards. You're never without them. And how did you get in here, anyway? I'd have detected the approach of a ship."

One of Hugo's graceful cousins slipped briefly into view then slipped out again, leaving a tray of food and drink on the table between them.

"Your fax," Tamra said, pointing at the dark orifice around which the little house was built. "It *is* the usual mode of travel, Bruno."

He pursed his lips. "Eh? My network gate is down, Highness. Nonfunctional, for years."

It was Tamra's turn to shrug. "I had it repaired last time I was up here."

"Really. Ah. Nice of you to inform me."

"You needn't be so offended," she said, with an air of both guilty humor and bruised camaraderie. "I've kept the secret, kept the override to myself. It's as I found it, with the exception that I can get word to you when circumstances demand it."

He nodded resignedly. "When circumstances demand it, ah. This isn't a social visit, then."

The shaking of her head was gentle, apologetic. "No. Did you expect otherwise?"

"No," he admitted. "Why should I? You've visited exactly once in sixteen years, and only then to tell me the Ring Collapsiter was falling into the sun."

The Ring Collapsiter: an annulus of collapsium encircling the Queendom's parent star, its interior a supervacuum shortcut through which telecom packets—such as the signals comprising a faxed monarch—might pass much faster than the vacuum speed of light. Only a third complete when last Bruno had seen it, the Collapsiter had already been the most breathtakingly beautiful of all the works of man. An impressive project to be sure, almost impressive enough to make him stay. A Queendom capable of such grandeur might have use for his peculiar drives and talents after all!

But in the end, he'd been lured back up here by the promise of an *arc de fin,* an arch through which the end of time itself might be observed. His bones quaked at the very idea. Here was an even grander project, so grand in fact that he expected to spend thousands of years working out the details. And yes, conducting those dangerous experiments—such as the Onion—that might eventually lead him there. Experiments even a bold Queendom could never tolerate in its midst, and rightly so.

Her Majesty smiled tightly and brushed a lock of hair from her face in precisely the way that had inspired the love of billions. "That was no trivial matter, Declarant-Philander Bruno de Towaji. You make yourself difficult to visit, and then complain that no one takes the quite enormous trouble to visit you anyway? We do have other concerns, you know. A whole society's worth. If a thought is spared for you every now and then, it's certainly not because you've encouraged it."

Bruno felt his irritation meter rising. Human genetics, though, had always included a mechanism for awe in the face of celebrity. This was the very reason for the Queendom's founding, the reason for all the peoples of all the worlds to *demand* that the tiny Pacific nation of Tonga yield up its young princess to be the Queen of them all. And against so deep an instinct, what chance did mere irritation have? He knew her as much more than a figurehead or celebrity, of course, but he'd long ago discovered just how little this mattered.

Bruno bowed his head. "You know me too well, Highness. Thus, you'll know that my apology is sincere. Have I wronged you? Questioned your right to demand audience? I have no explanation, save the lateness of the hour and my surprise on seeing you here."

"Accepted," the Queen said evenly, with a slight nod of the head.

Able to resist his hunger no longer, Bruno picked up one of the little dishes his servants had left and began popping peeled grapes into his mouth, one by one.

"Excuse me," he said around a mouthful of them. "I'm quite famished. Will you join me in a meal?"

She shook her head, but touched one of the glasses on the tray. "A drink, perhaps. This is lemonade?"

"Indeed," he said proudly, "fresh squeezed. Faxed juices may be identical to the taste, but who says taste matters more than principle? I grow the sugar, as well."

She smiled. "Your father would be proud. Your *robots* grow it, though, I hope."

"Well," he admitted, "I sometimes help. At any rate, it's clear you haven't come here to discuss agriculture. I'll waste no more of your time. What is it you require of me?"

Her Majesty sighed, looking suddenly tired and unhappy. Looking, actually, like she'd been concealing these things for far too long, and was relieved, finally, to let them out. "It's your expertise with the Ring Collapsiter, I'm afraid."

"Ah." Bruno nodded, only a little surprised. " 'Also grow tévé,' is that it?"

She flared visibly at the proverb, taking his meaning immediately. How many times had that hardy, bitter weed sustained Tonga's people in times of famine? The wise farmer set aside a little plot for it—the damned stuff needed no tending, just a bit of clear ground to stretch its leaves across. Bruno's barb was double pronged: On the one hand, Tamra was treating him as a kind of Royal Tévé, which seemed a fine way to repay his decades of adoration. On the other hand, *he* was the one who'd insisted on maintaining a palace vegetable garden, tévé and all, and he had little doubt it had vanished under shrubbery and elephant grass within a month of his departure.

Tamra eyed him silently for a few seconds before replying. " 'Plant a coconut and leave it alone.' "

"Hmmph," he said, and suddenly he was fighting off a smirk. A coconut was tough and hairy, difficult to reach without a good climb, and took years and years to produce anything useful when planted in even the best of soils. Bother it, Tamra was *good* at this sort of repartee—she'd have him tied up in neat little bows if he tried to outproverb her again.

His spasm of good humor quickly faded into worry. He'd left the Queendom with a solution, a means to stabilize the Ring Collapsiter and prevent any recurrence of the accident that had knocked it free. And once completed, once its final intricate shape obliterated all gravitational trace of its existence, the structure would be no more capable of falling into the sun than the Earth was of falling out of its orbit. But so long as it remained unfinished, the Ring Collapsiter was inherently perilous, inherently difficult to protect from the vagaries of time and space and chance. Every collapson weighed eight billion tons, after all, and even at a range of forty million kilometers, the sun's gravity was considerable. Precautions or no, nature *wanted* the two to come together.

"The details are complex," Tamra said, taking a sip of lemonade and glancing approvingly down at the glass. "I'm not entirely sure I understand them."

"Is Declarant Sykes still in charge of the project?"

"He is, yes."

"Then I shall get the details from him. But the ring is falling again? And our previous methods are unable to save it?"

She nodded. "I'm told that's so."

"Will it take six months, this time? Or is it free-falling under pure gravitation? Have I time for a night's sleep before faxing myself downsystem?"

Tamra appeared to consider for a moment, then nodded. "We have some time, yes. It's ten months before the crisis comes to a head, and I'm inclined to think we're in *very* deep trouble if you need every moment of that. So the answer is yes, you may remain here until morning. I'll send a copy of myself down with news of the delay."

"Where *are* your robots?" Bruno asked again. It was they who should do such messenger work, as well as their primary function as bodyguards. In truth, Her Majesty looked almost naked without them.

She laughed musically and rose from her seat. "Do I need them here, Philander? From whom are they to protect me? There are . . . times . . . when even the most discreet witnesses are unwelcome."

Bruno frowned. "I'm not sure I understand."

"Oh, Bruno," she said, stepping around the table to plant her lips on his.

chapter eight

in which the nature of time is explained

Bruno never could say no to her. Or rarely, anyhow, and last night they'd fallen together like randy teenagers, their decades apart like some kind of annoyingly long weekend. Still in love, damn them; all their fighting and sulking was for naught, a moment's tantrum in the long, long morning of their lives. But today—despite the way it had begun—was not about the two of them, but about the Queendom itself. Today was business *sans* pleasure, and what Queen and Philander didn't know how to separate the two? Formality seeped and hardened between them as they dined, dressed, and finally, traveled.

If Bruno expected to fax through to a work platform suspended picturesquely beneath the Ring Collapsiter, he was disappointed. Where they ended up instead was a vast, gloomy chamber of hulking gray machinery that hummed.

Tamra slipped her fingers from his, completing the separation. Bruno's hand felt curiously empty.

He sniffed. The atmosphere was thick and dry and warm, and reeked sharply of wintergreen and burning feathers, a sign that PCBs or other heavy, chlorinated oils were overheating in strained electrical transformers. A trouble sign, to be sure, but not half as troubling as that *hum*. Most of the basic tones were subsonic, sensed in the bones rather than the eardrums, but there were overtones and harmonics aplenty, a cacophony that somehow managed to seem both too bass and too shrill for comfort. The noise didn't seem loud until he tried to speak and found he almost had to shout.

"Where are we?"

Behind Tamra, a hemicylinder of gray metal hulked seamlessly atop a seamless metal deck, rising up into the slightly hazy air like a bald mountain.

"Grapple station," she replied in much the same tone.

"Ah."

The hum and reek now made sense: this place was an enormous gravity generator, a kind of God-sized cable winch holding up the Ring Collapsiter.[6] It had best *keep* holding, too; black holes inside the sun, even miniature "semisafe" ones, would collapse it to a cinder, assuming they didn't first tear it to shreds. But despite everyone's best intentions, despite precautions and failsafes and contingency plans, the ring of crystalline collapsium had slipped sunward again. And this grapple station, whatever its capability, was clearly straining past any reasonable endurance to slow the descent.

"Big," he said, unnecessarily.

"Quite," Her Majesty agreed.

The fax gate behind them quietly disgorged a pair of dainty robots, all silver and platinum and chrome. White caps adorned their heads, and white frilled collars adorned their necks. Their sexless torsos and faceless faces were smooth, unadorned expanses of bright metal. Their silver hands gripped ornate pistols of delicate—but nonetheless menacing—design. The robots bowed to Her Majesty and placed themselves at respectful distances on either side of her.

"You've changed guards," Bruno observed. "They used to be gold."

Tamra smiled, a bit wistfully. "That's right. They used to be

6. See Appendix A. Electomagnetic Grapple, page 371

taller, too, and thicker around the middle. But times change, you know. Fashions and preferences change. Even if yours do not."

"Oh, humph," he replied, walking past her leftmost guard, around toward the huge gray hemicylinder. He placed a hand on it, felt its desperate hum. "Who says I haven't changed? How would you know?"

She shrugged. "It's not an insult, just an observation. Your clothing, your words and mannerisms—all are decades out of touch. Your hair is different than last time, I suppose. Less wild, less gray. It suits you better. When I'm with you, though, I feel almost as if no time has passed at all. You bring my distant decades back to life."

Bruno humphed again. "What you call 'time,' Majesty, is more a social than a physical phenomenon. You don't perceive this, because you're inside the social structure that creates it. But watching clocks and calendars, indexing your memories by popular music—these are learned, unnatural behaviors. Mark my words: living alone is the ultimate exploration of inner truth. It's one thing to see yourself as a web of changing relationships: to others, to society, to material things and places. It's quite another to see simply *yourself*, to be your own companion, to talk to yourself and answer back honestly. *Your* times change because others change them for you. My changes come purely from within."

"Wait. Be quiet."

"Why," he chided, "because your illusions can't withstand a moment's scrutiny?"

She waved a hand in annoyance. "Bruno, be *quiet*. Someone's coming."

He followed her gaze. There in the distance, walking the kilometers-long avenue between hulking machines, was a pale young woman with tightly braided hair the color of metallic platinum. Bruno's vision was quite good—whose wasn't?—and for a moment he inspected her distant features, trying to identify the face. Was this someone he'd known, in the days before his exile? If so, it wasn't evident, but then again appearance

was a malleable thing, programmable through any fax machine.
She looked young but mature, which of course meant nothing at all.

"Oh," he said. "Do you know her?"

Tamra shook her head. The robots beside her faded back
into the shadows of machinery, their blank faces turned
toward the approaching woman.

"Hello!" Bruno called out.

"Hi," the woman said back, closer now, well within hailing
distance. "Welcome. I was told to expect you."

"Told? By Declarant Sykes?"

"Correct," she said, then made a skittish, nervous little
laugh. The toss of her shining braids was, he thought, calculated for nonchalance. "I'm Deliah van Skettering, Lead
Componeer for the Ministry of Grapples. Good day, Your
Majesty. And you, sir; you're Bruno de Towaji? It's an honor,
truly. I've studied collapsium engineering my whole adult life.
In fact as a student I used to keep a statue of you on my desk
for inspiration."

"Hmm," he said. "Yes, well."

He never had discovered a comfortable response for state-
ments like that one. Not that he heard them all *that* often,
but those little copper statues had been pretty popular for a
while until, mercifully, fashion had turned its attention elsewhere. Talented students and componeers seemed to prefer
living role models to dead ones, for which he could hardly
blame them. Less comprehensible were the ordinary citizens,
with no interest in collapsium or telecommunications or
telegravitic engineering, who nonetheless made him a subject of their public admiration. For his wealth, he supposed,
although many of the Queendom's plutocrats reaped as much
scorn and envy as actual respect.

So why Bruno? Who could say. Of such mysteries was society constructed. Tamra, at least, had always treated him
like an ordinary person. She'd liked the idea that he was
smart and famous and rich—with all of humanity to choose
from, it surely helped to have some screening criteria—but

having grown up a princess, she wasn't terribly *impressed* by
these things. Impressing her was a whole separate enterprise.
He truly wished he could return the favor, disregarding her
station and influence to deal with the woman herself, but
that was a trick he'd never quite managed in all their years together.

Not that he'd been deferential, exactly. She didn't go for
that, and in fact he'd been a real bum sometimes, pushing
her away, trampling her feelings half deliberately so she'd
send him off to "exile" in his laboratory. But even then he'd
been acutely conscious of her station. Perhaps that's *why* he
did it, or part of the why: to rebel against the obvious power
imbalance between them. And to have something to make up
for, yes. They were always a great pair for making up.

"He's pleased to meet you," Tamra said to this Deliah van
Skettering, meanwhile offering Bruno a lightly reproachful
elbow in the ribs.

"Er, yes."

Finally, Deliah presented herself before them. "Your
Majesty," she said, curtseying deeply, spreading an imaginary
skirt even though she was actually wearing trousers and work
boots and a heavy brown shirt made from some dense, wet-
looking material. "Declarant-Philander," she said to Bruno,
and curtseyed again.

Bruno couldn't help sizing her up: tall and sturdy, quick,
self-assured. But something told him she was maybe a little
bit hollow inside. Unfulfilled? She reminded him of a weaver
woman he'd known in Girona: Margaret something. Master
of a craft that was widely admired and very much in demand,
but difficult and rather dull in the practice. "The prison of my
talent," she'd often called it. Margaret's frustration had always seemed a terrible shame to Bruno, but if people could
choose their abilities he supposed the world would drown itself in athletes and guitar players and raunchy but lovable sex
artists. If you had a job you were good at and appreciated for,
well, sometimes that had to be enough.

He bowed.

"Doubly honored," Deliah said nervously. "Brushes with greatness, oh my. I've had this department for eight years, but *this* is the month people choose to notice."

"Naturally," Tamra said.

"I'm to take you to Declarant Sykes," Deliah added, casting a glance in the direction she'd come from. "Unfortunately, the station's only fax gate is on the opposite end from the instrument room. It's a bit of a walk."

"Marlon is mucking with instruments again?" Tamra asked in a disapproving tone.

"Um, well, we've been tuning the revpics, trying to bring the frequencies up. It's slow work."

"And rather beneath your rank," Tamra observed, falling into step behind her.

"Perhaps, yes."

The hum of machinery followed them as they walked.

"Well," Bruno said, "it's a very formidable station you have here. There are hundreds of others just like it?"

"That's so."

Bruno couldn't help but be impressed. Projects like this one, however ill fated, bespoke a Queendom far bolder, far wealthier and more ambitious, than the one he'd left. With death a hunted quality, faxed away with every minor journey, perhaps civilization was finally able to take a longer view. Was it easier to make such pipe dreams come true when the benefits were for the builders themselves, rather than some hypothetical "posterity?"

He traced his hand along an enormous and unpleasantly warm resistor.

"The main beam holds up the collapsiter. I'm guessing its complement is anchored to a star?"

Deliah turned and smiled at him, as if the question pleased her. "Several stars, actually. It's like sinking tent stakes into sand—the more you distribute the load, the less slippage you get."

"Ah. Of course."

"Partly my own idea, I'll confess. After all, we don't want to spend all our time tightening the, uh, tent cords."

"Indeed."

"It's only for a few decades, anyway, until the ring is self-supporting, like a bridge. That's the only reason we can do it this way. We couldn't build a permanent structure of gravity beams—the anchor stars would all crash together eventually."

"Obviously, yes," Bruno agreed, then wondered if his tone weren't a bit overbearing or dismissive. "I, uh, see you've worked out all the details."

That comment clearly didn't please Deliah van Skettering. Of course, yes, because she *hadn't* worked everything out, had not managed to prevent this newest disaster. Would she feel his words to be an insult? Bother it, people were so damned easy to offend. Especially the friendly ones. As always, Bruno could be offensive without lifting a finger.

"The Declarant's social skills don't see much use these days," Tamra said, touching both Bruno and Deliah on the shoulder. She sounded amused, though not entirely patient about it. "Do please forgive him."

"No, he's quite right," Deliah sighed. "Patience and mathematics. Patience and mathematics. If I've learned anything from his example, it's that. If I've learned anything."

"Here now," Bruno protested. Many notions could be drawn from his example, surely, but he'd hate to count self-pity among them. "Mistakes happen, young lady. Don't blame me for blaming you, because I haven't. If, at some point, I *do* blame you, you'll know it unambiguously. As you see, I'm not a subtle man."

Deliah ducked her head. "Of . . . course, Declarant. Forgive me."

"Oh, none of that," he said, waving a hand. "I won't hear of it; you'll have us tied in knots. So you're the director around here, are you?"

"For eight years now, yes."

"And you say you've had no other problems?"

"Major ones? There are always problems—"

He waved a hand. "Of course, of course. I'm not grilling you; I'm just, er, making conversation. Since it appears we'll be working together."

"Ah. Well, for what it's worth, I came to physics fairly late in life. And management. I'm from Africa."

Bruno wasn't sure what to make of that. "Is where you're from a significant factor here?"

She gave an uncomfortable laugh. "It can be, yes. Growing up on a photocollector farm, you don't think about much beyond the weather, the maintenance, and maybe a strong boy or two who'll keep the dust off and laugh at your jokes. But University changes you—that is its purpose, I suppose."

"Changes you? Leads you toward the sciences, you mean."

"Toward the management of sciences, yes. What a shock, to discover I was a shepherd of physicists! By my second year at KSPA I was the department gopher, organizing all the home conferences, and eventually *all* the conferences all over the solar system. My grades were good, too, and my thesis did win that prize. Suddenly I was 'Laureate van Skettering,' right when my kiddie marriage was falling apart and I needed a fresh start anyway. But from the moment I hit the job exchange, it was clear I was headed for administration, not math.

"Knowing the material is fine—it's common—but it's hard for one person to really move the world. Even *you* needed a cast of thousands in the end, Declarant, if I may say so. Turning prototype to product to end-user installed base is the real test of an idea, and knowing how to pull a team together—and *hold* them together when the going gets tough— is the key to that."

Bruno could hardly argue with that; if everyone were like him, there'd probably be no commerce or progress at all, at least in the conventional sense.

"And yet," Bruno said, groping to understand her point, "you're still surprised to find yourself here. Far from Africa, among monarchs and Declarants, plotting the salvation of a star and all its worlds."

"Exactly." Deliah nodded once, emphatically.

He cleared his throat. "You, ah, do realize that the rest of us feel that way too? I myself grew up in the apartment above a little Spanish tavern."

"I know," she replied quickly.

Well of course she did. She'd already admitted to being an admirer, and Bruno's life was in the public domain, open to all possible scrutiny. All at once, he was uncomfortable again, feeling exposed. Feeling far from *his* home, wherever that might be.

"Life is full of surprises," he added, more sourly than was probably wise.

Suddenly, they were at the instrument room, a narrow closet Bruno might almost have missed if a pair of silk-trousered legs hadn't been poking out of it. The walls and ceiling were of wellstone; a panoply of dials and gauges and keyboards and graphical displays raced and oozed and flickered around the flat surfaces, whose composition bubbled cubistically between metal and porcelain and various forms of plastic.

"What happened?" Deliah demanded of the legs. She was eyeing the wellstone surfaces with tired exasperation. Then, more respectfully, she said, "Can I help, Declarant?"

"No," a voice said from beyond the legs. They disappeared, Bruno saw, into a slot at the bottom of the closet's back wall. Big enough to hold a human torso, though probably not comfortably, not unless the space opened up back there behind the wall.

"You realize we're going to have to restart the calibration estimates from scratch," Deliah complained. "You do realize that?"

"I do, yes. Thank you." Presently, the owner of the legs shuffled and scooted and rocked out of the opening. Only when the face emerged was Bruno sure that this was, in fact,

Declarant-Philander Marlon Sykes. Awkwardly, Sykes straightened himself up to his full height. He wiped his hands on the blue velvet and fine, gold-white embroidery of his vest, leaving black smudges there.

"Marlon!" Her Majesty snapped. "What on Earth are you doing?"

The Queen's robots tensed on either side of her, but Sykes just flashed an easy grin and leaned back—carelessly, Bruno thought—against the madly shifting wall of the instrument room. "On Earth, I don't believe I'm doing anything at the moment. I do have copies on half a dozen grapple stations, probably all doing the same thing right now."

"Which is?" Tamra demanded, arching an eyebrow.

"Retrofitting the equipment, obviously."

Her Majesty's suede-booted foot tapped thrice on the decking. She seemed to consider for a moment before saying, "Declarant, the Queendom pays handsomely for your services. We expect handsome service in return. This—" She waggled a finger at his stained hands and clothing. "—is the best use of your talents right now? It must be, surely, or you'd be doing something else. Correct?"

"Ah." Marlon's smile faltered, then deepened. "Tamra, my pay is by the job, not the copy-hour. Consequently I find it easier to send my own copies to perform certain tasks, rather than having to explain these tasks to others, particularly since our laborers and technicians are operating at full legal capacity already."

"I'll issue a writ to waive the copy-hour limits," Tamra said. "I should have done it already, I see. How long has this been going on?"

He shrugged. "Not long."

"A week," Deliah van Skettering chipped in, her tone supportive and apologetic. "I may have requested . . . that is, my requests of Declarant Sykes may have been . . ."

"Be silent, Laureate-Director," Tamra said to the woman. Then, less haughtily, "All my conversations are official. Speaking out of turn is disruptive."

Reddening, Deliah bowed her head, saying nothing.

Bruno empathized: Deliah was no practiced courtier, after all, and she was—admirably—trying to take responsibility for her own job. But Tamra's role was equally clear: bureaucrats and functionaries must not be permitted to undermine her authority even in these tiny, offhand ways. A Queen must exude power and influence from every pore, yes? Else what good was a Queendom at all?

"Er, shall we . . . proceed?" he asked, when a few pointed moments had passed. It was a calculated risk: even *he* couldn't talk back to her in public. Not without paying.

"We shall," Tamra said lightly. And that was that.

"What is it you're doing there?" Bruno asked Marlon. "Manual labor? Couldn't robots help?"

"They *are* helping," Marlon snapped, in a rapid-fire voice. "Look, wellstone devices are almost infinitely configurable, but where no pathway exists at all between components A and B, as often happens when you're configuring large machinery for unintended purposes, we have to physically lay a line of wellstone down. Or copper, or fibe-op glass, but rarely, because we can program the wellstone to emulate those. So robots do the coarse installation, point to point, and the delicate final connections are completed by hand. And as I say, explaining the process to a technician requires refinement in both the theory and detail of what I'm doing, which would consume precious time. Until *I* know precisely what needs connection to what, I find it easier simply to tinker. Perhaps in another week, I'll have gained enough experience to pass instructions along."

"Hmm," Tamra said, unconvinced.

A touch of sullenness graced Marlon Sykes' features. His gaze flicked to Bruno for a moment. "*His* time costs you nothing, I suppose."

"He donates it, yes."

"I've little need for money," Bruno almost said, but stopped himself, realizing in time that it would probably antagonize rather than soothe. Marlon, the father of the Ring

Collapsiter, was just about as brilliant and wealthy and powerful a man as ever lived, his name writ large as any Edison or Franklin or Fuller. But through the twisting of fate, Bruno's name had been writ much larger, ridiculously larger. Along with his bank account, yes. It was a sore point between two Declarant-Philanders, and understandably so. What he did say was, "It pleases me to visit with friends again. I do it so rarely. I almost feel *I* should pay for the privilege. It's good to see you again, Marlon."

The first reply to that was simply a glower, but finally Marlon put his smile back on and reached out a hand to be shaken. "Your manners exceed my own. I've been immersed here; I'm not really in a mood for interruptions. You know how that can be, I'm sure."

"Indeed," Bruno said, and chuckled a little. He took Marlon's hand in his and clasped it warmly. It came away, of course, slick with machine grease, but that was of little consequence.

"You're well?"

"Well enough, thank you. And you?"

Marlon grumbled, nodding toward the malfunctioning instrument walls. "Could be better, alas. Have you made progress in your research? Are we any closer to an *arc de fin*?"

"Ah, well, that's difficult to say. Like you, I've been tinkering, although in my case the goal is True Vacuum. Results have been . . . mixed, I guess you'd say. Odd. I probably need some peer review at this point, isolation being an ideal breeding ground for foolish error. Perhaps we can discuss it while I'm here downsystem."

"Perhaps," Marlon said, not quite able to hide a sense of avarice and excitement. He wanted to share insights with Bruno, yes, but for whatever reason, he didn't seem to want Bruno to know that.

Tamra began tapping her foot again. "Will you explain our problem to de Towaji please, Declarant?"

Marlon sighed and crossed his arms. "Must I, Highness? I

really am quite busy here, and don't want to lose the thread of it. Perhaps you could visit me at home."

"When?" Tamra demanded coolly.

"Right now," Marlon said, making a kind of facial shrug. "I'm there. It's where I expected you, actually. Whatever possessed you to come here?"

"I don't know; it seemed like an appropriate starting point."

Marlon pursed his lips and shook his head. "Loud and smelly? For our dear friend de Towaji? His mind is a palace, Tam, a cathedral, unsullied by life's grimy banalities. Send him home to me, I beg you. I'll take proper care of him there."

"I'm fine here," Bruno protested mildly. "Banality and grime are novelties, remember. Though of course I'm happy to let you get back to work if that's what you need. Could I leave a copy here to help?"

"No, thanks," Marlon said too quickly, and though he clapped Bruno on the shoulder—leaving a noticeable smudge—there was little mirth in his eyes.

chapter nine

in which unexpected hospitality is offered

Sykes Manor was an exercise in water and white marble.
Spin-gee habitats were common enough in the Queendom,
spheres and cylinders that pressed their occupants to the inner walls by centrifugal force, in the age-old manner of carnival rides. Bruno had never seen a spin sphere crafted as a
single residence, though, and he'd never seen one in the
Athenian style before, nor imagined that such a thing might
exist. Where the classical Greeks had favored straight lines
and rectangles and squat isosceles triangles, Marlon's archi-
tects had substituted sphere-mapped chords and pie wedges
and truncated cones to good—though decidedly strange—effect. And where the inner surface of a typical kilometer-wide
suburb cylinder might be dotted with homesteads and ringed
with a greenbelt or two, draining into faux-natural streams
and ponds, Marlon's house, only forty meters across, contained a system of rigidly geometric gardens and fountains,
zigzagging between looming walled structures that reached,
in some cases, almost to the spin axis. There were no external
windows looking out into planetary space, either; instead,

bright, yellow-orange light slanted down from a tiny, illuminated dome at one of the hubs.

The overall effect was completely startling: an immaculate palace or temple complex as glimpsed at the moment of sunrise, but folded in on itself until inner and outer walls met, creating the dreamlike sensation that one was neither inside nor outside, neither above and looking down, nor below and looking up. No matter where one stood or where one looked, one was, it seemed, perpetually *about to enter* some grand, vaulted inner space that in fact couldn't possibly exist.

All this said something important, Bruno felt, about the psychological workings of a certain Declarant-Philander, though exactly *what* it said he wasn't sure. There was a kind of ostentation here: modest wealth conspicuously displayed. Well, modest by Bruno's standards, at any rate; probably very few people could afford to live this way, and fewer still would do it if they could.

"Many people," Bruno had observed shortly after entering this place, "are too timid or oblivious to shape an environment to their own true hearts. You, Marlon Sykes, are not one of them."

Marlon, reclined on a couch and plucking at the strings of a mandolin, had laughed pleasantly, clearly taking the comment as Bruno had intended it.

"You flatter me," he'd said, and his robots had handed Bruno a mug of chilled green tea. This other Marlon, relaxing at home, seemed far more at ease than his counterpart at the grapple station, far happier to greet the man he regarded as a rival, on the arm of the woman he'd once loved.

We all have multiple faces and aspects, Bruno mused, *but rarely is the contrast so obvious.* That was life in the Queendom for you; the Iscog joined every fax machine to every other, reducing all of space, topologically speaking, to a single geometric point. This permitted—in fact demanded—the encountering of innumerable rareties and ironies and stark, polar opposites, all superimposed atop one another. Impossible, of course, without the transfinite self-recursions of collapsium-based computing devices.

He supposed he could permit himself, at such a moment, to admire his handiwork.

Now the three of them lounged on soft couches in the slanting light beside a softly chattering cascade, clear water spilling down stairs of white marble in the shade of a line of olive trees. Tamra's slender silver robots stood guard on either side, like statues.

"How they got there isn't clear," Marlon was saying. He'd put away his mandolin and was tracing with his index finger on a wellstone slate. "But this whole segment of the ring is contaminated with muons, in tight little orbits around the collapson nodes."

On Bruno's own slate, Marlon's tracings were echoed, and quickly became solid, detailed, three-dimensional-looking images. The sun blazed, and the Ring Collapsiter—its thickness exaggerated by several orders of magnitude—glittered around it like a two-thirds completed crown. Fully half the structure, though, showed not the soothing blue of Hawking-Cerenkov radiation, but a kind of dingy brown glow. Presumably, this was as fictitious as the ring's thickness; Bruno couldn't think of any collapsium process that would create a visible signature like that one.

Bruno sipped from his mug, nodding. The tea was a little sweet for his taste, but he wasn't sure it would be polite to ask the mug to change it for him. Not right in front of Marlon; not when he was being so friendly.

"I see. And the ring is slipping because the EM grapples would damage the contaminated region? By pulling its lattices out of phase?"

"Just so. We dare not disturb it further."

"You're distributing the load across the remainder of the ring, yes? What there is of it, I mean. Your stations remain operational, just aimed differently, at the undamaged arc segments?" He studied the drawing. "Yes, that *would* produce a side force, wouldn't it? But you can't turn the grapples off, either, cutting the puppet's strings, as it were. The whole thing would fall into the sun in a matter of days!—And you can't attach a wellstone sail to the contaminated area, because the orbiting particles would smash through it precisely where the stress is greatest."

"We tried it," Marlon said, shaking his head ruefully. "The sails collapsed immediately and fell into the black holes. Theoretically the holes are semisafe, too small to swallow even a proton, but if you jam one in there hard enough, it'll go. And that's the beginning of the end, because it increases the size of the hole, making it ever so slightly easier for the next particle to penetrate. And of course, any mass change disrupts the equilibrium of the crystal lattice, so already, the collapsium is inherently unstable."

"Ah," Bruno said, beginning at last to understand. "That's why you want higher frequencies on the grapples: so you can grab hold right where you need to. The collapsium is in a precarious state, and gravitic disturbances are to be avoided at all costs. But frequencies *higher* than those of gravitation won't set up the same sort of destructive resonance."

Marlon's smile was only a little tight. "Your edge remains keen, Declarant. In minutes, you reiterate the analysis of weeks. Yes, it's exactly as you say."

"The work progresses poorly, though," Her Majesty interjected, in cool tones. "The collapsiter builds momentum with each passing moment. Even if Declarant Sykes' plan works perfectly, there may not be time to stop its fall. And if we're lucky enough to stop it just *above* the sun's surface, rather than below, I still think the result is unlikely to please us. Your services, Bruno, are very much in need."

Bruno sighed, as uncomfortable as ever with this notion that the unsolvable problems were somehow his to solve. "My 'services' seem to have come up with precisely the same solution that Marlon's did. It's the right solution, Tam."

Her Majesty said nothing, but put on a faux vapid smile that meant she found his comment foolish.

Grumbling, Marlon threw his tea mug into the little cascade, where it clanked and splashed and skidded to a halt, resting half submerged on the marble bottom. "We've enough force to lift this thing, Majesty. It's simply a matter of applying that force where it's needed. As I've told you, the math is really quite straightforward."

"Undoubtedly," she agreed, nodding once.

"You *can* be infuriating sometimes, Tam," Bruno said to her, not unkindly. In decades past, he'd sometimes spent whole days, even weeks being infuriated by her. Truthfully, there were worse ways to spend one's time. But Marlon did not seem so amused.

"Just think about the problem for me," she said, nestling back into her couch and closing her eyes, as if basking in warm sunlight, though in truth the glow of the illuminated dome was rather cool. "Both of you."

They were all silent for a few seconds.

"I do mean now," she noted.

Both men grumbled and, taking advantage of her closed eyes, made sarcastic faces. Then, seeing each other, they laughed, the tension going out of them. Bruno hurled his own mug into the fountain, causing a brief ripple of alarm in Tamra's robots, and then he leaned back with his arms behind his head. Might as well assume a comfortable thinking position, yes? Leather and wood creaked pleasantly beneath him.

"Hmm, yes. A pickle indeed. So how long until we're rid of these particles?"

Marlon sat up on an elbow. "Rid of them how? By decay?"

"Right."

A detailed discussion ensued.[7]

"Eleven months," Bruno mused, when they'd kicked it around for a while. "That's odd. May I examine your raw data?"

Marlon's good cheer faded a bit. "Of course, yes. What data we have is yours."

With their two wellstone drawing slates slaved together,

7. See Appendix A: Muon Contamination, page 373

Marlon walked him through several layers of menus until he'd pulled up the database of measurements his paid observers had collected in recent weeks. Mere samplings, of course, indirect measurements scattered here and there along the Ring Collapsiter's considerable length. Bruno pondered them for a while—apparently a *long* while, since both Marlon and Tamra got up to use the bathroom a few times while he was doing it—and finally he called up a little hypercomputer in a corner of the slate and fed it some quite horrific equations to solve. The answers were, of course, available almost immediately.

"Eleven months," he confirmed, with an approving nod in Marlon's direction. "And how long, again, until the collapsiter penetrates Sol's chromopause?" That was the accepted benchmark for irretrievability; soon afterward, the collapsons would have swollen with gobbled star matter to the point where their crystalline structure became unsupportable. The whole thing would, no doubt slowly and elaborately, crush down into a single large hole, and eventually pull the sun in after it.

"*Ten* months," Marlon replied, looking and sounding unnerved.

"Well, well," Bruno said. "That's what I call inconvenient timing. Had you been assuming this was a natural phenomenon?"

Marlon's voice was hollow, frightened. "I had, yes. Indeed I had. But the odds against such a coincidence . . ."

Her Majesty opened her eyes and sat up, as if only now realizing the implication. "What are you saying, Declarants? That there's a *saboteur* afoot? That someone has done this *deliberately*?"

Bruno shrugged. " 'Saboteur' is the right word, I suppose. A muon is a highly unstable particle about a tenth the size of a proton, and it results from the decay of an even more unstable particle called a pion. My guess is that electrons from the solar wind were struck with a high-powered and precisely targeted stream of coherent neutrinos—a nasen beam, we call it—and this converted them to pions. It's a graduate-level transmutation exercise, performed on an enormous scale."

Marlon Sykes had turned almost completely white. "Good Lord, Bruno, I think you must certainly be right. What else *could* it be? What else could scatter such short-lived particles over such a wide area? I am, as always, dwarfed in your shadow. In an *hour* you've deduced this."

"Well," Bruno grumbled, trying to think of something self-deprecating to say.

"Well nothing," Marlon insisted, somewhat angrily.

"A *saboteur*?" Tamra said again, rising to her feet so she could stamp one of them. "You suggest that a subject of this Queendom is capable of such villainy? A subject of *mine*?"

"I suggest nothing," Bruno said innocently.

A loud noise, like a gong, echoed through the sphero-Athenian spaces of Sykes Manor. Marlon looked up sharply. "Yes?"

"A message," the house said to him, in tones much louder and slower and flatter of affect than Bruno's own house would dare employ.

"I'm holding a slate," Marlon said, testily.

In his hands, an image appeared: a square-faced man of deeply serious expression, clad in the stiff uniform of the Royal Constabulary. That uniform had not changed one bit since Bruno had last seen one, thirty years before: a wellcloth coverall, programmed to act like beige smartcotton festooned with strips of white numerals. And of course, the obligatory monocle over the left eye.

"Yes?" Marlon demanded of the face.

"Declarant-Philander Sykes, is everything all right?"

"It is as far as *I* know. How can I help you?"

The policeman's expression managed, somehow, to grow more serious. "Sir, there's been an incident on Grapple Station 117. Two dead, apparently very recently, apparently by homicide. Are you sitting down, sir?"

"Why are you calling me?" Marlon asked, trying now to

disguise the annoyance in his voice. "Who was homicide, er, was murdered?"

"You were, sir. And a woman, one Deliah van Skettering."

"Oh," Marlon said, going paler then before. "Oh, shit."

"Yes, sir. Exactly. I'm sorry to ask it, but I wonder if you could come to the site and answer a few questions."

chapter ten

in which a crime
is reconstructed

In some sense, the first ten thousand years of human his-tory could be described as a steady climb toward freedom. Not the doomed, hapless freedom of short-lived beach and savanna apes, but the enlightened democracy of a fit and educated humanity that recognized—and indeed, meticulously cataloged—the value of individual action. Society, it was thought, should work to maximize the power—and with it the accountability—of each of its members, so that success and failure and happiness and misery might be had in direct proportion to the effort invested.

Turns out this was a load of hooey all along; people *hated* that sort of self-responsibility. Always had. Only when it was inescapably universal, when there were no more corrupt or uncivilized "third worlds" to flee to, did it become clear that what people *really* wanted, in their secret hearts of hearts, was a charismatic monarch to admire and gossip about and blame all their problems on.

Unfortunately, over the millennia Earth's monarchies had been deposed one by one, and since deposed monarchies had a habit of creeping back into power it had been necessary to murder them all—not simply the monarchs and their heirs and assigns and spouses and bastard cousins, but also their friends, supporters, beloved pets, and the occasional bystander, leaving as little chance of a miraculous restoration as possible.

There were *de novo* monarchs here and there, micronational leaders who'd declared their kingship or queenship on a lark, or in dire earnest and questionable mental health, but by the twenty-fifth century the only real, legitimate, globally recognized monarch left, the only one whose lineage extended back into sufficient historical murk, was King Longo Lutui, of the tiny Polynesian nation of Tonga. And as luck would have it, shortly before the scheduled Interplanetary Referendum on Constitutional Reform, King Longo, sailing the shark-filled straits between the islands of Tongatapu and Eua, chased a wine bottle over the side of his boat and was neither seen nor heard from again. He had left behind a single heir: one Princess Tamra.

You know what happened from there: Her coronation became the talk of the solar system, the duly modified referendum was held, and Tamra was elected the Queen of Sol by a stunning 93% supermajority. And since everyone knew that power corrupted, they were careful not to give her any, and to install a special prosecutor to chase after what little she managed to accumulate. Much was made of her sexual purity as well, and it was thought good and proper that she be humanity's Virgin Queen for all time thenceforward.

The only trouble was, nobody had particularly consulted Tamra about any of this. Really, they were just taking their own burdens of personal accountability and heaping them onto *her*, which hardly seemed fair, and this whole virginity business had more to do with her being fifteen than with any inherent chastity of spirit. She just hadn't worked up the nerve yet, was all. And while the immortality thing hadn't quite happened by that time, the writing on the wall was clearly legible, and the thought of retaining her supposed purity for literally "all time thenceforward" did not amuse Tamra in the least.

So, once installed as Queen, once crowned and throned and petitioned for the royal edicts everyone so craved, her first act had been to Censure everyone responsible for putting her there. Her second act was to compel her physicians to see that her physical purity could regenerate itself in the manner of a lizard's tail or a starfish's arm. And her third had been a deliciously shocking call for suitors—low achievers need not apply.

The rest, as they say, is history.

So understand that the officer in charge of the grapple station crime scene, one Lieutenant Cheng Shiao of the Royal Constabulary, did a commendable job of not acting flabbergasted or starstruck when the expected First Philander stepped through the fax gate with the quite unexpected Queen of Sol in tow, plus a pair of dainty metal bodyguards, plus an extra Philander who was quite famous in his own right. Shiao bowed to each of them in turn and explained with perfect professionalism that in light of the victims' rank and occupation, a more senior investigator had been called and was expected on the scene shortly. In the meantime, if he could just ask a few questions . . .

Marlon Sykes, for his part, did a commendable job of answering without visible emotion. Had he had any reason to expect violence? No. Had any threats been made against him? No. Did he have any enemies? Certainly, yes. A man in his position could hardly avoid it. But *mortal* enemies? He'd have to think about that one. He *had* just uncovered evidence of—

Presently, the fax gate spat out a disheveled young woman Bruno took a moment to recognize as Deliah van Skettering. Dressed not in work shirt and trousers but in a rumpled saffron evening gown, she sported an arch of flowers above her off-kilter platinum braids and looked as if she'd been crying.

Her first words were, "This is a fine hello, isn't it? Talk about going from bad to worse!"

"There there, miss," Cheng Shiao consoled. His voice could

be, all at once, soothing and professional and yet loud enough to drown out the whine of machinery.

"Hi," Marlon added, disspiritedly.

"When you're ready, miss, a few questions?"

"Oh. Of course, yes. Hello, Your Highness. It's very nice of you to be here."

Tamra inclined her head in acknowledgment.

The fax gate, its entrance already crowded, hummed for a moment before expelling another figure, this time a young girl in what looked like a school uniform: beige blouse, dark gray necktie, beige pleated skirt, dark gray socks, black shoes. Her eyes—the left one half-hidden by a VR monocle—fixed immediately on Shiao, then swept the rest of the assembled persons coolly. She looked, to Bruno's inexperienced eye, about ten or eleven years old, on the threshold of puberty but still girlishly proportioned. Her carriage and posture and gait were all wrong, though. Or partly wrong, anyway, as if she'd spent too much time around grown-ups and had forgotten how to move like a child.

"Commandant-Inspector," Shiao said at once, throwing his shoulders back, his chin up, his chest forward. "Thank you for relieving me. It will please me to assist you on this case in any way I can."

Astonished, Bruno looked at the little girl again, more closely this time, noting that Shiao had made no such display of obsequity to a pair of Declarant-Philanders, nor even to the Queen of Sol herself. Commandant-Inspector? He'd always assumed that was a rank for octogenarians, senior police officers with decades of crime-fighting experience.

He noted, too, Tamra's and Marlon's and Deliah's lack of surprise at the policeman's reaction. They knew this girl, or knew *of* her, if indeed the word "girl" applied in any but the most outward sense. Perhaps it was a disguise, an invitation to underestimate the person beneath?

"Thank you, Lieutenant," the girl said. Then, curtseying to Tamra, "Good evening, Your Majesty. Sorry to meet you under these circumstances; I hadn't heard you were at the scene. Declarant Sykes, Laureate van Skettering, allow me to express my condolences."

And this perplexed Bruno still further, because the voice was very much that of a young girl trying hard to act mature, and while she was speaking, her right foot twisted and dug at the floor's metal decking, and her right hand grabbed a corner of her skirt and twisted it, then dropped it, smoothed it, and finally grabbed it again.

Bruno couldn't help himself. "You're the senior investigator?" he blurted.

The girl looked at him, again with that same sort of rapid, confident assessment that said she knew a thing or two about human beings. She didn't appear overawed with what she saw. "Have we met, sir?"

"Er, I think not. I'm de Towaji."

"De Towaji who?" Her voice was unimpressed.

Tamra came to the rescue then, stepping sideways to touch a hand to Bruno's shoulder. "Declarant-Philander Bruno de Towaji, dear. He's the inventor, among other things, of collapsium." Then her voice dropped an octave, filled out with genial warning. "Bruno, this is Commandant Vivian Rajmon, a senior inspector of the Royal Constabulary and a personal friend of mine."

"Senior?" he couldn't keep from saying.

Commandant-Inspector Vivian Rajmon's sigh was loud and short, an exclamation of impatience. "The worst part is always having to explain it. Can I *pleeease* take a leave of absence, Tamra?"

"Not a chance," Her Majesty said, with stern amusement. "It would encourage the criminal element too much."

"Explain what?" Bruno asked, still stuck on the girl's appearance.

Inspector Rajmon sighed again, eyeing Bruno gloomily. "I've heard of you. You're rich. You own your own private planet."

"Er, a small one, yes."

"What are you doing here? Wait! Let me guess: you were called in to consult on the fall of the Ring Collapsiter. You visited Marlon Sykes, and were with him when news of his murder arrived."

Bruno thought to bow. "Your deductions are accurate, uh, mademoiselle."

She pursed her lips, and looked him over as if weighing the intent of his words. Finally, she said, "I don't care to explain myself to you. I don't have to." Then, to Shiao, she said, "Has the scene been fully documented?"

"Nearly complete, Commandant-Inspector," Shiao said, stiffly. "We should have a reconstruction in a few minutes."

Vivian nodded. "Good. Thank you." Then her voice became amused. "At *ease,* Lieutenant."

"Yes'm." Shiao's posture slumped just enough to show he was complying with the order.

"Declarant, Laureate," Vivian said then to Marlon and Deliah, "do you feel up to viewing the bodies?"

Marlon Sykes nodded.

Deliah, for her part, straightened her back, pushed her hair into closer array, and said, "Why not? Nothing could make this evening much worse than it is already."

"Let's go, then," Vivian said, then nodded to Shiao. "Will you keep the news cameras away, please?"

Shiao went rigid again. "Absolutely, Commandant-Inspector. I won't budge from this spot."

She nodded, apparently satisfied with that, and set off down the length of the grapple station with the rest of them trailing behind.

The place was *crawling* with figures in white spacesuits, dozens of them, some on rolling ladders, some on hands and knees, some dangling from roof beams on harnesses of optically superconducting cable so that they seemed to float unsupported in the air. All of them were sweeping every available surface with instruments of various design and purpose.

When Vivian's entourage had gone far enough and spread out enough that the station's hum would hide a discreet voice,

Bruno touched Tamra's elbow and leaned in close to murmur, "She's got that fellow well cowed, hasn't she? It seems odd."

"They *adore* her," Her Majesty murmured back. "These constables, all of them, they have such a hard time letting go. Vivian's situation is very sad, very unfortunate. She hasn't always been so young."

"A disguise, then?"

"Hardly. She died in an accident last year, and we've had a terrible time tracking down her fax patterns. She wasn't *afraid* to fax herself, but she did prefer to travel in that little spaceship of hers. How she loved that ship! But it blew up one day and took her with it."

"How perfectly horrid," Bruno said, meaning it. "And this . . . young version was the most recent you could find? That's peculiar; even if she rarely faxed, there should be buffer archives stored *somewhere*."

"In theory," Tamra whispered back. It was difficult to whisper here and still be heard, but Vivian had cast a suspicious glance backward. She knew, obviously, that they'd be talking about her, that Bruno required *some* explanation before taking her at rank value, but she just as clearly didn't like the idea.

"The theory fails to model reality?"

"Uh, right. Even the Royal Registry for Indispensable Persons didn't seem to have a copy, not that they've admitted to it yet. 'Still searching, Your Majesty. We're quite sure it's around here somewhere.' Even if that's *true,* it only means their search algorithms are defective. This is what I get for awarding contracts to the lowest bidder."

"Hmm," Bruno said, digesting that. There'd been no "Royal Registry" during his time in civilization—at least none that he'd ever heard about—and he was certainly an infrequent traveler himself. Other than his home fax machine, did anyplace have recent copies of *him*? Did this station, or Marlon's home? What might happen if he died suddenly? He tended not to pay attention to such concerns, but perhaps that was foolish of him. Things mightn't always work out in his favor.

Finally, he asked, "How is she able to perform her duties at all? You thought my robot Hugo to be a cruel experiment, but it seems far crueler to ask a young girl to act with a lifetime of experience she never had."

"Oh, Bruno, it's just not that simple. Vivian was always good about keeping mental notes, and after the accident she insisted on downloading all of them, all at once. The result is a very well trained, very confused little girl. In retrospect, it probably wasn't a wise idea, but there you have it. She complains about her work now, yes, but she was miserable—I mean genuinely despondent—until I ordered her back to it. And since the Constabulary was clamoring for her anyway, it seemed the kindest course of action."

"Hmm," Bruno said, unconvinced. Mental notes—essentially neuroelectrical snapshots of a particular moment of understanding—were something he'd always found to cause at least as many problems as they cured. What use to recapture the exact steps of a derivation or insight, when what you really wanted was to take the *results* of it and move forward, upward, to the next level of understanding? Notes could too easily set you in circles, working the same problems over and over to no clear purpose.

Now he was willing to concede that his example might not be a typical one. Quite possibly, a profession like criminal investigation relied on memory and habit in a way that note-taking could complement. But it was quite a step from there to the idea that an eleven-year-old could be programmed to perform the job as well as a seasoned adult. And even if *that* were granted, the question of whether such a thing *should* be done . . .

On the other hand, it *had been* done. Bruno's approval wasn't required, and his opinion was not an informed one. If Her Majesty and the Royal Constabulary wanted Vivian Rajmon back at work, well, perhaps they knew best after all.

Vivian slowed; the knot of walking people drew closer together. Over her shoulder she asked, "So, do I meet with your approval, de Towaji?"

He answered quickly, and with a fortunate evenness of tone. "You meet with *Her Majesty's* approval, mademoiselle. My own opinion hardly matters. As you surmise, I'm here only to assess the sabotage of the Ring Collapsiter."

Vivian stopped so suddenly that Deliah van Skettering collided with her. But her voice was dignified enough in speaking this single word. "Sabotage?"

"Indeed."

"We've worked it out," Marlon Sykes cut in, his voice weary but hard edged. "The pattern simply isn't consistent with a natural event. Someone deliberately destabilized the gravitational links, apparently for the express purpose of knocking the ring into the sun again."

"How long have you known this?" Vivian asked impatiently.

Marlon shrugged. "Twenty minutes, maybe."

"Nearly coincident with the murder."

"Well, yes. I'd guess the two subjects are related."

Vivian sighed, and started twisting at the hem of her skirt again. "Were you going to *tell* me about this? Were you waiting for me to figure it out on my own?"

"Er, you've only been here a minute."

"Indeed," Tamra said, in mildly commanding tones. "Let's not expect too much of the victims, dear. They're distraught."

Vivian bowed her head momentarily. "Of course, yes. Excuse my error." When she raised it again, her eyes were clear. "Are there other copies of you two around the Queendom?"

"Yes," Marlon and Deliah answered together. "Several,"

"At all the grapple stations in the Capricorn arc," Marlon added. "We're attempting to tune them for operation at higher frequencies. I believe I'm on Mars right now as well, though I wouldn't swear to it."

Nodding distractedly, Vivian took a little wellstone slate out of a pocket in her skirt, touched a lighted circle, and said into it, "Lieutenant Shiao, would you please have your people check all the grapple stations in the Capricorn arc? Let me know if you find anything unusual."

"Yes'm," the slate said without delay. "Right away."

She touched the little circle again and put the slate away. "Where on Mars?"

"I couldn't say, exactly."

"Can you call yourself there?"

Marlon shrugged. "Not easily. I can send a message, and reply when I get it."

Vivian nodded. "Good. Do that. Now I'm afraid we're going to have to view the bodies. This may be unpleasant for you. If either one of you want to change your minds, now would be the time."

"I'm all right," Marlon said, shaking his head grimly.

"I'm saturated and therefore imperturbable," Deliah answered, less confidently.

"Well then, let's proceed."

The instrument room was only a little farther on, surrounded by a knot of white-suited technicians. Cheng Shiao was here as well, presiding over the evidence collection, gazing into a slate of his own and nodding at something someone was saying. At the sight of Vivian, he jerked to attention.

"Commandant-Inspector! A pleasure. You're looking well."

"I've aged a month," she replied, a little snottily.

Marlon and Deliah crowded slowly forward, their curiosity battling a sense of reluctance and, to all appearances, defeating it. Police technicians parted solemnly for them.

"Oh," Marlon said, in flat tones.

Deliah was less sanguine. "How completely rude! Look at this! Do I deserve this? Gods, the inconsideration. This must have *hurt*!"

By craning his neck, Bruno was able to see around her, to see what she was looking at: herself and Marlon lying in heaps on the floor of the instrument room, with their toes pointing down and their faces pointing up. Someone had twisted their heads completely around, leaving wide, ugly, red-black bruises all around their necks, almost like burns. In the doorway, a lacquer-black robot sprawled, powerless and inert. It was small, probably not more than a meter and a half in height, though its arms and hands and especially its fingers were of disproportionate length. Its glossy exterior betrayed no dents or scratches or other signs of violence; it seemed to have just dropped there, perhaps while exiting the room.

"That doesn't belong here," Tamra said unnecessarily. "That's not government issue."

Vivian examined the scene for several seconds, pursing her lips and nodding. "Homicide, two counts, officers on the scene. Murder weapon is possibly a robot. Lieutenant, do we have a reconstruction yet?"

Bruno was surprised to see a heaviness around the edges of her eyes, as if she were suddenly holding back tears. Her lip quivered a little, although her voice had been firm and clear. Perhaps dealing with this sort of carnage wasn't as easy for her as Tamra might like to believe.

"Yes'm," Cheng Shiao said at once. He held up a wellstone slate. Vivian clicked her own, smaller one against it, and the two units chimed. An image appeared of the murder scene, exactly as it lay before them all but without the crowd, without the police and technicians and royal entourage complete with silver bodyguards. There was only Marlon, and Deliah, and the enigmatic little robot.

"The time is twenty-eight minutes ago," Shiao said. "Both victims are clinically dead, in the presence of an inactivated autronic device of roughly anthropoid design, as seen here." On the displays, in three-dimensional miniature, the faces and bodies of the two prone figures began to twitch. The movements were slight, but the time scale was clearly compressed, so that the corpses seemed to take on a kind of manic quiver reminiscent of an AC electrical shock.

"Death throes, approximately four minutes for the woman and three for the man, may be considered mercifully brief. Neural and circulatory connections between brain and body have been completely severed, and both brains have suffered additional, acceleration-related traumas, owing to the great violence of the event. Organized memories not related to smell or emotion should be considered irretrievable in both cases. Whether this damage was deliberate or incidental is a matter for speculation.

"Continuing backward in time, we find the autronic device, colloquially a 'robot,' showing its final signs of activity. Central processing shuts down last, following the termination of emergency and backup power. Here the memory is wiped and erased, and shortly before that, primary power shuts off, most likely under CPU command."

On screen, the robot twitched, then rose to its feet like a marionette. It stood still for a moment, then turned around suddenly and brought its hands out parallel in front of it, raised slightly above the level of its head. The body of Marlon Sykes, twitching more violently now, rose from the floor and placed its head between the robot's hands. Its neck was still twisted, though there was now no sign of the burnlike discoloration. If it could be said that there was any facial expression at all, it was one of simple discomfort, of skin and muscle hanging crooked and rudely pressed, like the face of a sleeper propped awkwardly in a chair not meant for sleeping.

That was only for a moment, though. In the next instant, the body's head was rotated sharply, with such speed that Bruno didn't see it happen, and afterward Marlon stood there, looking over his shoulder with what was now very clearly an expression of fear and startlement.

Then, in quick succession, the body of Deliah van Skettering first hurled itself upward into the robot's waiting hands, then twisted its head around similarly, then turned, intact, to face the information-rich wall of the instrument room. Bruno noted that the walls were not randomizing, as they had been when he himself had last seen them.

"The second and first murders occur, to all appearances, a premeditated and in fact calculated attack. Here the robot enters and approaches."

The black machine leaped backward out of the room, landing lightly on its feet, and then commenced a stately—if accelerated—backward stroll along the grapple station's main avenue. The viewpoint followed it all the way back to the fax gate, where it vanished.

"Curiously," Shiao said, "the fax has no record of this transaction. We deduce it purely from the age and placement of molecular traces left by the robot's feet. From this point, the scene remains largely unchanged for sixteen minutes, forty seconds, at which point there *is* a record of passage for two persons—Her Majesty Queen Tamra Lutui and Declarant-Philander Bruno de Towaji—and their accompanying guards."

On the two slates, a little Bruno and Tamra walked backward out of the fax, led by one stocky little silver robot and followed by another. They continued backward at a brisk walk until arriving at the instrument room, at which point a conversation ensued between them and the figures of Marlon and Deliah, both alive. And this time, the walls were randomizing as Bruno had remembered.

How did the police know to include that in their simulation? What storage devices or subtle electrical traces told them that? These reconstructions, corroborated now by his own observations, seemed all but perfect. He resolved to learn more about police procedures, and particularly the physics underlying them.

The conversation was brief, and finally Marlon's hand sucked a grease stain off Bruno's jacket, and Marlon himself settled down onto his back on the floor and scooted headfirst into the recess where Bruno had first found him. Then Bruno and Tamra and the guards walked backward to the fax gate again, this time with Deliah van Skettering trailing behind. When they had gone, Deliah backed alone to the instrument room again.

"A brief visit," Shiao said, "preceded by another period of relative inactivity. We jump behind. Two hours, five minutes and thirty-six seconds earlier, the van Skettering woman arrives, and eleven minutes before *that*, Sykes does. Again, for some reason the fax does not maintain any record or receipt of this singular transaction, but shed skin cells and residual ghosting tell us almost precisely when it must have occurred. Prior to this arrival, the station appears to have sat unattended for a period of twenty-nine days, and shows no prior visits by either Sykes or van Skettering at any time. This completes the first draft of our reconstruction. A final, admissible draft will be completed within twenty-four hours."

Shiao clicked his heels together and waited.

"Excellent work," Vivian said, nodding. "I'll note this in my report. Regarding a motive, we—"

Along the avenue, another Shiao came sprinting toward them, shouting, "Commandant-Inspector! Commandant-Inspector! I'm reporting trouble at six other grapple stations!" He pulled up and stopped, puffing. "Murders, Commandant-Inspector, all almost exactly like this one. Two bodies, one robot, some of them fresher than those found here. And Commandant? One of me has failed to report back. It isn't like me, if I may say so. If I may say so, I fear the worst."

Frowning, Vivian nodded. "Rightly so. Send a full armed detail and report back immediately. Try to capture the robot alive, if at all possible."

"Yes'm!" The new Shiao turned and sprinted back toward the fax again. He was passed on the way by still another Shiao, who, while less agitated, was if anything in an even grimmer mood.

"Commandant-Inspector!"

"Yes, Shiao?"

"Commandant-Inspector, there's been an accident of some sort. Cislunar traffic control just came through with a debris anomaly; the home of Declarant-Philander Marlon Sykes has apparently been damaged. My attempts to raise him there have been unsuccessful. House software does not appear to be responding. I fear the worst."

"Darn it!" Vivian squawked, suddenly eleven years old again. "That's no accident. Darn, darn, darnit! This just isn't how we do things in the Queendom. Somebody's being systematically *mean,* and that *just isn't how we do things.*"

"No'm."

She relaxed a little, perhaps by force, then nodded to Her Majesty. "This situation is obviously volatile, Tam. With your permission, I'd like to remove you all to a safer location."

Tamra bowed her head. "I defer to your judgment, Commandant-Inspector."

"Good. Shiao, escort all these people to headquarters under maximum protection. Are you still guarding the fax gate?"

"Yes'm. I'm there now."

"Good. On your way out, tell yourself to seal it behind us. Official access only. And while you're at it, find out more about these unlogged fax transactions. There's something very uncanny about that."

chapter eleven

in which the
rubble is sifted

"So this unidentified 'saboteur' of yours—" Vivian sighed, looking out the headquarters window at a distant line of palm trees. "—either a person or an organization, is not only trying to push the Ring Collapsiter into the sun, but also to eradicate any persons able to stop it. I don't get it. I don't get a motive for this. I mean, we haven't received any kind of threats or demands."

"Indeed," Bruno said. "It's difficult to imagine an outcome useful to *anyone*. And yet, the tricks being played here are extraordinarily clever. This is not the work of a madman."

"Madmen aren't necessarily stupid," Marlon pointed out sullenly. He had good cause to be sullen: as the investigation spread, it had quickly become apparent that *no* fax machine anywhere in the Queendom had record of him. He'd been erased, in the ninety minutes leading up to the destruction of his house. There was only one copy of him currently in existence, and if not for the discovery of the bodies on Station 117 and the timing of his visit there, *no* copy would exist. Even the Royal Registry, when asked to produce him, begged "a slight delay, owing to technical difficulties."

It seemed to horrify Tamra and Deliah at least as much as it horrified Marlon himself. Bruno, who'd been single-copy for most of his life, couldn't easily grasp their mood. Marlon was still alive, right? But for those accustomed to multiplicity, that seemed little comfort. This much was apparent to all: that the greatest of rarities, a murder in the *first* degree, had been attempted, and had very nearly succeeded.

No one seemed to notice that Bruno himself had nearly been obliterated in the same stroke. Had hunter-killer apps gone looking for his fax image in the collapsiter grid? Were the police investigating that? Perhaps they assumed he'd left a live copy at home, as many people did while traveling.

"Nor are stupid men invariably hapless," Deliah added, with a sort of low anger. "The gravity projector was invented by a moron. Half the senate are fools, but see how they come alive when crossed!" She was standing at the window, looking out at coconut palms and bamboo and beach sand, and the distant breaking of ocean waves. She'd been quietly outraged, Bruno thought, to find that her murder was an afterthought, that she wasn't the target, that she was merely standing next to Marlon Sykes at the wrong time. She, the Lead Componeer for the Ministry of Grapples, had not been seen as a threat to the Ring Collapsiter's fall. The idyllic island of Tongatapu had done little to assuage her indignation; she stood guywire taut, hands clasped firmly behind her buttocks.

"Boyle Schmenton was hardly a moron," Bruno felt compelled to point out.

"Oh, dry up."

"That's enough, Laureate-Director," Tamra said coolly.

A collective sigh or yawn went through them all—all except the robot guards, who stood like anchored chrome statues, gleaming in the sunlight. Royal Constabulary Headquarters, on the northeast edge of the city of Nuku'alofa, was a pyramid of yellow-white glass, nearly as large as Bruno's whole planet and really far too bright inside for an office building. But the temperature and humidity were just right, and the air smelled brilliantly of ocean and wood smoke and vanilla. *Wild* vanilla, probably—nobody really farmed anymore, or fished, or roasted pigs and turtles in pits on the beach.

In some ways, Bruno had always felt he was more Tongan than the Tongans themselves. His father, Enzo de Towaji, had won a lot of money flying kites, and sunk it all—against every bit of advice—into a restaurant that served only "natural" foods and beverages. A stupid idea, yes, but it had not only caught on, but spawned a whole range of subindustries to support and complement it. Bruno had grown up in the retro-Girona of gentlemen farmers and butchers and vintners, and eventually even weaver women and chandlers to complete the ambience. Back-to-basics was always an easy sell in Catalonia—Enzo was no fool. Of course, the Sabadell-Andorra earthquake had ended that era rather decisively, but Bruno had never really shaken off its influence.

Still, he'd forgotten how much he missed *Tonga,* how very many memories he had tied up here. The noisy palace, the quiet beaches, the secret harbors of Eua accessible only by catamaran . . . He'd come to Tamra's court at the age of thirty, and remained for thirty years more, fighting always for the time to seclude himself, to lock these sultry islands away behind white laboratory walls and *work.* The *arc de fin,* the *arc de fin!* But now he'd been away and alone for nearly as long, his life neatly trisected by this residence and birthplace and ancestral capital of Queen Tamra Lutui.

He moved his chair closer to hers, and would have reached for her hand if they'd been anything like alone together. As it was, there were seven people in the room here, and dozens more visible in the rooms nearby, and hundreds or thousands of news cameras swarming like thirsty mosquitoes at the cordon line, three hundred meters out. But Tamra seemed to sense his thoughts, and nodded sidelong at him: Yes, Philander, I remember it too.

Vivian set down her wellstone slate and rubbed her eyes with her thumbs in a very unchildlike gesture. "I need more information. This isn't falling into place for me. You, Sergeant," she said, singling out one of the uniformed officers standing guard. "Find me Cheng Shiao, with a reconstruction of the attack on Sykes' house. No excuses—I want whatever he's got. And bring me a soda, also."

"Yes'm. Right away."

To Bruno, for some reason, she said, "It's like something I've learned in school but mostly forgotten."

"Mademoiselle?" Bruno said, in a tone meant to convey incomprehension.

"My life. My job. I feel as if I know them until it's time to *do* something, and then I'm never sure what. I keep expecting people to laugh, to say I'm doing it all wrong."

Bruno felt a little smile plant itself on him. "I've often felt that way myself, mademoiselle. It's more normal than you might suppose. I do think you're being too bossy, though. You might tone that down a notch."

"My name is Vivian, *sir*."

"Ah. Well. I shall call you that in the future, and if you like, you may call me Bruno. Understand, I've never met a person in your . . . circumstances before. We're making up the protocol as we go along, both of us."

"Hmm." She considered that answer, or perhaps the smile behind it, and finally seemed to find it good.

"You're doing a splendid job," Tamra added sincerely. "Believe me, I'd remove you if you weren't. The Queendom deserves no less."

"Hmm." After a moment's reflection, Vivian seemed to like that answer even better.

They all fell silent. The hum of ventilators and lighting seemed, somehow, to match the rolling and crashing of the ocean, too distant to be audible behind the wellstone glass of the windows.

Half a minute later, Cheng Shiao strode into the office, a glass of dark, fizzing soda in his hand. He set it down in front of Vivian, then stood at attention. "Cola Five-Two, no ice. Regrettably, I'm unavailable with the full reconstruction at this time, as my cruiser is presently docking with the remains of Sykes Manor. Only the gross reconstruction, based on our last radar assay, is available yet. I've taken the liberty of uploading it to your pads."

"Thank you, Lieutenant. Will you walk us through it?"

"A pleasure, Commandant-Inspector, though I'm afraid there isn't much to it." Images appeared on all the little pads, and on a backlit holographic rectangle that appeared in the center of the table's smooth surface, like a glass window looking down on outer space, on the golden-white sphere of Marlon's house spinning silently against the starscape, lit mainly by floodlights but with a sliver of bright sunlight illuminating one side. "A directed energy stream approximately six meters wide strikes the house in a single pulse at fourteen hours fifty-two minutes, penetrating *here* and exiting *here*. Although the structure remains largely intact, atmospheric containment fails immediately—note the venting gases—and power distribution fails within seconds."

The little house shot gouts of debris and glittering crystals of frozen air from a pair of circular openings that appeared in it. The mangled Athenian structures within showed clearly.

"Power distribution failed?" Marlon asked angrily. "There's wellstone all through that house—more than enough redundancy to keep it alive."

"Yes sir. Apparently it was the embedded computing structures themselves that failed."

"Secondary radiation?" Bruno speculated. "A shower of charged particles released by the sudden energy flux?"

"Possibly, sir."

"What sort of beam was it?"

"Unknown, sir."

"Hmm." Bruno pinched his chin between thumb and forefinger, as was his habit when attempting to concentrate. "I don't suppose you have the precise time of impact? Coupled with the rotation rate of the house, that could be used to trace the beam back to its source."

"We have timeline only to the half minute, sir, based on long-range radar tracks of the larger debris. I expect to refine that figure through proximity scan and direct assay of the impact site."

"This is police business," Vivian noted impatiently. "Shiao *does* know what he's doing."

"Please," Tamra said, holding up a hand in what was either a scolding or a beseeching gesture, or perhaps both. "The Royal Committee for Investigation of Ring Collapsiter Anomalies does share jurisdiction here. Their investigation precedes yours, in fact precedes the murder itself, and I daresay their business is the more urgent. You're to provide de Towaji with anything he asks."

"Oh," Vivian said, with surprising equanimity. "Okay."

Bruno, who hadn't realized he was a member of any sort of official committee, said, with some embarrassment, "Er, what's the soonest you could get us a full reconstruction?"

Shiao shrugged. "Unknown, sir. Since the investigating cruiser is some seven light-minutes distant, I haven't communicated with myself directly. For a precise figure, you'd have to ask me there yourself, in person."

"Ah. An excellent suggestion. Your cruiser is fully equipped? Can I fax myself there?"

Shiao looked alarmed. "Well, um, technically yes, sir, but in actuality I was attempting a joke. You'd need to be certified for shipboard operations. Have you even had any spacesuit training?"

Bruno laughed. "Breathe in, breathe out, and keep your boot grapples engaged? I've seen it in the movies."

"Sir, emergency procedures alone require eight weeks of intensive immersion. I'm afraid I can't authorize—"

"You *can* authorize it," Her Majesty said firmly. "Was I unclear about this? De Towaji is operating under full royal dispensation, and shall have whatever resources he requires. His safety is *my* responsibility, not yours."

Nervously, Shiao pressed. "Sir, have you ever even *worn* a spacesuit?"

"No," Bruno admitted, "but I grew up in a back-to-basics community where primitive skills like that were highly prized.

I'm adaptable. Don't worry, son; I intend no unwarranted risks, and you'll be held blameless for any foolishness on my part. I do think this merits my attention, though. And yours, Marlon, if you feel up to accompanying me."

"It's my house," Marlon said unhappily. "Of course I'll go."

"And I," Tamra said, stifling Shiao's protest with a stern look. "It's my Queendom at risk. And I *have* had spacesuit and spaceship training—in fact, I'm a level-one instructor." Shiao looked surprised at this, which only made Her Majesty grow sterner. "You think I'm a twit, like my dear departed Queen Mother? All my life I've had the finest doctors, the finest fax programmers, the finest tutors and trainers. I'm as fit and as fast and as wise as modern science can make me, and I've been certified with more tools and vehicles and weapons than you've probably ever heard of. It's not Tamra Lutui who'll step aboard that cruiser, but the Queendom of Sol itself, and your approval, Lieutenant, has not been solicited."

Bruno noted that Marlon, who'd been Tamra's childhood mathematics tutor long before he'd been anything else, swelled with pride at these remarks. Shiao, though, gasped, bowed his head, and dropped to his knees.

"Meaning no disrespect, Your Majesty! My concern is only for your safety!"

"And appreciated as such," Tamra conceded. "But over-ruled. Vivian, have *you* retained any spacesuit training?"

"Um, I think so."

"Excellent. Will you accompany us?"

"Sure."

Bruno watched Shiao's down-turned face, thinking he'd never seen someone actually *bite back* a protest before. He wondered if it was anywhere near as uncomfortable as it looked.

It took less than fifteen minutes for the Constabulary ward-robe to dress them all in custom-fit, top-of-the-line vacuum-safety equipment, by which time Shiao admitted that his docking maneuvers were complete and that he was dutifully awaiting the Royal Committee in what remained of Sykes Manor.

Bruno flexed his fingers and elbows and knees experimentally. The silvery-blue garments weren't nearly as heavy or stiff as they looked, and the helmet dome, when he commanded it to swing shut over his head, was optically superconducting, invisible except for faint silver marking dots applied to it—he supposed they were there so he'd know where the dome was, so he wouldn't accidentally try to put his gloved fingers through it.

They each had their name emblazoned on their rebreather backpacks—literally *emblazoned*, in dully glowing red letters. Bruno's said TOWAJI, an error or abbreviation he hadn't seen fit to correct. And here around him, as they crowded into the fax atrium, were SYKES and SKETTERING, a miniature RAJMON and a couple of hulking SHIAOs.

Tamra's suit alone was nameless, bearing only the royal seal, but it was unmistakable from any angle, being purple in color, with bright gold trim that seemed to—possibly *did*—glow with its own inner light. It also managed, despite its bulk, to look sexy on her, the cut somehow exaggerating the hourglass of her waist, the curve of her calves, the gentle swell of rump and bosom. Crisscrossing reinforcement straps, their placement engineered to look coincidental, contrived to emphasize each perfect breast in a way that made Bruno feel almost as though he were imagining it, as though he were a lecher and a boor unworthy of the Virgin Queen's chaste presence. Doubtless, she'd downloaded the pattern from her palace wardrobe, which had designed it for exactly these qualities. Of such silly but powerful subtleties was court life constructed. Perhaps it was a kind of joke.

The royal bodyguards alone remained undressed, looking almost vulnerable alongside their armored Queen. Nonetheless, pistols at the ready, they stepped through the gate to prepare the way for her. She followed closely; Bruno, right in tow, felt compelled to study the heart shape of her purple armored behind.

Seven minutes' travel time vanished in a faxed instant; stepping through a curtain would have provided a greater sense of travel.

The inside of the police cruiser was surprisingly large, a gravity-free cylinder twice as wide as Bruno was tall, with token "floor" and "ceiling" of waffled rubber and all the rest an expanse of wellstone, smooth gray panels set with deep, breadbox-sized niches every couple of meters, and larger, coffin-sized ones interspersed less frequently. The thing appeared to be about a hundred meters long, somewhat larger than the shattered sphere of Marlon's house visible outside the round, di-clad portholes. The ship's setup was enviable and no doubt expensive—a complete laboratory that could, on a moment's notice, be reconfigured for nearly any purpose, and that could simultaneously protect or confine dozens of human beings, be they SWAT troopers or prisoners or refugees plucked from some civil disaster.

A Cheng Shiao stood, waving uncertainly, in the aisle a dozen meters ahead, next to what was probably an air-lock hatch. Tamra, with her robots on either side, advanced toward him, her improbably swiveling derriere beckoning Bruno to follow, which he did. The others appeared behind him one by one, clearly visible in the small rearview mirrors projecting forward from each of his shoulders.

"Any warning lights in your suit collar?" Shiao asked anxiously. "Any unfamiliar noises or sensations?"

"No," Tamra answered him with apparent good cheer. Their voices rang in Bruno's helmet as intimately as if they were right in there with him.

"Er, no," he said, though in fact the weightlessness—despite the fax filters that had conditioned his body against space sickness—was already making him a bit queasy. The food and drink Marlon had served him earlier now seemed to be rocking back and forth as a single, fluid mass in his stomach.

"Nope," Vivian said behind him.

"No," Marlon said more sullenly, echoed by an even more sullen Deliah van Sketterng. Why she'd insisted on accompanying them Bruno was not at all sure—she'd seemed to regard the prospect with a mix of resentment and dread. But she'd died already; little worse could happen now. Perhaps she just wanted to feel included, to be present in case anything important happened. Or perhaps she had something material to contribute—she was, after all, a Laureate in the sciences and a Director in the bureaucracy. But that didn't mean she enjoyed the idea. Like Bruno, she had no spacesuit training of any kind, so her obvious fear of space's vacuum was well founded, more sensible really than Bruno's own nonchalance.

He flexed his hand, trying somehow to feel the absence of air around him. He realized, with a twinge of worry, that he'd once again neglected to leave a copy of himself behind. He wouldn't want to *be* left behind, so the idea hadn't occurred until now, to make a copy and mistreat it that way. Was this unwise, given the risks he was taking? Ah well, done was done, and the fax machines at both ends should retain his pattern in their buffers, at least until something else overwrote it.

He followed Her Majesty around the corner and into the airlock, both of whose doors stood open. Beyond it was some crude hardware—a kind of metal tunnel that seemed to have been jammed straight through the hull of Marlon's home. Bruno's sense of up and down did a little cartwheel, making him queasier still. Where the floor of the police cruiser had been "beneath" him and the airlock "in front," now the airlock and its hatchway seemed to point "up" through the floor of Sykes Manor. And Bruno was clinging to the wall by the grapples on his boot soles! If the police hadn't stopped the house's spin "gravity," he'd be falling backward right now, pivoting on broken ankles—his boot soles still clinging—until he finally bashed the back of his helmet against the wall below. But if not for the weightlessness, he wouldn't be so disoriented in the first place. He'd be climbing a ladder or something.

The police had stopped Marlon's house from spinning, he realized, for safety reasons. With centrifugal "gravity" pressing everything to the hull—or out through the holes the energy beam had punched in it—there would be a risk of flung debris or even outright disintegration of the house, like a merry-go-round whose bolts had all come undone.

"You've despun it," Bruno said to one of the Shiaos, and though the Shiao was "below" or "behind" him and had no direct cue that he was the one being spoken to, the reply was immediate. "Yes, sir. To facilitate docking. Watch your step, please."

This exchange of words had a soothing effect on Bruno, who hadn't realized he was in need of soothing, hadn't realized quite how difficult and uncomfortable and not-a-game this business was going to be. He wondered if it mightn't be easier to disengage the boot grapples and simply launch himself up the tube, to rise like a soda bubble through the hole in Marlon's floor. But probably, if that were easiest, they'd have told him to do it. There was of course the problem of stopping.

Her Majesty's first robot walked up the side of the tube and around its upper lip as if this were the most natural thing in the worlds, and then Tamra herself did likewise, and then the other robot. Bruno, when his turn came, found the maneuver less difficult than it looked. Really, it was a matter of ankles and calf muscles, of letting the boots pull flat against whatever surface was handy, and of keeping one's leg—and with it the rest of the body—aligned. He marveled again at how supple these suits were. Thick enough to feel sturdy and safe as two winter coats with a suit of armor in between, they nonetheless flexed and twisted quite readily, as if shrinking away from the areas under compression—such as the insides of joints—and in turn rushing to the areas under tension, somehow adding length there, so that the fabric needn't stretch or tighten.

Marlon's house, alas, was a mess inside. Power had failed, leaving the interior dark save for starlight streaming in through one gaping hole, and sunlight tinting the edges of the other, and between them the wandering flashlight and headlight beams of white-space-suited evidence technicians, a dozen of whom swarmed the wreckage like bizarre creatures of the deepest ocean. Where a few hours ago there'd been marvels here, or at least architectural curiosities, now there were simply floating debris and the stubs of pillars and the empty foundations of buildings.

It looks more like Athens than ever, he thought suddenly. He nearly said it out loud, to God knew what effect on Marlon, but keeping the observation inside made it seem all the more insistently true. The *real* Athens, the contemporary one, preserved its temples and Acropolis forever in their twenty-first century state of ruin, lighting them up at night with floodlights and search beams . . .

Well, in an earlier age, at least. Bruno hadn't been to Athens in more than eighty years, almost before the Queendom's founding, and hadn't heard even the slightest news of it since moving up to his little planet in the Kuiper Belt. By now, he supposed the city could look like anything: a dome or a beehive or a forest of sky-scraping towers, perhaps even a restoration of its dusty classical grandeur. There was no limit to what people could do these days, or at any rate there *shouldn't* be.

"Wow," Vivian said as she clambered up beside Bruno. "Look at this place. What a terrible shame."

"You should have seen it before," Marlon, who was right behind her, said. The words came slowly, and the bitterness fell away from his voice in midsentence, leaving only surprise and regret and, it seemed, finally some giddy realization that he was lucky to be alive.

Time doubled back on Bruno for a moment; he recalled the Sabadell-Andorra event, ninety-two seconds of explosive shaking that had toppled trees and structures throughout the Ter valley. There'd been so much fear, so much damage, so much injury and death, a whole population battered out of its smug, suburban complacency. He remembered his neighbors standing on broken alley pavement, bitterly arguing and complaining about this and that crack in their house's foundation until a man from across the street—whose name they had never known—walked over and handed them a peach.

"Bruised," he said. "Won't last an hour. Better eat it quick." And then he'd walked back to his own house, a pile of shattered brick, to continue shoveling for anything salvageable. Then his neighbors had noticed Bruno looking at them, and had turned away with a funny kind of shame or guilt in their faces. Guilt at having survived. Bruno, overcome with quiet, unfocused affection, forgave them for it immediately.

That was how it had gone: the ones who lost everything, whose lives were separated completely from the material possessions that had seemed to define them, were the ones who somehow managed to take it in stride. Himself included, in a way, although it took some time to realize that Enzo and Bernice were not disgraced or somehow forgotten by his pursuit of happiness. That had been a terrible year—being a fifteen-year-old University student without parents, without a home—but by the following spring it had begun to seem like they'd simply stepped back, giving him the room he needed to grow.

He doubted there would ever be another disaster of comparable scale, on Earth or anywhere else—the Queendom was simply too safe a place for that. But perhaps, one way or another, there'd always be this scene: a man surveying the ruins of his home with sudden, passionate equanimity.

"You should have *seen* it," Marlon said again, now with pride. He raised an arm to point. "I had olive trees over there. All down through here was running water and marble walls. Actual marble; I had it shipped up from Earth."

"We'll rebuild it," Tamra promised, laying a purple-gloved hand on Marlon's shoulder. "I'll send my finest architect."

Marlon managed a laugh that was only partly hollow. "There are no backups, Majesty—no complete record of the structure anywhere. Some photographs were published in my last biography, but that's all. I didn't want it duplicated, you see. Imitated, perhaps, but never duplicated. Even *I* don't remember every detail. Ah, damn it, I'll miss this place."

And then his eyes misted with tears, and Bruno suddenly remembered *that* from the earthquake as well. Equanimity could be a fragile thing.

"We'll build something different, then," Tamra said gently.

"Yes. I suppose we will."

Tamra's hand still rested on Marlon's thick shoulder padding; he probably couldn't feel it, but certainly he could *see* it in his rearview mirrors. He knew it was there, and indeed something seemed to pass between the two of them, using that arm as a conduit. Bruno was uncomfortably reminded that Marlon Sykes had been Philander before him, and had, cumulatively, spent decades longer in Tamra's presence than Bruno ever had.

"Come," Bruno said softly, bending close to little Vivian as if to whisper in her ear. "Let's, ah, examine the area, the two of us."

One can't whisper over an open frequency, though, not to one person. Marlon and Tamra both looked sharply at him, annoyed about something. Well, humph, what was he supposed to do? It seemed like a private moment, one they were certainly both entitled to, but was he to pretend he didn't exist? To ignore their business here and stand around quietly until they were finished?

"Switch to Police Five," Vivian said, in a tone that echoed Bruno's murmur but was simultaneously commanding and self-conscious, as if she were covering or apologizing for a mistake he'd made.

"Excuse me?"

"The channel. We're on Police *One* right now. The knob is *here*." She jabbed a gauntleted finger at his forearm.

"Ah, I see." Once they'd completed the switch and walked a few paces away he added, "That wasn't very grown-up of you."

"Well, I never said I was grown up, did I?"

"Tamra seems to believe it."

Wood and marble chips crunched beneath their feet, trapped between boot soles and deck plates drawn together by the spacesuits' safety grapples. They were strolling along a darkened . . . avenue, he supposed, their head- and hand-lights illuminating jagged stubs of building on one side and, on the other, the shattered remains of a canal, ice crystals glittering along what remained of its sides and bottom. Above, a pair of evidence technicians drifted by, their own lamps setting aglow the fragments of column and slab that spun slowly through the hanging dust.

"Tamra is benevolent," Vivian said, "and inclined to see strengths. She's very dear to me—I remember that much—but I'm not sure I'm quite the person she used to know."

"Er, I'm sure they'll find your full pattern eventually."

"Perhaps," she agreed, "but I've lived that life already—*her* life, the older me. I remember a lot about her. If they did find and reinstantiate that pattern, I'd feel very close—very, um, empathetic—but whether I'd want to *be* her, to be reconverged with her, I'm not so sure. Nobody has really asked me that."

"Oh. I see."

Vivian's tone became sharp. "Do you? I don't see how. People act like this is some kind of unfortunate setback for me. They act like they understand how hard it is for me right now, which they couldn't possibly."

"Hmm, well." Bruno wished he could pinch his chin. "We all have our problems, I fear. I don't suppose anyone *understands* the ones that other people have, but it shouldn't stop them from trying. They know what *a* problem feels like, anyway. Your police do seem to understand a bit, to be making allowances for you. Even I, an outsider, can see how highly they think of you."

"Or of her," she said, making a face. When they'd crunched along a few paces more, she turned and asked him, "So what's *your* problem? You're rich; you own your own planet far, far away; and you once saved the entire Queendom from calamity. What makes you think you know the first thing about people's troubles?"

"Brat," he said to her, not unkindly. "If you *were* an adult, you wouldn't ask a question like that. I get lonely sometimes. Often. It's my wealth and my fame, far more than distance, that isolate me. People always seem to expect something of me, some wisdom or eloquence or leadership I've never known how to provide. I used to study history, looking for an archetypal figure to emulate when these occasions arose. A tycoon? A philosopher? A military conqueror? I even tried to dress the part, to *look* historical. But one day, I finally realized how absurd that was. There wasn't anyone to emulate; civilization had changed too much, and human beings along with it. Changed because of me, I mean, because of things that I'd done. There were no other Declarant-Philander shatterers of worlds, certainly no immortal ones. No other men like me, ever. So really, *I'm* the archetype for future histories to deconstruct, and I fear that's a lot of responsibility for one man to bear. Really, a lot."

They'd stopped walking, and behind the dome of her helmet Vivian pursed her lips and considered his words for several long seconds. "You're a megalomaniac," she said finally.

He burst out laughing. "Ho! From the mouths of babes. Indeed, I do think highly of myself. But others do, as well, and not in quite the right way. They admire—too well!—a person who isn't really me."

Vivian looked thoughtful. "So you don't know how to be yourself, without letting other people down. That's your problem. You feel like everyone's looking, like they know more than you do about how you should act or what you should do. That's *our* problem, both of us."

He nodded. "All right, that seems a fair comparison."

The smile she offered him then was self-conscious and self-deprecating, though not actually apologetic. "I suppose a lot of people feel that way. There's probably nothing so special or unique about it. We all share the same neural architecture, right? Approximately? How embarrassing, to think my traumas and tragedies could be so banal."

"Shocking indeed," Bruno agreed, deciding that this girl was every bit as formidable as Tamra and the police seemed to think. "You're beginning to understand. That's what growing up means: a good understanding of one's own banality. But of course, we're all different and special, too."

"Oh, joy." She laughed.

He laughed with her. "Does that sound trite, Vivian? I don't mean it that way. Whatever *unique* gifts we possess — things that can't be had from any other source—those are things we should cultivate. Even if they're absurd, even if they're downright *counterproductive,* they're the only true signs that we, our own unique selves, were ever here at all. I suppose that's why crimes are committed; sometimes, that's the only calling card a person knows how to leave."

Vivian flung her arms out and tipped her head back inside its clear bubble. "Ah! Right! We should simply let people blow up their enemies and throw Ring Collapsiters into the sun. Thank you, Declarant. To think I've been wasting all this effort enforcing laws. Why, it's all so clear to me now!"

"Ah, you're a rotten child. I suppose we're all rotten children, though. In a thousand years, you'll look back on this conversation and laugh. A young de Towaji, presuming to lecture. On *manners,* no less!"

Her giggle was pleasant. "You're funny. Did you know that?"

"Funny? Hrumph," he replied, feeling a gate slam down suddenly on his good cheer. Tamra used to think he was funny, too, used to laugh along with his observations and suggestions and spontaneous displays of good cheer. What had happened to those days? Why had he found them unsustainable? So many of his archetypes were curmudgeons, or at least he imagined them that way; but was there anything as ridiculous as a curmudgeonly *child?* What a thing to look back on, a thousand years hence. A young de Towaji, presuming to curmudge.

Vivian eyed him and frowned, looking ready to scold. He *deserved* a scolding for letting his mood collapse like that, for being so damnably self-conscious that a simple compliment should shut him up. But what she said was, "I wonder if *she* did this, if she had a conversation like this one at this exact point in her life. I don't see how she could have. It's all very illuminating, very opinion shaping, and unfortunately that means I really am diverging, becoming a noticeably different person than her. Bruno, what if they *do* find her? What am I going to do then?"

For all its suppleness, the spacesuit didn't seem to permit much of a shrug. Not one that she'd see, anyway. "I think you can decide that when it happens. Why worry now? There's no need to be hasty, not when we're going to live forever. Perhaps you could be her daughter, or her younger sister, and you could live together in Boston or Calcutta or Cairo, one of the Children's Cities."

"I already have a mother. Where do you think I live?"

"Ah. Well, perhaps you'll find this woman *is* you, or the part of you that you feel is missing. You could even combine, the two of you, into a third distinct person, and all three go on with separate lives. The physical barriers to that sort of thing were all broken years ago; imagination really is the only limit."

"Hmm." She mulled that over, nodding slowly. "You *are* wise, in a way. Nobody else has suggested any of this. I'll consider it; I really will. And meanwhile, I do have my work to keep me busy."

"Ah, yes. Your work."

She thrust her chin out. "I do enjoy it, you know. Nobody will play games with me anymore, but an inspector's role *is* a game. Even if everyone *does* insist on treating me like a grown-up, I find the mental challenges stimulating. Take that brick over there." She pointed at one as it drifted through their beams a few meters ahead. "It tells a whole story, if you know how to read it. Marble, right? But it's darkened; it looks foamy and waxy and brittle. Something's happened to it."

"To all the stone," Bruno agreed, looking around. "It's probably secondary radiation. The energy beam struck a channel through solid matter from one side of the house to the other, presumably vaporizing it, and the vaporized matter re-released some of that energy in a different form."

"Different how?" she asked, her face growing more animated, more interested.

"I don't know," he said, attempting another shrug. "Something charged, I'd expect. That wreaks chemical havoc with most materials. There's no measurable radiation *now,* so it'd have to be something with a very short half-life, like maybe pions. Actually, that makes sense: neutrons decaying into protons and pions would transmute some of the calcium to scandium, the oxygen to fluorine, and the carbon to nitrogen. Some of the protons, stripped away by the impact of high-energy pions, simply become hydrogen atoms, and finally the whole mess recombines at high temperature, creating . . . what? Fluoroapatite, scandium formates, and tar? Is that consistent with what we're seeing?"

Vivian's eyes glittered. "What would cause that? What would make those particles act that way?"

"A nasen beam," Bruno answered, feeling the hairs prickle up on the back of his neck. "It'd have to be a powerful one; the overwhelming majority of neutrinos wouldn't interact at all."

"I see. And weren't you looking for a nasen beam projector already?"

"Indeed," he said. "Indeed. It needn't be *large,* just an oblate, monocrystalline diamond with wellstone emitters at either end, and a very good heat sink attached. You could easily fit one in your police cruiser, although the energy to fire it would have to be stored somewhere. A superconducting battery holding . . . what? A petajoule? *That* would be substantial. Larger than this house, I think. A little larger. So you'd need a big ship, or a ground base somewhere. Tracing from Shiao's reconstruction we might . . ."

He realized he was talking to a dead channel; Vivian had just jabbed the frequency controls on her forearm, and while she was nodding and looking right at him, she was suddenly *speaking* to someone else, in a voice Bruno couldn't hear. After a moment, she took out a wellstone pad and studied it.

Bruno tried Police One. "Something interesting?"

She looked up and nodded. "Yeah. I've relayed your deduction to Shiao. He's backtracking to the time of impact. Is there any way to know how *far* the beam traveled before arriving here?"

Bruno again tried to pinch his chin, and was frustrated by the invisible barrier of his helmet dome. "How far? Let's see. Nasen beams focus tightly, but disperse over large distances. Six meters wide at the impact site? Is there a difference in diameter from one hole to the other? I suppose we don't know which is the entrance wound and which is the exit, but if one is wider than the other—by a very small amount, you understand—the resulting cone should point straight to the source. Well, coupled with the exact impact time and rotation rate."

"Shiao?" Vivian prompted.

"Processing," Shiao replied. *A* Shiao. His voice was deep, and if not completely humorless, then at least solidly professional. His tone made a promise of the word, a reassurance to the many victims of this crime. Light beams swept and flashed the ruins as evidence techs—apparently communicating on some channel of their own—swarmed to take the appropriate measurements.

"Patience is the hard part," Vivian remarked, with a sidelong glance at Bruno.

But it was Shiao who replied. "Of course, Commandant-Inspector. I apologize for the delay. I'm refining the reconstruction, and should be finished right . . . now. I have the position: three AUs distant, in the asteroid belt. Referencing ephemeris data. Confirmed: no charted celestial object would have been in that location at that time."

"A ship, then?" Vivian asked.

"Most likely, Commandant-Inspector. I'll send out an all-points. Do either of you have suggestions regarding a description?"

"A solid battery somewhat larger than this house," Bruno answered. "Either moving very slowly, or carrying an even bigger tank for tritium fuel. It should be fairly unmistakable, actually."

And then Marlon's voice came through. "Hello? Did we miss something? I believe we're looking for a spaceship carrying large batteries, and a nasen projector."

chapter twelve

in which a strange creature is discovered

After that there was a great deal of radio traffic with Earth and Mars and a number of space traffic control stations, as the police sought a ship of the appropriate dimensions speeding— or drifting—away from the appropriate coordinates. But it was *slow* traffic, light-lagged, some of it routed the long way around the sun, to receivers way off on the other side. Bruno began to appreciate how the Bureaucracy, painfully efficient in so many other regards, could finally chafe against this barrier— the speed of light—that no persuasion or fiat or veto could soften for them.

It was as if Mars and Earth existed in a different time, in some parallel universe whose clocks ran perpetually behind. How distracting, when one's work demanded prompt coordination! Hence the Ring Collapsiter, first link in a network of supraluminal conduits that might finally join the disparate worlds together in a single moment. Or an entirely smaller span of moments, at least.

"While they're settling this," Tamra said to Bruno, with an offhand wave at Vivian and Cheng Shiao and the evidence technicians, "would you please go have a word with the press? They're massed outside by the thousands, understandably curious. I think a word from you at this point would be reassuring."

Bruno opened his mouth to protest, to point out how generally poor he was at that sort of thing, but the words didn't form. He couldn't convey the idea, because in fact he didn't *believe* the idea. How surprising! Yes, he *was* the expert here, the person who could best explain what had probably happened. Any claims to the contrary would go beyond modesty, into simple cowardice and obstruction. And anyway, the police were busy and Tamra herself was still consoling Marlon, while Bruno had no obvious duties just now.

Finally, he nodded. "Of course, Highness. I'll be back in a few minutes."

He dithered for a moment, wondering where exactly he should go, until he spied starlight through the one of the gaping holes the nasen beam had left. He strode toward it, crunching over dust and rubble and swaths of bare metal hull, swinging wide around the now barely visible foundations of a couple of structures. The dissolution of Sykes Manor was still ongoing, the remaining bits and pieces slowly losing cohesion and joining the nebula of floating debris. As he approached the hole, he saw there was a good deal of garbage floating outside as well, slowly leaking from the hull's double wound, forming expanding clouds that would, eventually, become rings encircling the sun itself, like a kind of miniature, invisibly diffuse asteroid belt.

The last few steps were more difficult; he couldn't suppress the idea that the opening pointed *down*, that another few steps would cast him, screaming and helpless, into the infinity of space. Rubbish, of course; his boot grapples would simply swing him around, pulling in whatever direction they happened to be facing, until finally he stood on the *outside* of the hull looking "down" into the inside. But still, the bottoms of his feet tingled, and he wished he could wipe away the mist of sweat that sprang nervously from his forehead.

As promised, the eyes of the news cameras glittered at

him like a wall, hundreds or possibly thousands of them hovering right at the limit of their invisible, three hundred–meter cordon around Her Majesty's person.

He switched the control on his forearm to the PRESS/PUBLIC ACCESS setting. "Hello?" he uttered tentatively.

Questions besieged him instantly, a hundred voices all yammering at once, with a sound like amplified static. He thought he heard the words "queen" and "house" and "collapsiter" in there a few times, but perhaps those were just his expectations, overlaid against the noise.

He held up a hand and shouted. "Please!" The noise quieted somewhat. "Oh, for goodness' sake. Be silent! Silent!" Within a few seconds, the hubbub stilled. He lowered his hand. "Thank you. Good afternoon. I am de Towaji, summoned here as part of the Royal Committee for Investigation of, uh, Ring Collapsiter Anomalies. There is reason to believe this structure was damaged by a coherent energy burst called a 'nasen beam,' fired by a spaceship the police are still trying to locate. This ship may also have been involved in the most recent disruption of the Ring Collapsiter's suspension mechanisms, although we have no direct proof at this time. Investigation is of course ongoing. I have no predictions as to when, uh, any resolution may come about. And now, if you require more specific information, I'm willing to answer a few questions."

To avoid a tsunami of replies, he thought to point toward a specific region of the flattened swarm, a cluster of four or five cameras, and to say, "You, yes."

The response was immediate. "Sir, have you resumed sexual relations with Her Majesty?"

Bruno sighed. "Is that all you people ever think about? The Queendom *is* in peril, you know. Are there any serious or technical questions?"

There almost certainly *were,* but something in his tone put them off, made the cameras worried or confused. Sykes Manor sat halfway between the orbits of Earth and Venus and was not, at this time of year, actually *close* to either of them. So the cameras were almost certainly autonomous, loaded with their owners' instruction sets and stripped-down personality images and fired off on absurdly hasty trajectories to gather up what news they could. Given a few seconds to collect their miniature wits, or a few tens of seconds to confer with their distant owners, the cameras' processors might well have come up with an intelligent question or two; surely *some* of them were from research or educational outfits, or other nontabloid press.

But Bruno, already bored with his role as spokesman, didn't give them a few seconds. Instead, he waved a dismissive hand and said, "Bah, you have the gist of it already. The details, when we know them, will be released in some sort of interactive document. Meanwhile, Marlon Sykes and Deliah van Skettering are coping with their misfortune, while their murderer is sought."

"Declarant," one brave camera finally asked, "will this report include your solution to the Ring Collapsiter's fall?"

"I have no solution to that," Bruno said grumpily. "At the moment, I'm not certain there is one."

The cameras met that remark with stunned silence. Oh. So much for his being reassuring.

"Er, that is, I've only been here a few hours. And as such things go, they've been rather busy hours. When I've had time to study the problem more completely, I'll . . . Well, it's just premature right now."

Bother it, he *was* bad at this. Annoyed, he cut the channel and walked away. Tamra should have had better judgment than to send him out here like this, unsupervised.

On his way, he nearly walked into one of the many Cheng Shiaos that filled Sykes Manor; the Shiao was standing there in the gloom, his back turned, his lights pointing up at distant rubble, and Bruno half mistook him for a pillar until the lights turned suddenly toward him.

"Goodness, Shiao, you startled me."

Shiao gave a ritual nod. "Excuse me, Declarant. The fault is mine. To update you on what's happening: the suspect vessel has been pinpointed, and has refused radio contact or else been unable to establish it. Its registration number, which we've been able to read optically from the exterior hull, shows ownership by something called the Titania Mineralogical Concern. This registry may be forged or stolen, though; the application was filed eighty years ago, for an eight-berth personnel ferry much smaller than this vessel, by the name of *Lupin II*."

"Ah," Bruno said. "I see, yes. And this other ship, the one you've actually spotted, does it have a name?"

Shiao looked troubled. "It does, sir. HMS *De Towaji's Bane*. You'll, ah, be pleased to know that the nearest Constabulary cruiser is already en route toward it, with a SWAT boarding party and a full suite of armaments. ETA five hours, twenty-two minutes."

"Ah," Bruno said, taken aback. "My own bane, is it? I should be flattered, I suppose. And a boarding party, you say? You'll certainly want to identify the nasen beam projector—it should be *outside* the hull, possibly in a pod of some sort, with its heat sink located opposite the projection aperture. The device also needs to be completely free of mechanical vibrations for several minutes before it's fired, so if anyone aims it at your cruiser there should be ample warning to move out of the way. You needn't move far—even a few meters would suffice. Just enough that the beam will miss if it isn't realigned."

"Thank you, Declarant," Shiao said, sounding impressed and concerned and genuinely grateful. "That advice could well save lives today."

"Think nothing of it," Bruno returned, waving a hand. "My own life may well be among them, as this bears directly on the Ring Collapsiter investigation. You're prepared to fax the Royal Committee aboard for the encounter?"

Shiao's jaw tightened visibly, but all he said was, "Absolutely, sir. Arrangements are already underway."

. . .

A Constabulary boarding action turned out to be a remarkably dull affair. This one did, anyway, since the "suspect vessel," Bruno's very own personal bane, his *hashashin,* his self-styled mortal enemy, never once engaged its engines or aimed its nasen projector or reoriented its hull in any way. It might almost have been a derelict, a ghost ship drifting empty through space, if not for the winking of running lights, clearly visible through the new cruiser's telescopes. Too, the cruiser's captain reported that the suspect vessel did occasionally fire a puff of gas from its maneuvering thrusters. "Momentum wheel desaturation," he explained cryptically. "For control of their altitude, which appears to be fixed in inertial space."

Ordinarily, Bruno would have pressed for a more detailed explanation, but he'd been drawn into a royal game of doubles poker and dared not let his attention wander too far for too long lest young Vivian kick his armored shin with the remarkably armor-rattling toe of her space boot. They'd all taken a quiet dinner and fresh-air break back on Tongatapu before coming here, but they'd been back in suits and helmet domes for over two hours now, and it had been getting somewhat tiresome. Finally Vivian had faxed up a set of magnetic playing cards and convinced Tamra to make their use an Official Business of the Royal Committee.

Ordinarily, Bruno would have objected to such gross misuse of his person at a time like this. He'd done so often enough in his days at Tamra's palace, when matters were—to put it mildly—a good deal less urgent. But he couldn't quite bring himself to refuse Vivian Rajmon; if the Queendom could put its children to work in such hazardous circumstances, chasing after their elders' banes and suchlike, then said Queendom should at least indulge, when possible, said children's need for play. He'd even surprised himself by enjoying the game a little. He and Vivian had narrowly won the match with three games out of five, although Deliah and Marlon had won the other two, and the odd pairing of Tamra with Cheng Shiao had presented substantial resistance throughout. Vivian seemed more childish than ever, or perhaps the term would be child*like,* since she manifested it mainly in pleasant ways. Even Tamra seemed to notice the difference, and to look on her little Commandant-Inspector a bit more thoughtfully.

But another hour later even that was finished, and the SWAT robots were strapping them all into recessed acceleration couches as the final rendezvous and boarding action approached. The ship's bulkheads swam with wellstone designs, hypercomputers forming and reforming and vanishing and forming again, their innards no doubt buzzing with strategic and tactical analyses. Ironically, this superficial turmoil required nothing of Bruno and was in fact his first real chance to sit still and think. He took full advantage of it by refining, in his mind, the exact scenario by which a single ship, with a single nasen beam projector, might weaken and contaminate nearly a third of the Ring Collapsiter's arc. He came up with a number of plausible mechanisms and finally settled on one that best fit the observed facts: the ship had sat up here in the asteroid belt and fired almost tangentially, the most glancing of blows, cutting a chord about half a kilometer sunward of the collapsiter's rim.

At that range, the beam would be about twice as wide as the collapsiter itself, but the sun's gravity—and indeed the collapsiter's own gravity—would pull the beam out of true, curve it around like a stream of water firing out of a hose. If the top of the beam's arc touched the Ring Collapsiter *just so,* then instead of punching two neat holes through the ring, as it had through Marlon's house, it would instead follow the ring's curvature around, plowing a swath right through it, perhaps for millions of kilometers. Hmm. He'd have to work the actual math on that one; curiosity aside, the results might be needed as evidence in court.

Cheng Shiao settled into the berth across from his and was instantly immobilized by straps and webbing.

"So," Bruno asked him, "if you don't mind my asking, how does one rise to the rank of lieutenant in the Royal Constabulary?"

Shiao, still attempting to settle into a more comfortable position, looked puzzled. "Rise, sir? I was appointed to this rank directly."

"Truly? With no prior experience?"

"Correct."

"How strange. On what . . . basis was this appointment made?"

"Exam scores, sir. And general inclination. I won't bore you with the story."

"No, indeed, I'm asking you to. I begin to realize how little I know about the modern Queendom."

Shiao met his gaze. "Are you certain you want the full details? Because there's some violence involved. I was in Qingdao, walking along the Yanan Lu on my way to the job interview, which was well outside the business district, in a warehouse area I didn't know well. It was two-ten in the afternoon; there wasn't much traffic. As I was walking, I passed what appeared to be an abandoned building, with two males standing on the front steps. They were dressed in reflective jackets and sunglasses, and appeared unusually alert."

"Nervous, eh?"

"No, sir, just the opposite. My strong impression at the time was that they were guards. Not professional security, you understand—they were kempt and well dressed, but there was no impression of legitimacy about them. It seemed to me that they were posted there explicitly to intimidate passersby. I suspected that some business was going on inside the building, and there was a desire to prevent interruptions."

"Or witnesses."

"Exactly, yes."

"So what did you do? You weren't a police officer at all at that point, were you?"

"I belonged to a neighborhood watch organization in Xingtai. But you're correct: I had no official standing in the city of Qingdao. I wasn't licensed to carry weapons or interfere with lawful enterprise. But the situation looked bad, like someone could easily get hurt."

"Including yourself," Bruno noted.

"Yes, sir. I was acutely aware of the fact—any suspicious action on my part could tip them off. Even simply walking past might do it; the smart thing would have been to just turn around the moment I saw them. But I believe in the law. I believe that no one has the right to violate it, especially in flagrant ways that breed disrespect. Calling the police would have been an option, but I worried the suspects would be long gone by the time an officer materialized."

"A curious worry. What did you do?"

Shiao shrugged. "I called myself at home, and then while the line was open I rapidly approached the two suspects. 'I need your help,' I said to them. 'Someone is chasing me.' It's doubtful they would have believed this story for long, and possibly they saw at once what I was doing, which was capturing their coordinates and their images to a remote location. But what certainly gave me away was my own voice on the telephone, screaming that I should get out of there immediately. I was younger then, more impulsive, but it turned out to be good advice: the nearer suspect drew a laser pointer and burned the left side of my face straight through to the bone."

"Good gods!"

"He was aiming for the phone," Shiao explained, "and he hit it. At that moment I myself was still an incidental target. Since I was already running, I took advantage of the distraction to engage the suspect physically."

Bruno didn't know whether to be impressed or appalled. "Surely you must have been in agony!"

Again, Shiao shrugged. "I assume so. By the time the city police arrived, I was dead, so I never did learn how it all turned out. We didn't have the kind of scene reconstructions that we do nowadays; it became something of a town mystery. All I can say is that one suspect was picked up at the scene, having been detained there by an injury, and the other was identified and arrested later based on the video I'd captured. No other associates were ever explicitly identified."

Shiao's voice had never once wavered from the precise, restrained, overpolite monotone that had marked good police officers for centuries, perhaps forever. There was no room for boast or modesty in that tone: the account was purely factual and devoid of emotional overtone, laid out plainly for Bruno's evaluation. Shiao's eyes had not looked clouded or sentimental as he told the tale of this major turning point in his life.

"I daresay these gentlemen benefited from the lesson," Bruno ventured.

Shiao nodded. "I like to think so, sir. A policeman's job is to chill and frustrate crime—merely punishing it is a symptom of failure."

"I suppose so, yes. Very insightful. I'm surprised they didn't promote you directly to captain."

Again, a factual monotone. "I failed the aptitude, sir. I hope to grow and season with age, but today the Constabulary has dozens of better cops than myself."

"Dozens? Really?" Bruno blanched inwardly at the thought. With forty billion citizens to choose from, the Queendom certainly had no shortage of compulsive savants to fill its payroll. Better than filling it with incompetents, obviously, but there was something frightening about a really gung-ho interplanetary police force. "I shall be very careful to obey the laws, I think."

"That's the idea, sir." Then, catching something in Bruno's look, Shiao said, "It makes some people nervous, this kind of concentrated authority. I understand the feeling. But I can assure you of the Constabulary's complete intolerance for bad cops. Any crook or bigot in our midst, or even a well-meaning authoritarian, would be disowned and prosecuted immediately. Of the seven thousand, six hundred, and eight applicants for the position of lieutenant, more than eighty percent failed the moral aptitude screening."

"Seven thousand!" Bruno said, surprised. "Goodness, that's a lot of applicants. What happened to all of them?"

"A few are taken on each year as sergeants," Shiao replied, "and since local and regional forces have less stringent entrance criteria, they absorb a lot of our near misses."

"Mmm. How many is a lot?"

Shrug. "Probably a few hundred, that year."

"And the rest?"

Shiao considered for a few seconds before answering, "I would guess many of them found work in support roles: admin, theory, equipment testing. And there's always a need for critics and advocates in the policy arena. And actors for the training demos, and I suppose for commercial movies as well. Actors who really *understand* the police are rare."

"And the rest?" Bruno persisted.

Now Shiao began to look uncomfortable, and Bruno sensed he was edging into taboo territory. In a meritocracy, what happened to people who lacked merit? People who were lazy or impulsive or foolish could change, up to a point, but could they *want* to change?

"Neighborhood Watch is a respectable job," Shiao answered finally. "And they'll take almost anyone."

"Almost," Bruno mused. "Mmm. And the rest?"

Shiao sighed. "There's always crime itself, sir. It's not generally a career choice for geniuses."

"Ah. I suppose not. Seems a bit unfair, though."

Shiao, to Bruno's surprise, seemed to find that funny. "*They* certainly think so, sir. But good and evil are choices, not fates handed out at birth. We're talking, probably, about fewer than a hundred of those seven thousand applicants, and if you actually *met* them, you might find your sympathies reduced."

"Ah. Maybe so. You've little hope of promotion, then? It sounds like an awfully rigid structure."

"They all are, sir. To get promoted I'd have to displace someone more experienced, which is a huge effort even to attempt. And my own job goes open for recompetition every decade, so I could well be *de*moted if I start to get sloppy. In theory, we're encouraged to see demotion as a positive career move—point of maximum competence, as they say. But that's a fairly new idea. 'Rigid structure' is an accurate description. But of course, we're planning for the long term these days."

"Mmm. Indeed."

Shiao had nothing further to say. Neither did Bruno. The conversation was at an end.

The actual docking and boarding were so uneventful Bruno nearly missed them; the cruiser simply pulled up alongside the suspect vessel, selected a standard docking adapter, and mated airlocks with nary a thump. Only when Shiao's harnesses retracted and vanished and the SWAT robots started running in puppetlike synchrony toward the hatch, flicking on their optically superconducting outer jackets so that they vanished from sight—only then did Bruno realize what was happening. Hastily, he unstrapped himself, prepared to follow once the area was "secured." This had been explained to him at length—whether he left a copy behind or not, he was neither to risk himself nor interfere with tactical or evidentiary procedures unless some very clear and pertinent reason presented itself.

It took a whopping forty-five seconds to secure the suspect spaceship.

"One occupant," the human SWAT commander stated flatly as he materialized to usher the royal committee from their berths. "A modified human, male, deceased."

"Modified?" Bruno asked, curious and a little afraid. "Deceased?"

"You'll see."

"Hmm."

The inside of the ship was remarkably cramped and colorless, like a half dozen prison cells strung end to end. The ship was much smaller on the inside than the outside, since after all it was mostly engine, fuel tank, and superconducting battery. But it was so *dim*, so *ugly*. There were no windows of any kind, and no effort had been made to smooth or pad the many corners, nor to hide the various plumbing and wiring that connected the ship's systems. It looked like a utility closet, and would have been an inhospitable place even without the twenty black-shelled SWAT robots crowding it.

The "one occupant" lay on a kind of acceleration couch near the ship's bow, from which all manner of hoses and cables radiated. The couch appeared to be the ship's only actual furnishing. The "deceased" status of said occupant was obvious; Bruno's external air pressure gauge read a flat 0.00, and the figure was naked, somewhat shriveled looking, and was both covered and surrounded by odd pools and knobs and jagged crystals of red-colored ice. "Male" was there for anyone to see, and as for "modified human," well, that was unequivocal as well; there were wires and tubes feeding into every part of the dead man's body. The ones running into his head looked blackened and scorched and melted, as if they'd carried a brief but enormous electrical surge.

The fact that he had six arms—each gripping its own joystick on the wide, gray shoulders of the couch—was actually one of the least disturbing things about him. People hadn't done this much in Bruno's day, wholesale modifications of their body forms, but even then, the absence had been recognized as a matter of fashion. The idea itself was hardly a shocking one, given that the capability was there in any fax machine.

What did shock Bruno was that the face, shriveled and bloody and burned as it was, looked painfully familiar. "I know this man," he said, and his voice sounded unnerved even to him. "I've seen him. On my last visit to the Queendom, I think. On Maxwell Montes, on Venus."

"It's Wenders Rodenbeck," Tamra agreed, and her voice sounded unnerved as well. "The playwright."

"Activist against collapsium," Deliah added. "Yes, we hear from him frequently at the ministry. I've never known him to wear six-armed body forms, though, nor to travel in space. He's the typical hypocrite: faxing himself daily through the collapsiter grid he claims to despise. He's pleasant about it, though—a natural charmer. I actually like him. Can this be the same person?"

"Where are his injunctions and restraining orders now?" Marlon murmured, as if to the body itself. "Is this his final settlement, a head full of burnt wires? I'll wager I know Wenders better than any of you. A happy prankster, yes. Now a killer? Now lying here with six arms, and blood all over his face? Is this a trick? God, excuse me, I think I'm going to vomit."

And so he did, inside the bowl of his helmet. Familiar with the hazard, the SWAT robots slapped his purge valve, then whisked him away to the fax machine before he could move wrong or breathe wrong and suck down a choking glob. Crystals of purged, rapidly freezing vomit spun after him, as if terrified of being abandoned here without him.

"Cause of death," Cheng Shiao said gently, looking down at a wellstone pad, "probable suicide. He left a note. An entire log, actually, detailing his activities for the past seven years. Assuming it's accurate, this would appear to be our man."

Vivian regained her maturity and summoned Wenders Rodenbeck right there to *De Towaji's Bane* for questioning. Did he know anything about this ship or its business? Did he wish any harm to the Queendom, or bear a grudge against any of its officials or luminaries?

Rodenbeck, bleary eyed, hanging there in zero atmosphere in a spacesuit he'd never been trained to use, could only stammer his replies: No, no, not at all. Never!

The Queendom recognized no right to remain silent under questioning; every response was compulsory, and subject to analysis by the finest lie detectors, stress analyzers, and personality emulators of the Royal Constabulary. If he was innocent of the crime being investigated, all records of this conversation would be purged from the interrogators' minds, leaving them to speculate about any other infelicities or malfeasances he might have revealed under questioning. And any distress he suffered would be measured with exacting precision, and a proper compensation calculated and dispensed. But in the meantime, the twin priorities of public safety and swift justice held sway, and his brain was theirs to pick.

Bruno had never imagined himself in such a position before; it troubled and embarrassed him, dirtied him in some ill-defined way. Perhaps the experience would be erased, though; Rodenbeck *did* appear both innocent and distressed. "I'm an artist," he protested repeatedly. "I love the Queendom—I've gone to considerable pains to protect it against its own excesses. And always within the framework of the law! Well, nearly always . . ."

"Ah," Vivian said then, with a knowing look. "Yes. Indeed."

Bruno figured that would have been an unnerving thing under any circumstances, to be addressed that way by a Commandant-Inspector of the Royal Constabulary. Hearing it from an eleven-year-old girl, though, seemed to tip Rodenbeck into hysteria. "Hey, I watch the news!" he shouted. "I'm not stupid. I know why I'm here! You think this Ring Collapsiter thing has anything to do with me? Do you really?"

"You *have* spoken out against it on lots of occasions," Vivian pointed out. "And against its creators."

"Of course! Its creators are guilty of the grossest irresponsibility and negligence, *as demonstrated* by their current difficulties. I protest the use of collapsium *because* it's dangerous, *because* it poses a huge safety risk. I'm on the side of the angels, here, little girl. Why *would* I, why would I *possibly* do anything to enlarge that risk?"

Vivian, examining readings of some sort on her little wellstone pad, frowned at that. "*Have* you done anything to enhance the threat?"

"No."

"Have you harmed anyone?"

"No."

"Do you plan to?"

"No!"

She sighed then, and clunked her hand against the dome of her helmet in a manner all too familiar to Bruno—she'd been trying to touch her face. "Come look at a body with me, sir. You may find the experience disturbing."

"Why? Whose body is it?"

"Yours."

They strode the length of the ship, slipping past SWAT robots and royal bodyguards until they'd reached the strange acceleration couch. It had been fitted with a crinkly black plastic cover, but at Vivian's nod the attendant Shiao unhooked its fasteners and peeled it away, revealing the body beneath.

Rodenbeck recoiled. "Eew. Is that real? Is that supposed to be *me?*"

"It is you, sir," Vivian said. "Bioassay confirms it's an accurate copy whose pattern began divergence from yours approximately seven years ago. It shows several fax markers in that first year, each with body modifications associated, and nothing at all after that. Reconstruction shows it's been physically grafted to that chair for sixty-two months, nine days. Unfortunately, the brain suffered extensive damage in the surge that killed it, so its memories are not available to us. Do you have any idea what this . . . individual . . . might have been up to?"

Rodenbeck started to say something, but fainted instead.

Vivian sighed, and said to Shiao, "Get him out of here; take him home. He doesn't know anything."

Shiao straightened. "Right away, Commandant-Inspector. I agree with your analysis."

"Relax, Lieutenant. Please."

"Yes'm. Absolutely."

When Shiao had gone, Tamra whirled around and pointed an angry finger at the body. "This creature did well to kill itself—I'd see it jailed for a million years! Yet Rodenbeck, who *is* the creature, is innocent? Explain this to me, Vivian. Why did you let him go?"

"Because he's innocent," Vivian said simply, attempting a shrug inside her suit. "We see this sometimes: compartmentalization of intent. We all have copies running around, true? Sometimes, one of them will diverge, and decide it's not part of the canonical individual anymore. Could be a traumatic experience, could be almost anything, really. All of a sudden, you have this person with Wenders Rodenbeck's history and knowledge, but not his actual sense of identity. Maybe he's smug, he figures he knows something that's fundamentally changed him. So he changes his body, changes his name, stays out of fax machines—which would not only log his existence, but might eventually report his movements back to the *real* Rodenbeck and charge him transit fees for every step!

"So this copy lives in the shadows for a while, without the social pressures or accountability he's accustomed to, and whatever funny ideas he has in his head start to seem reasonable. Rodenbeck isn't a criminal, but this—all right, this *creature*—isn't Rodenbeck anymore. It hasn't been for a long time."

"And this happens *often*?" Tamra demanded, her tone indicating just how well she liked this sort of thing going on under her nose behind her back.

"Not often," Vivian said. "But sometimes. I remember maybe, like, three cases of this since human-capable faxes first became available. I'm not really sure; you'd have to ask Shiao for the details."

Bruno, finally moved to speak, said, "I don't think I like the implications, here. Living alone causes genocidal mania? Do you think *I'm* at risk, mademoiselle? I'd resent that notion very much!"

Vivian eyed him clinically for several seconds. "Well, I would say you're at a higher risk for it than someone with equivalent intellect, but who's better socialized. Don't take that as an insult; genocidal mania is remarkably rare, even among hardened sociopaths, and you haven't shown any of the marker behaviors."

"Well. Humph. If I do lose my mind, perhaps you'll be the first to know about it. This whole experience has been unsavory, and we've nothing to show for it, no villain to punish."

"And the collapsiter is still falling," Tamra pointed out angrily. "You *do* need to address that at some point, you know."

Bruno gasped. "Goodness, I'd almost forgotten! It came to me, while the ships were docking; what if the ring were spun?" He turned to Marlon, who was drifting in dour silence at the other end of the ship, by the airlock. In an atmosphere he'd have been too distant for anything but a shouted conversation, but over suit radios it hardly mattered. "Marlon, the grapple stations all point straight down at the ring, yes? As much as possible given the damage, I mean. But imagine skewing them, pointing them a few degrees off to one side. That would create a torque which would spin the ring in place."

"And reduce the upward pull on it," Marlon said, straightening. "It would just fall in that much faster, until the attachment points had swung around to be underneath the grapples again."

"Ah!" Bruno said, waving a finger at his colleague. "But we'd keep moving them, attaching to new points that were off to the side again. Like pushing a merry-go-round. If that torque were applied for long enough, the collapsiter would simply go into orbit around the sun."

Marlon's frown was clearly visible. "It's fragile, Bruno. Until that muon contamination burns off, we hardly dare to *touch* the ring."

"Really? Assuming any significant vibrations could be damped, we'd actually be reducing the strain on the collapsium lattice with every bit of velocity we added. It should take . . . what? A little over ten to the sixth meters per second to orbit it? It'd be self-supporting then, like the rings of Saturn, needing the grapple stations only to shepherd and stabilize it. At a tenth of a gee acceleration, that speed would take less than three weeks to achieve. Since we have *ten months* to play with, we could go all the way down to fifty milligee and still have margin to spare. I'll need the math to be certain, but surely the lattice ought to tolerate *that*."

"Gods of fucking algebra!" Marlon exclaimed. "It certainly should! It certainly should! Does it take a Declarant to see *that*?"

And here, the police files recorded a distinct clunking noise over Marlon's radio as he tried to slap himself in the forehead but hit only the solid helmet dome instead.

chapter thirteen

in which a brilliant
first step is taken

To Bruno's surprise, the investigation didn't stop there.
"We have old fax records to pore through," Vivian explained in
their parting conversation. "It's possible there are alternate
copies of the creature out there that may at least be acces-
sories by foreknowledge. The original divergence may even
have happened against Rodenbeck's will, which would be a
kind of kidnapping. And we have so many unexplained fax
anomalies surrounding this thing. This could well take *years*
to sort out, assuming it's possible at all. But our duty is to try."

"Well," Bruno told her seriously, "far be it from me to stand
in duty's way, but do remember to act your age now and then,
while you still have it. Enjoy your plight, for my sake if for no
other reason. Most of us are only young once!"

That wasn't a particularly funny comment, but they chuckled together at it just the same, and Deliah and Tamra and
Cheng Shiao chuckled with them. Marlon simply glowered,
apparently having decided yet again to be jealous of Bruno,
after his recent whirlwind of media appearances had—to everyone's surprise—actually gone rather well. Marlon himself had
been invited to appear only as an afterthought or sidekick, or

to answer for his errors, or as a substitute for Bruno when Bruno was unavailable.

Fortunately, Bruno's availability was about to drop to zero; he was returning home tonight, delayed only by Her Majesty's insistence. This was the last official meeting of the Royal Committee for Investigation of Ring Collapsiter Anomalies—thankfully abbreviated to RoCIRCA—and Tamra had assured all of them that attendance was compulsory. Thankfully, the location she'd reserved for it was Fangatapu, the Forbidden Beach near Tamra's Tongan palace, where she'd arranged that the warm summertime sun should set through three separate layers of patchy cloud, making—they'd all agreed—for one of the most striking sunsets any of them had ever seen. And the blankets somehow never got sandy, and the drinks were just intoxicating enough that Bruno could quench his thirst pleasantly without fear of overindulgence.

"It's been nice getting to know you," Deliah said, filling an opening in the conversation. "I wish it could have been under different circumstances; it's fair to say you haven't seen me at my best. I'm actually a fairly together person."

She'd expressed this sentiment before, so Bruno smiled for her and used the reply he'd rehearsed the night before. "Madam, it's been a pleasure, and if it's your worst side I've seen this past week, I suspect I'm unworthy company for the real you."

She actually *blushed* at that, a fact in which Bruno took some satisfaction. Not bad for a recluse. Actually, he didn't feel that his style or behavior had changed all that much, but people did seem to respond to him better these days, to find more enjoyment than discomfort in his company. Perhaps he'd simply been born with an old man's personality and was finally growing into it, or at least learning to walk in the oversized shoes society had chosen for him.

"You'd make an excellent investigator," Cheng Shiao told him a little while after that. "I've learned some things by watching you."

Bruno suspected that was one of the highest compliments the man had at his disposal. His first impulse was therefore to brush it off, to deny it or make a poor joke of it, but with effort he restrained himself, nodded once, and returned with, "Your talent at reconstruction would serve brilliantly in any field of science. If Vivian here weren't immortal, I'm sure you'd have her job someday."

Shiao made a visible effort to smile at that. "I'm quite glad she *is* immortal, sir."

"Naturally, yes. As we all are. But it does crush any hope of ambition, doesn't it?"

"I suppose so, sir. I suppose I'm fortunate not to have any."

"As am I." Bruno laughed. "And look where it's got me. Still, I imagine your childhood on a bitter plateau somewhere, all rocks and weeds and poisonous snakes."

Shiao smirked at that. "Sir, I grew up in a posh Xingtai suburb, with lemon-tea summers and snow-dragon winters, and everywhere the smell of roasted meat. Superstition thick enough to dance on—we had thousands of little gods running around, but no one particularly believed in them, not with *fear* and *awe* like a proper god should inspire. It was just one more lazy game to play; the whole place was a game. I like my life now because it's serious, because what I do matters.

"It has nothing to do with place, really. You look at me and you see a stiff policeman, which is entirely correct. But it's not an affliction, right? It's an aspiration. There are personable, easygoing police as well, and we need them, because it takes a certain variety to balance out a force. From an early age, I guess you could say I cultivated myself to be the person I am, and really I'm very pleased it's turned out so well."

"Choosing to isolate and deprive yourself," Bruno mused. "Why does that sound familiar?"

Shiao politely waved a hand. "Quite the opposite, sir; I enjoy being this way. It's very rewarding."

"It also suits his face," Vivian added. "He has such stern features. You know that cartoon show, 'Barnes and Manetti'? He looks just like Manetti sometimes. Talks like him, too."

Shiao looked surprised. "Is that show still on? It's true: Manetti was an idol of mine. Barnes always had it easy; he would just bend the rules more and more until a solution finally fell into his lap. Intimidation, tampering, unauthorized surveillance . . . He's supposed to be the hero, right? Manetti is just an obstacle, this infuriating person standing between the perpetrators and their hard-won justice. But Manetti actually *obeys the law,* which is much harder. Doing the right thing is always harder. Barnes wouldn't last two weeks in the Constabulary."

"No," Vivian agreed, "he certainly wouldn't."

A seagull screeched nearby, drawing everyone's attention. For a while, they just watched the sunlight on the waves.

Finally, Tamra turned to Marlon. "Do you have any parting words for our guest of honor? If not, we might as well get on with this."

"Thank him for his services," Marlon said, with a good solid attempt at sincerity, "and wish him well in his research. I've little doubt there'll be many more breakthroughs with his name attached."

"Is that all?" Tamra prodded.

"I think so, yes."

"No good-byes?"

"No. Life is long. The Queendom is small. He and I will be seeing each other again."

She looked ready to respond to that, but finally shrugged. "All right, then. Bruno, I've kept the media away this time— cordon set at twenty kilometers—but I'm sure you understand, we can't let you out of here without another Medal of Salvation."

"No," Bruno agreed ruefully, "I don't suppose you can. Is this a ceremony, then?"

She shook her head. "You've earned the right to have this your way. But I will say thank you; you didn't have to come help us again."

"Oh, pish," he said, not bothering to hide his irritation. "Of course I did. I'm not half the misanthrope you seem to believe, dear. I do wish for people to be happy, free of harm, all that sort of thing. It's just that usually I can best accomplish this by being far away; Rodenbeck is correct about one thing: collapsium research *is* fraught with perils. Marlon is braver than I, to risk his reputation so close to home."

"That may be," she conceded, silencing Marlon's protest with a look. "And we wouldn't dream of depriving you of your passions, nor of depriving *ourselves* of the benefits thereof. But we do miss you; surely you understand that."

"I've never doubted it."

"Well, then," she said, and stuck out her hand, a little gold medallion dangling from it by a length of green ribbon. "Here's your medal."

He took it from her. It was heavier than it looked, and warm from having been in her pocket. Somewhat embarrassed, he nonetheless slipped the thing around his neck and let it hang.

The Royal Committee applauded politely for a full minute, at which point Tamra said, "All right, everyone, thanks for coming. Now I'll ask you to excuse us."

They all rose with a chorus of good-byes, to which Bruno responded with, surprisingly, a little lump in his throat. And then, without further ado, they were all walking away, blankets in hand, their rising conversation now with one another, rather than with Bruno. In another minute, he and Tamra were alone. They rose, leaving their own blankets behind for beach attendants to clean up, and made their way toward the fax gate that stood by the washrooms, just beyond the tree-line.

"You're more regal than you used to be," Bruno remarked. "More comfortable with your regality."

She shrugged. "The people expect no less: elective monarchy is basically a scapegoating tactic."

Bruno smirked at this; in Girona, the word "scapegoat" had meant, literally, a *goat* on whom the city's problems were blamed. Every year, in a grand festival, the people would stack themselves into human pyramids—a prize for the highest! the widest! the jiggliest!—and then they'd throw this poor goat off a tower. No one particularly disputed the cruelty of the practice, but centuries of tradition weighed heavy then, as they probably did today.

Tamra, who knew all about the goat but apparently hadn't made the connection, continued. "Once upon a time, democrats overthrew monarchs for the promise of freedom. What a laugh! As if responsibility and accountability were something people wanted for themselves! Freedom means finding someone else to worry about all the little details for you, and all the *big* details you're too immersed in your life to see. People don't want a dictator, obviously. Quite the contrary; they want a *dictatee,* a conscripted functionary who can be endlessly blamed and imposed upon. It *is* democracy, for all but the monarch herself."

"Ah, but we love you in return," Bruno pointed out. "And there's a lot of money and privilege involved."

"Yes. Yes, there is. And it's my duty to enjoy and appreciate that, up to a point. But if I begin to feel *entitled,* I undermine the very principles of my office, and wherever I go I find myself sharply and impatiently reminded of the fact. They aren't shy about it, these subjects of mine. Isn't it the least bit ironic, Bruno, that a Queendom which seeks to match jobs to people for optimum happiness and efficiency also insists on, at best, grudging leadership at its highest levels? Isn't that an odd thing?"

Bruno mused, then slowly nodded. "It is ironic, yes. But it's hardly the only such irony. And I doubt it's quite the conspiracy you suggest. People probably just want their money's worth, and haven't really reflected on how it affects you personally. Or perhaps they *have,* but they still feel—rightly, I think—that *someone* has to bear the responsibility. It's not always for us to choose our fates."

"Not for me, at any rate. I do like to imagine I've bought some freedom of choice for other people. But anyway, it's not like I have anything else to compare my life to. I'm content enough, yes, through long practice and long experience. And like everyone else, I reserve the right to complain sometimes. You will attend me in this, Philander."

"As you wish, Highness." Bruno couldn't quite hide his smirk. "You know, I wasn't always so suave. You're just about the only person who accepted me, in those days, exactly as I was."

"Suave!" she laughed. "Well, that's one word for it, I suppose, though not one that leaps most readily to mind. But seriously, Bruno, I don't *accept* you. I never have; you're not a very acceptable person. I *love* you, and that's a very different thing."

"Indeed," he agreed. "Very different. I wouldn't know what love *was* if not for you. It's difficult to leave you here and go about my business; surely that's understood."

She looked sad then, which made him feel guilty. He almost decided right then to stay in the Queendom forever. Almost.

"Unfortunately," she said, "even twenty kilometers away, news cameras have an alarming ability to resolve fine details. If we were, say, to duck into one of these washrooms for even a moment, the headlines would last the rest of the year. So I'm afraid you must kiss me chastely on the lips, just once, and take your leave of me."

"Yes, Highness," he said, ever the obedient one, and complied exactly with her instructions.

"Oh, phooey," she said, punching him lightly on the chest. "Is that the best you can do? Do my hints and temptations mean nothing?"

"That wasn't very grown-up of you," he said, feigning both pain and indignation.

"Who ever said I was grown up?" she returned, and pushed him bodily through the fax gate.

For once, he experienced a distinct sensation of travel; her laughter cut off instantly, and the cool touch of her hand seemed very distant indeed. Sweet sorrow? Pah, there was nothing sweet about it. On the other side was full daylight and a decidedly chilly breeze. The trees around him swayed, and the clouds scudded overhead like speeding aircraft, and the breeze became a wind that ruffled and flattened the meadow grass as he hurried toward his little white house.

Hurried, because he knew what happened next; even as the house opened a door for him, even as his staff of robots swarmed to pull him inside, the ground tilted beneath them all, then straightened, then tilted again the other way. The Onion! Blast it, he'd nearly forgotten. How *was* he going to dispose of that thing? Saving the Queendom was trouble enough, but this, *this* was difficult!

"Welcome, sir," the house offered as gravity gradually returned to something approaching its normal magnitude and direction.

One of his robots fell over.

The others seemed not to notice it, except as an obstacle to be danced around or avoided altogether as they hurried to bring him food, drink, fresh clothes, or whatever it was they thought he needed right now. But to *fall*—such clumsiness was unheard-of, even in the face of the Onion's disturbances. The one that had fallen had a scuffed, somewhat battered look to it, and presently it turned its blank metal face up toward Bruno in what could only be described as a pitiful manner, and emitted a sharp, questioning mewl.

Forgetting all else for the moment, Bruno cried out in surprise and delight and extended an eager hand toward the robot. "Hugo! Good God, man, you've learned to walk!"

book three

thrice upon a
schemer's plotting

chapter fourteen

in which an ancient question is revisited

Though Isaac Newton is best known for his pomiary inves-tigations into the nature of gravity, he was in fact quite troubled by his findings. Action at a distance, an effect with no explicable cause? The idea would be preposterous if its truth weren't so readily demonstrated. And while gravity was bothersome, inertia was by far the deepest thorn in his aristocratic hide, a thing he itched and scrabbled at right up to the final hours of his life.

A ship, he reasoned, must part the waters ahead of it, must push the waters aside to make a place for itself to move forward into. This requires energy; hence the need for sails, or oar-wielding galley slaves, or some other means to *push* against the water's resistance. So perhaps the air and Earth and even the space between planets were permeated with a kind of fluid? One which resisted the acceleration of the bodies within it, creating this phantom "inertia" that seemed to constrain the motions of every object in God's strange universe?

But if that were true, why would those selfsame objects, having been accelerated into motion, then remain in motion indefinitely? Why was the amount of force needed to decelerate an apple the same as that used to accelerate it in the first place? No ship had ever sailed thus; no fluid had ever allowed it. What properties would such an intangible fluid possess? Newton realized the question was fundamental, but after decades of pondering and wondering and quietly beseeching the powers of Heaven he was still no closer to understanding, and so he died.

What he didn't know, of course, was that the "fluid" was none other than *light*, the half-filled photon states of the zero-point vacuum churning in a perpetual storm of electric and magnetic potentials, which in turn resisted—and continue even now to resist—the acceleration of quarks and other charged particles. Since this field is isotropic, or uniform in all directions, and Lorentz-invariant, or uniform at all velocities, a force is required to alter the path or speed of any charged particle, on any trajectory at any time, anywhere in the universe. And since the interaction of charge with the zero-point field is precisely what gives rise to the illusion of "matter," the force required to accelerate an object winds up being directly proportional to its mass.

For nearly three centuries after Newton, philosophers were content to regard this "inertia" as some inherent property of matter, axiomatic and therefore inexplicable, where in fact Newton's strained speculations had been much nearer to the truth.

In the tenth decade of the Queendom of Sol, on a miniature planet orbiting at the middle depths of the Kuiper Belt, there lived a man named Bruno de Towaji who, at the time of our final attention, was brooding over an aspect of this very problem, and wishing to God he could be half as smart as Newton about it. He was in the habit of maneuvering very large masses with very great precision, and the energies involved—a direct consequence of Newton's inertia—were straining the limits of his infrastructure.

He was a sort of chemist or materials scientist, but the particles he worked with weighed a billion tons each, and swallowed light, and bent and twisted the spacetime around them. They were known classically as "black holes," industrially as "collapson nodes," but in Bruno's private lexicon they frequently adopted the names of anatomical features or bodily fluids or social functions best left unmentioned here.

It was daytime on Bruno's little planet, but the planet's little sun was dark, a shadow against the starscape, its nuclear fires encapsulated by a photoelectric conversion shell so that only its invisible heat escaped. Bruno lay on his back, on a chaise longue, in a meadow beneath a sprawling, hot, dew-dripping canopy of stars. The atmosphere was only a few meters thick because, yes, the planet really was that small, and so the stars didn't twinkle at him, but rather glared down with a hard, steady light that gave little doubt as to their nature. Had cavemen seen such a light they'd have guessed immediately that the stars were little suns, or large ones seen from a very great distance. The constellations would have been perfectly familiar, too, save for the bright yellow star off the tail of Sagittarius. That was Sol, the Queendom, the whole of humanity huddled around that pinprick of warmth. An ordinary star, and at this distance not really any brighter than Sirius.

But the stars didn't interest Bruno just now; he was inspecting, for perhaps the hundredth time that month, the ring of collapsium—of quantum-repulsion black-hole matter—with which he'd encircled his dark little sun. Once upon a time, that matter had comprised an ultradense "moon" of di-clad neutronium. Later, it had been an Onion of vacuum-rending collapsium shells, and afterward a disc and a cube and a series of interlocking equilateral triangles. From each configuration he'd learned a thing or two—mainly about how ignorant he really was, and how mysterious the inner workings of God's universe could be at their most fundamental levels.

Perhaps someday those collapsons would form an *arc de fin*—an archway through which the end of time could be observed, for purposes that Bruno had never really been able to articulate. Because it was there, he supposed. Because he felt like knowing. He'd managed, over the years, to confirm the theoretical possibility of such a device, and to derive some vague, half-baked notions as to how it might be constructed. But it was a long way from there to actually *building* the thing. It would be the work of centuries, he feared, perhaps even millennia.

Pinching his bearded chin thoughtfully, he studied the "ring," which was actually a quite complicated arrangement of scallopy, sinusoidal ripples, one upon the other, like a lace apron or tutu strung across the sky. It glowed the bright, pale color first glimpsed by Pavel Cerenkov in the twentieth century; the blue of supraluminal particles shedding energy as they dropped below the speed of light.

Had he surrounded the *planet* with it, the ring might have appeared as a peaked arch linking one side of the horizon with the other. Well, perhaps not—Bruno's planet was so small that it sloped away like a hilltop beneath his lounge. As a result, his horizons were not only close, they were visibly *down*. At any rate, there wasn't nearly enough collapsium to encircle the entire planet. He'd need three or four kilometers of it to accomplish that. But the "sun" was much smaller, and the collapsium looked like exactly what it was: a frilled ring a few centimeters thick and fifty meters around, encircling a dark, spherical body orbiting some seven hundred meters above the planet's surface.

The inside of a warehouse would be as inspiring.

Or perhaps that was merely the contempt of familiarity speaking, or Bruno's own long frustration; perhaps the scene was more wonderful and wondrous than anything Isaac Newton—in his plague-ridden, wattle-thatched world—could possibly have imagined. Bruno feared, suddenly, that this was so. He sat up, looking around him at the steamy, starlit darkness, wondering if, through years of neglect and overwork, he'd burned out his capacity for wonder. What a thought! What if he *made* the *arc de fin, glimpsed* the fading lights of the end of time, and could muster no more than a weary "eh"? How awful!

He made an effort to see the scene with fresh eyes: the planet like a little benighted Eden, the stooping robot field-workers like peasants of a land so wealthy its very *citizens* were made of gold. And over there, his little cottage with its wellstone walls all turned to white glass, a pretty trick indeed. And above it all, the collapsium, glowing blue as the ghosts of drowned sailors. Soon enough, that scalloped ring would be gone, replaced by some new assembly, some new experiment. It was a fleeting thing, a blossom.

There was the problem, though—the very reason for Bruno's frustration. He'd long ago run out of fresh neutronium and had for years now resigned himself to recycling his collapsium over and over again. Every experiment had to be dismantled to make way for the next—carefully, to prevent its structure from collapsing into a single, ordinary hypermass. Such dismantling required phenomenal precision, and thanks to inertia it also required such vast amounts of energy that he'd been forced to harness virtually the *entire output* of his miniature star.

The star—his own invention—was simple enough; a neutronium core wrapped securely in superreflectors, holding down an outer sheath of hydrogen in self-sustaining nuclear fusion. But it was for *light*, damn it; it was meant not only to warm but to *brighten* this little world at the fringes of interstellar space. So thanks to inertia, he lived in the dark, and while he could certainly build a new sun, and even a new moon to go with it, the difficulties of contacting the Queendom to arrange for neutronium production and delivery would consume his attention as surely his experiments consumed light, possibly for years. Bah.

He could, of course, hop into the fax machine and duplicate himself, but he knew himself too well; the duplicate wouldn't want to deal with logistical headaches any more than he did. Within hours it would be commandeering his precious resources for some new harebrained experiment, and his attempts to argue the point would prove worse than fruitless, for the duplicate would believe itself to be *him*. And it would be right. He'd played this drama out enough times to know the pointlessness of it.

And yet . . .

Was it any better to live in darkness? To cast aside the final pretense of comfort and live as a perfect troglodyte scientist, with no human needs left to neglect? How Tamra Lutui—the Virgin Queen of All Things—would recoil at that! As he himself should recoil, hearing it reduced to those terms.

He sighed, musing darkly: if only inertia could be overcome; if only he could really *proceed,* unhindered and happy. If he could crowd the zero-point field aside, or deaden it with complementary waves, then the tiniest flick would send his billion-ton billiards wherever he chose, at whatever velocity, and another infinitesimal tap would suffice to stop them. Was such an idea feasible? Ridiculous? He should give it some more thought, he thought, but of course *that* would mean suspending his current work, too. The idea made him tired, or perhaps he was already tired and the idea simply helped him to realize it.

He lay back again, to resume his study of the collapsium. It *was* beautiful, really, but also coldly menacing, distorting not only the spacetime around it but the life of one Declarant-Philander Bruno de Towaji as well. He'd never asked to be marooned out here, never asked to live in darkness and isolation, never asked for any of this. Or perhaps he had, in seeking the *arc de fin,* but why did it have to be so *hard*? Why did he have to sacrifice so *much*?

He supposed the thing to do was to resign himself to an idle period—a vacation, in effect—during which he could solicit production bids. Or perhaps one could simply *buy* neutronium these days—heaven knew the Ring Collapsiter's demand for it had to be a good thirteen or fourteen orders of magnitude larger than Bruno's had ever been.

He could probably use the time off, anyway. Didn't Tamra have the hundredth anniversary of her coronation coming up sometime soon? Surely she'd be upset if he let *that* go by without comment. Perhaps he could visit. There were other friends he'd been wondering about as well. Vivian Rajmon, Commandant-Inspector of the Royal Constabulary? Goodness, she must be over sixteen by now! And Marlon Sykes, his fellow Declarant-Philander? Marlon might not be happy to see him—probably not, actually—but they could talk about physics, maybe hash through some of these inertia problems. Surely he'd be happy to do *that,* at least.

With some unpleasant sense of surprise, Bruno realized that except for a handful of emergencies in which the whole of humanity was threatened, it had been almost three *decades* since he'd had any contact with the Queendom at all. Was that what it took to interest him in the affairs of everyday life? Total calamity? Even his broken network gate had gone unrepaired, except for Her Majesty's unauthorized access portal. And she hadn't used it to visit him since the last calamity. Who could blame her, when he'd never sent so much as a letter?

It was like waking up underwater, yes. How did *that* happen?

He felt his blood stir, and wondered, finally, if this was what he'd been needing: *human* interaction to keep his physics problems in balance. No man was an island, the saying went. Never mind a whole planet. Indeed, he could fix his network gate immediately and send a message down into the Queendom, asking which of his friends would consider forgiving his long silence. Perhaps it would cause a stir in the media— they'd always had a strange interest in his affairs— but for God's sake, why should he let that bother him?

He shot to his feet and, leaving the chaise lounge behind, marched homeward with more determination and enthusiasm than he'd had for much of anything lately.

"Door," he said as he approached the house. Obligingly, the nearest wall formed a stained-glass door and opened it for him. He stepped through, and the interior lights came on dimly and began easing him from darkness to full interior light.

Robots danced out of his way, offering nothing in the way of food or drink because lately he'd been yelling at them for that, but one battered thing, far less graceful than its peers, moved directly into his path and spread its arms.

"Hugo," he said, with a warmth that surprised even him. "Hugo, old fellow, have I neglected you as well? Have a hug, then, yes. Are you well this morning?"

The robot's neck squeaked audibly as its head nodded, twice, and then the thing was stepping clumsily out of his way and looking around the house as if bewildered. Hugo was an experiment of sorts: an ordinary household robot not controlled by the household, not controlled by anything except its own desires and intentions. In general these were minimal and quite peculiar, unlike the desires of a person or a pet or an invading insect, but on occasion—perhaps by sheer coincidence—its behavior could be touchingly childlike.

"There, there," he told it, and patted its head a few times. He'd felt a stab of guilt, thinking of young Vivian. She could be childlike, too, but even five years ago she'd been uncomfortably adult about some other things, and by now she was a young woman, her quite charming girlishness probably a thing of the past, or else taking on the overtones of adult affectation. How dreadful for him, that he could let such a thing slip by and feel guilty only now, when it was too late to do anything about it. Had he really tried to teach poor Hugo to play shuffleboard? That was a poor idea from the start, and if playing against the *house's* robots was no fun either, well, had he never considered that Vivian might like to play? Or Tamra, or *somebody*?

"House," he said sternly, turning to face the central fax orifice, "I require network access as soon as possible."

"Planetary maintenance?" the house asked, perhaps thinking he needed to access the little world's store of raw materials—water, air, pure element stock for the fax's matter buffers . . . Perhaps that seemed likelier than the alternative: that he needed people. His house knew him too well.

"No, no," he told it, "the Iscog."

"Acknowledged," the house said, and he could have sworn

it sounded surprised. Iscog: the Inner System Collapsiter Grid. The Queendom's telecom network.

Bruno, feeling somewhat indignant at that perhaps-imagined reaction, said, "I did build the thing, you know. The Iscog. I've a right to take an interest in the people using it."

"Of course, sir," the house agreed, and *now* it sounded imperturbably mechanical. "Gate repair is in progress. Estimated completion time, nine seconds. Gate repair is complete."

Bruno frowned. That was too easy—a further indictment of his neglect. Had it waited all these years, for him to say those few simple words? Well, bah. There was no help for it now; the thing to do was to move forward.

"Record a letter," he said.

But before the house could answer, the fax gate sizzled and glowed, and a human figure tumbled out of it and fell, sprawling, to the floor.

"Oh!" it said, in a voice—a male voice—like a sob. The figure reached out a hand, and stroked the floor as if caressing it. "Oh, can it? Can it be? Have I s-s-spilled at last to the feet of de Towaji?"

Nonplussed, Bruno took a step backward and sputtered, "Sir, my goodness! Have you been authorized to access this portal? What are you doing here?" And then, belatedly, "Are you all right?"

"All right?" the man sobbed giddily, looking up from his face-down sprawl. "All right? The concept eludes. No pain is being applied. Is that an answer?"

"Are you injured?"

"Injured? Mortally! Or not at all; the distinction is less important than you probably imagine."

The question was far from frivolous; fax gate filters were supposed to strip the injuries and illnesses and general wear-and-tear of life from the bodies that passed through them. Conversely, they were supposed to leave affectations like baldness and pierce-holes alone, especially if the subject's genome appendices commanded it. In the case of this man, though, the fax seemed to have had a very hard time making up its mind; his clothing hung off him in tatters, even its software apparently defunct; and beneath it, where the skin should be exposed, there was instead a varicolored and decidedly lumpy surface, like tattooed scar tissue. The hands appeared crooked and malformed, as did the feet projecting from the remains of a pair of suede knee boots, and the face . . . Something odd had been done to the face, it had been flattened somehow, the nose pushed upward and the cheeks drawn down, creating a piggish sort of look. And yet, for all that, the face looked worryingly familiar.

"Do I know you, sir?" Bruno asked. His voice trembled; he had the distinct feeling that the answer would upset him.

The sprawled man looked up at him and smiled in a most horrific way. "Do you not recognize me, de Towaji? I'd hoped not, actually, for I'm no fit thing for your remembrance. The only claim I have to usefulness—the only claim!—is that I was once your-s-s-self. Look upon me, de Towaji, and despair: I am precisely as low as you can sink."

chapter fifteen

in which the clarity
of hindsight is reaffirmed

Bruno's household managed to get the stranger washed and into fresh clothing, over repeated and strenuous protests.

"This thing? I'm no fit inhabitant for a garment like this. No! Away! Don't touch me. Please!"

The robots, dashing about in their usual poetic blur, nonetheless betrayed a curious deference or solicitousness toward the stranger, and by using their bodies in conjunction with strategically held towels and clothes, they managed to keep the surface of his body almost completely hidden. Bruno caught glimpses of ridged or puckered flesh, colored over with strange designs, and he very briefly observed a complete word calligraphed along the stranger's leg. "PENITENT," it looked like, though he was far from certain about that.

Finally, the protests died down, and the stranger said, "Ah, who's myself to argue? It's your generosity that's given me these doublet and tights, not my own deserving, of which there is—take my word of it—none whatsoever."

"Oh, nonsense," Bruno said carefully, unsure what to make of a remark like that. Unsure what to make of this person at all, wondering what had happened to him and why he'd chosen to come *here* in what seemed to be an hour of quite desperate need.

But the stranger only laughed. "You haven't grasped the tenth of it, Declarant-Philander, you who've never yet made acquaintance with the lash. Ah, what a lordly figure you cut! Your knees unbent, your eyes unaverted. Do you crawl? Do you plead? Do you think yours-s-self incapable of it?"

The stranger wasn't mocking him, but seemed actually to be sort of pitying or even pleading, like someone who'd stumbled on a suicide attempt in progress and had no idea what to say. But there was a kind of *self*-mockery going on there, the voice reedy and whining, its tone deliberately obnoxious, as though its owner feared to speak with any decisive clarity or strength.

"What in the worlds has happened to you?" Bruno asked, and was relieved to hear more concern than disgust in his own voice. As the robots finished their work and danced away one by one, he stepped forward to offer the man a hand up. "Why have you come here?"

"What's the date?" the stranger asked him in return. He declined the helping hand and stood up on his own, though he wobbled slightly. Were his knees weak? Injured, perhaps? As for dates, Bruno didn't generally keep track of such things, but the house answered for him. "Sunday, February 28th, Year Ninety-Five of the Queendom."

"Ah," the stranger said, nodding. The look on his face was full of excitement, though of a stilted, unpleasant, untrustworthy variety. "Then I've been trapped in the grid for over two weeks, waiting for your port to open. I was afraid it *mightn't* open—I know you too well!—but faxing to nowhere was much preferable to the alternative. And betrayer that I am, I did dare hope to reach you."

Bruno's frown deepened. "I don't grasp your meaning, sir. Where have you come from?"

"From damnation itself!" the stranger said, cringing, and squeaked out a manic sound that was neither giggle nor sob.

"You think I'm jesting? Speaking in metaphors? He has a lot of anger toward you, and by extension toward myself, for having *been* you. Whips, chains, direct stimulation of the centers of s-s-suffering? These are merely appetizers. The most disagreeable treatments you can possibly imagine are inadequate, mere infantile shadows of the truth, because you haven't spent a lifetime reflecting on it, as He has."

But Bruno was still shaking his head. "What do you mean, 'having been me?' Are you saying you're Bruno de Towaji? A copy of myself?"

"Was," the stranger spat. "Was. It's a name I'll sully no further. But yes; He pirates fax patterns out of the Iscog, and instantiates them in secret, in dungeons hidden away from civilized eyes and sensors. He's particularly fond of *your* pattern—there've been dozens of us in His clutches at one time or another—but He keeps others as well: Rodenbecks, van Sketterings, Kroghs . . . He even kept a Tamra for a while, though it didn't seem to please Him. He's kept a few others on occasion. Not that they last long, of course, the way He uses them up, but they can always be freshly printed, the s-s-same pain recipes tried over and over until they're perfected. I represent an unbroken chain, decades long. In the midst of our sufferings we pass down the histories and lore, from one generation to the next. He encourages the practice, as it deepens our despair."

Bruno could only stare. Was the stranger mad? Was he speaking from delusion, or some demented sense of jest? The two men stared at each other, the one unbelieving and the other unbelievable, for a long string of moments.

"May I sit?" the stranger finally asked, in the same whiny, ingratiating tones. He sounded tired, though. More than tired. Exhausted, in the literal sense: a container that had been squeezed of its contents. His knees quivered beneath his scrawny weight. He looked ready to faint. "I shudder to contaminate your furnishings, Bruno, or even your fine little floor, but my s-s-strength is limited."

"Are you really myself?" Bruno asked, horrified to his very

core, unable to reconcile a single trait or feature of this exhausted container with his own self-image. But the question needed no answer—the house would have corrected the lie already, would never have admitted the stranger in the first place if he were, indeed, anything other than what he claimed. "My God, my *God,* yes, sit down over here! Lie back! House, bring us hot soup and blankets. Immediately!"

Steering the stranger—steering *himself*—toward the couch, he realized that it was warm enough in here, that there was no *literal* need for soup or blankets. But the house and the stranger seemed to understand; the gesture was symbolic. Robots brought woolen bedclothes, with which the stranger permitted Bruno to cover him, and a mug of steaming broth, from which he dutifully sipped.

"Ah," the stranger sighed, "you're too kind. *Literally* too kind, for I've betrayed your secrets and bartered off your dignity more thoroughly than you could ever know. He knows what moves you, what hurts you; He knows everything about you. He knows how you wipe your ass! I told Him all of this, over and over. I deserve none of your s-s-sympathy. And yet here I am, seeking it. Further proof of my unworth!"

"No, no! My God, Bruno, who's done this to you?"

The stranger sat up angrily. "Do not call me that! I am not a Bruno! Call me Shit, or Remnant, or Betrayer."

Bruno, leaning forward against one arm of the couch, shook his head. "I'll do no such thing."

"Sir," the stranger pleaded, "do not call me Bruno. Unless you seek to upset me, sir. I deserve that, but I don't desire it."

Hugo let out a sudden mewl. In a corner of the room, trapped between a table and the wall, it stood perplexed, contemplating its golden legs and the prison that held them, perhaps considering an act of self-mutilation—Hugo had removed a leg more than once, sometimes for less reason than this. Once it had even managed to remove both of its arms, and had stood over them forlornly for a solid day, ignored by the house software, until Bruno had finally taken pity, broken off his experiments, and taken a screwdriver to the poor thing.

But even Hugo possessed a measure of self-respect. Barely sentient, barely knowing it was alive at all, the "emancipated" robot nonetheless managed to find and fulfill the occasional desire. It managed to play a little, learn a little, live a little; this fact was clear in its bearing. The stranger, who had no such air about him, eyed the thing, suddenly, with an envy that looked like hunger.

"Come," Bruno reassured, and wished there were someone else here to reassure *him*, or better yet that he'd wake up and find this whole incident to be a particularly loathsome dream, the result of a too-early bedtime after much too heavy and spicy a meal. "Come on, uh, friend. We'll get you calmed down, and then the two of us can climb in the fax together and reconverge."

Even as he said it, the idea struck him as a poor one.

The stranger's reaction was violent. "Are you mad? Are you *mad*, Bruno? I am every imaginable poison and pathogen! Look at this wreck, this wreckage of yourself, and ask what these memories will do to that proud bearing of yours. I know your weaknesses, sir; I know them far better than you, and I say keep your distance. I am your worst imaginable betrayer, and even *I* recoil at the idea! I'll never join with you. Never!"

Bruno pulled back a little, seeing the huddled figure in still another light: a man who *had* been himself, but was himself no longer. A man whose harrowing experiences set him apart, entitled him to a sense of identity quite distinct from Bruno's own. Suddenly, he felt ashamed for having suggested otherwise.

"I will call you Brazowy," he said gently. "Or perhaps Kafiese. Those are translations; they mean 'brown' or 'brown haired,' as Bruno does."

"I know what they mean," the stranger snapped. "But I warn you, sir: you overestimate the dignity I'm able to s-s-sustain. Those names are fair and pretty; I couldn't bear them. Call me Fuscus if you must."

" 'Muddy?' "

"Muddy! Yes, call me Muddy! That's exactly what I am: the flooded, silted ruins of a once-grand mansion. I am clotted with muck from a distant source, and I'll reek of it to the end of my days."

Bruno nodded grimly. "Very well, then; Muddy it is. But you must tell me, who is this villain? Who dares to kidnap and torture the images of innocent people? He has the *Queen*, you say? Unthinkable!"

"You know who it is," Muddy said.

"I don't."

"You can guess who it is, Declarant."

"No, I couldn't possibly."

Muddy pushed a wild, gray-white lock of hair back over the rutted battlefield of his scalp, and cringed. "I can say the name, sir, but you'll feel no surprise on hearing it. My tormentor is none other than His Declarancy, Philander Marlon Fineas Jimson S-S-S-Sykes."

And it was true; Bruno felt his hair stand on end, his skin go clammy, his feet begin to tingle and sweat. He felt disgust, and anger, and betrayal, and above all, a deep sense of embarrassment for poor Marlon, that he should take his petty envies and covetousnesses so deeply and seriously and personally after all. But he felt no real surprise. In some sense, he supposed he'd known all along that Marlon was no good, that there was something really wrong with him.

"The really odd part," Muddy said, and the whiny tone in his voice, while stronger than ever, seemed more forgivable, "is that he does it to himself as well. You'll see him dragging his own copy down into the caverns, and the copy will be s-s-screaming, 'Oh God, it's *me* this time! It's a mistake; I'm on the wrong side! I'm supposed to be you!' and His Declarancy will lock it down and torment it in the most savage ways, all the while yelling 'Stupid! Stupid! Stupid! Why do you have to be so *stupid*!' He's harder on himself than he is on others, if such a thing is possible. There's a kind of nobility in that."

"No, there is not," Bruno stated flatly. "The man is clearly ill, and these ghastly infractions of his must be stopped at once. It's fortunate you escaped when you did."

Muddy, pulling the blanket up a little higher under his chin, looked blank. "Escape? I didn't *escape*, Bruno. There is no escape from a place like that, from a man like that. One dreams of death, not freedom. Truly, I tell you, he's thought of everything."

"Then . . . how are you here?"

Muddy laughed sourly. "I was released, in the manner that a projectile is released from a cannon. I was s-s-sent here to you, sir, and like an obedient wretch I've complied. I bring a message, and the message is myself."

Bruno shook his head. "I don't understand."

"Don't you? I thought you were so smart! The message of myself is that *you can be broken*, that your spirit and your flesh are far weaker than you've ever guessed. You can be made so abjectly miserable that in the end you'll betray your principles, your dignity, your Queendom, and your Queen with frightening complicity and ease. There's nothing in yourself to stop it from happening, no inner strength or reserve that can possibly suffice. Even you, Declarant. Even you can be turned into me. His Declarancy wanted to be sure you understood this."

Bruno got the message. He looked at Muddy, and finally he *did* see himself inside there somewhere, and the sight filled him with disgust and terror. Was there so little to him after all? He tried, not very convincingly, to give this wretch a reassuring clap on the shoulder. " 'His Declarancy,' as you call him, is no doubt going straight to jail. We'll contact Vivian Rajmon of the Royal Constabulary; she'll know exactly how to proceed."

And here, Bruno felt his disgust deepen; Vivian a young woman already, and himself calling her only because he'd been the victim of a crime. He'd claimed more than once to be her friend, but would a friend require *this* before finding, finally, the time to place a call? Surely not. So in fact he was no friend at all, and never had been, and all his claims to the contrary were the worst sort of self-congratulatory hypocrisy.

But what Muddy said was, "I'm afraid that'll be impossible, Your Lordship. He's seen to that."

"I beg your pardon?"

"Contacting this friend of yours. It'll be impossible. He was planning to smash the Inner-System Collapsiter Grid; I was s-s-supposed to be one of the last messages it was permitted to carry."

"Smash the Iscog? Why?"

Muddy's sour laugh echoed through the house again. "To isolate you, sir. To trap you at the very summit of the solar system while he carries out his plans below. And, as an amusing aside, to trap me here with you, as a permanent reminder of your talent for failure. I'm truly sorry it had to be this way, Bruno. I'm sorry I had to help."

"The Ring Collapsiter!" Bruno said, slapping himself on the head, feeling like a perfect fool. "All those problems, accidents, all the sabotage. It was Marlon all along! He's *trying* to destroy the Queendom."

"Of course he is, sir. Always has been."

Thinking of a corpse he'd seen once on an unlicensed space freighter, Bruno asked, "Does he ever alter the body forms of his victims? Does he add or remove limbs?"

"Constantly, sir."

"God, I've been a fool!"

"You certainly have, sir. Believe me, I know that far better than you."

"But why would he do such a thing?" Bruno was pacing now, waving his arms. "Even a sick, vengeful man needs *somewhere* to be sick and vengeful, doesn't he? He's no fool; he's not *stupid*. What could he possibly stand to gain by destroying the Queendom?"

"I wouldn't know, sir. You'd have to ask him that yourself."

Finally, Bruno felt himself get truly angry, angrier than he'd been in years, or maybe ever. "Is that the way of it? Is that his message to me? I *will* ask him myself, then. We'll find

a way down there, and we'll show you right back to him as a
message that we're not so easily beaten, you and I!"

At this, Muddy laughed again, his voice sadder and nastier
and whinier than ever.

"What? What's funny?" Bruno snapped.

"Nothing, sir. It's just that I t-t-told him you'd say that."

And in that moment, Bruno *hated* Muddy for all that had
happened, and he knew this meant that he was actually hating himself—all the weakness and stupidity and vulnerability
in himself. And then he felt like an even *bigger* fool, because
it meant that Marlon's bullet had hit its target dead-on, and
he, Bruno, had been powerless to dodge it.

"Right ascension ninety-one degrees, eleven minutes, forty-
seven seconds," Bruno said. "Declination nine degrees, zero
minutes, three seconds."

"Nothing," Muddy answered.

"Right ascension ninety-one degrees, eleven minutes, forty-
seven seconds. Declination nine degrees, zero minutes, six
seconds."

"Nothing," Muddy said again. He was bent almost double,
peering into a brass eyepiece. Strange markings, perhaps Chi-
nese, were visible on the back of his neck. Above them both,
the ceiling had arched itself into a dome of glass, through which
the faxed telescope could observe the heavens. It looked archaic, this telescope, almost a thing Galileo himself might
have employed, but its lenses were of wellstone rather than
glass. The filtered, enhanced, broad-spectrum images they produced could easily rival the finest products of twenty-first century astronomy.

In fact, there was little need for a human operator at all; a
few murmured instructions to the house and every celestial
object of note would be mapped within the hour. But they *had*
let the house find Iscog fragments for them, boulder-sized bits
of collapsium ejected starward by the grid's obviously quite
messy demise. Whatever sabotage Marlon performed had

been swift and decisive. One shuddered to contemplate the dynamics: so much mass interacting with so much violence and chaos! And so Bruno had determined that they should inspect the fragments—at least a few of them—with their own eyes. Or with reasonable proxies thereof. Perhaps it would help them to understand what had happened, and how.

"Nothing," Muddy said again. "No wait," he then amended. "It's there at the edge of the frame."

"Center, please."

"Yes, sir."

The one good thing about this wretch, Bruno decided, was that he had no pretensions of any kind. Unlike a *real* de Towaji, Muddy made no attempt to conscript or control or second-guess. He didn't seem to feel any sense of ownership here, or any urgency about their task or their precarious position. In fact, he seemed content to follow orders without the slightest reflection. Perhaps it gave him a sense of peace.

"Oh. Goodness," Muddy said. "You should have a look at this, Your Lordship."

They traded places, and Bruno leaned over to peer into the eyepiece. He saw nothing there but a scattering of stars. "I don't see it."

"It's moving," that whiny voice complained. "I don't know how to make the telescope track it."

"Moving against the starscape? An arc-second and a half in thirty seconds? It's five AUs away!"

"It's fast," Muddy agreed. "Whatever ejected it must have been—" He cringed slightly. "—a violent event."

"Mmm."

Indeed, Bruno's sensors had been triggering all afternoon, reporting magnetic and gravitational anomalies passing through the area. If even a few of these had originated in the Queendom a mere week ago, then they must be moving very fast indeed, fully 10% of the speed of light. That meant crushing accelerations: hundreds or thousands of gees. He imagined a handful of collapsium structures falling together over planetary distances as the Iscog was fractured, then spinning apart in a hundred little gravitational eddies, flinging bits of themselves in all directions while their cores were crushed into a single useless hypermass. Such an event *would* be violent—exceedingly so.

"You adjust the tracking with this," Bruno grumbled, pointing to a brass-shod button on the side of the telescope. "Center your target, and then press. To turn tracking off, center on empty space and press again. If you have questions, you know, you *can* ask them. Which direction is the object moving?"

"Down. Er, south."

"Hmm."

He bent to the eyepiece again, and adjusted the declination until something appeared at the edge of the frame: a dark, metallic object that looked vaguely like a castle, its turrets pointed back down toward the sun, glittering dimly in its distant light. It was moving south by southeast, actually; he centered it and locked the tracking function. Immediately, the stars behind the object began crawling across his view. It *was* moving fast.

"Good Lord," he said, "that's not a collapsium fragment; it's one of the EM grapple stations!"

"Yes, sir."

"It should be deep inside the Queendom, holding up the Ring Collapsiter!"

"Yes, sir. It certainly should. The event that ejected it must have been extremely violent."

"Indeed," Bruno said abstractly. Fussing with the dainty brass controls, he managed to magnify the image and adjust its wavelength compression until the object became translucent, a flying palace of smoky glass. The gravitic machineries were visible inside, glass within glass, some components glowing warm shades of orange, while others, shown in blue, either absorbed heat or channeled it away. Even a cursory inspection showed that the station couldn't be entirely functional; power and heat and buffer mass flowed through it, but fitfully, via components that sat askew, bent and twisted and shaken out of true by what surely must have been titanic forces. Actually, it was amazing the thing had survived at all.

He zoomed in on one of the smaller warm spots, and gasped.

"My God. My God! There's a *person* onboard!"

"Not possible," Muddy whined. "The gee f-f-forces would have been too great."

"One would think so!" Bruno agreed, straightening and stepping away. "One most certainly would expect so. But see for yourself!"

Muddy shuffled forward again and, sighing as if in pain, bent once more to the telescope. He drew in a breath immediately, then put a tentative hand to the controls. "He's moving. He's alive. I don't understand. No wait, it's a woman. *She*. Is this the wavelength control? These two? Ah. She's holding a wrench. She's disassembling something."

"House!" Bruno called out. "Contact that station!"

"Network resources unavailable, sir," the house replied apologetically.

"Then build an antenna, damn you. Use radio waves."

"May I compromise roof transparency?"

"Do whatever you must. That woman is in terrible danger, exiting the solar system at relativistic speed! When her power reserves fail, she'll suffocate or freeze to death, assuming she hasn't already starved by then."

In the next moment, the glass roof was spiderwebbed with silvery conformal antenna elements, a network for focusing and gathering electromagnetic radiation in the longer wavelengths, centimeters and meters and even tens of meters.

"She's doomed," Muddy said matter-of-factly. "No one can reach her. No one will even try. Radio contact is pointless, p-p-perhaps even cruel."

"Blast!" Bruno cursed, and nearly knocked the telescope over. "The chaos below, in Queendom space, must be of immense proportion. There must be tragedies like this one playing out all across the solar system. Damn your Marlon Sykes; he *knows* what he's doing!"

"*My* Marlon Sykes?"

Bruno sighed, ran a hand through the long ripples of his hair, and finally threw himself down on the sofa. "Are we so helpless, Muddy? We, the Queendom's favored consultants? There's more than enough material here—" He spread his arms to indicate the planet beneath their feet. "—to fax a fleet of the swiftest and noblest spaceships."

"As His Declarancy no doubt anticipated," Muddy said, sniffing.

"Indeed," Bruno snapped. "Indeed. Whatever is transpiring below, he doesn't expect us to be able to intervene. At a full gee acceleration, assuming our propulsion system could sustain that, it'd still be two weeks before we could reach the Ring Collapsiter. Twice as long, if we wanted to stop when we got there!"

Muddy nodded, groaned a little, then plopped down cross-legged on the floor beside the telescope. "He knows you'll try, sir. The fact amuses him."

Bruno felt a bomb-burst of rage. "Does it? What in God's name is *driving* this man? Why can't he just *accept* things as they are? I could kill him! He pretends to be merely jealous, a little bit bruised and snooty, a little bit nasty when crossed. And it's fine! People like him for it, or at least in spite of it. His wit and charm serve him well enough, and his genius. Why can't he just *be* that person? What's so savagely difficult, so brutally unfair about that?"

Muddy's laugh sounded like the rattling of pebbles in a jar. "Lordship, do you understand so little? The sociopath, as known by s-s-society, is only a mask. Usually, one which has been perfected over a period of decades and which serves as an interface to the wider world which cannot accept—or in many cases even understand—the true face underneath. Think of the puppet theater in the old marketplace. Could you tell, simply by watching the puppet, if the puppeteer was kindly or vicious? Did you ever consider the puppeteer at all? Who crafts a mask if not to please, if not to present a likeness every man and woman and child can be captivated by? We may ask the basement torturer to become the model citizen he emulates so skillfully, but it's like asking the shell to be an egg; it's a meaningless question. It's all the pieces together, the villainy and greatness and everyday human foibles, that we must use to take his measure."

"You look up to him," Bruno said, eyeing his counterpart with disgust.

"I know more about him than you do," Muddy said darkly. "I know a lot more than you, about a great many things. In some ways, I'm finding it easier to think of you as a child than as a full-grown veteran of worldly politics and strife. I can reconcile your behavior that way, your attitudes."

Bruno sighed. "So I'm a fool, am I? Because my mind has never been shaped by humiliation or pain? What a pitiable creature you are, Muddy. I'll remain a fool, thank you."

"No, sir, no!" Muddy cried, throwing an arm melodramatically across his eyes. "Not a fool, a *child*. A s-s-sweet, bright-eyed little boy that Enzo and Bernice would be proud to show off! It isn't a bad thing, sir. I never said it was."

And Bruno felt ashamed then, because tears were soaking Muddy's sleeve, rolling down his gaunt face, and his voice, never strong to begin with, had broken through with high, squeaky sobs. And, more shameful still, Bruno himself could think of no response, no comfort, no apology save another cup of hot soup. This was what he'd become: a hermit unable to comport civilly, even with himself.

Perhaps Marlon was right to despise him.

chapter sixteen

in which a restless
spirit is appeased

Bruno sat up in his bed, suddenly wide awake, his body as rigid as a gravestone. Such a dream. Such a *dream* he'd had!

He'd never been much of a dreamer, had never put much stock or faith in a state of mind so confused and cluttered with false associations. A duck asks if your latest calculations are thorough enough, and the wall becomes a floor beneath you, and suddenly it's raining macaroni. Rubbish! But tonight he'd dreamed with strange clarity: his skin shivering as if electrified, his mouth dry, his eyes hot with the energies of the zero-point field, laid out *visibly* before him. Or perhaps "visibly" was the wrong word, since he was simultaneously aware of the intensities at every wavelength, the half-infinite energies filling each photon state . . . The view should have been nonsense, infinitely bright or infinitely dark or else infinitely *transparent*, as the vacuum between islands of matter was usually thought to be. But in the dream he'd walked through his house, through the gardens and meadows of his empty little world, and he'd seen not only the *things*, but the rippling vibrations of charge that gave rise to them, and the zero-point vacuum that inspired the vibrations, and the true vacuum beneath that.

And in the dream, he'd pulled a special glove down over his hand, and the glove was made of billion-ton black holes the size of protons, and its color was neither the phosphor green of gravitational binding nor the Cerenkov blue of mature collapsium, but the optically superconducting *nothing* of True Vacuum, for the black holes were not arranged in three-dimensional lattices, but in ripples of semi-random, four-dimensional, open-celled foam. Vibration-damping foam, just exactly like what you'd find muffling the walls of a broadcast studio, although fantastically smaller. The four-dimensional structure was easy, simply a matter of timing the placement of certain elements. A child, he'd thought, could do the math.

And in the dream, the storming vacuum energies had shrunk away from his glove like wax before a torch, and the space before him had filled with nothingness, and he'd glided through it without effort, skating through the hills and meadows without moving his feet, without any sensation of *moving* at all. In the dream, the *universe* had moved, or seemed to, while he stood motionless at its center.

And he'd realized, all at once, that this was no talking duck or pasta rain, that this was something he could *actually do*. And so, in the dream, he'd sat bolt upright in his bed, and the dream had blended so seamlessly with reality that he'd wondered, in a deep and literal sense, if the two were really such separate things after all.

For a moment he felt paralyzed, glued in place by the bogus "inertia" of the vacuum pressing in on him from all sides. It seemed impossible that he should be able to breathe, that his blood should pump and his nerves fire, that he should be able to exist at all. But he did exist, and his blood pumped, and his nerves fired, and as the moment passed he was kicking his covers off, leaping to the floor in his bare feet, screaming "Door! Door!" at the wall and running right on through, trusting it to open for him in time.

"Muddy!" he shouted, racing toward the bony figure curled

up on the couch beneath a heap of blankets. "Muddy, wake up! I've had an idea!"

Muddy, it seemed, was no stranger to sudden, screaming awakenings in the dead of the night. He sat up immediately, latching onto Bruno with quick, terrified eyes.

"I've had an idea!" Bruno repeated. "A big one, a wonderful one!"

"Yes?" Muddy said warily, making a visible effort not to scream or retreat or clutch at his chest. "A *helpful* idea?"

"You be the judge," Bruno said quickly, and launched into an account of his dream.

"Oh," Muddy said when he was done. His finger probed at the air, as if trying to feel the vacuum energies there. "Oh. Oh, yes, that s-s-sounds like it should work. That's very good, Your Declarancy; the simplicity of the math is a very good sign. I think you must be onto something."

"I have work to do," Bruno said excitedly. "Lots of work! It's another damned invention, I suppose. We'll see all of society turned on its ear again, bent and twisted around these momentary insights. What a strange thing that is, to cause such trouble and be adored for it. The Queendom should hang us both for our crimes, and save itself any further turmoil! But I'll say, even the worst outcome is bound to improve on what Marlon has in store."

"Likely so," Muddy agreed, "if it has come in time to stop him. I don't suppose this is the sort of thing even He can anticipate. A bolt of inspiration, s-s-striking from nowhere? Our muse usually comes when it jolly well pleases her, without regard for when she's actually needed."

Muddy seemed far more saddened than intrigued, and at this, Bruno felt genuine pity for him, for perhaps the first time. Was his counterpart *so* broken that even the lure of discovery couldn't enliven him? He must have suffered grievously indeed.

"Come," Bruno said, extending him a hand. "You remember the boat I built—that *you* built—on the yard at Talafo'uo?"

"HMS *Redshift*," Muddy said wanly. "By gods, it seems so long ago."

Indeed, it did. Bruno had been fresh to the islands of Tonga, and the task had seemed simple enough: design and fax the parts, assemble them, and motor away on a full-planing hull that would leap from one wave crest to the next, barely touching the water at all. But Bruno had—as a matter of principle—refused both robotic and human assistance. That old Girona stubbornness again, so that even with the best tools and guidebooks money could buy, even with his modular, snap-together design and hundreds of real-world examples to compare his work against, the little boat had wound up taking a full week to come together, and another three to really start performing well. There were a lot of variables to control; the experience had been both humbling and uplifting, after his larger and more troublesome successes with the early telecom collapsiters.

"I would ask you to repeat that experience," Bruno said.

"That? It took weeks."

"You'll let robots do the work, of course. It must be done quickly. But be a hero, Muddy: build me a spaceship. I haven't time to do it myself; this idea demands attention. But when we're both done, perhaps we'll ride to the Queendom's rescue." When there was no reply, he went on, "Are you able to face your puerile, damnable little nemesis? Has he left you with any ability to oppose him?"

Now Muddy shrugged with weary sadness, and wiped a teardrop off his cheek. "Who can say, Declarant? I'm permitted to hate Him, and to wish innumerable harms upon Him, but I never have r-r-resisted Him. I suppose I've never had the opportunity."

"Well, here you have it: together we can work this out, this challenge of Marlon and inertia both. Will you build a ship for me, Muddy?"

Sigh. "You're right to question me, sir, and quite wrong to place any faith in my abilities. Or yours! The one gift he gave me, the one true thing I've learned from his attentions, is a confidence in our fallibility. What argues in your favor is that you're asking for mere engineering, which is banal. Pluck any two people at random, deposit them on a planet somewhere, and inside of an hour they're a design team, finding new ways to put up a roof. They don't have to be friends; they don't have to communicate well, or even at all, because the whole process is coded in their genes. It may be that I can fumble through it, as humans have always fumbled, and produce some half-assed but workable product, as I did with *Redshift*."

"That's the spirit," Bruno said, trying to sound encouraging. He clapped Muddy on the shoulder, this time with some genuine affection. "Nothing fancy, nothing hard—just a hull of iron and the weakest, mealiest of engines to push her."

Muddy bowed his head. "Very well, sir. I'll do as you ask, though perhaps not for the reasons you would wish."

"Eh?"

"Sir, have you examined the converse of engineering? We fall into it so naturally, but in the end every project expires, and one way or another every team is dismantled, and *that's* something we're not wired to deal with. It saddens, even traumatizes us. *That's* where geniuses are needed, to engineer the conclusions of things. We let things wither, collapse, decompose, when we should be murdering them gently and artfully."

Bruno frowned. "What is it you wish to murder?"

"An age of mankind," Muddy said cryptically. "The innocence of an entire society. People believe themselves to be the masters of creation, when in fact they're barely participants. Better that they learn this now." He looked up at Bruno as if hoping to be questioned for that remark, or doubted, or accused.

Bruno looked askance at him. "You wish the people harm?"

"No. I wish for them to internalize His Declarancy's lessons, and to do that they must live. Horrid, to think they might die without first understanding their lives."

There was much to disagree with in a statement like that, but Bruno, still awash with excitement, declined to take the bait. "Just get started, all right? I'll be in my laboratory. House: see that I'm not disturbed."

"As you wish, sir," the house replied, in its usual, coolly solicitous voice, deep yet subtly feminine. With a start, Bruno realized it was his mother's voice, or something not terribly different from it. Strange that he'd never noticed this before, but from the look on Muddy's face, Bruno gathered he'd noticed it as well, and seemed to find it significant in some way. Disturbing.

Well, hopefully there'd be plenty of time to consider the matter later, assuming it had any importance at all. Now was hardly the time to worry about it, not with the laws of physics coming down around the Queendom's ears. He strode resolutely toward his study door, thinking that he could always change the house's voice when he got back from the Queendom.

If you get back, Muddy's whining voice corrected in his mind. Well, all right then. If. He went to work.[8]

"Sir," the house said to him sometime later, its mother voice sounding anxious at the need to wake him, "I'm receiving a signal from the runaway grapple station."

"Hmm, what? A signal, really?" He sat up, rubbing his eyes, putting a hand to the crick in his back. A signal, goodness; he hadn't expected any such thing. His contact effort had been . . . a formality, really, because what were the odds that the station's castaway would think of *radio,* out here in the wilderness of the Kuiper? Even assuming the necessary devices could be instantiated and configured, what would be the point? Bruno was the only one out here, his tiny planet the only inhabited object in . . . What? Half a million cubic light-hours of space? Long odds indeed!

"Play it," he instructed, coming fully awake.

Obediently, the house formed wall speakers and piped the

8. See Appendix A: Defeating Inertia, page 375

signal through them, distorted but clearly intelligible. "Hello, Mayday, Mayday. This is Deliah van Skettering of the Ministry of Grapples, responding to your ping. Hello. Can anyone hear me? This is Deliah van Skettering calling Mayday. Repeat, Mayday. Radio source, please respond. I require immediate assistance . . ."

He jerked a hand across his throat, and the house cut the signal. Deliah! Laureate-Director and Lead Componeer of the Ministry of Grapples! What was *she* doing aboard a runaway station? And given her presence there, what were the odds of a passage within even a few AU—hundreds of millions of kilometers—of Bruno's position? Unless perhaps she'd been on *all* the stations for some reason, and they'd *all* been flung off into the outer darkness, and this was simply the one that passed nearest to him on its way to infinity.

Did she know that he was here, that the radio beacon signaling her was, in fact, his? Through the heavy distortion—no doubt caused through some combination of long-range, enormous velocity differential, and poor transmitting equipment—her voice sounded perfunctory, not eager or hopeful but *bored*. And then he understood: the poor woman was a victim of slow drowning. She grasped dutifully at corks and straws, not because it was likely to help but because it was all she could do, other than simply admitting defeat.

"House, what's the light-lag between here and the station?"

"Seven minutes, fifty-six seconds."

"Sixteen minutes round trip? Hmm. I hadn't counted on this; I really hadn't. Well, send a reply: 'Laureate-Director, this is Bruno de Towaji. Repeat, this is de Towaji. Perhaps you'll recall meeting me a number of years ago, shortly before your murder? Now, as then, I offer my heartfelt condolences on your situation. Still, I am very curious as to how it came about! Can you report your status? Over.' "

"Reply sent," the house said.

Bruno nodded, and settled back into his calculations where he'd left off. Not that he'd forgotten about Ms. van Skettering—

far from it!—but she'd hardly benefit from his sitting around waiting for something as frightfully slow as *light*.

He was worried about this new "hypercollapsite"—although the material itself was proven feasible, there was the matter of gross structure to contend with. What shapes must he mold the stuff into, to achieve the desired, inertia-foiling result? The question turned out to be nontrivial in the extreme. He could well envision himself scrabbling at it for hours or days, looking for a conceptual "edge" to start from. It was one thing to *speak* of EM vibration-damping foams, quite another to design them.

"Return message received," the house said, after what couldn't possibly have been sixteen minutes.

"Yes, already? Let's hear it."

"De Towaji!" Deliah's clipped, tinny, strangely muffled voice said. "I'd hoped that was you; I'm glad it is. My situation is that I'm in very serious trouble. I think you know that. The station's grapple lock on the Ring Collapsiter was disrupted—I'm not sure how—but the complement beam was left intact, pulling us straight out toward Aldeberan. It took me three days to get it shut off. I have *casualties* here, Declarant—three technicians dead! We saw the other stations going off-line, and we tried to wrap ourselves in impervium before the same thing happened to us. It . . . wasn't a good solution."

Bruno's fingers dug at the wellwood edges of his desk. Had he been unwise to establish this contact? Was there anything, really, that he could do?

His voice was tentative but, he hoped, compassionate. "Deliah, ah, not to put too fine a point on it, but are you hoping for rescue? You see, I'm rather engaged at the moment, and a lot of lives may hang in the balance."

Her reply, a thousand seconds later. "It's very kind of you to ask, Declarant, but I am realistic about my situation. Even assuming anything could be done—which I doubt—the Queendom's peril is obviously much more important than my own. The Ring Collapsiter is falling in *again*, much faster this time, and mostly in pieces. Something has also happened to the Iscog, although I'm not sure what. There's loose collapsium and neutronium *everywhere*—the planets may actually be in as much danger as the sun!"

She paused, then continued. "Are you able to travel, de Towaji? When I last saw Her Majesty, she was adrift on a workman's platform spinning perilously close to the sun. It sounds like you have some sort of . . . plan or something. Is that the case? We are lucky to have you, we really are. Meanwhile, I'm absolutely kicking myself that I let this happen. I just wish I knew what went wrong."

"Deliah," he reassured her, "this calamity was engineered by Marlon Sykes. I can't imagine what his reasons might be, but his *methods* are more thorough than you probably imagine. I doubt you've erred in the slightest, although it's commendable that you're willing to consider it. Even more commendable is your bravery. I'll be sure to tell you about it when next we meet."

"Marlon?" her voice came back, incredulous. "Why would *Marlon* sabotage the collapsiter? I mean, I know the man—in several senses of the word—and he does have a temper sometimes, but it's *his* collapsiter. It always has been."

"The man is apparently acting from pure malice, Deliah. Evil, one might say. God, what a petty, small-minded thing that is! Of all the things to do, of all the infinite possibilities, to choose *that*! Why not paint, or dig holes, or sing off-key when nobody's listening; *there's* nobility for you. Hurting people is just dumb. It's vandalism in its lowest form."

"I'm glad I knew you, de Towaji."

"Call me Bruno, please, and know that the honor is mine. I'll be sure to tell you this when we meet again someday."

Her voice was weary and resigned. "Bruno, we're not going to meet again. The Iscog is smashed, and all my copies were on these grapple stations. I may be the last of me already; if not, it's just a matter of time."

Bruno was aghast. "There's the Royal Registry for Indispensable Persons, isn't there?"

"What? Oh, no, the Registry closed its doors years ago.

Corrupted storage media; toward the end, they couldn't keep a gnat."

"Personal backups?"

"You've been gone a long time, Bruno. We've had virus storms, datavore infestations, Flying Dutchman faxes circling endlessly through the network . . . A clean backup is only possible if the *system generating it* is clean, and we haven't had that luxury in recent years. I'm not sure we ever did."

Bruno was even more aghast. "Do you mean to say your *only copy* is flying off into interstellar space?"

"Worse than that," she replied, her voice going stern. "I think *Tamra's* only copy is down there on that ceremony platform; Tongatapu was one of the islands that got drowned by tidal waves. Literally *drowned,* no survivors."

Bruno tried to parse that statement. Like most of Tonga's islands, Tongatapu was a coral atoll, very flat. Geology had tipped it slightly, raising its southern edge out of the waves and submerging parts of the north completely, but even the heights of Fua'amotu rose no more than about fifty meters above sea level. And if something truly massive, a ball of neubles or a stray telecom collapsiter, grazed close enough to the Earth, it could raise local sea levels by several times that much. No survivors? Tongatapu had over eighty thousand residents!

"There are others down there on the platform with her," Deliah continued. "Wenders Rodenbeck, for one, and Vivian Rajmon and her pet police captain. We were rehearsing for the completion ceremony next year, when the last segment of Ring Collapsiter was to be towed into place."

Pet captain? Would that be Cheng Shiao? Bruno tried to remember if that too-competent constable had been a captain or not. By all the little gods, he really *had* been away too long.

"Damn it," he said. "Damn that Marlon; he's timed this entirely too well. It's what malice does, I suppose—sit around calculating minimum effort for maximum harm. Well, he shan't get away with it. You sit tight, Deliah; you'll be rescued

in the next couple of days. I shall personally guarantee it."
The words surprised even him as he said them. To keep from
blurting anything else, he quickly added, "Over and out."

He'd been continuing his work throughout the five hours
or so of that slow conversation, and now he set into it more
fiercely, with the energy of total outrage. Gross structure! He
must find a gross structure for his hypercollapsite!

But the work progressed slowly, and it was in this area that
he encountered his first major disappointments: truly effective damping of the zero-point field would require enormous
assemblies, towering cities of foam many thousands of miles
wide, and massing enormously more than Sol herself. Perhaps
mankind could one day conceive of projects so grand, but for
the moment Bruno had some very sharp time and material
limits to contend with, and little patience for daydreams.

With sensors fine and coarse, he studied the ring encircling his tiny star. Such was the pool of his actual resources:
ten trillion tons of collapsium. He assumed an equal mass of
hypercollapsite—implying a completely error-free rearrange-
ment scheme—and fed it into a permutation algorithm to
plumb what forms, if any, could be crafted that might do any
good at all.

Here, finally, he got lucky again—almost. The key was that
the zero-point field's energy was known to rise as a function
of frequency; its highest energies occurred at the shortest
wavelengths. With limited mass, Bruno's damper could only
block out absorption "windows" of the field's full spectrum,
but by concentrating on windows at the higher frequencies, it
could maximize its otherwise limited effect. And the higher
frequencies, he found, were by far the easiest to damp; it was
the low ones, the cosmological subwoofers, that penetrated
every simulated barrier he could think to erect.

So he put his head down for a little more sleep, trusting
the machines to do their work. He was exhausted; this was
exhausting work, wringing his brain like a sponge. As he
drifted off, bright flashes popped behind his eyelids, as his
ocular muscles flinched to the beat of Muddy's spaceship

work outside. Even through the wellstone walls, there was no mistaking the muffled *clang! clang!* and occasional bursts of stacatto speech, like the cursing of a man who's just hammered his thumb. Bruno's last vague thought was that the boat gods must be in need of appeasement out there, and perhaps—worryingly—in here as well.

His sleep was troubled—one might say *haunted*. He woke a few unsatisfying hours later, produced more flashes by rubbing his eyes, then opened them and learned from his hypercomputers that there was a rilled dome shape, like a meter-wide mushroom cap turned inside out, that when cast in hypercollapsite foam would block out some very high energies indeed. Such higher-frequency energies were also the greatest contributors to Newton's inertia, so in fact the computer-designed device would behave as if it contained less than a gram of matter, or $1E-19$ times its actual mass. Objects in its immediate wake would experience an enormously weaker damping effect, but nonetheless would feel the effects of acceleration reduced by a factor of 1081.3901.

In other words, a ship outfitted with such a cap would feel less than one-thousandth of the actual gee forces it was subjected to. More significantly, it would require less than one-thousandth of the fuel and travel time of a conventional ship. This was hardly the magic glove of his dream, but this hypothetical spaceship could—with barely a whiff of fuel in its tanks—accelerate at a thousand gees or more without damage or even discomfort to its occupants.

The problem—found only after an initial, ill-advised burst of smug excitement—was that immeasurably tiny rounding errors had gradually accumulated in the hypercomputers' innumerable calculations. He'd never have believed it possible, but when he painstakingly worked out a closed-form solution to confirm the final design, his direct calculations yielded a mass fully 15.028% larger than the iterative solution had yielded. Perhaps no one had ever pushed a computer so hard, forced *so many* calculations based on calculations based on calculations, to achieve a result so weirdly inaccurate. He'd never heard of such a thing happening before.

Here, though, the error was critical: Bruno's collapsium reserves were right at the ragged edge of useful size. Actually, on the wrong side of the ragged edge—he was nearly 1.5 *trillion* tons shy of the mass required to achieve any measurable effect at all.

The boat gods were angry indeed. Absently, he murmured a little prayer to appease them.

Then he permitted himself a discouraged sigh. Sinking down into superstition was not a good sign right now. That the boat gods weren't "real" made little difference; the human brain was wired for animism and anthropomorphism as much as for monarchy. Hammered by billions of years of evolution, it had learned to devote most of its enormous pattern-matching power to guessing the moods and likely actions of prey animals, and predators, and fellow human brains, which of course were the most complex and dangerous of all. And like any hypertrophied athlete, it had lost generality in the process, so that it tended to turn the same sort of attention toward natural phenomena—especially pseudo-random or chaotic events—treating them as entities to be studied and modeled and, if at all possible, appeased.

So even in mono- or atheistic cultures, you inevitably found Mother Nature and Grim Reaper analogs, along with whole pantheons of other demigods and spirits and patron saints inspired by the myriad processes of the world around them. In the early ages of rationalism, these beings were often dismissed as either idle fantasies or as a kind of shorthand for pseudo-mystical concepts like Murphy's Law and Karma and Fate, which were themselves a shorthand for rigorous, statistical observations about the fate of individuals in society. And if science had long recognized that the mind *did* model them as entities, that made them real enough to cause real problems, even if these problems were quite separate from the phenomena that implied them.

Blast it, Bruno had hardly spared a thought for the boat gods in sixty years. At Talafo'ou they'd made their presence known, grudgingly rewarding his *Redshift* labors but also decisively punishing all hubris and presumption. And demanding, yes, a steady sacrifice in disappeared tools and fasteners. Tonga's old gods were officially dead—not even Tamra had been eager to share their names or histories with him—and it had taken time to arrive at a nonverbal understanding with them, once they'd shown him for sure who was boss. But this time he hadn't considered their needs at all. Nonexistent or no, they were bound to take that personally. And they had access to his brain.

He rose from his chair, prepared to curse or pray or go looking for something tangible to sacrifice—but gasped at the sensation of gravity pulling down at him. A full gee's worth of gravity, created by fifteen hundred neubles at the planet's core! Why, if he could simply extract those, then perhaps the situation could be salvaged after all!

Encouraged, he plopped into the chair again and rattled some more calculations into the hypercomputers, deeply informed now by all that he had learned. He confirmed that this was—just barely!—enough.

All right, then, little gods be praised. All of this was finally, actually possible.

Bruno let out a long sigh.

It seemed Marlon's taunts had done their work too well, goading Bruno to the point that he actually *could* interfere. He suspected that anger alone could never have carried him this far. Folk wisdom had always held that love was more powerful than anger, and folk wisdom had proved so right about so many things. But what happened when love and anger were wedded together, when they served the same end?

Leaving aside all the other enormous issues at work here, the simple fact was that Tamra-Tamatra Lutui's *life* was in danger, and as her friend and lover Bruno would be damned— literally *damned* to an eternity of suffering—if he let her freeze to death in the sunless dark, or vaporize in a nova flare, or burn away on a workman's platform, or any such disagreeable thing. So perhaps the old adage was true: love really *did* conquer all. It conquered inertia, anyway.

Wary of displaying any actionable hubris, he gave the boat gods a solemn nod and then sat quietly for a minute, though his insides were doing a little jig.

Then impatience finally caught up with him; the house, when queried, informed him that he'd been cooped up in here for almost seventy-three hours. How long did the Queendom have left, before the collapsium started falling into the sun? Miraculously, it hadn't happened yet; the house had been keeping a close eye on Sol ever since Muddy first told his mad tale, and the unmistakable signs of collapsium intrusion had yet to manifest on that dear old star. All the whirling fragments had missed, had been flung off in other directions. But how long could such fortune hold?

The final stage of this endeavor, the actual *construction* of the vacuogel hypercollapsite cap, was a matter of excruciating precision, properly the subject of several weeks' simulation and preparation in its own right, but Bruno—in perhaps the most shocking lapse of his career—thrust his hands into a set of EM grapple controllers to attack the problem manually. One shudders to think how close to the brink he might have come, how many times he nearly slipped or erred or performed key steps out of sequence. Were the odds—and the gods—in his favor? All we can say for certain is that de Towaji completed the entire process in less than twenty hours, his fingers hopping from island to island, one stable form to the next, and that disaster did not, in fact, strike.

Rome may not have been built in a day, but for better or worse, the first crude hypercollapsite was. Sometimes it works like that; simply knowing that a thing is possible sometimes leads you straight to it. If you're a genius, at least. If you're desperate and angry and don't have time to fail. If the higher powers, such as they are, seem inclined to take your side.

As the day progressed, the collapsium shrank, withered, brightened briefly as its nodes fell into denser and denser arrangements, and finally lost its color altogether and became invisible, an optical superconductor. Then came the final step: a jerk here, a flourish there, a picosecond's delay, and . . . the structure ceased to be a part of the Newtonian universe, its mass folding in on itself, its charge vibrations damping out in self-eradicating sympathetic waves.

Still useless, of course; without that penultimate, trillion-ton cap's cap, the eye at the top of the pyramid, the device could no more block inertia than a boat with a hole in it could float. But that was a simple matter, easily corrected when the time came—or so Bruno hoped, at any rate. If it weren't, if problems occurred at this point to crush the hypercollapsite or otherwise prevent it from functioning, there was little to be done about it. The time had come, to do or die.

His final acts in the study that day, partly practical and partly symbolic, were to capture the forces and movements and stages the collapsium had gone through in its transformation to code them into a single wellstone jewel embedded in the hypercomputer wall, to form a little wellgold ring around the jewel, and to pluck that ring from the wall and place it on the middle finger of his right hand, where it looked very smart indeed.

"Door," he said then, and stepped out to meet his destiny.

chapter seventeen

in which the bravery
of houses is demonstrated

"*That's* our spaceship?" was all Bruno could think to say, upon seeing what Muddy had done with the past four days.

"An iron hull and an engine to propel her," Muddy quoted back at him, cringing and whining. "That's what you told me."

And that was very nearly all there was; the pressure vessel itself was windowless and barrel shaped, tapered slightly at the top and bottom, and the sheets of iron that comprised it were exceedingly thin, almost like foil. Bruno figured he could easily puncture them with a screwdriver. The rivets holding them together were tiny and weak looking, too; perhaps he could breach the hull with his *bare hands*. The "engine" consisted of a pair of man-sized EM grapples at the top—the bow, Bruno supposed—each with a man-sized superconducting battery to power it, and the life-support system was simply a di-clad tube of supercondensed oxygen strapped to the side of the barrel, with a valve and heating coil at one end and a plastic tube running through into the hull.

The interior was nearly as spartan: a flimsy "hatch" led

through to a chamber with two chairs and a little fax machine, plus an iron toilet whose plumbing was apparently just some sort of airlock for dumping wastes overboard. The only civilized concession was the inch of wellstone Muddy had laid—or more likely asked the robots to lay—around the inside and outside surfaces of the hull. For the moment, it was inert, its fine-threaded structure translucent as smoke. This, too, reflected poor judgment: a stiff breeze could damage it in that state.

"I hardly know where to begin," Bruno said, goggling at this monstrosity that hulked, in the warm starlit darkness, on his front lawn.

"It's precisely what you ordered, sir, and the gods have been most forgiving in its creation. How was I to s-s-surmise you wanted elegance?"

Bruno's sigh was almost a laugh. Almost. "Muddy, this thing is flimsy as a kite. If the wellstone loses power or integrity for some reason, what's to hold the ship together?"

"It's *light*. I wanted it to be *light*, so it could travel even if your . . . project didn't work out. And if the wellstone fails, won't your hypercollapsite destroy the hull anyway? Regardless of its composition?"

"Hmm. Yes, well, what about the life support?"

"That oxygen bottle is the *backup* system. In *operation* we'll use wellstone scrubbers to crack exhaled CO_2."

Bruno shook a finger, unwilling to be appeased. "The interior space? We're to rescue a Queendom in a ship sized for just the two of us?"

Muddy squirmed under his gaze. "I made four folding chairs for extra passengers; I was going to put those in before we left. They attach to special brackets in the walls. But surely we can't rescue *everyone*, no matter how big a spaceship we bring. One does have to draw the line s-s-somewhere."

"Why is the wellstone inactivated? You've left this ship frighteningly vulnerable."

"To permit your inspection, sir. I'll switch it back on once you're done."

"If I tripped, I could fall right through the hull!"

"The robots have been instructed to prevent that, Declarancy."

Bruno had saved his worst for last: he pointed up at the bow. "All right, you, look here; look at these grapples. This is supposed to be our propulsion system?"

Muddy cast him a bruised look. "That's the b-b-best part, sir. Efficient: a hundred percent conversion of stored energy to kinetic, with thrust limited only by the available power. *Much* better than rockets, if you're in a hurry. Never widely employed, because the targets you grapple to are dragged and disturbed in the process, ditto anything that passes through the beam incidentally. Actually, it's probably *illegal* to travel that way in the Queendom, but under the circumstances I s-s-suppose they'll forgive us."

"Muddy, rockets push, from the rear. That's what we need here! Good God, man, grapples *pull* from the *front*. We have a zpf-damping cap on the front of the ship; the grapple beams will vanish into it without a trace. What do you think a grapple beam *is*?"

Finally, for the first time Bruno could recollect, Muddy gathered himself up, straightened his spine, and returned something approximating a steady gaze. "I know exactly what a grapple beam is, Declarant. You forget yourself. You forget that I *was* yourself. In the first place, we can expel oxygen for emergency propulsion, accelerated electromagnetically through wellstone channels in the hull. From the *back*, yes. In the second place, I watched you put the ertial shield together."

"Ertial?" Bruno asked.

"The opposite of *in*ertial. I coined the term while you were working. Anyway, I watched you assemble the thing, and I know it's got a hole in it. As it happens, these grapples are positioned to emit right through that hole."

Bruno smacked himself on the head. "Damn me! Damn us both, we should have coordinated this better. Muddy, that hole is there because I ran out of materials. I was planning to fill it with mass from the planet's core. It's strictly temporary."

Muddy's composure collapsed immediately. His arm went up to cover his face, and he commenced a hoarse sobbing. "Oh, sir! Oh, sir! You know how badly I wanted to please you. I can't manage even that, can I? Did I ever doubt that history would judge me h-h-harshly? If so, that doubt is removed. Please don't yell at me anymore, sir; please don't. The weight of my own disapproval is all I can bear!"

For the umptieth time, Bruno felt ashamed, both for upsetting Muddy and for *being* him, this miserable creature who was so easily upset, and so overly dramatic when it happened. Was he really so weak? So sniveling? Marlon Sykes had his number, all right, had his every shame and insecurity mapped out. That was, of course, the whole idea, but that didn't make it easier to face. Well damn Marlon, anyway. Did it matter what he thought? So what if Bruno and Muddy were a pair of folding cravens? At least they weren't hurting anyone, weren't, for example, destroying the Queendom for spite's sake.

"There, there," Bruno said awkwardly, stepping forward to embrace his tortured self. "It's all right, Brother. It's all right. Let me try some more calculations, and see what I can come up with. You finish outfitting the ship, all right? I'll be back in a few minutes."

"All right," Muddy said, sniffing, and burst into fresh sobs. "God, I'm *so* broken it surprises even me. Go, sir. Please. Observe me no further."

It seemed that Bruno should have said something heartening at this point, but instead he turned away from Muddy and, taking him at his word, slunk away into the house. This was just too difficult, too awkward, too shaming. Muddy would understand his reaction, right? Better than anyone else possibly could.

He continued on into his study. Fortunately, it hadn't cleaned itself up since he'd gone outside; everything was exactly as he'd left it. This made it easy to drop right back into his chair and pick up the "ertial shield" calculations right where he'd left off. Clearly now, time was running out.

He worried about the number of workable geometries, this close to the lower mass limit. He supposed the number of solutions could well be infinite, or at least very large, but in a severely restricted domain—the same little mushroom cap, with an infinite number of trivial modifications. Were there any solutions with holes through the middle? He began with the hypothesis that there *were,* and began formulating a proof.

An hour later, his efforts had borne fruit, yielding an ertial shield solution with a hole of nearly the right size, in nearly the right place. To create it he'd have to use *all* the neutronium from the planet's core, and from the core of the little dark sun as well, but that couldn't be helped. He rose from his chair and bolted through the house.

"Muddy! Muddy, warm up the grapples; we leave at once!"

Outside, the little spaceship had turned to impervium: a smooth, barrel-shaped, superreflecting mirror. Impossibly light and impossibly strong, it would no doubt break his toes if he kicked it. Muddy stood beside it, looking toward Bruno. As before, tears filled his eyes. Were they fresh? Had they been there for the entire hour?

"It's only just occurred to me," Muddy said sadly. "You mean to destroy the planet."

Hurriedly, Bruno nodded. "And the sun, yes. It can't be helped. Do we have everything we need to rescue a stray grapple station?"

"D'you hear that, house? We s-s-seek to destroy you for our own gain."

"Ah. Do be careful, sirs," the house replied in its calm, mother's voice.

"Does it bother you?" Muddy pressed, shifting his weight from foot to foot. "Would you rather live?"

"As you wish," the house said, equally enough.

Muddy appeared distressed by this. "Shall we at least say good-bye? You've been *home* to me, a reassurance, a place to dream of returning to. It isn't lightly that one abandons such a place to . . . the torch."

The house, unmoving and unchanging, seemed to consider

this for a few moments before replying, "I've uploaded my gain states to your ship's memory, sir. Should you ever desire to rebuild me, that image awaits your command. I'm sorry that my destruction troubles you; shall I clean up first? Can I offer you some soup?"

"No." Muddy said, weeping afresh. "No, thank you."

"Are we ready to lift off?" Bruno asked, trying to be gentle but needing to hurry things along.

"Not quite," Muddy said, a little angrily. "A solar IR laser is charging the batteries, and if we're headed for the *grapple station* instead of the *Queendom*, our own grapples will need a few minutes to change target lock."

Bruno waved a hand. "Muddy, you can handle these things while I'm installing the ertial shield. We've got to *go*, man."

Muddy's sobs strengthened, and his arm looked ready to leap up and cover his face again. "Oh, sir, can't we walk around the world? Can't we see it one last time? I've dreamed of this place for too long, to have it s-s-snatched out from under me so soon!"

"All right," Bruno snapped, then softened his tone. "All right, yes. If we haven't got at least a *few* minutes to spare, it's my fault for taking too long in the study. And this place *has* been a fine home, hasn't it?"

For a few seconds it seemed Muddy might reply, but he didn't, and finally Bruno turned to lead the way down the meadow path away from the house. Darkness hadn't been kind here—the grass lay dead and crisp in some places, dead and limply moldering in others. His gardens lay in neat, lifeless rows. At the meadow's far end, his dogwoods and honeysuckles had gone dormant, shedding their leaves in a carpet that squelched and crumbled beneath their boots.

The little bridge was intact, and the stream beneath it babbled as happily as ever, but the barley fields beyond it held only harvest stubble and a pair of stoop-backed robots dutifully uprooting the tiny white mushrooms that were springing up all around. The rocky desert looked all right, and the beach, and the sea. These things he hadn't killed yet. Not yet.

"What would Enzo have made of this place, I wonder?" Muddy asked, pausing where the stream widened out into foul, rotting bog at the ocean's edge.

Bruno snorted. "It's no world for kites, I'm afraid, though he'd have liked the fields and vineyards."

"And hated the silence. He wouldn't have understood this, would he, Bruno? Crawling off on our own like this, messing around with *theories* and *things*; he'd never have stood for it if he'd been alive."

No, indeed. Enzo de Towaji had been the ultimate people person, a man who seemed to exist *only* in the thoughts and reactions of others. Strange that he'd been so happy with Bernice, who *did* like the quiet. How often would she be staring into the fireplace, or setting off to hike in the hills, or playing a game of chess against herself, when Enzo would kidnap her along on some foolish errand? But perhaps she needed that—needed someone to drag her mind from its pure, Machiavellian pursuits.

"Mother might have understood," Muddy said.

Bruno nodded. "Indeed. Indeed, yes, although she'd find the place awfully confining. We really should be going, Muddy. There are live people who need us. Deliah van Skettering, for starters."

Muddy pursed his lips. "She's the woman on the station?"

"Yes, and she's probably single-copy. Her death could well be as final as Enzo's and Bernice's, if we're late in preventing it."

"Do we have the *time*?"

Bruno puffed out his chest. "I daresay we *must*. If nothing else, she knows where to find Tamra, who, incidentally, may also have been singled in this calamity. But I *hope* we'd have saved her in any case."

"To spite Marlon?" Muddy asked, in a particularly whining tone.

"To spite God," Bruno answered sincerely. It was the ultimate superstition, the last and most powerful he could tap. If spirits and demigods were a shorthand for all the pseudorandomness of nature, then God was a shorthand for all the spirits taken together. If silly "boat gods" could derive some statistically measurable reality from dwelling even fleetingly in Bruno's subconscious, then God himself—who dwelt in nearly everyone—must derive enormously more. So to blame God, to beseech God, to *invoke* God was an act not only of desperation, but of ultimate rationality.

He expanded. "This business of *evil*, of *murder*, has no place in civilized society. Deliah does not wish to fly off into outer darkness, and so she shall not. And she'll have you to thank for it, Muddy, and God to curse for letting it come down to your actions, and mine. Has Marlon broken your heart, along with your pride? Come! Saddle up our steed and let's away!"

To his relief, Muddy did seem infected by that enthusiasm; together they trotted along the beach, along the pebbled pathway that led back into meadow again. The house appeared over the horizon, and suddenly they were upon it.

A hundred robots lined the way ahead of them.

There were fifty robots on either side of the path, gleaming gold and silver and glossy black in the starlight, their left arms raised in formal salute, forming an arch. Bruno skidded to a halt, Muddy coming up short beside him. Together they stared for a few silent moments, before starting forward.

Two by two, the robots turned blank faces toward their masters and seemed to convey a sense of exultation, untainted by sorrow. Two by two they bowed, bodies clicking and whirring with impossible grace, arms extending downward to brush the withered grass. Two by two, they collapsed the archway, a good-bye as eloquent as any poet had ever penned.

"Farewell, old friends," Bruno murmured as they came to the end of it, as the last two robots swept into their bows. Muddy burst out crying again.

"It's been a privilege, sir," the house said.

"I thank you," Muddy sobbed, "from the very bottom of my wounded heart."

Then Bruno touched him on the shoulder and steered him toward the ship, and together they climbed through the little hatch. Inside was a miniature palace of diamonds and green velvet, of blue-and-white veined lapis and green-and-white veined jade. The two little chairs had become slick, stylish acceleration couches in black leather; the toilet had turned to gold.

"Good night!" Bruno exclaimed on seeing it. "Did I accuse you of shoddy design, Brother? I retract every word!"

"It's just library patterns," Muddy said, shrugging, his sobs trailing away into sniffles again. Then he straightened. "Oblivion! Aren't we forgetting your pet?"

"My pet? My pet?" Bruno felt his eyes widen. "Ah, God! Hugo!"

He leaped through the hatch, catching his boot toe on it, and fell sprawling in the rotting grass, narrowly missing smashing his nose. He needn't have bothered, though; the battered robot stood outside, looking as if it'd been just about to climb in.

"Mewl," it said distinctly, looking down at Bruno in an oddly human—if faceless—way.

"Yes," Bruno agreed, rising, brushing himself off, "mewl indeed. Climb aboard, you, and quickly. There's much to do, and little time!"

chapter eighteen

in which numerous
laws are broken

Of the world's destruction there is little to say; grapples cleft the planet in twain, exposing its core of prismatic-white neubles, and the neubles were collapsed into proton-sized black holes, and the black holes were formed into collapsium, and the collapsium was squashed into a torus of vacuogel hypercollapsite and positioned atop the ertial shield.

The destruction of the sun was somewhat more delicate, somewhat more involved, but only slightly. Muddy, staring upward through the wellstone "window" of the bow, wept and moaned inconsolably throughout the process, until Bruno, who was none too happy about all this himself, finally snapped at him to shut up. Hugo mewled once and fell silent, and as the ertial shield *whump*ed into place atop the spaceship's impervium bow and the propulsion grapples locked onto their distant target, there was only the sound of the two men breathing: one raggedly, the other not.

The star field—and the debris field of their former home— rippled only slightly; the ertial shield was transparent to visible light, transparent in fact to nearly every phenomenon the universe could throw at it. It existed primarily as an absence, a damping, a silence in the zero-point field's infinite screeching.

"Engage the beams," Bruno said, when all systems were ready.

"Aye, aye, Captain," Muddy acknowledged in sullen, childish tones. In place of a standard hypercomputer interface he'd designed a late renaissance control panel, with all manner of gilded switches and levers and dials, and with his hands he now manipulated these controls.

The transition from weightlessness to weight was immediate; the debris field dropped away against the unmoving stars, and Bruno felt his lungs compress, the air forced out of them by the weight of his own breastbone. The acceleration wasn't enormous—the system was set for precisely 1.00000 gee—but it came on as a step function. Its time derivative, known to physicists as "jerk," was nearly infinite, lurching them from zero to full throttle in a millionth of a millionth of a microsecond. Funny how, in their hurry, they hadn't considered the *effect* of this on tender flesh and blood; it hurt. Not a stinging or a burning or a bruising kind of hurt, but a *pressing,* like having a soft, heavy couch dropped on you.

"Ah, my bones!" Muddy shrieked. "My ribs! I've broken my ribs!" And then he vomited over the side of his couch and shrieked again.

"Steady," Bruno said, unfastening restraints and sitting up. The movement was unwise. The ertial shield swept away the zero-point field immediately ahead of them, leaving behind a medium one thousand times less energetic; in theory, plowing through this sparser field at one thousand times the acceleration should have been completely equivalent to 1.00000 gee, indistinguishable in every way from normal gravity or thrust. But a bow-heavy structure weighing trillions of tons, however cleverly disguised, poses some minor practical difficulties. What was really going on, in this air-filled space behind the hypercollapsite? Was it surprising that inner-ear fluids might misbehave?

While these thoughts raced through Bruno's head, his

body slid off the acceleration couch and onto the floor. He felt there was something strange in the way he fell, and stranger still in the way he landed, as if the fine hairs on his skin were solid rods growing out of a light, solid, cleverly articulated doll. He attempted to rise. The floor had a comforting traction, at least, but it seemed his mass—his *weight*—rose too quickly for the press of gravity. Something a little off, a little light, with the inertia?

His dizziness continued, along with an odd, pressing sensation in his chest. The heart? He imagined inertialess blood pumping through inertialess veins. Pressure and viscosity and muscular contraction weren't functions of inertia; the heart *would* pump. The blood *would* flow. But strangely, yes.

Beside him, Hugo lay where they'd strapped it to the floor. It held a worn metal hand in front of its face and made small movements with it every few moments, seeming somehow fascinated with the results. Had Hugo discovered inertia, by virtue of its sudden reduction?

With great concentration, Bruno managed to regain his balance and rise slowly to his feet, standing unsteadily between Muddy's couch and his own.

"My bones," Muddy whined tearfully, "my organs. My *eyes*."

He was rolling back and forth as much as his restraints would allow, as if in a kind of slow seizure, but Bruno immediately had the sense that the movement was voluntary, that Muddy wasn't seriously hurt, that the tears were of misery rather than outright agony.

Bruno reached out with uncertain fingers to probe at Muddy's chest. "Does this hurt? Here? Here?"

Muddy cried out each time, but the bones themselves felt perfectly intact. "Ow! Ow, sir, you grieve me!"

"I don't think there's a fracture."

His groaning intensified. "No fracture? God, you'd think after years of torture a person would become inured to pain. The truth is otherwise! Opposite! Bruno, if you knew the indignities these bones had been s-s-subjected to. Split with wedges? I only wish. It's that legacy that haunts me now."

Bruno frowned down at himself. "The fax should have healed any injuries. You should be every bit as fit as I am."

"Should I?" Muddy's face was miserable, ashamed. He tried to turn away. "I've been cunningly redesigned, sir, in ways the fax has little ability to detect and still less to repair. Primarily in the synaptic wiring, but he took some liberties with my s-s-skeleton as well. To move is to suffer; to hold still is to suffer more."

Bruno, who was getting tired of feeling aghast, merely sighed. "We'll undesign you, then."

"Easy to say. Someday, yes, no doubt we'll overcome his cleverness. Meanwhile, I suppose I deserve these miseries."

Here was a clumsy move, an attempt to make Bruno deny it. He declined again to take the bait, saying instead, "There are pressing concerns and limited resources, and anyway that little fax"—he pointed—"won't pass a human body. So perhaps it *is* necessary for you to be patient until the situation has stabilized. I'm sorry for that, particularly since your suffering doesn't appear to build character."

Muddy managed—with visible strain—to scrape out a chuckle. "Ah, a touch of bitterness, of condescension. Go with it, Bruno; be human. Your respect is forced; honor me instead with your heartfelt disgust. There's a good lad."

Bruno sighed again. "Can I offer you a drug?"

"A drug! How novel. Indeed, yes, I'd be powerless to refuse some of Enzo's Christmas brandy. Reduce this pain in me, sir. Your inertially corrupt s-s-spacetime disagrees with me!"

"Brandy is not a painkiller."

"Ah, but it is, Declarancy. It is."

"Not the proper sort, and you know it. I'll get you something . . . strong."

Bruno glanced up, half expecting to see the stars themselves moving outside the wellstone "window" of the bow. But the star field was inert, unimpressed with their meddlings. The turning of his head left him dizzy; he nearly fell again, but caught himself with a hand on each of the two couches. Moving carefully and with many pauses, he extricated himself from between the couches, turned toward the fax, and pulled up a hypercomputer interface beside it so he could search the onboard libraries for a suitable painkiller. There were, it turned out, many thousands to choose from.

"We're . . . really . . . moving along, aren't we?" Muddy mused.

Turning slowly, Bruno looked up, and followed Muddy's gaze to the instruments. Specifically, to the "Distance to Target" gauge, an old-style digital readout made from rows of illuminable red bars. It read in tenths of a meter, and at present its lower five digits were all flickery eights, changing too rapidly to register on the eye. The higher seven digits counted down smoothly, their speed increasing even as he watched.

"Indeed," Bruno agreed. "We'll reach the halfway mark in a couple of hours."

This was no small feat; though the runaway grapple station had passed just over eight light-minutes of Bruno's little planet—greater than the distance between the Earth and Sun—at its closest approach, it had since hurtled another fifty light-minutes toward infinity. Poor Deliah had probably traveled farther than any human being before her.

The fax made a little coughing sound and spat a pill into Bruno's hand. He extended the other hand and extracted a glass of water, whose contents sloshed from side to side with even the slightest jostling as he rose to approach Muddy.

"Chair upright," Muddy said, then screamed as the chair complied.

When all was ready, Bruno handed his counterpart the pill and the glass, watched him carefully ingest the one and sip from the other, then wince as if the act of swallowing caused some new pain of its own. He drank from the glass several times more, grimacing each time, and also complaining that it was "merely water." Then finally the chair was reclined again, and the glass was carefully returned to the fax, and Bruno climbed awkwardly back into his own couch, managing to step on Hugo's head twice during the process. Hugo mewled at this, but otherwise didn't seem to mind.

"Sorry, old thing. I'd break the floor if it weren't impervium."

"Will this take effect quickly?" Muddy asked.

"It should, yes." Bruno carefully strapped himself back in and cinched the straps tight. "Ah. Ah, yes. It's much better to lie still."

Muddy snorted beside him. "She *is* a fine ship, isn't she?"

"For a cobbled-together prototype on her first shakedown cruise, I'd say she's a bloody miracle."

"Shall we name her?"

Bruno grunted; he hadn't thought about that. Anthropomorphic instincts aside, he wasn't much for naming inanimate things, or even semianimate ones like houses and small planets. But a ship was a different matter—it *was* animate, by definition. And it would need a name for legal registration if for no other reason. *There* was some optimistic thinking.

"All right, yes." He ran through a few possibilities in his mind: the *Redshift II,* the *Tamra Lutui, The Grappleship Old Girona.* Then, belatedly catching a hint in Muddy's tone, he asked, "You, ah, have something in mind?"

"I do. I thought perhaps the *Sabadell-Andorra.*"

That gave Bruno pause. Absurd on the face of it: by nature, spaceships were gracile and swift, where tectonic plates were among the slowest and heaviest objects ever manipulated by humans. And anyway, did anyone outside Catalonia even remember the pocket catastrophe of that earthquake? Then again, in component form this little spaceship massed considerably more than all the fallen hillsides of Girona, possibly as much as the Iberian plate itself, and the technology certainly was—well, earthshaking in its implications.

"All right," he said finally, nodding, "*Sabadell-Andorra* it is. And *we'll* know what it means, at least."

"I feel the medication working."

Bruno turned to look at his . . . brother—his battered, mistreated counterpart. "Good. Excellent. Is it helping?"

"It is, yes. Ah. To be without pain, for even a moment . . ."

Muddy's eyelids began to droop. Through thousands of years of civilization, mankind had yet to invent a reliable pain-suppression chemical that didn't also proportionally suppress consciousness. Pain was simply too fundamental, too *necessary,* to be banished so easily; it bound itself up in every system of the body. There were various "nondrowsy formulas" Bruno might have tried, milder analgesics tempered with stimulants and euphoriants, but the ship's library gave these much lower effectiveness ratings. Of course there was always the brute-force approach: simply deadening the spinal nerves. Muddy didn't need to move for a while anyway, right? But sleep seemed a much kinder side effect than total paralysis.

"Thanks," Muddy said blurrily; Then his eyes closed, his breathing slowed, and he just sort of faded away. It was a peaceful thing to watch, a hundred little tensions sliding out of that tortured body to leave it—finally!—at peace. Bruno almost feared he'd *died* until his chest rose and fell again slowly—and again, and again—his breathing shallow but steady. Muddy would awaken in four or five hours, just in time for the rendezvous with Deliah's grapple station.

Bruno, seeing these hours stretching dully before him, wished *he* had some means to slip away so easily. All the hard hours in the study had taken their toll; he didn't relish any further isolation. He spent fully twenty-eight seconds considering this before he, too, fell asleep.

He awoke to gravity fluctuations—a sense of rotation and weightlessness—followed by the slamming jerk of acceleration again. The first sound he heard was Muddy's weeping—not a shriek or howl or moan this time but a quiet, private, sniffly sort of weeping that engendered immediate sympathy. He opened his eyes, saw Muddy lying there on the acceleration couch, his skin and tufted hair pale against the black leather.

His shirt had loosened in the night; the word "savage" was clearly visible on his shoulder in fluorescent green.

"Are you all right?" Bruno asked him gently.

Muddy jumped a little, startled. "What? Ah, Bruno. I was savoring a dream."

Above, the bow afforded a view of Sol, at this range barely distinguishable from the stars around it.

"Mmm. A sad dream?"

"A dream about His Declarancy. Not sad, no; I dreamed he held a whip in his hand."

"How terrifying!"

Muddy snorted. "Not at all. No, the whip is a personal, almost intimate expression between two people. It means he wants to talk, to exchange. But in my dream, he was whipping the sun, and flares were spinning out of it with every stroke, and he was saying your name over and over again, and when I asked him what he was doing, he turned to look at me. His face was blank, like a robot's. I woke up."

"That sounds horrible, Muddy."

"No." He was shaking his head. "To me it was touching. Sweet. I suppose I'm crying because it *should* have been horrible, because I've come so far from where I started. Ah, Bruno, if only you could *know* him. He admires you so very much. He's not such a bad man, in some ways. Just very, very driven."

"How sad for him," Bruno said, then loosened his straps a little and raised his seat back. "Muddy, you don't have to play his games anymore."

The tears ran freely down Muddy's face. "Perhaps I do, sir. These things aren't so easily undone as you seem to imagine. Perhaps they can't be undone at all, except in death, but he's made such an obedient little coward of me I doubt even *that* is an option. There's little doubt I'm doing his work right now, one way or another. You should lock me in this chair and drug me for the duration, sir. I would, in your place."

"Yes? Well, that's precisely where you and I differ. I'm very sorry for all that's happened to you, but *enough* already. Right?

You've made a fine ship to fly against him, and you're using it. Revel in that. Have we turned around yet?"

"Indeed," Muddy said, in sour imitation of Bruno's own voice. Or perhaps the "imitation" was literal, and his voice really was that growling and brusque. "We've been decelerating for hours. We'll reach the station in eleven minutes."

He pointed to a diagram on the instrument console, a little brass plaque engraved with black letters and symbols, which showed the arrow-straight trajectory of the station and the slightly curvier path of the *Sabadell-Andorra* intersecting it. Curvy because the ship's only means of propulsion was the runaway station itself, the electromagnetic anchor they'd tied to it. There was nothing else to anchor to out here in the so-called Kuiper Belt, a space so huge and empty around them that the nearest other object was probably the planetary debris field they'd left behind, or perhaps a flake or two of very lonely methane ice.

At any rate, since they couldn't aim for where the station *would* be, but only where it *was,* their path was a classic "stern chase." Actually, it was worse than that, because they'd had to place themselves directly between the station and the sun, so the latter could be used as a deceleration anchor. Their final rendezvous—indicated in miniature on the little brass plaque—involved a lot of flip-flopping toward the station and back, for course correction, while Sol, on the other side, did all the heavy lifting. Bruno had been awakened by just such a flip-flop. It was hardly an optimal arrangement, but it did seem to be getting the job done. As Bruno watched, the little black indentations labeled SHIP and STATION inched forward in their tracks, dotted lines turning solid in their wake. And indeed, if the display was accurate then rendezvous was very nearly at hand.

"Have you made radio contact?" he asked Muddy.

"With the s-s-station?"

"With Deliah, yes."

"I hadn't thought of it. Shall I?"

"Allow me. Ship? Hello?"

A hypercomputer earpiece appeared on the hull beside him.

"Ship here," was the immediate—though somewhat tentative—reply. The poor thing was probably growing a consciousness emulator for the first time, opening its metaphorical eyes and ears, the demands of an impatient de Towaji being its first-ever experience of *experience*. The ship itself wouldn't mind, of course; it would be eager for any task, but still Bruno found the idea depressing. This week had been filled to bursting with depressing ideas.

"Can you make radio contact with that grapple station?"

"The object ahead of us? Certainly, sir. Can you recommend a frequency?"

Bruno gave it one—the one he and Deliah had used in their conversation at closest approach. "Analog," he added, "not digital."

"Very well, sir. Receiving reply."

"Play it."

"Bruno!" Deliah van Skettering's voice said. "*Malo e lelei*, it's about time you answered. I've had you on radar for over an hour. Hello?"

"I'm here," he acknowledged. "Two of me, actually, though one would deny it. How are you holding up?"

"Splendidly," she said, and he couldn't tell if she was being sarcastic or not. He supposed not; *he'd* certainly be delighted at the prospect of rescue after a week of lonely terror out here, the sun shrinking steadily behind him. The light-lag and vocal distortions, at least, had dropped almost to zero.

"Right. Well, we'll be there in a couple of minutes. I'm not sure that we have an actual rendezvous plan, but we'll work something out."

"What is the condition of the station?" Muddy interjected, in a voice less sour than before.

"Condition? Why, it's a mess. Every non-wellstone component has been smashed out of true, and there are *lots* of those components. Big, too. I feel I'm in some carnival funhouse. I'm actually amazed the hull's held up so well: I've got leaks, but they're about eighth on my hierarchy of problems to worry about. The floor here is neutronium filled, for local gravity. My biggest fear is losing cohesion in the diamond cladding— I'd survive about a microsecond."

"Is the station functional?" Muddy pressed. "Can you produce a grapple beam with it?"

Deliah paused. "Bruno? Is that still you? You sound funny."

"I'm Muddy. A de Towaji relative on the Quisling s-s-side of the family."

Quisling: traitor. Deliah didn't appear to catch the reference. "Attitude control is out," she said evenly. "Power distribution is out. I've got hypercomputers running in several locations, but there isn't a lot for them to *do*. The emitter cavities are wellstone lined, so it's possible the revpics still have full range of motion. If I can route power to them, I could probably get enough vibration out to muster some measurable gravitation. Not enough to save me or anything. Why? What did you have in mind?"

Muddy shrugged, then seemed to realize she couldn't see that. "I, uh, thought we might simply take it with us. The whole thing. I thought it might come in handy."

"It might at that," Bruno said, impressed with the idea. "Goodness." He turned to the nearest hypercomputer and tapped in some quick calculations. "Hmmph. Not feasible. The ertial shield's wake is essentially cone shaped, and could only accommodate the station if it were more than a kilometer behind. But at that range, most of the zpf has filled in again. It's like digging a hole in water—it doesn't last long at all."

Muddy looked ready to cry again. "It was just an idea," he whined, cringing back in his couch as if expecting violence.

"A *good* idea," Bruno agreed quickly, "just not a workable one. At best, we'd yank a core sample out through the station's middle."

"I have no idea what you're talking about," Deliah complained. "If you can *think* of towing something this size through space, then you're either crazy or . . . Well, we've got some talking to do when you get here."

A gentle but very solid *whump* came up through the floor, and suddenly all the sensations of inertialess motion vanished. They weren't accelerating any longer, so the aft deck was no longer "down." But they weren't weightless, either. Instead, the di-clad neutronium deck liners inside the grapple station tugged at them sidewise. The deck seemed to tilt beneath them now, as on an ocean ship that was sinking.

"Huh. I believe we *are* here," Muddy said.

The view above them was still of Sol: a bright star among the many stars, none of them moving. But at the edges of the view, just barely visible, was a lighted red circle in a curve of well-metals. It flicked off and then on again as Bruno watched. Not part of their own ship; it was the only sign of the massive station hulking below them.

"Ship," Muddy said, "display a schematic of the station, including yourself upon it, and clearly indicate the positions of all living persons."

Obligingly, the brass plaque erased itself and became instead a plate of holographic glass, behind which a little grapple station appeared, as if modeled in translucent brown plastic. Two dots of brightly contrasting pink appeared in one lobe of the structure—Bruno and Muddy in the *Sabadell-Andorra*. A third dot hovered nearby, perhaps fifty meters away.

"Okay, I have you on scope," Deliah said. "The nearest air lock suffered minimal damage in the accident—air leakage shouldn't be a major problem if you mate there."

"Mate?" Bruno asked stupidly.

Muddy slapped himself on the forehead, not playfully or symbolically but *hard*, as if he meant to raise a welt. "Little gods, I'm so stupid! *So* stupid!"

"We have no airlock," Bruno said, echoing the obvious. "Steady, Brother—I didn't think of it either. We're not the most brilliant of sailors, you and I. Deliah, there's a problem. Have you any sort of spacesuit to climb into?"

"No," she said, "nothing like that. All the faxes are down. Do I hear you correctly? If you're airlock-free, I don't see how a spacesuit would help. The vacuum would kill you both the moment I opened your hatch."

"Indeed," Bruno agreed ruefully. "We have a *door,* and an ample supply of oxygen, but that will do us little good if we must suffocate to admit you. An idiotic quandary. Let's think on this a moment. My humblest apologies, madam."

"Can you fax yourself into storage for a few minutes, while the hatch is opened and closed?" Deliah asked.

"Alas, no, our fax is much too small to admit a person. Let me think about this."

Muddy had, of course, started crying again, but presently his eyes brightened, his snuffling quieted, and his hands lashed out for the control panel above him.

"An idea?" Bruno asked, feeling startled.

"Indeed, yes. Deliah, move as far away from us as you can. Can you seal yourself off with an independent air supply?"

Her snort of amusement was unmistakable. "You overestimate the conditions here, de Towaji."

"I'm Muddy."

"Oh. Well, I can put some distance between us, but it's all one crumpled volume. Is the danger really any greater if I'm close?"

Muddy considered. "I suppose not, actually."

"I'll only go a little ways, then."

"Stay clear of the walls, at least."

The floor had begun to make a new noise—a kind of low, sizzling hiss.

"What are you doing?" Bruno asked. Well, demanded, actually, and then immediately felt bad for it. He'd been telling Muddy all along to act like a man, to use the brains and initiative he'd been born with, to be helpful rather than help*less,* and yet here he was getting unnerved and suspicious the first time it actually happened. He supposed it was another response from humanity's deep wiring: Muddy had acted subservient for long enough to place himself "beneath" Bruno in some imaginary hierarchy. And now he was . . . What? Exceeding that role? Getting uppity? Was Bruno entitled, in this age of self-repair and self-reconstruction, to blame him for that, and then excuse his own behavior as a quirk of evolution? Surely not.

These things, Muddy's voice reminded him, *aren't so easily undone as you seem to imagine.* Perhaps it was like the wiring for pain: subtle, pervasive, intimately tied to vital functions. But was *that* an excuse? Goodness, if Bruno couldn't treat *himself* with dignity . . .

"I'm sorry," he said to Muddy's cringing form, with as much sincerity as he could muster. "Please proceed."

Slowly, Muddy uncringed himself and moved his hands back toward the controls. "It's a chemical reaction. A s-s-series of them, actually."

"Ah!" Bruno said, grasping the idea at once. The hull's outer layer was wellstone; it could be programmed into all manner of absurdly reactive forms that would decompose—atom by atom—the absurdly nonreactive substance of the grapple station's wellstone hull. Such reactions could be timed in waves, so that each atom of silicon substrate, once liberated, could be carried away in the chemical equivalent of a bucket brigade. And at the edges and interfaces, the two hulls could be pseudochemically *merged,* to keep the air from leaking out around the sides. The *Sabadell-Andorra* was melting its way through the defenses of the runaway station, melting through into its cozy, air-filled interior. Already, the sizzling sound had climbed half a meter up the sides of the *Andorra's* barrel hull.

"My God!" Bruno exclaimed, and if he weren't secured and awkwardly tilted in his leather couch, he'd have leaped to his feet to grasp Muddy's hand and pump it. "How brilliant! What a *tidy solution* that is. And quick! Why, it took you hardly any time at all."

"Careful, sir," Muddy warned. "You endanger your modesty. To claim me as part of yourself, then praise my brilliance? It's mightily suspicious." His voice was partly sour, partly sarcastic, partly amused and wry. But he seemed to appreciate the compliment just the same. He relaxed visibly, his frame filling out a little as his muscles slumped and his chest expanded.

"Oh, piffle," Bruno answered, in much the same tone. But he took the hint, and declined to praise himself further. "How long until we can open the door?"

"Another minute."

Deliah's voice broke through again. "Holy Philadelphia! My station! My beautiful station, what are you doing to the hull of my beautiful station?"

She, too, sounded amused. What a jolly band of jokers they were up here, ten thousand million kilometers above the sun. Bruno supposed it was a reasonable defense mechanism, given the chaos below and the impossibility of their intervention there, at this particular moment. He thought of Tonga, the cliffs of Fua'amotu washed away, and felt guilty for his humor.

"I see the door," Deliah said in a bleaker, more serious tone. "It's about halfway in. No signs of air leakage yet. For an impromptu solution, this seems to be working rather well."

"You know," Muddy said, "technically we could do the same thing to our *own* hull: pull the iron aside bit by bit as a temporary measure, and make a wellstone door anywhere we like. Not even a door, a semipermeable membrane. I suppose fighting your way against the air-pressure gradient might be difficult, but we could compensate by . . . Well, hmm."

"It hardly matters," Deliah said. "Your real hatch is almost through. Just stay clear of that cladding! You do realize I'd never approve this as a safe operating procedure. You could *so easily* kill us all right now . . .

"All right, another two centimeters and it looks like the hatch will open. And . . . it's . . . there. Can you go a little further inward, just to be safe? Good. Can you see this? It looks perfectly clear from where I'm standing. Can you open the door?"

"Indeed," Bruno said.

But it was Muddy who was closest, and so he was the one

who unstrapped himself, slid down the now-diagonal floor, and threw the latches. There was a huffing noise as the equalization valves kicked in. Bruno's ears popped; the pressure was lower on Deliah's side.

The door swung open, and a platinum-haired woman in a grease-smeared yellow pantsuit burst through. With hardly a glance, she threw her arms around Muddy and kissed him soundly on the cheek. "My hero!"

Muddy squawked and tried to pull away. "I'm Muddy, madam. Your hero is over there. Please, *please*, you're hurting me."

"You're *both* my heroes," she insisted breathlessly, and launched herself uphill at Bruno who, to tell the truth, reacted much as Muddy had. They were neither one of them too comfortable with displays of gratitude. Some heroes.

in which the
lawbreaking accelerates

Deliah's face betrayed more curiosity than concern. "I don't understand, Bruno. Why did you change your name? What exactly did Marlon do?"

Muddy tensed at the question but, to his credit, did his best to answer politely. "That's a more personal inquiry than you suspect, madam. Pray you never discover the answer."

Bruno, who'd been ignoring the two so he could feed calculations into a pair of hypercomputers, looked up now and saw the need to intervene. "Ah. Deliah, you've hit upon a . . . delicate subject. Muddy has, until quite recently, been accumulating what we'll politely call 'deep psychological injuries.' All things considered I'd say he's coping rather well, but it's unwise—not to mention unkind—to press him. Once he's seen proper medical attention, he may feel more inclined to share his story, but for the moment even *I* don't know it. And perhaps we should take him at his word, that there are things we really don't want to know."

Muddy, not surprisingly, burst out crying at this.

Deliah blushed. Her folding chair—now a slim couch of padded white leather secured beside the fax machine—

creaked a little as she moved within her restraints. "I'm . . . sorry, uh, Muddy. I had no idea your troubles were so . . . That is to say . . . Urgh. When I first saw you, I thought you looked, um, festive, and so I . . ."

"Festive. Festive!" Muddy fingered the several gray tufts of hair sprouting from his wrinkled, mottled scalp, then touched his upturned nose, which was somewhat redder and wider than Bruno's own. His cheeks were ruddier, too. Muddy wasn't restrained at all; he sat upon his couch, and through his tears an awkward chuckle escaped, and an unhappy smile, and he even managed a little bow in this sickening environment of *Sabadell-Andorra* under full sunward acceleration.

"I didn't mean—"

"No, no, the lady is most perceptive. Indeed, among . . . other activities . . . I was employed exactly as you surmise. You may say the word—I grant you my leave."

"Here now," Bruno tried. What he wanted to say was that Muddy might prove useful in the hours ahead, and his delicate-but-functional emotional state should not be tweaked or tampered with. But that sounded so cold, so calculating. If Muddy were Bruno himself, then fine; he could do whatever he pleased. People made copies for purposes both monumental and banal, and reconverged them with equal aplomb. Some even destroyed the copies after certain rough uses, with no reconvergence, no exchange of mental notes, or else they designed sacrificial copies that willingly destroyed themselves. *That* was a bitter pill for any enlightened society to swallow, but indeed, under Queendom law Bruno would be well within his rights to command Muddy's erasure as "spoilage."

For that matter, the Queendom itself could make such a ruling, and poor Muddy would have no recourse. This could hardly be called justice—indeed, such scenarios had inspired some of the century's most wrenching songs and dramas. And yet, the government *must* hold these powers, or all its planets would be stuffed pole to pole with cranky, unwanted faxes. If *that* wasn't a form of criminal trespass, then what was? A hundred million of the same compulsive, neurotic narcissist? No thank you!

But still, he found reason to doubt. From the look on her face, it seemed clear that Deliah knew exactly what Muddy was talking about, while Bruno himself had no idea. This was hardly the rapport one expected between duplicates, or even brothers.

"Say the word," Muddy repeated.

Deliah struggled with it for a few seconds before finally giving in. "Jester."

Still weeping, Muddy bowed again, then carefully slid off his couch until his feet were on the deck. "Jester. Indeed. I *am* festive, a plaything, a joke between friends. Shall I defy my nature, and gallivant about the solar system with *this* foul hero?" He jerked an elbow in Bruno's direction. "Or shall I drug myself insensible, and spare you both my company? The latter, I think. This place is filled with pain."

As he spoke, he tiptoed gingerly over the supine form of Hugo, still strapped to the floor and apparently content there. He advanced on Deliah, or rather on the fax orifice beside her, and she pulled away as much as her restraints allowed, her face betraying a familiar mix of guilt and mortification.

Ignoring her, Muddy extended a hand to the fax, which anticipated his request and spat a pill into his waiting palm, along with a glass of something that definitely wasn't water. He popped the drug into his mouth and gulped it immediately, then winced in pain and downed, in two big gulps, the amber fluid in the glass. His sobbing renewed as he put the glass back in the fax again. Then, head down, he trudged back to his couch, settled down on it, and strapped himself in.

"Apologies, Laureate-Director," he said to Deliah, through his tears. "It isn't you. I'd no doubt embarrass myself no matter what you did or said. I'm *intended* to embarrass a certain de Towaji, but I've disowned him. Let him find his own humiliations."

Then he closed his eyes and feigned sleep, and soon enough the heavy rise and fall of his chest was no act.

"I'm so very sorry," Deliah said, to no one specific.

Bruno was gruff. "Blame your friend Marlon. If you doubt the malice of his intentions, there's your proof right there. That any human being should be so mistreated . . ."

"Marlon's not like that, Bruno. He really isn't."

"He is," Bruno insisted. "Unless someone a thousand times *more* evil has constructed Muddy to frame him. False memories, false Iscog trace . . . I know of exactly two people bright enough and patient enough to pull off that trick, and one of them *is* Marlon."

"Who is the other?"

Bruno's face grew warm. "Oh, all right then; possibly several others could do it. If we're to live forever, no doubt any number of surprises and infamies will assail us. People can accomplish anything, given sufficient time. This isn't the last sick fantasy we'll see played out in our lifetimes."

"No," she mused, "I suppose it isn't. But *Marlon?*"

"Occam's Razor would convict him; his guilt is the simplest explanation. And Deliah, I'm sorry to inform you that he keeps copies of *you* in his dungeons as well. I have Muddy's word on it, at any rate."

That clearly knocked her back. Perhaps he could have broached the matter more delicately. Ah, that worlds-renowned de Towaji charm.

The two of them were silent a long time.

Finally, Deliah said, "I had a personal relationship with Marlon at one time. He was upset about the way it broke off, and I suppose in some sense I don't blame him. But I couldn't help it; I really couldn't. Love is the bane of the immortal, I've always said. Are we cheating God by living forever? If so, he gets us back with nagging doubts, and silly dreams of silly perfection. It must have been easier in the days when marriage meant a decade or two of hard work and squalor, then a simple, horrible death. All choices would be permanent in that time, and thus simple. You want to grow old and die alone? No? Then grab a hand and hold it tight! Today, the question is a lot harder to answer, because we know *someplace* there's a perfect mate, or at least an optimal one, whom we have only to find and meet. Perfect love! So the thought of spending eternity with anything less becomes appalling. But are we supposed to meet everyone? Shake every hand, kiss every mouth, listen to every bit of passionate nonsense until we're *completely, viscerally sure*? What a stupid, lonely quest that is."

"Finding such love can be as bad, I fear," Bruno said morosely. His chin was resting on his hand. "Perfect love, yes: it bends and compels you, it crowds out every other passion. Love is sublime, truly, a precious gift. But also, alas, one of God's little pranks. It's naive of you to confuse love and happiness, as if they were somehow the same thing. In fact love, once found, is more akin to gravity: too strong, too close, and it will crush you. Unless you're careful, always."

She twirled, absently, one of her platinum-colored braids. "There are so many theories about why you and Tamra split up."

"Theories, humph." He leaned back and crossed his arms. "It couldn't be simpler: we fought too much. We did come from opposite sides of the Earth, after all. The antipodes, as she used to say. Love does nothing about the friction of misunderstanding; if anything, it exacerbates the problem. And thirty years really is a long time to spend with one person. Back then it seemed like a lifetime, but of course that was a foolish perception. We were young, and the lives ahead of us so long."

"I didn't know you fought," Deliah said, surprised. "You always looked so happy together."

"Didn't we?" Bruno agreed. "But there was just so much baggage there. My family wasn't wealthy—a restaurateur and a small-time politician—but at University, after the earthquake, I started to have some money. Far more than any teenage orphan should have, really, and by the time I was thirty, even before Tamra's lawyers got behind me, it had mushroomed beyond all sense. My reaction was predictable: an excess of excess. Drugs, women, miniature planets . . . It was just a phase, but I was still in it when she summoned me to court. She was so vulnerable—I mean, *her* parents had just died, one right after the other, and like me she'd been thrust into a very public role which small-town life had never groomed her for. I was older, and I'd been through all that, and she turned to me in, just, absolute desperation. I suppose I took advantage."

Seeing Deliah's querying look, he sighed and expanded, "It was two or three years before she had the courage to demand my fidelity. I found it difficult to refuse a beautiful woman, and they were *all* so beautiful, so drawn to that complex of youth and wealth and power . . . I had no charm, no guile, no 'sizzle,' as we used to say back then. But I had brains and money, as well as Tamra herself: I was that forbidden morsel from the Queen's private garden. But none of those ladies were ever worth the pain they caused. It makes me physically ill to think of it now."

"But you're the one who left," Deliah said, looking as if she was struggling to comprehend. Bruno, who'd been summarily classified and pigeonholed and speculated about for as long as he cared to remember, was flattered that anyone would actually struggle to comprehend him.

"You're a good friend," he said, nodding. "I've never talked about this. It feels good to get it off my chest. Yes, I was the one who left. By then I'd been faithful and accommodating for two decades, but my work had been suffering for it. And I drank too much. I always drank too much."

"Alcohol?"

"Indeed. Crude, I know, and I always expected the media to expose me for it. But like the womanizing, it was something they just didn't want to find out about. I never understood that. I never understood much of anything back then, and the *arc de fin* was beckoning, and I had this *whole planet* to retreat to. So I left, yes. Some would call it an escape; some would say I ran from my problems instead of solving them, but that too is naive. In solitude, I found the clarity I needed. My work flourished, my vices fell away like child-hood. I'm a better person today; I truly am. Or a bigger fool, perhaps, but that's nearly as good."

"But we miss you, Bruno. Everyone misses you. There's never been another Philander, not really."

"Oh, pish. I was always an embarrassment. Like that time on Maxwell Montes, when I threw up at the banquet table. Drinking again, after all those years. Throwing money around, insulting the hostess . . . What a wretched night!"

"That *was* embarrassing," Deliah admitted, cracking a doleful half smile. "You had toilet paper on your shoe, also. And that silly hat of yours was in fashion for all of about three months. But we followed you up that mountain, Bruno. All of us did."

He cocked an eyebrow. "You were there?"

"Yeah, that was right after my laureacy. I took over the Ministry of Grapples only a few years afterward, from this really pleasant man who wound up doing cryoastronomy in Russia. Talk about your happy demotions! But, I mean, yes, I was there. And you were brilliant, you really were. You proba-bly are a terrible manager, but you're also the sort who makes footsteps other people want to follow in, constantly—it's your default state."

Bruno had nothing to say to that.

She pressed. "Bruno, is hiding away on your private planet really the best thing you could be doing? I don't personally need an *arc de fin*—I'm not sure anyone does. And, seriously, we do miss you."

"The planet's gone," he told her. "Destroyed. Used up."

"Oh. Well, I'm sorry."

He shrugged. "Perhaps it served its purpose."

"Tamra misses you," she added thoughtfully.

"We have forever," he said, and shrugged again. But that felt shallow, unjust. "I miss her, too. I wish I'd been better for her."

Deliah stared at him for several seconds, her eyes growing sad.

"We all make mistakes. Marlon was one of mine, I guess. But I think you're wrong about him, Bruno. I . . . God, I'd like to think I'm not *that* stupid."

Bruno should have offered some words of comfort for that, some reassurance. He *wanted* to reassure her, this good friend he hadn't really known he had. But what could he say? That it was all right? That she'd failed to recognize the monster because she had no monster in herself? He couldn't bring himself to say that; the lapse was inexcusable. Not only on her part, but on his, on everyone's.

Seeing that he wasn't going to answer, Deliah turned away.

"I'm sorry," he offered. It was the best he could do.

In times of distress, Bruno retreated into his work. This day was no exception. And he could *use* the work, too, because in retrospect there were all kinds of things wrong with the ertial shield and the design of the *Sabadell-Andorra,* and for clarity's sake he wanted to know exactly where he and Muddy had gone wrong. It wasn't a vain undertaking—a detailed understanding of the ship's flaws might well save their lives in the coming hours.

"I'm very happy to be rescued," Deliah said after a while. Her tone was more serious now, and Bruno turned to face her. "From the . . . depths of my heart I thank you for that. But I was *this* close." She held up two fingers, pinching the air between them. "Death and I were on speaking terms. He'd taken three good people right in front of me, and afterward I had a lot of time to contemplate, and not much else to do. People don't have that experience anymore, and I definitely wouldn't recommend it as recreation or any such thing. But still it's a very purifying thing, to finally look at your life from the outside. And to be reborn afterwards!

"Maybe it's like your decades of solitude, only more compressed, and more urgent. I don't think I can go back to being the same person I was. Or I *could,* maybe, but what a waste it would be! Of hard-won insight. This whole Laureate-Director thing has been very interesting—I've learned a lot about so many different things—but am I supposed to do it *forever*? Or until someone better comes along and replaces me, I guess, but even that . . . I'm more *person* than that. Every person is so much more than the paths they've taken, those few particular paths we choose on the spur of the moment, with no information. So much of it is mistakes.

"I'm not saying this very well. It's a straightforward thing, though: I want to change, not what I am but what I *do* with what I am. Surely it behooves us, as immortal people, to find the time to start over. Otherwise, we're just living the same time, over and over again."

"There is the small matter," Bruno reminded her, "of rescuing the sun from collapse." He was suddenly cross, and hadn't the energy to conceal it.

"Oh," she said, seeming to come awake. "Yes, there is that." Then she frowned, not at Bruno but at herself. "Here I'm blithely assuming you've figured it all out. You must get so tired of that! To be so relentlessly relied upon, when inside you're just like everyone else. Smarter, obviously, but there are lots of smart people who don't get . . . I don't know . . . scapegoated that way. Even myself, who should have known better than to let this all happen."

Bruno nodded, somewhat mollified. "To be relied upon, yes. It's burdensome. Maybe *that's* why I left."

"Hmm. I never thought of it that way. I suppose you probably have a lot to say on that subject."

"Er," he hedged, not wanting to be drawn in again. "Perhaps a little later."

"Oh." Deliah, who'd had some small experience dealing with physicists, smiled a little and clapped him on the arm. "You've started working. I wasn't disturbing you before, but I am now."

That only made him feel sheepish. "It's not that I don't want to talk, Deliah. I do. It's very rude, I know."

"Can I help with what you're doing?"

Bruno thought about that. "You probably could, if we had more time. A week, perhaps. But I'm too many layers deep, in matters I'd be very poor at explaining. As the designated scapegoat, I need to press on with this alone."

She nodded. "I understand."

"I suppose you do," he said sincerely, "and I appreciate it. It's quite uncommon."

He turned back to his analyses.

As often happened when he was engaged in such activity, time passed. Quite a lot of it, actually, until Deliah became restless and—against all advice—unstrapped herself to "stretch her legs." This involved her pacing back and forth in the cabin's quite narrow confines, which of course Bruno found very distracting, and couldn't quite keep himself from complaining about.

"Well," Deliah said, trying to be polite but with frustration and boredom written all over her, "I appreciate the rescue; I really do. But it's difficult to lie still on a couch for sixteen hours with no one to talk to and nothing to do. Sixteen hours is splendidly fast for such a monumental journey—five hundred light minutes, almost sixty AU. And I thought *I* was moving fast, covering that same distance in a week! But I'm a person who needs to be busy. With the Iscog down, I can't access libraries or entertainments or anything, and with you and this 'Muddy' down I can't have a conversation . . ." She looked around the cabin, her eyes settling on Hugo. "What's this thing? A servant?"

"Oh, uh, actually a sort of pet," Bruno answered distractedly.

"Mewl," Hugo answered, as if aware of the attention.

"May I release it?"

"What? Er, I'd rather you didn't. It tends to get into trouble, which under present circumstances hardly seems a good idea. It seems content enough where it is, yes?"

Deliah sighed. "The perfect pet for you, Declarant; it requires no attention. Shall I redecorate the cabin, here? It's really . . . Well, I guess 'spartan' is hardly the word for something done up in gold and lapis lazuli, but it's not very *pleasing.* You're hoping to rescue Her Majesty in this? It ought to be more regal, then."

Hrumph. Her Majesty could be rescued in a clear plastic bag for all Bruno cared. Still it might be nice to surprise her, particularly if he didn't have to do anything special himself. She *would* find this ship ugly. "Do you know her tastes?"

Deliah shrugged. "Probably not as well as you do. I see her palace in the entertainments and such, but the closest I've been in person is the beach outside."

Bruno waved a hand. "Well, then you know more than I. The decorations I recall are all forty years out of date. No doubt they've become mortifyingly ugly in that time. Are you at all fashionable?"

Deliah blushed a little. "I come from an African sun farm, Bruno. And I grew up to be a shepherd of physicists. *I* like my styles, anyway."

Bruno laughed. "Ah. Well. *Having* a style makes you more fashionable than I've ever been. Have at it, yes, by all means, although I'll ask you to leave Muddy's control panel as it is, along with these interfaces." He indicated his dual hyper-computers. "And try not to jerk the couches out from under us."

"I'll work around them," Deliah agreed, less enthusiastically than before. Suddenly, he understood: redecoration had not been a serious suggestion. She'd been pressing him with its absurdity, hoping he'd suggest something else, or maybe just talk to her. But now, with his approval, she was stuck with actually doing it. He sympathized; it *was* hard to get excited about busywork. But at the moment, he had no other suggestions for her. At least they weren't dying yet.

After that, they left each other alone for a good long while. There were some noises, and Deliah talked to herself occasionally, but soon he was engrossed enough not to find it distracting. Actually, it was he who eventually distracted himself, when a rumbling in his belly reminded him how long it had been since his last meal. Reluctantly, he pried himself away from the work, and unfastened his harness.

"Well hello," Deliah said as he rose—slowly and carefully—from his couch.

"Hi," he muttered back to her, then realized he should probably be more polite. "Good, ah, afternoon."

He looked around, and immediately wondered just how long he'd been working. The place looked utterly different; where there'd been lapis walls and decks of jade, now there were cedarwood panels and bricks of red clay, and carpets and cushions in the pattern of animal skins that seemed, oddly enough, to go very well with the existing controls. A folding screen of black wood and white paper hid the little toilet, and opposite that, beside where Hugo lay, was a crackling fireplace, wooden logs blazing merrily behind a pane of sooty glass. There was *heat* coming out of it in considerable quantity.

"Good night!" he exclaimed. "What have you done? Is that *safe*?"

"The fire?" she asked, following his gaze. "Oh, sure, perfectly. It's a broad-spectrum holographic panel. I thought it was a little cold in here anyway; the temperature control loops for life support were fairly primitive."

"We were in a hurry."

"I'm sure. But this is nicer, don't you think?"

Thinking about it for a moment, he found he had to agree. "It is, yes." He walked over to it, careful not to lose his balance or step on poor Hugo. He held his hands out. "The heat is unevenly distributed. It seems to come from the coals and flames themselves."

"Oh, sure," she agreed, "the hologram includes thermal IR in the five to twelve-micron range, where it radiates best through air. It's distinguishable from a real fire—you can't open the glass, for one thing—but it's just as nice for our purpose. You've never seen one before? There used to be a folding variety you could carry in your pocket. You'd charge it up with sunlight and set it anywhere you liked."

"Carry in your pocket? Without being burned?"

She smiled. "The heat-emitting surfaces activate when you open it, silly. Wouldn't you design it that way?"

"I suppose so," he allowed. As if he'd ever stoop to designing something so inane. But life was *long,* as he'd said. With eternity stretching before him, perhaps he'd do all manner of silly things. Perhaps he'd be known, in future times, as an immensely silly man who once invented a few big things, in his overly serious youth. What a thought! Then again, perhaps he'd be killed in the next few hours. Perhaps the Queendom would fall, and save history the trouble of remembering him at all.

"I need food," he observed. He walked to the fax and demanded a walnut-and-celery sandwich, which it surrendered readily enough. A glass of milk soon followed, and an apple, and a Venusian plibble, and a basket of sliced potatoes fried in pork grease. Gods, he *was* hungry.

"With any luck," he said when he was done eating, "Tamra has already been rescued, and we can turn our attention immediately to the Ring Collapsiter."

"Unlikely," Deliah answered seriously. "The last communications I overheard were a good five days ago, but there was a lot of complaining among the spaceship captains and crews. They kept dying, or being ejected from the solar system like me. There were just too many mass anomalies slinging around, on chaotic trajectories. No way to navigate, no safe place to rest. Maybe it's improved since then . . ."

"But probably not," Bruno concluded. Probably, a lot of collapsium *had* been ejected, and he supposed some of it might have overcome the odds and collided with a planet or other body, perhaps the sun itself. Indeed, they might already be too late! But the bulk of it would still be down there in interplanetary space, interacting chaotically but nonetheless trapped in gravitational contours.

He glanced up, expecting to see the pinpoint of Sol through the window. No such luck: the view was dim, dappled with stars he couldn't immediately identify.

"We've turned around already? We've crossed Neptune's orbit?" he asked, surprised.

"Uh-huh," Deliah said, surprised by his surprise. "I'm

pretty sure we cross *Uranus'* orbit in a few minutes. You really have been in a trance, haven't you?"

"So it would seem."

"Grappling the sun is a felony, by the way. If you didn't know. What's our deceleration anchor? I've been wondering. I suppose we're simply attached to my station?"

"Correct," Bruno said, nodding distractedly. "Yes, we're pulling on it pretty hard. In spite of its mass, it may well have been dragged below solar escape velocity by now. Perhaps it'll fall back into the inner system as a comet someday."

"Oh, what a charming thought! It wouldn't have a tail, though, would it?"

"No. Not unless it picks up some volatiles between now and then. And I can't imagine where it would find any. I was referring more to the shape of its orbit. Highly elliptical, like a comet."

Bruno looked over at Muddy's trajectory display, still an engraved plaque of wellstone bronze. Indeed, the orbit of Neptune was hours behind them, with the orbit of Bruno's own former world several hours beyond that. And the ship really was about to cross the orbit of Uranus. In fact, on the scale of the display it looked like they'd cross the actual planet itself.

"Er, ship," he said mildly, "how close are we going to come to the planet Uranus?"

"Eight hundred twenty thousand kilometers," the ship replied immediately.

"I see. That's within the gravitational sphere of influence, isn't it?"

"Affirmative," the ship agreed.

"Hmm. Probability of striking particulate matter in the vicinity of the planet?"

"Eleven percent, for objects one microgram or larger." The ship's voice was cheerful, gender neutral, unimpressed.

"I see. And when, exactly, will we be crossing the planet's ring plane?"

"Five minutes, nineteen seconds." It paused. "Danger is minimal, sir," it then offered. "Probability of damage to the impervium is two point six times ten to the minus eleventh percent. Is that acceptable?"

Relieved, Bruno snorted. "It sounds like the least of our problems. Indeed, yes, it's acceptable. Will we be passing close to any other planets?"

"Negative," the ship replied.

"Good. Excellent. Keep it that way. Oh, and ship?"

"Yes, sir?"

"Your name is *Sabadell-Andorra*."

"Excuse me, sir, library search. Sabadell and Andorra are geographic localities in northeastern Iberia, European continent, planet Earth." It paused for a moment, then cited a reference: date, Greenwich Mean Time, latitude and longitude of epicenter, and then a series of geological measurements intended to convey a sense of the magnitude and manner of the associated shock and vibration. "My library contains no other reference to a *Sabadell-Andorra*. Am I named for this event? An earthquake?"

"Uh, yes. Indeed."

"Acknowledged. Thank you, sir."

Deliah cleared her throat. "There's a library on board, Bruno?"

"Evidently. I mean, Muddy put the thing together; you'd have to ask him all the details, but it isn't the sort of thing *I'd* leave out. One needs these things sometimes."

"So I can watch movies? Read books? Peruse technical articles?"

"Er, well, old ones, yes. Was that not clear to you?"

Her annoyance, fortunately, was cheerful. "No, Declarant, it wasn't." Then, catching his own grumpy look, she said, "Serves me right, does it? Well, if I'm too much trouble, you can always put me back where you found me."

"Later," he said, in mock warning. "There isn't time for it right now." He grew more serious. "There really isn't. Marlon sent Muddy to me almost three weeks ago, and it was a taunt he expected me to answer. Or hoped I would, at any rate. If my network gate had been functional when Muddy's image was transmitted, I'd've had time to build some more conventional means of transport. Three weeks isn't a long time to travel fifty AU, not in a fusion-powered ship that has to lug its own fuel along, but it certainly *could* be done. So he must have had some schedule in mind that would prevent my interference. Whatever grand finale he has in store, it can't be very far off."

Deliah sobered as well. "You lost more than half a day to come get me, going *away* from the sun rather than toward it."

Bruno shrugged. "It couldn't be helped. You knew where to find the Queen."

"No, I could have told you that over the radio. You could have let me die; it's what any reasonable person would have done." She waved a finger in his face. "Your heart is soft."

"Soft enough to endanger the Queendom," he grumbled. "All right, then. If we *are* too late, there's no one to blame but myself."

Deliah, seeming surprisingly immune to the effects of the ship's lopsided inertia, came forward and kissed him on the forehead. "There's Marlon to blame, as you keep reminding me. Bruno, I'm not sure people actually *expect* you to come swooping in to save the day. We're in the middle of history's greatest calamity, and *I* certainly never expected to survive it. If you're not finally able to salvage anything, well, at least you've tried."

"I should have seen this coming," Bruno brooded.

"So should I," Deliah said. "So should Tamra. So should everyone else who's ever been friends with the man. And the police, too; tracing his involvement in all the grapple accidents is their job, not yours. But I guess Marlon's outfoxed us all."

"Humpf," Bruno said, which pretty well summed up his opinion on that matter.

Deliah's eyes widened, drawn upward to something above and behind Bruno. "Look!" she said.

He turned, and immediately regretted the wave of nausea this sudden movement brought. But he saw what she was pointing at: a little dome of blue at the bottom edge of the window, with three brightish pinpoints hovering above it. Uranus and its moons? The dome climbed and grew in the view; in half a minute, the whole planet would be visible.

He reached out to give Muddy's leg a shake. "Wake up. Wake up! You'll want to see this. At least, I think you will . . ."

Muddy, who was fully reclined in his couch, groggily opened his eyes. "What? What's that? Oh. Mmm. You're very kind to wake me, Lordship, but actually, I've seen planets before." And with that he turned away and fell back into stuporous sleep.

Impressive views have a way of saturating the mind; the planet was visible for a good twenty minutes, but never so large or close as that first stunning glimpse. And really, the planet didn't have any features to speak of, just a uniform, powder-green haze sinking down for thousands upon thousands of kilometers. The world was huge, able to contain a dozen Earths, but it shrank quickly, becoming a little ball and finally a bright green speck before disappearing down the other side of the window.

An hour and a half later, they crossed the orbit of Saturn, which of course was completely uneventful since the planet was nowhere nearby. An hour after that, they passed Jupiter's similarly empty orbit. Against the starscape soon afterward, they spotted a few bright, fast-moving specks that proved, under the enhancement of wellstone telescopes, to be asteroids. That was good for a few minutes' distraction, in the hour and a half it took them to reach the orbit of Mars.

Then the pace of things started to pick up. The ship was slowing down dramatically, now cruising at barely an eighth of its thirty-thousand-kilometer-per-second peak velocity, but the inner planets were a *lot* closer together than their outer cousins. Earth was barely twenty minutes beyond the Red

Planet, and *Sabadell-Andorra* had started picking up random bits of radio noise. Nothing useful—just data bursts and occasional, panicky voices—but it made clear that they'd reentered civilization, and that civilization, though deprived of both its communication networks and the more primitive means of physical travel, nonetheless still had some fight in it.

They encountered their share of gravitational anomalies, too: Iscog fragments and free-floating neubles ejected from some industrial site somewhere. Their course jinked around in a way that worried Bruno. Finding the sun was not too difficult, but finding Tamra's little di-clad neutronium work platform in the sun's glare might very well be. Especially if their own course was misplotted. It wasn't like they could ping the Iscog for their precise location. These thoughts made him impatient.

Still, the view above them was naught but stars, the sun invisible below their feet, the planets hidden by distance and geometry. Even civilization was large, consisting mostly of empty space. Even an inertialess grappleship needed some time to cross through. To reach the orbit of Venus took them another twelve minutes, by which time they'd shed 95% of their velocity and were rapidly shedding the rest. Mercury was deep in the sun's gravitational sink, farther from Venus than Earth was. They'd need thirty-six minutes more to reach it. From there, though, it should only be a few more minutes to reach the platform where Tamra and her entourage supposedly awaited rescue. Assuming their course was proper . . .

Once again, Bruno shook Muddy awake.

Once again, Muddy responded groggily and tried to go back to sleep.

"Oh, no, no," Bruno said this time. "I don't know what you took, or how much, but I'll wager it wasn't what *I'd* picked for you. So okay, you've had a little break from yourself, but you get up and fly this ship now, Declarant-Philander; you've yet to teach me how to do it myself. Go on, take something to wake up if you like, but we need you at the controls."

"Hmmpf," Muddy replied, opening bloodshot eyes to peer at him. "Where are we?"

"Just sunward of Venus. We've just about half an hour to go, and you'll need to start scanning for Tamra's platform."

"Hmmpf," Muddy said again, though in a livelier, more interested way. "That far, are we? Yes, I s-s-suppose I *should* be getting up, despite all the misery that entails. I can take a pill, you say?"

"Muddy, so long as you're awake and alert you can take any damned thing you please. We'll sort your problems out later, right?"

"All right, yes."

He struggled out of his couch, fell squarely atop a mewling Hugo, and made his way to the fax machine, which insisted on giving him a chilled electrolyte solution before dispensing any medication. From the look on Muddy's face, it tasted none too wonderful.

"All right?" Bruno asked, when Muddy finally settled back down into his couch.

"Please, if you would, wait for the drugs to take effect." Muddy's voice was thick and slow.

"I'll do no such thing. Begin scanning, please."

"Well, aye, Your Lordship."

"You've learned sarcasm in your years away."

"And you've learned to be a prick. Beginning scan, sir. The ship is perfectly capable of doing this by itself, you know. Navigation and helm control, too. The instrument panel is just for fun, as I'm sure you've probably guessed. Well, it does make a *few* things easier—whoa. Scan complete; I've found a platform. Would you like a telescopic image?"

"Please."

A holographic window appeared in the brick wall beside Bruno's head. On it, he could clearly see a thin disc of opaque but gloriously shiny white. Di-clad neutronium, yes, spinning slowly in the sunlight. And, pinned to the bottom of the disc as if glued there, the somewhat larger shape of a police cruiser, whose battered hull had apparently reverted to native iron, its wellstone sheathing dead or inactivated.

"Is the dome intact?" Bruno asked rhetorically. The clear

dome that held in the platform's air was pointed away from them at the moment, pointed straight down at the full fires of the sun.

"Looks like someone *did* get to them," Deliah observed. "It must have been a hell of a trip."

"And an unfortunate one," Bruno said. "It doesn't look as though that cruiser set down there peacefully. Look at that hull: the bending, the stress ripples. Do you see any lights on it?"

"I'm compensating for sunlight," Muddy volunteered. "We're looking almost straight down. There may be lights that are simply drowned out. But I'm doubtful—that iron looks partly melted to me."

"Indeed," Bruno said. "Any signs of air leakage?"

Muddy checked. "No, sir. No signs of air at all, not even traces in the immediate vicinity."

"They might have spacesuits on," Deliah said.

"There'd still be traces," Muddy sniffed. "That hull's been devoid of life for at least a day. Probably longer. The air blew out and crystallized, and the s-s-solar wind has carried away the evidence."

"Well, then," Bruno said. "Rest in peace, brave men and women of the Royal Constabulary. Here's yet another tragedy to lay at the feet of Marlon Sykes."

Deliah pointed. "Here comes the dome. It looks intact!"

The platform's slow rotation was turning the shipwreck back down to face the punishing sunlight, and turning the dome—the only place that might yet harbor survivors—toward the cold blackness of space. Bruno's heart sank. Intact or no, the dome's contents would undergo brutal thermal cycles, heating up probably to several hundred degrees at peak, and then bleeding it all away again, bottoming out probably well below freezing. Living tissue did, of course, have its compensating mechanisms, its exothermic metabolism and its evaporative cooling, its circulatory system to refresh chilled or overheated tissues with milder fluids from the body's interior. Ironically, human beings stood up to such punishment better than many inanimate objects, better even than the clothing and shoes that should nominally be protecting them. Indeed, the Queen and her people had allegedly survived at least six revolutions of the platform before Deliah had lost contact with them. But *two weeks*? It seemed impossible that even the hardiest of humans could survive *that*.

Could the neutronium's enormous mass serve as a heat sink? No, of course not—it had been basking out here in full sunlight for years! Its temperature would have equalized long ago, probably to something uncomfortably warm. Well, at least diamond was a good thermal conductor—it *would* pull heat from the sunward face, and radiate it away on the opposite side, in the cold shadows. That might help, though just how much . . .

As the platform continued to turn, its habitable side swung slowly into view, and Bruno could see—to his incalculable relief—that beneath the diamond dome were a handful of loose, soft-looking silver cones, like little tents made of reflective fabric.

"What's inside those?" he demanded, pointing at them on the display. "Is anyone alive?"

"I'm not able to tell," Muddy answered gruffly, with no real sign of relief or concern in his voice. This was one of his symptoms—apathy regarding anyone but himself and Bruno, who still *was* himself in some very meaningful ways. But apathy even about Her Majesty?

Bruno waved impatient hands. "They're what, sheets of impervium cloth?"

"Bunkerlite, I think, or some near equivalent. Super-reflectors, anyway."

"They must have gotten their fax machine working," Deliah said, and at least the relief was evident in *her* voice.

"So they could be alive," Bruno dared to say. "*Sabadell-Andorra*, please attempt to establish radio contact. Muddy, are we on course to arrive there?"

"Nearly," Muddy said. "We'll need a minor adjustment. I'm moving the grapple anchor to Venus . . ."

"Not the inhabited areas, surely?"

"Uh, checking. No. Not the inhabited areas."

"Still illegal," Deliah noted.

The ship bucked around them; if they hadn't been strapped to their couches, the companions would all have tumbled like tenpins.

"Now we are on course," Muddy said. "Arrival in twenty minutes. There's a problem, though—our course intercepts a loose fragment of Ring Collapsiter. What happens if that contacts the ertial shield?"

"Oh, I'm not certain," Bruno admitted. "And I doubt very much that we want to find out. But we *do* have to pass this way. For my comfort, let's miss this thing by at least a kilometer."

"Aye, Lordship." Muddy said. Then, "Unfortunately, we appear to be headed directly for it. We'll miss by meters, if at all."

"Heavens! Is there anything to hook to for a plane change? North or south, it doesn't matter; we just need to get some small distance between ourselves and the plane of the Ring Collapsiter."

"Oh, sir. No. We've spent the last sixteen hours pulling ourselves ever more precisely *into* that plane, and no, there isn't anything near at hand we can grapple to, to pull us out of it again."

"The poles of Venus, perhaps?"

Muddy burst into tears. "Alas, no! We have to strike our targets with a nearly perpendicular beam. Venus itself is out of our plane, but not *enough* out of it. We could attach to its equator, and given enough time . . . Pointless. We haven't enough time."

"Blast. Can we *stop*?"

"Not quickly enough, sir." Muddy wiped at his tears—a futile gesture, since the flow of fresh ones hadn't abated. "Remember, we're at full deceleration already. Oblivion, what a miserable ass I am. What a perfect servant of Declarant Sykes. I've killed you at last, sir, within reach of your goal."

"Oh, nonsense. Everyone makes mistakes. You've *my* distracted brain to do your thinking with, and that's a burden I wouldn't wish on Sykes himself. Time to impact?"

"Um, seventeen minutes."

"Enough time to think of something. How about your emergency propulsion system? The compressed oxygen apparatus?"

Muddy brightened. "I'd all but forgotten about that. Yes! What a thought, that something of my design should prove useful." He hammered a series of calculations into the interfaces before him. "There is enough time, yes. It's very low thrust, in comparison with our present velocity, but if we activate it immediately, we'll miss the collapsium by half a kilometer. Is that enough?"

Bruno tried to think of some way to confirm it, and finally—to his deep chagrin—was forced to shrug. "I don't know, Muddy. I guess it'll have to be."

in which old
demons are faced

Bruno sweated some as the wayward fragment approached.
He pulled up images of it on a gravitational anomaly scanner;
a thin loop of collapsium a thousand kilometers long. It
should have appeared arrow-straight, just the tiniest slice of a
huge circle stretching clear around the sun, but the piece had
begun to pull in on itself, to twist, to curl. It seemed to be
part of a ring much smaller than the collapsiter itself, one
that might fit around the equator of Earth's moon, or even a
medium-sized asteroid. It was kinked in places, too, its structural rigidity slowly failing. In another few weeks it would
probably curl enough to double back on itself, with probably
calamitous results. Did it *have* a few weeks? He checked its
trajectory and found it was indeed in a rather sedate solar orbit, with perihelion nearly a million kilometers above the
chromopause. An orbit that might continue indefinitely, in
the absence of disturbing influences.

There *were* influences, though; the nearby construction
platform, for one. And his sensors picked up all sorts of other,
indistinct mass concentrations at the edges of his detection
range. No doubt there were a thousand other fragments just

.

like this one, caroming about in the limited space inside Mercury's orbit. Eventually, this fragment would run afoul of one of those others, and its orbit would ratchet upward or downward. Eventually, one of them would surely fall straight in. There could be no doubt of that.

The backup thrusters hummed; hundreds of tiny, temporary channels through the wellstone outer hull, accelerating heavy oxygen ions, one by one, to relativistic speeds. This, too, was probably illegal: an exhaust much deadlier than the typical fusion helium, and deadlier at a much greater range, too. They could probably cook a human from a light-second away.

"Thirty s-s-seconds to closest approach," Muddy warned.

"Hmm. Here we go, then."

"It's been an honor working with you, sir."

"Likewise," Deliah chipped in.

"Oh, nonsense. I couldn't have done any of this alone. We all have the greatest respect for each other, et cetera, et cetera."

"Twenty seconds."

He became acutely aware of his breathing. He wondered if it was loud, if it maybe should be a little slower and quieter.

"Ten seconds. Five. Four, three, two . . ."

And then, suddenly, there it was in the window above them—a long, slender piece glowing brightly with the familiar Cerenkov blue. The ertial shield hadn't twitched in the slightest, hadn't reacted at all. The collapsium itself seemed similarly unaffected, not falling in on itself in their wake or anything. They continued past, seeing more and more of it, the fragment growing longer and dimmer and loopier in the window view. Then the last of it trailed by, and they were in clear space again.

"Backup thrusters off," Muddy said. The humming stopped.

Deliah let a long breath out. "That wasn't so bad."

"No," Bruno agreed. Not bad at all. Some day, he'd have to work out the theory of it all, the precise interactions between collapsium and hypercollapsite. The weak link was surely the collapsium, it being so much less dense, so much more subject to gravity and inertia and the various other interactions of the zero-point field. His fear had been the crushing of its lattice, and its resulting reversion to a chain of heavy, disconnected, uncontrollable hypermasses capable of all sorts of harm. But perhaps the two could live together in harmony after all. At half a kilometer's distance, anyway!

"Platform contact in two minutes," Muddy said. He seemed to enjoy counting down event times—a task at once useful and easy and safe.

"Good," Bruno acknowledged. "Can we have the telescope image back?"

Wordlessly, Muddy reached for his interface. The window reappeared, now showing a much larger, more detailed version of what they'd seen before. The dome was there, and the mirrored tents beneath it. Now there were other things visible as well: light-energy conversion panels with cables running across the diamond deck until they slipped under the edges of superreflective cloth. Discs of various color arranged in neat rows outside the tents, as if occupied in some sort of experiment. And one image that was both horrifying and uplifting: the blackened, burned skeleton of a human being. Horrifying because, well, it was the blackened, burned skeleton of a human being. Uplifting because there was only one. Had the survivors dragged a fallen comrade outside, to burn rather than rot? It lent credence to the idea that there *were* survivors down there.

"My God," Deliah said.

That initial view had been oblique, almost edge-on, so it was difficult to make out any telling details as the platform turned away, turned its other, blank side to face them.

Now the shipwreck as well betrayed new details; he could clearly make out the lines of an airlock in its iron skin, and a seam where two plates had warped apart. There was a neat, circular hole through the side, too, down low where it was nearly hidden by shadow. As the platform revolved—and grew, for they were approaching it rapidly—he could see a matching hole down low on the ship's other side.

He experienced an instant chilling of the blood. He'd seen holes like that before, in the ruins of Sykes Manor. Holes created by a weapon, a nasen beam. That ship hadn't *crashed* onto the platform, hadn't limped its way here and quietly expired; it had been *murdered* in the very act of rescue!

"This is a trap," he said, as coolly and evenly as possible. "Someone is watching the platform, waiting to pick off any ship that approaches."

"My God!" Deliah squawked, with much greater conviction.

"I knew it!" Muddy wailed, suddenly tearful again. "I knew I'd get us killed! Declarant-Philander, there's nothing we can do! No place else to grapple to, not in the time allotted!"

"To the collapsium fragment above us?" Bruno suggested quickly.

"No!" Deliah said. "It's muon-contaminated—it'll come apart in seconds."

"We *will* rendezvous with the platform," Muddy insisted. "Nothing can prevent that now, no matter what we grapple to. Inertia can only be bent so far."

Bruno pounded a fist into his palm. "Blast it, a nasen beam isn't easy to aim! How's our oxygen supply?"

"Fine, sir," Muddy wearily replied.

"Good. Set your thrusters on a program of random firing. Stay on trajectory, but let our arrival time float, plus or minus a few seconds. That may confuse the targeting mechanisms. They don't have to miss us by much, so long as they miss us!"

Soon, an annoyingly staccato hum commenced in the outer hull. As before, no sense of motion resulted from it.

"Where is this nasen beam?" Deliah wanted to know.

Bruno shrugged. "I couldn't say. On a ship, probably, and not too near, or we'd've detected it already. It *could* be quite distant, in which case it likely wouldn't fire until we'd matched

courses with the platform. A known position—you see?—
regardless of light-lag delays. If we complete our rescue quickly,
the beam's . . . controller may not realize we're gone until after it's fired."

"Thirty seconds to contact," Muddy whined. "I'm *scared*,
Bruno. I don't want to do this!"

"Turn us!" Bruno shot back, with sudden inspiration.
"Make sure our hatch is facing the dome! And try to hit as
close to the dome's base as possible, without endangering the
neutronium cladding. It's all right to hit a little harder, just be
sure we *stick* when we hit, so we can start melting through
immediately. This is for your safety, Muddy; as you say, we
will hit."

"Ten seconds. Oh, God, can't we just let them die?"

The impact was sudden and severe; Bruno was thrown
against his restraints and slammed back into his couch again.
Muddy shrieked, and even Deliah cried out in distress.

Bruno's own fear was a brusque, impatient business. He
was frustrated, more than a little bit angry at being forced to
such extremity, and there was a substantial part of his mind
that dreamily refused to believe any of this was happening at
all. His thoughts, such as they were, were focused on Tamra.
In those hurried moments as he threw off his harness and
leaped for the door, his own safety concerned him mainly to
the extent that it was linked with hers—he couldn't very well
save her if he got himself killed. So he moved very quickly until he was poised to open the door, then froze in place.

He welcomed the sizzling sound when it began; this wellstone chemistry would get him through to Her Majesty as
quickly and safely as possible.

Muddy continued wailing. Hugo mewled. Deliah, rising
from her own couch, asked, "Is there anything I should be
doing right now?"

Bruno, in his singularly single-minded state, ignored them
all. "Ship," he said, as another inspiration struck, "are your
grapples still locked on Venus?"

"Negative," the ship replied. "The rotation of the platform makes that impossible."

"What's the largest object handy? The sun? Obviously, yes. Can you lock onto that?"

"Intermittently," the ship agreed.

"Good. Do it, and engage the grapples as soon as possible. This platform is damned heavy, but with the ertial shield we may be able to drag it out of place. At least a little. Perhaps a little is all we need. Now then, please paint a line on the interior to mark the thickness and position of the dome."

"Instruction unclear," the ship replied apologetically.

Blast it, his old house had been well accustomed to half-nonsense commands like that. "Paint a line, you! Show me where the dome is, the edge of the dome against your hull!"

"Like this?"

A pinkish red area the size of Bruno's torso appeared on the inner surface of the hatch. Was this what he wanted? He waited for a moment and verified that yes, indeed, the circle was growing. Soon it became a hollowed-out oval, roughly as deep as Bruno's hand and encircling an area as large as his body. It swelled outward slowly as the side of the ship sank its way in through the diamond structure of the dome.

"When this completely encircles the hatch," he said, pointing to the pink line, "stop burrowing and await further instructions. I'm going to open this door and exit the ship. Er, exit *you*. When I come back in and close the door, break contact immediately and take us out of here. Let the dome decompress, and just grapple to anything you like. If there's no target handy, use the backup thrusters."

"Understood, sir."

The outside of the painted line advanced past the corners of the hatchway. The inside of the line soon followed, leaving the hatchway completely clear. The sizzling sound switched off; the door was fully inside the dome, and so, with hardly a thought in his head, Bruno threw the latches back and heaved the door open, then leaped out.

Sunlight struck him like a physical blow. There is heat, he

had time to think, and there is *heat*. Solar energy at fourteen thousand watts per square meter—ten times Earth normal—was something the body had no immediate response for. It was exactly like being thrown into a fire; his eyes pinched closed of their own accord, his hair singed and crisped and smoked on his scalp, and he collapsed immediately to the di-clad neutronium deck, thrashing and gasping. Fortunately, the deck was relatively cool, and his shirt and tights—which were cream colored and fairly reflective—had some minimal climate-control capabilities that saturated right around the time his sweat glands finally opened up and began pouring out rivers of lukewarm saline. These factors helped keep him from more serious injury for the six seconds it took the sun to "set" behind the platform's edge.

He heard voices nearby. "It *is* a ship; look!" "What's that door doing there? Who is that? That's not a robot; that's a man!" "My God, I think he stepped out in the daylight."

Bruno sat up and, to his surprise, let out a very undignified scream. "Ow! Ow! Goddamn it, that hurts!" His face and hands felt sunburned already, and his eyes, when he opened them, were blinded by sweat and huge, glowing blobs of color.

"Sir?" a voice said, now just a meter or two away. "Are you all right?"

"I'm fine," Bruno said, though this was far from certain. Once again, his thoughts settled on Tamra. He picked himself up. "Bruno de Towaji, at Her Majesty's service."

His vision began to clear slightly, and the burning of his skin eased somewhat as the air began to cool. His sweat-soaked clothes began to feel heavy and cold, which was wonderful. He looked around. In the glow of wellstone lights set around the dome's perimeter, he saw four shiny tents surrounded by solar collectors and neat rows of scorched, plastic discs the size of dart boards. Various charred debris—shoes and hats and crumbly brown scrolls of paper—littered the deck around him. Nearby was the skeleton he'd seen, and a little ways off, in the lee of a tent, was another skeleton he hadn't. And immediately surrounding him, crowding right up against him, were four figures dressed head to toe in suits of thick, silver-white cloth that left only their faces exposed. He took each of them in with a hurried glance.

It'd been a long time. The first face he identified as belonging to Wenders Rodenbeck, the playwright-cum-lawyer. The second—identified more by his hulking body than his Asian features—was the policeman Cheng Shiao. The third was one of Tamra's courtiers, the woman named Tusité. Hardest of all was the fourth, a quite familiar-looking young lady. She had the same copper eyes and sandalwood skin as young Vivian Rajmon, and with a start he realized it *was* Vivian, grown up nearly all the way.

But where was Tamra? Putting all else out of his mind, he pointed to the open hatchway of his ship, which hung ridiculously outside the dome, like some shiny, barrel-shaped lamprey. "This way," he said. "Climb aboard, and quickly. I'll assist Her Majesty. Where is she?"

Cheng Shiao stepped forward and grabbed Bruno firmly by the elbow. "Philander," he said in quick, precise tones, "it is my sad duty to inform you that Her Majesty gave her life in the effort to save others. Let's away from this place, quickly. You're in terrible danger."

Bruno felt as though he'd been slammed in the chest with a croquet mallet. "What? What? Instruction unclear. What did you say?"

Shiao's face was grimly serious. "Her Majesty Queen Tamra-Tamatra Lutui, in the person of her last known copy, is dead. I'm more sorry than you know, Philander."

He said some other stuff after that, various irrelevancies about ships and danger and impending death, none of which registered on Bruno. If not for Shiao's firm grip on his elbow, he'd have sunk to the deck and stayed there, waited for the sun to come and burn him away. But Shiao's grip didn't compromise, didn't allow him to fall. He was dragged back toward the waiting ship and pulled through the hatch.

Only when the hatch was closed, and *Sabadell-Andorra* broke contact with the platform's dome and lurched toward the sun at a thousand-gee acceleration, and the sickening inertial imbalances caused Shiao to lose equilibrium . . .

Only then was Bruno de Towaji permitted to faint.

Of historical note is the fact that within milliseconds of Bruno's head striking the edge of the fireplace, a nasen beam passed through the diamond cladding of the platform, breaching it. The resulting neutronium spill eradicated all traces of the structure itself, including the bones of one Tamra-Tamatra Lutui, and had the *Sabadell-Andorra* been propelled by any of the technologies that were standard at the time, there is little doubt that *it* would have been eradicated as well.

Bruno knew he wasn't dead when he heard Muddy wailing. Oddly, though, what Muddy was saying was not "Poor me," or "I am afraid," but "Tamra! Tamra!! Oh, God, how I've failed you!" This was how he knew he and Muddy weren't really so different after all.

"He's waking up," a too-husky version of Vivian Rajmon's voice said. "Cheng, come here; he's waking up."

"No," Bruno said without opening his eyes. "No, there's no point in that."

"Are you all right, Bruno? We've put some salve on your burns, but your hair will need to be shaved . . ."

Resignedly, he opened his eyes, which already ran with tears, and promised to run with many more before they were through. "Hello, Vivian. God, how beautiful you've become! What a young lady! It's good of you to care for me, really; thank you. It's quite unnecessary, though; my life is over. I'm about to kill myself."

Muddy shrieked again, and leaped from his own couch to throw himself atop Bruno's body. "No! Declarant, Lordship, you mustn't consider it! To lose Tamra *and* you, how unthinkable. No! I won't allow it!"

"Ah, damn it," Bruno said, struggling under Muddy's weight. "Get off me. Get *off*. I'll do as I please, damn you!"

"You will *not*," Muddy snarled. His breath was hot on Bruno's cheek; the bristles of his beard dug into Bruno's flesh like needles. "The Queendom still rots with collapsium, its sun is in imminent danger of swallowing a hypermass, and I have suffered a blow far worse than any torment of Marlon's. We all have. God, I'm able to *empathize*. I'm able to feel the pain of all the worlds' billions, because my own pain is finally too huge to contain.

"Will you not avenge her, Bruno? Will you not fight for her Queendom's safety, as she'd command you to if she were here? Have we traded places, you and I? Because *I* would save her worlds if I could. *If I could*."

"Let me up."

"Listen carefully, damn you: I'm weak and damaged and years behind your knowledge of collapsium. I *will* save the Queendom, but I've only yourself to use as my instrument. There is no other r-recourse. Let you up? By God, you'll *get* up. Now!"

His weight lifted off Bruno, but suddenly his hands were there, grabbing the ruff of Bruno's shirt, hauling him up by it.

"Say it," Muddy instructed, thrusting his face once more into Bruno's own. "Say you will live."

"Let go."

Bruno tried to shake off Muddy's grasp and saw the wince of agony there on his brother's face, his own face. Muddy's weakened body struggled against pain and fatigue and despair, but his grip was surprisingly strong, the conviction behind it being much greater than Bruno's own. It was that more than anything—that wobbly but determined strength in the face of total calamity—that altered the trajectory of Bruno's heart.

"All right, damn it. I'll live," he agreed, his voice heavy with despair. To be bested by this most pathetic of creatures, to find that he himself was the lesser man after all . . .

But with nothing left to live for, he could at least, indeed, spend his life in the act of vengeance. He could, at least, do his level best to crush Marlon's face between angry fists, to put an end to these evil plans, to sweep up every last bit of stray collapsium before irreversible havoc could be wreaked on the Queendom and its people.

"Or die trying," Muddy added with a sudden, strangled laugh. He released Bruno's shirt ruff and stepped away, and suddenly tears were rolling down his face. His strength—limited, as he'd so often said—was finally expended, and he staggered and slumped against his acceleration couch.

Not limply, though—the ertial space around them seemed to discourage that. Instead, he bounced away and collapsed in a heap beside the supine Hugo, who mewled in delight. *Hello, friend!*

"Attention," the voice of *Sabadell-Andorra* said. "I am receiving a radio transmission, analog voice."

Dear God, Bruno thought, was there no rest? Would there be no rest for him, ever? "Play it," he said, raising the back of his couch to a working position. The whole ship smelled of sweat and scorched cloth, and his own sun-fried hair. He looked around, thinking: so crowded in here. What are we doing?

"De Towaji?" a crackling voice asked from the ether. It was Marlon Sykes' voice, unmistakable after all these years. "Bruno de Towaji, is that you?"

Bruno sighed, too tired for the moment to feel a proper sense of hatred. "Reply: Yes, Marlon, you pathetic bastard. I'm here."

"I hoped you'd come," Marlon said, after only a few seconds' delay. He must be somewhere close by. Bruno scanned the trajectory display but saw no trace of a base or spaceship or other structure there, just another loose end of Ring Collapsiter swimming into view.

"End reply," he said. "Ship, can you localize the source of that transmission?"

"Negative, sir. Range is indeterminate, and the signal appears to be coming from a broad region, fully half the sky."

Bruno frowned. "Which half?"

"Opposite the sun."

"Hmm. And it all arrives at the same time? It's a clean signal?"

"Affirmative, sir."

"How unique. It's as if it were coming from an enormous shell antenna, symmetric about our position. But *that's* unlikely, isn't it? He's got some trick he's employing."

Marlon's voice came again. "Bruno, are you still there?"

"Reply: I'm here. You say you hoped I'd come?"

Again, the delay. Then Sykes said, "I did, really. You're my hero, sir. Didn't your tattooed friend tell you?" The odd thing was, Marlon didn't sound snotty or sarcastic or evil with that remark. He sounded like plain old Marlon Sykes, meaning every word he was saying.

"Declarant Sykes," Cheng Shiao said urgently, leaning over the radio console in an ill-considered lurch. "I must insist that you surrender yourself immediately. You've broken the *law*, sir."

Sykes laughed at that, and suddenly he *did* sound evil. "Who've you got down there with you, Bruno? Some policeman? No one fit to judge *us*, certainly. We make our own laws, we Declarant-Philanders. Even *physical* laws can be ruled in our favor, if we prepare the proper defense."

Bruno sighed, weary of all this. "What is it you want, Marlon?"

"To business, eh? No time to catch up on the personal side? All right, then; be that way. I've contacted you to ask you to join me. Not quite as a *full* partner—I'm really not prepared to share the conceptual credit—but I could certainly use your help in the detail work. Frankly, I could use your company, too, if you're willing to lend it."

Bruno was aghast. "Marlon, are you insane? Well, clearly you are, but are you stupid as well? Tamra is *dead*. You *killed* her, you . . . you . . . fiend!" There didn't seem any better word for it. Words had simply failed him.

"Fiend?" Marlon sounded genuinely hurt. "I'm as much a victim as you, sir. Remember, I loved her first. I didn't kill her—why would I do that? She killed herself. Ask your little friends there."

Killed herself? Killed *herself*?

"It's true," Vivian said hollowly. She'd stripped out of her quilted bodysuit and now wore only a kind of slip or underdress that served to emphasize her all-but-grown-up figure. But her face—her grown-up face—was heartbreakingly sad. "We'd gotten the fax working again, intermittently, but it kept malfunctioning and going offline—none of us knew enough about it to say why. We had only two reflective blankets at that time, and there just wasn't enough room for everyone underneath them. We tried taking turns that first day, but it was clear that that was just going to slowly kill us all.

"So we tried drawing straws, but Her Majesty somehow rigged the draw. She lost five times in a row. We didn't let it stand, of course, though she kept insisting it was her duty, that 'not one more citizen' would die in her stead. But what was *our* duty, if not to protect her? Then Cheng Peterson died—we found him with his skin burned black and his tongue all puffed out—and she just . . . walked out into the sunlight and cut her throat. I don't know where she got the knife; I never saw it before. We tried to save her. We *tried,* but you can't fix a carotid artery under those conditions; you just can't. So she . . . died. And the next day—"

Vivian, clutching tightly at the wellwood mantelpiece, choked momentarily, her beautiful face streaked with speedy, inertialess tears. The strain of the long ordeal showed clearly in her features. Finally, she found enough composure to continue. "The next day, we got the fax working again for nearly an hour. We got the tents up, and the moisture condensers . . . She would have lived, Bruno. She would have. The Queen of All Things sacrificed herself for *nothing*."

"Not for nothing," Muddy said, struggling to rise from his heap on the floor. He looked dizzy. He looked, truthfully, like he should just stay put. "It was a gesture of, of . . . d-d-defiance. Perhaps she knew she was bait in a trap."

"No," Shiao said, shaking his crew cut head sadly, "the cruiser didn't try to rescue us until five days after that. She couldn't have known."

"An affirmation of life for the rest of you, then," Muddy said harshly. "Ill considered, perhaps, but she l-l-loved all of you enough to do it, and that's the thing that counts. She died—f-fittingly—of an excess of love."

"You see?" Marlon piped up from the radio speaker. "I was as shocked and shattered as any of you. I'd roll back time to that moment if I could." Then, more ominously: "Perhaps some day I shall."

Bruno's weariness had been subsiding, replaced bit by bit with a deep, sustaining anger. Now it blossomed. "You created the situation, *Marlon*. You put her there in harm's way, and you could have *removed* her from it when you saw the way things were going. You're twice the bastard I thought, for laying the blame on chance when you know perfectly well it's your own damned fault. Why would I possibly want to join you? What hope or endeavor could we possibly share?"

There was a long pause, until finally Marlon answered. "I was never sure if you knew, Bruno. When I had the idea, I figured *surely* it was one you'd considered and discarded. But the math checked out, so I guessed you'd just been squeamish about it. Perfectly in keeping with your character, right? You actually *care* about people on some level, which is great. Really, I mean that in a nonsarcastic way. But you were all alone up there on that little planet, your research going off in these weird directions, and I saw it'd be thousands of years before you actually got anywhere with it.

"That first time you came back to the Queendom, I thought you'd call me out for what I was doing. When you didn't . . . Well, I was full of resentment then. I was happy to see you go, and happy to capture your image for . . . well, malicious purposes. And the image confirmed your ignorance! The second time, though, I figured you *must* have worked it out. You were very methodical, so when you said nothing, I dared to hope you were secretly on my side. It made me feel better about you, about how great everyone thinks you are. If *you* were working on *my* idea, well, that would make it all worthwhile. And if not, then maybe you weren't so smart after all. And that would be an important discovery, too."

His voice sped up, becoming almost giddy. "I watched your world through telescopes, you know, and when you finally made a *ring* of the collapsium— around a star, no less!— I thought surely you *must* have figured it out. I waited for your network gate to open; I even sent you a present. But you hadn't worked it out, had you? You still haven't. I really am way ahead of you on this one. How extraordinarily affirming that is, of all my years of effort!"

Bruno felt he couldn't possibly be more bewildered. "Marlon, what in the damn worlds are you talking about?"

Another long pause. Then: "The *arc de fin,* Bruno. Your window to the end of time. There's a shortcut, an easy solution, to produce it *this year.* This very month. It requires a lot of mass, and an energetic collapse, but those have finally been arranged."

"Oh. Dear God," Bruno said. "The sun!"

"Exactly. I need it. Oh, I suppose any equivalent star would do, but there'd have to be a thriving industrial civilization there to help me collapse it in the proper way. So we'd be back to waiting thousands of years again, until these Queendom slackards expand beyond this one meager system. It's too long. History should know its own end, to be able to make sense of its present. And history *will* record that it was I, not you, who opened that window."

Bruno couldn't help laughing a little—a sour, bitter, furious chuckle. Grief hovered beside him, waiting its turn, but for the moment he was simply angry. "History will die with the Queendom, Marlon. There'll be no one left to remember how damned smart you were."

"Oh, please." Marlon's voice was impatient. "I disrupted the Iscog to keep small minds from interfering; I didn't realize *yours* was one of them. There'll be more deaths, of course; that can't be avoided. Probably most of the people on Earth, certainly all the ones on Venus. The flares of the dying sun *will* be impressive, it's true. But come on; you know as well as I how trivial it is to create miniature stars. We could be circling the planets with them, using them for power, heat, light, industry . . . Why should we settle for nature, when a handful of neubles, some wellstone, and some hydrogen will match what nature requires a billion billion billion tons to accomplish? A sun! I say it's inevitable, that we should dismantle the stars for our own purposes and replace them with something of our own device. History will credit me with *that*, as well."

"History will label you a monster," Bruno said darkly.

After a pause, Marlon grumbled. "Bruno, I realize nobody *owes* me greatness, but if I can *seize* greatness, why shouldn't I? The Queendom provides the framework and the labor, and I provide the ideas and the careful flow of information to control it all. At the top! People suffer as a result, but what's so unnatural about that? This idea that people should be safe and happy, that's a very distorting idea. Look to history: Most societies have agreed that people should be *useful*, to men of vision like myself. Who remembers the happy nobodies? My future is grander than yours, Bruno; I swear it. Your so-called 'monsters' are simply the flesh of humanity's ambition to create a history worth recording."

"You're brainsick, Marlon. Something's come loose in your base pattern. When was the last time you were medically validated by anything but a fax filter?"

"Damn yourself! God, why is there always this confusion between ambition and madness? The two aren't even related. I've *created* various mad versions of myself, just to see if that would be useful. Better than complacency, at any rate;

sometimes I think the very *purpose* of the Queendom is to crush away all dreams of greatness, to stuff them into a single individual and then rob her of any real power, just to show it can't be had."

"The Ring Collapsiter was ambitious, Marlon."

"More than you know."

"As described! What a fine idea it was, and *is*. What a shame to so pervert it! I'd thought you were a builder, Marlon, a creator. I'm ashamed to be so wrong."

"Oh, listen to yourself. Listen to that pompous, stupid voice! I *know* you, sir. Don't forget it. I know you when you're proud and fresh, and I know you afterward, when you've broken. I'm *well* aware of your limits. Don't *presume* to think, for even a moment, that you have the same knowledge of me."

Sykes paused, then continued in a milder voice. "All right, I suppose I am a monster. I suppose that goes without question at this point. But a *visionary* monster, and that's what really matters. You and I have clashed enough, Bruno. I'm done hating you; I'm prepared to write your name in next to my own. Consider: if not for you, I'd have no peers at all, and how's a man with no peers supposed to fit in? Ah? Ah?" He invited a friendly laugh, and seemed to expect that he'd get one.

Bruno sighed a final time. "You know I can't let you do this, Marlon. Do as Captain Shiao says: Surrender yourself now. They won't prosecute you; you clearly have some kind of illness. Once cured, you'll see the madness in all this. For your own sake, not to mention poor Tamra's, you should help me clean this mess up and start setting things right."

"Oh, dear. Oh, dear, oh dear. I had to try, Bruno. Don't say I didn't try. I'm sorry to tell you, this conversation is over."

Suddenly, the space around them was filled with pulsing light. Great blossoms of pure energy—each one easily the size of Earth's moon—flicked into existence, remained just long enough to register, and vanished again.

"Good night!" Bruno exclaimed. "Ship, what's the distribution of those flashes?"

"Stochastic, sir, a Gaussian white-noise pattern."

"Centered around us?"

"Centered ten million kilometers to the solar east of us. Eigenvectors are nonorthogonal; the distribution is shaped like—excuse me, library search—a banana, sir."

"A banana? Gods, what now? What's the standard deviation?"

"Along which axis, sir?"

"Along the *relevant* axis, you! The one connecting our position to the centroid of your banana. How *close* is this phenomenon to *hitting* us?"

"Ah," the ship said. "Five million kilometers, sir."

Bruno frowned, pinched his chin. "We're at the two-sigma dispersion contour? That's odd. Is the centroid stationary?"

"Negative, sir. It's matching our acceleration, and exceeding our velocity by a constant two hundred thousand kilometers per second. It is gaining on us."

"Ah," Bruno said, finally beginning to understand. "Add the phenomenon to the trajectory display, please. All known flashes to date."

The result was quite alarming: here was the grappleship, hurtling directly downward, toward the vast luminous plains of the solar chromosphere. And off to one side was a crescent-shaped pattern of dots, marching and smearing its way toward them. Off to the other side was that stray Ring Collapsiter fragment he'd glimpsed a few minutes ago: a ropy, kilometers-long chain of collapsium.

Despite the ertial nausea, everyone crowded forward, eager to see and understand the new display, eager to know what was happening to them. Their bodies stank of sweat; even Deliah's, he realized. Even his own. Impervium or no, it was getting hot in here. No material was superreflective at all wavelengths, after all, and the hull was necessarily pierced by certain openings, for the grapple beams and the emergency exhaust ports and of course the hatch itself. So it leaked, slowly letting in the heat. How close to the sun could they *get* before they were cooked in place? He noticed that the little faux fireplace had extinguished itself, probably figuring its warming-the-place-up job was done.

"Blackbody temperature of the flashes?" Bruno asked.

"Ten million kelvins, sir."

"Ah." That told him nothing useful.

"We're being herded," Cheng Shiao said, pointing at the display. "The sun on one side, the weapon pulses on the other. No way to move up or down out of the ecliptic plane. No place to go but *here*."

"Toward the collapsium," Bruno agreed angrily. "Deliah, can we grapple to it?"

"Not without shredding it. The whole thing will still be muon-contaminated, Bruno. Very fragile."

"*How* contaminated? How long will it stand up to our tugging?"

"I don't know. Seconds, minutes . . . I don't know how to measure or calculate it. Do you?"

"Not offhand," Bruno admitted. Then he said, "Bah. Enough. We grapple to it, at once. Ship? You hear me? Grab the *end* of that fragment, if you can—that'll direct the tension along its strongest axis."

"Acknowledged, sir."

Gravity flickered and lurched, then restored itself. The view outside the bow wheeled and locked, centering itself on the distant, powder-blue tendril of collapsium.

"It's too hot in here," Tamra's courtier, Tusité, complained.

"We're all hot," Muddy answered her faintly, from his place on the floor. Evidently he'd decided to remain there. "We're diving into the sun, for God's sake."

"Environmental controls at maximum," the ship said in its own defense.

"Vent some oxygen from the emergency tank," Bruno suggested. "It's supercompressed—its expansion upon release should provide some cooling."

The temperature nudged down a bit. A sigh went through

them all. In the window above, the collapsium grew larger, closer.

Sabadell-Andorra spoke again. "Receiving a transmission, sir. Playing it."

Then Marlon's voice, crackling heavily with solar-wind static. "Bruno, what are you doing? You leave that fragment alone! Its placement is very precise! What are you *dragging* it with?"

"No reply," Bruno instructed.

"Bruno," Marlon warned, "stop this at once. Blast it, I've given you every possible chance, and see where it gets me. Good-bye, sir."

"Centroid of the flashes has shifted to our position," the ship said. "It is now tracking us directly."

Under his breath, Bruno muttered something history does not record. "All right, what's our probability of being flashed?"

"Of being inside one of the flashes when it appears?" the ship asked.

"Exactly."

"Approximately one-half percent, sir, every second."

"I see. And how long before we collide with that collapsium fragment?"

"Forty seconds, sir."

"Ah." He looked around, at the assembled friends and acquaintances, at the robot and the copy of himself. "Well, I'm very sorry, everyone, but Marlon appears to have killed us all. My humblest apologies to every one of you."

Then a thought struck him. "Ship, what part of the fragment are we approaching? The middle?"

"The end, sir. It's where we grappled to, per your orders."

"Indeed." He turned to Deliah and spoke quickly. "The Ring Collapsiter is *hollow*, yes? A *tube* of collapsium, with an open conduit down the center. That's the whole point of it: a tunnel of supervacuum through which light can travel unimpeded."

"Yes," Deliah said uncertainly, her eyes widening.

"How large a conduit, again? Six meters? Wide enough to admit this vessel?"

"Bruno, you can't—well, perhaps you can."

"Ship, can you dive straight down the center of the fragment?"

"I can try, sir. Contact in five seconds. Four, three, two, one . . ."

in which the predictions
of a doomsayer are fulfilled

Is this death, Bruno wondered? There was certainly a lot of screaming, or rather, a lot of unearthly, uncanny whispering sounds that *reminded* him of screaming. He also heard clear, high ringing sounds, like hundreds of little bells. And these flitting, translucent entities ... Were they souls? Angels? Devils? Were they the ones screaming? The sounds were impossible to localize—they seemed to come from within his own head!

Simultaneous arrival in both eardrums, the voice of reason whispered, and that voice actually *was* in his head, purely imaginary, giving him something to compare these actual sounds against. The difference was, so to speak, pronounced. So perhaps he was in a real place after all. In his ship, alive inside the Ring Collapsiter? That seemed as unlikely as Heaven itself.

His senses told him nothing familiar, filled him with confusion and terror and nothing more. Start with vision: he saw, or seemed to see, a dim, sourceless, colorless light all around, like a fog. Within the light he perceived movement, rapid and repetitive. He perceived shapes, or rather, shapeless regions with a different sort of translucence. Some of these moved; others did not. Some were close; others were not.

Aha! So stereo vision still worked in this place. Bruno still had two eyes, which were capable of angling inward or outward to judge distance. That was something, a major clue! But what were those two eyes *seeing*? Not ordinary light, certainly. Start with the assumption, then, that he was inside the collapsium. What would that imply? A greatly reduced zero-point field, for one thing. Like the ertial shield's wake, but symmetric all around him? With no acceleration to restore some grudging sense of inertia? The speed of light would be much higher, meaning the *frequency* of light would be much higher for a given energy. Visible light photons would phase off into the gamma-ray portion of the spectrum, without gaining the energy wallop of true gamma rays. And low-energy photons? Might they become visible?

Try sound next: He couldn't localize it, the way he could localize light. But while stereo vision was related to angles, independent of anything else, stereo *hearing* relied on differences in a sound's arrival time from one ear to the other. This related directly to the speed of sound—the higher the speed, the vaguer the perceived direction. Yet he *did* hear human voices, or something like them. So perhaps the speed of sound—and thus its frequency—wasn't *that* different, maybe increased by a factor of a few hundred. Perhaps friction and viscosity played a larger role in sound waves than inertia did. If he spoke in low tones, could he make himself understood?

"HELLO!" he rumbled in his deepest, loudest bass, and indeed, he felt and heard a scratchy whisper that was faint but— at least to him—reasonably intelligible. He was rewarded with a renewed cacophony of sounds, urgent sounding but otherwise devoid of meaning.

He was still furious and afraid, still awaiting his chance to grieve, but now he was *fascinated* as well. Rarely did physics problems present themselves in such dramatic and tangible ways!

All right, then; try the sense of touch: He felt light impacts all around him, like puffs of air. There was no feeling of weight or motion, but the touches on his skin did seem to correspond in some way to the dancing translucences all around him. He reached out a hand, and it flicked out like a whip and then stopped as quickly. To his astonishment he felt the shapes of a human nose and cheek touch it lightly, for an instant, then bounce away. The face had felt rigid, as if carved out of wax, but it *had* been a face, warm and sticky-slick with natural oils. For an instant it had even *looked* like a face in a vague, watercolor sort of way, before it flickered off into the fog again.

Finally, his senses began to integrate. To give them a few moments' peace, he took a breath and closed his eyes. *Those* actions felt normal enough, at least. When he looked again, things were clearer.

He could make out the insides of the *Sabadell-Andorra*, yes, her hull all but transparent in this foggy light. Inside that space were the many human bodies he and Muddy had collected, but they were bouncing around off every surface, like ping-pong balls. Sometimes they spun, sometimes not. Sometimes they'd *stop* suddenly, and then be knocked into motion again by the collision of someone else. All their transitions were instantaneous, rigid. Bruno himself was not bouncing, since he was strapped into his ghostly-clear couch. Another form—Deliah, in her folding chair?—was also motionless, though the body twitched in a quick, unpleasant, insectile way.

The screams continued.

"ER, TRY TO REMAIN CALM," he rumbled at them. "SEE IF YOU CAN GRAB ONTO SOMETHING."

Almost immediately, one of the bodies stopped bouncing. Bruno peered at it, trying to make out details. A person, desperately gripping Muddy's control panel with arms and knees?

"it works," a faint, whispery voice, barely audible sounded. "you can stop yourself you can catch yourself"

Another body froze in place against the hatchway. Soon

someone else was clinging to *that*. Then a pair of bodies were bouncing together, clinging to each other but not to anything else.

Suddenly there were voices rather than screams. "where are we hey that's my hair i've got you don't let go we are inside the ring collapsiter i thought we were dead for sure . . ."

"SHIP?" Bruno tried.

". . . because i can't reach it that's my eye you will have to climb over . . ."

"SHIP!"

"Y-r-mnk-str-hhhhhhk"

"*SABADELL-ANDORRA,* CAN YOU HEAR ME?"

"C . . . d not pro . . . d"

"SHIFT YOUR AUDIO FREQUENCIES. TRANSMIT LOWER. LISTEN HIGHER. THE SPEED OF SOUND HAS CHANGED."

"C . . . nsating. This is a test signal. Can you hear me, sir?" The voice was tinny but clear.

"YES! CAN YOU REBROADCAST OUR VOICES IN A FREQUENCY-SHIFTED DOMAIN?"

Now in a stronger voice: "Th . . t should be possible in a moment, sir. I'm experiencing an enormous number of intermittent computational malfunctions, but I have established sufficient redundancy to compensate. Shift and rebroadcast is enabled."

Bruno cleared his throat, then tried to speak normally. "Hello?" His voice, despite an echoey, underwater quality, sounded much better. And with much less effort, too.

"Hello!" four or five other voices called back.

Then a new burst of chatter broke out.

"I can *hear*!"

". . . got my voice back."

"I feel really sick."

"Help! I don't like this!"

"Excuse me, Madam, I need you to move a little to the left. Yes, that's helpful. Thank you."

Outside the weirdly translucent hull, Bruno could just barely make out stippled rows and columns of pinpoint brightness in the fog: the collapsium lattice that surrounded them. Curiously, it moved only slightly, vibrating a few centimeters back and forth in irregular bursts. Was the ship *stuck* against it somehow? It was not easy to see, to perceive any details at all, but there did seem to be some sort of kink in the tunnel ahead of them.

"What do we do now?" someone wanted to know.

An excellent question! This was no comfortable place—it was weightlessness and ertial travel, fever and sensory deprivation, hallucination and drowning all rolled into one. Bruno had felt more at ease on rickety sailboats, riding the stormy seas of Tonga! But how to escape? And where to go?

"Sykes may believe we're dead," Cheng Shiao's voice said tightly, through tinkling bells and underwatery echoes. "That's something."

Vivian Rajmon's voice replied. "I half believe it myself, Cheng. Is that your hand? It feels like wood!"

Bruno peered and squinted, trying to perceive the two, to tell them apart from the others. Were there visual cues when a person spoke? Did translucent angel-amoebas have a discernible body language? He picked out two figures huddled together by the fireplace and decided that was probably who they were.

Annoyingly, one figure still bounced around the hull's interior. The body was difficult to focus on, almost too quick to see at all.

"Declarant," another male voice said, "I don't feel too well right now."

"I'm sure none of us do," Bruno agreed. "Who is that? Wenders Rodenbeck?"

"The man himself," Rodenbeck's voice agreed.

"Is that you bouncing around?"

"That's right. My hands've gone numb; I can't seem to make the fingers work. I feel sort of *poisoned,* if that makes sense to you."

Bruno's face threw itself into an inertialess frown. "Seriously ill, hmm?"

"Seriously," Rodenbeck agreed, in steady but frightened tones. "Whatever's . . . happening to us in here, I think it must be very unhealthy. Getting out of this seems like a pretty necessary thing, if you don't mind me saying."

Bruno, fearing Rodenbeck had suffered some sort of inertialess whiplash injury to his neck, suppressed the urge to nod. "I quite agree. Try not to move, sir. Your symptoms are troubling, and without knowing their cause, there's no telling whether you could exacerbate them, or indeed, whether the rest of us could be similarly affected. But haste will likely make things worse. Can you remain calm for a few minutes?"

"De Towaji is right," Shiao said. "We don't even know what sort of weapon was used against us back there. Explosive projectiles of some sort?"

"There were no projectiles," Bruno said. "Just bursts of energy."

"Energy doesn't just *appear*," Deliah objected.

"Indeed. It's puzzling. Perhaps Marlon was locally inverting the photon states of the zero-point field? That *would* create energetic bursts, but they'd be short-lived, and since this would also carve equivalent holes in the vacuum, which the energy would immediately rush back in to fill, the *net* release would still be zero. I suppose that is consistent with what we've observed."

Then came Muddy's voice, only slightly whiny. "Pulsed gravity lasers, if they were *crossed*, should create brief p-peaks of intense gravitation. Potentially, eight crossed beams could create the equivalent of a collapsium lattice, for picosecond intervals."

"Ah. Clever thought."

Shiao made an optimistic grunt. "It's not dangerous, then? It's a trick, an illusion?"

"Oh," Bruno said, "I don't know about that. The net energy of a knife is also zero. Better a knife than a bomb, I'll wager, but finding ourselves in the middle of such an inversion would almost certainly be harmful."

"Fatal?"

Bruno's inertialess shrug nearly dislocated both shoulders. "I really couldn't say, Captain. I'm speculating enough as it is. It would get inside our superreflectors, I'm sure. It would *appear* inside, without having to penetrate. But he would have to score the hit on us, first, and that appears difficult. For whatever reason, the timing and position of the flashes don't appear to be precisely controllable."

Shiao persisted. "Why would he use such an ineffective weapon? Because this ship is too nimble? Too difficult to target with a nasen beam?"

"He does seem to have a lot of devices at his disposal," Muddy agreed. "At least one nasen projector, probably eight or more gravity lasers, and oblivion knows how many s-s-standard EM grapples, to pull the Iscog and the Ring Collapsiter apart as he has. The energy he's expended in the past five minutes would fill a battery twice as large as this ship. How much has he expended in the past *week*? The past *three* weeks?"

"We should be looking for a very large ship, then?" asked Shiao.

"Or a base," Muddy said. "He's a deeply private man, fond of s-s-secret facilities buried in rock. And if he *is* using gravity lasers in the way I've imagined, there would need to be two banks of four, spaced a considerable distance apart. Look for a good-sized asteroid whose sunward face is c-covered in wellstone energy converters. Dead black."

With great effort and concentration, Bruno fought inertialessness to lean as far forward as his straps would allow, and peered at the translucence of the control panel. He knew exactly where the trajectory display should be located, so it wasn't hard to train his eyes on that spot. It *was* hard to make anything out there, though. Were those the edges of the plaque? The dashed and dotted lines upon it? He tried to remember where the planets had been, when they'd last seen a glimpse of . . .

"Mercury," he said. "It's close enough—the radio time-lags match. It's certainly *big* enough. And I can't imagine a larger, emptier source of concealment."

"Or a better source of raw materials," Muddy agreed. "Mercury, yes."

"I really don't feel well," Rodenbeck complained, in a weaker voice than before. "My limbs have gone entirely numb."

"All right," Bruno said, with an accidental and quite sickening nod. "Ship? Why have we stopped?"

"I stopped us," the ship replied. "The tunnel ahead of us bends too sharply to admit my outer hull."

"Hmm. You used backup thrusters to do this?"

"Yes. I'm also currently using them to maintain attitude and position. It's difficult, sir—required thrust is very low to effect a velocity change, but the counterpulse required to damp it is itself a function of position and velocity. The resulting control space has no closed-form solutions."

"So you're improvising."

"Correct, sir. Fuel consumption has stabilized, but remains disconcertingly rapid."

Rapid? *That* wasn't a good thing. "Estimated time of depletion?"

"Two minutes, twenty-four seconds, sir."

"Oh, dear. Is there enough fuel to back us out of here safely?"

"Negative, sir."

"Blast. Use some imagination, you! Bring matters like this to my attention before they become irrevocable!"

"I am extremely taxed," the ship said in its own defense.

Bruno sighed. "All right, then, turn around and pull us out with the grapples; without a fuel supply we're in more danger in here than we are outside."

"Acknowledged, sir."

There was no sense of movement, but the jittering lattice of pinpoints outside the hull began—slowly and jerkily—to rotate. With a yelp of surprise, Wenders Rodenbeck settled at once to the deck beside Bruno's couch and remained there.

"Ah, good. You've managed to grab hold," Bruno said, looking down approvingly.

"Actually, friend, I appear to be stuck." Rodenbeck's voice was alarmed.

"Stuck?"

"It feels . . . like gravity. Pretty much exactly like gravity."

Oh, goodness. Oh, goodness! "Ship, cease rotation!"

But it was too late. The walls hummed with activity, oxygen atoms accelerating near-inertialessly and being expelled at velocities that probably exceeded the vacuum speed of light. But the rotation continued—even began, ponderously, to accelerate.

"I don't understand," Deliah van Skettering protested. "The gravity inside a cylinder should cancel to zero, regardless of position or orientation."

"A *continuous* cylinder of infinite length," Bruno corrected. "Ours is kinked and twisted, and composed of discrete masses, and filled with a Casimir supervacuum that dulls momentum! I'm a fool. Hold on, Wenders, I'll fish you up."

"No!" Muddy shrieked. "I forbid it, sir! Keep your hands where they are!"

"Muddy, I—"

"You'll be killed," Muddy insisted. "Needlessly, pointlessly killed! You can't save him in time!"

"You're saying I'm going to die?" Rodenbeck asked, his breath now coming in gasps.

"Blast it," Bruno said, quietly, hollowly, because he almost certainly *would* be killed if he intervened. But perhaps Rodenbeck—an artist, an innocent in this madness—could be saved. With numb fingers, he undid his safety harness. Already he was feeling the beginnings of weight, as the stern of the ship swung close to a collapson node. And for so small a black hole, the gradients would be exceedingly steep. Wenders Rodenbeck was probably already feeling more than a gee, the equivalent of Earth-surface gravity. And in the next thirty seconds . . .

There was no way to avoid this; the ship couldn't go forward, couldn't drag itself backward with grapples, couldn't go *anywhere* without turning around. But Bruno should have foreseen this difficulty, should have seen where the danger would occur and then ordered everyone away from it. Steeling himself, he leaned over the side of his couch . . .

And was whisked, with an instantaneous, all-but-inertialess flicker of movement, to the bow of the ship.

"I f-f-forbid it," Muddy said, his hard, solid-wax torso bouncing and skating over Bruno's own. He held on tightly to something, pinning Bruno to the window there, preventing him from escaping. Muddy had leaped the length of the ship, apparently, to ensure this.

"Let go," Bruno said urgently. "Let *go*! I must help him. This is my fault!"

"It isn't. We've never done this before. What man has walked inside collapsium like a tunnel beneath a river? What man can foresee every problem? You saved him once, but this time, Marlon has him for certain."

"Oh! God!" Rodenbeck cried out, weakly.

"Release me," Bruno insisted. "We've seen deaths before, but I can *do* something this time. Listen, you coward! You sniveler! Am I really so weak, so selfish? Am I really so capable of being *you*? *Release me!*"

"I will not."

Below, Bruno was just able to see Rodenbeck's struggling form, pinned to the deck now by several gees. There was no expression on his amoeba face, but the expression in his gasping voice was plain enough: "I told you . . . this stuff was . . . dangerous, de To . . ."

And then he died, his lungs' strength insufficient to lift their own tremendous weight. He suffocated there at the bottom of the ship, while Bruno and the others, hanging only a few meters away, feeling only the merest stirrings of gravity, did nothing. Terrible sounds rose up from the body as its bones snapped, then shattered, then powdered, until finally Rodenbeck was nothing but a leathery, vaguely man-shaped pancake on the floor. Five hundred gee? A thousand? The gradient itself must have been terrible, a difference of hundreds of gees just between the deck and the space a single centimeter above it. Bruno could *see* the collapson node there behind Rodenbeck's body. He watched it pull the remaining remains into a circular mass and drag them along the floor as it rotated by.

And still the jets hummed; still the faint bells tinkled in the air.

"My God," Deliah said, and began to weep.

Bruno finally stopped struggling.

The rotation continued another fifteen seconds, until finally *Sabadell-Andorra* proclaimed the maneuver complete. "Eight seconds to fuel depletion," it added.

"Right," Muddy said. "Grapples on full. T-take us out of here."

"Acknowledged, sir. Destination?"

"The planet Mercury."

in which history's
great wizards clash

There was a lot of talk, once they'd entered normal space again.

"All the things people are doing when they die," Vivian said quietly. "The things they're *just about to do* at the moment the strings are cut. Sometimes nasty, sometimes wonderful, sometimes perfectly ordinary. My grandmother used to say these were things God wanted for himself. She was a kind of Muslim, I suppose—her God was always needy and bitter like that. Not remote, though—he was right there looming over her all the time, like a drunk uncle. But when she died she wasn't doing anything special, just sitting by the window in her rocking chair, wrapped up in an old blanket."

"Maybe God needed that," Shiao suggested matter-of-factly.

Vivian gave an absent nod. "Yes, that's what Mother said. But couldn't he just, you know, create his own moment of peace? Why should he need to take Grammy's? When I was older, I think I would wake up sometimes, wondering if that God of hers were looming over *me*, ready to steal my dreams or my morning breath or something. What a puny motive! He doesn't get to do much of that anymore, and I'm glad about it.

History's greatest thug; phooey, I disown him! The day I stand at his throne I'll place him under arrest; I swear I will." She cast a gloomy look at the bloodstained deck. "Rest in peace, Wenders Rodenbeck. Rest, all the victims of this atrocity."

And there was other talk as well: Was Declarant Sykes still looking for them? Should they attempt to render the ship invisible? That wouldn't work, of course—it'd simply let the sunlight through, to poach all the remaining people inside.

Bruno's grief had now become unbearable; finally it commanded his attention. He ignored the whole discussion, simply throwing an arm over his face and weeping, weeping, his tears seeming to come from an endless reservoir somewhere. He'd been powerless, all those years ago, to save Enzo and Bernice de Towaji when the Old Girona Bistro fell down on them. He *knew* they were dying in there, *knew* there was time to save them if only, if only . . . And so, today, had he been helpless to save Wenders. And Tamra, yes—how very grievously he'd failed *her*! Perhaps he was, quite simply, powerless after all. Perhaps all his deeds and accomplishments were so much illusion, just chance and foolish self-deception. It seemed a plausible enough notion, at that moment.

"What do we do with the . . . body?" someone asked.

"It seems to have gelled. Look, it's a solid mass. Weird. Into the fax with it, I'd say."

"I'll do it. Here."

"Oh, God! Oh, God! Save us! Hasn't there been enough? Deposit us in some safe location before you dash off on this mission!" That sounded like Tamra's friend Tusité. Bruno forgave her the outburst; Tamra surrounded herself with all manner of silly people, but very few of them were *weak*. It didn't imply weakness, to bend and break under the strain of these events. Indeed, quite the reverse—it was only *human*, part of the basic mammalian wiring, to feel terrified when helpless. And to grieve for one's Queen, yes, as for no other thing except, perhaps, one's own children.

He wanted to comfort her. He wanted to be comforted. He wanted comfort, period. But he sensed, he knew, that no one would have anything to offer but their own grief, and perhaps some platitudes. *Such a tragedy. We all loved her so well and so personally, each in our own way.* How trite! How monstrous! Platitudes existed for this very purpose; to underscore the dreary, hopeless banality of human suffering. Should he carve a pyramid with his bare hands? Circumnavigate a world? Would that *help*? Even for himself, he had no words or thoughts of wisdom, only platitudes.

And then Muddy's voice spoke up. "There *are* no s-s-safe places, madam, and no chance to look for them if there were. Time is of the essence if we're to foil this . . . madman's plot."

That got on Bruno's nerves: Muddy's tone was, as ever, grating and whiny and filled with terrified self-pity. And yet, there he was, acting to save the Queendom while Bruno himself sniveled and sobbed on the couch. How humiliating! How base! The thought only made him cry harder.

"Mercury isn't a small place," Vivian Rajmon observed.

"Indeed," Muddy said, "and we've only a few minutes to decide where to begin."

"We look for deep-black solar collectors, you said. Superabsorbers?"

"C-c-correct. But even those will be small, compared to the size of a *world*. Even with the best sensors and algorithms, we are hindered by simple geometry. Searching the entire surface could take hours."

"Hours," Cheng Shiao brooded. "With Sykes ready to open fire upon us at any time. I'm surprised he hasn't already!"

"Perhaps he isn't looking," Vivian said. "Perhaps he's busy hatching some new villainy." Then she paused, and came over to Bruno's bedside. She put a hand on his shoulder, squeezed. "It must be hard, Declarant: all of us drawing upon you so desperately, in *your* hour of need. Even your own duplicate is doing it! But we'll be there very soon. Will you join us for a moment?"

Finally, at these words, Bruno felt the flow of tears begin to ebb. Not so much because Vivian had requested it—although he'd had a little soft spot in his heart for her since she was eleven years old—but because he didn't want to arrive at their destination and have Marlon see him weep. Absurd, of course, since Marlon had probably seen *Muddy* weep for twenty continuous years, had in fact coaxed tears from a Bruno until he *became* a Muddy, over and over and over again. But he supposed the mind didn't need to work rationally, so long as it worked.

"Oh, forgive me." He sniffed, wiping his eyes and nose with a sleeve.

"Of course," she said gently. "Of course we do."

He consoled himself with one thought: that the Sabadell-Andorra Earthquake had been an accident, an act of God. Inevitable, really, and buried back in an age when death—especially by accident—was still the norm. These more recent deaths were something else entirely: *caused.* He glanced up: Mercury was fully visible, already as large as a mottled gray apple in the view, and growing visibly.

He sat up and tried wanly to bring some of the iron back into his voice. "Do . . . forgive me, please. The loss of so many, including Her Majesty, has . . . well. Yes. You know as well as I. But of course we'll be to the planet in a few minutes, unbalanced or no. An unfortunate property of time is that it can't be made to wait."

Then, after a moment's reflection, he said, "Our enemy, of course, has the same problem. Things are moving quickly. If *we're* as quick, we may very well land safely. Visually, Marlon will be looking straight into the sun for us, which ought to confuse even quite sophisticated sensors. And gravitationally . . . well, let's just say this ship has an unusual—and decidedly minimal—signature. And if he really isn't looking, if he *does* presume us dead, we may be able to slip right in."

"He'll see us in *orbit*," Shiao protested, "if we're forced to scour the surface for signs of him."

Bruno, still sniffling a bit, pinched himself on the chin. "Hmm. Well. We needn't search the *entire* planet, surely. He must have his energy converters on the daylight side right now, after all. And his beam weapons as well, since they can't fire through the planet." He sat up straighter. "In fact, he must have had collectors on the daylight side *continuously* for the past several weeks. Either that, or very, very large batteries, and since the former is much easier . . ."

"What's to say the power source is near the base?" Shiao asked skeptically.

"Efficiency," Deliah said, ticking the answers off on her fingers. "Safety. Cost. Time. Light-lag. Marlon may be a good faker, but in private he is—demonstrably!—not a very patient person. He's gone to a lot of trouble over this, but I doubt he's gone to any *extra* trouble, or put up with any suboptimal equipment, or otherwise made things harder on himself than they absolutely need to be."

Fighting dizzy nausea, Bruno nodded. "Indeed. I quite agree."

Muddy was huddled at one of the hypercomputer interfaces, tapping figures in madly. "Mercury completes a revolution every fifty-eight days, an *orbit* every eighty-eight. Daylight lasts eight and a half weeks at the equator, so we're looking pole to pole in an arc from the eastern terminator to thirty degrees west of the noon line. But to be consistent with observations, the g-gravity lasers couldn't be within, er, thirty degrees of the north pole, whereas from the *south* . . ."

Bruno looked up again, saw the planet there in the bow window, fully illuminated from edge to edge like a full but strangely altered moon because they were flying toward it almost straight up out of the sun, their grapples locked on the planet's equator. Indeed, the planet was as wide as a dinner platter, and widening rapidly.

"The base should be s-s-somewhere in here," Muddy said, and on the window a green, crosshatched area the shape of a kidney bean appeared, covering less than a fifth of the planet's sunward face. "Initiating telescopic survey."

Shiao glared up anxiously through the window. "How long will this take? Should we think about plotting an orbit solution?"

"I am still experiencing widespread malfunction," *Sabadell-Andorra* answered. "Gravitational stresses have fractured millions of my wellstone fibers."

"Oh, God," Deliah said. "Is hull containment in danger?"

"Not imminently. Unless there are further stresses. But my computing power and reliability are markedly degraded."

"Oh, well, no problem about *that*." Deliah's voice dripped irony.

Then Muddy spoke up. "Survey complete. There are a number of reflective prominences right *here*, surrounded by a bank of s-s-superabsorbers."

On the window, superimposed over the planet's surface and the bean-shaped highlight, a red X appeared.

"Yes? Goodness, lock the grapples to it," Bruno said, his blood rising. Part of him hadn't really expected to find anything—their chain of suppositions *was* rather long—and another part had expected, long before now, to be burned out of the sky by some silly weapon or other. But logic existed for a reason, because it carried you inexorably toward truth. When properly applied, of course, but by now that was a matter of long habit.

"Grapples may harm the base," Deliah said excitedly. "Disrupting local gravity, interfering with *his* grav-projection mechanisms . . . It could be just the edge we need."

"A double edge," Shiao cautioned. "It'll alert him to our presence, and in fact pinpoint our exact location."

"Irrelevant," Muddy said. "Unless we mean to d-destroy the base using *ourselves* as a projectile, we must begin deceleration at once."

Indeed, moments later the gravity switched off, and everyone went flying into the air as the *Sabadell-Andorra* wheeled around them, orienting its grapples toward the sun. Above, the window dimmed again to prevent the sunlight from searing them all. Then gravity returned, and they all came crashing back down in an assortment of uncomfortable ways.

"Blast," Bruno said, pointing vaguely. "Everyone into your

couches, please. Unfold those, yes. We now have—alas!—enough seats to accommodate everyone."

"Are we still heading for this 'base'?" Tusité asked.

"We are," Muddy confirmed. Then, in a rare display of manners for a de Towaji of any sort, he stuck out his hand. "I don't believe we've formally met, by the way. I'm Muddy."

"Tusité," she returned quickly, accepting his hand into her own dark fingers with a reflexively dainty, ladylike grip. "No last name."

"Me either," Muddy said.

She looked puzzled by that—clearly she thought he was another Bruno, or at least another de Towaji. But what she said, albeit somewhat brusquely, was, "Charmed. I . . . apologize for screaming, a minute ago. It's frightening, all this running and fighting and dying. But I do owe you my life."

"Oh, none of that," Muddy clucked. "We've all had our share of b-bad moments on this trip. Anyway, you owe *him*." He nodded sideways at Bruno.

Tusité looked in Bruno's direction and inclined her head. She looked as if her fright were only barely contained, but she nonetheless turned back to Muddy. "Mercury is hostile wilderness, true?" she asked. "So hot it's full of molten metal? If we come down in the wrong spot, it could mean our deaths."

"Indeed," Muddy agreed. "But we're aimed right for the center of the Declarant's base. As we approach, I'll be scanning for dangers. I'll look for hollows beneath the rock, too—natural or otherwise—because that's where we'll find him. I'll do my b-best to set us atop one of them."

"Steering how?" she pressed anxiously.

"The guidance algorithm adjusts its course by sliding the grapple target to different parts of the sun."

"I'll bet we're disrupting *that*, as well," Deliah noted. "It's illegal to grapple the sun because it can whip up flares and proton storms which affect the entire Queendom. I doubt anyone has ever given our poor photopause the sort of thrashing we're giving it now."

"Indeed," Bruno said, "we have much to answer for."

Everyone burst out laughing at that. Tight, anxious laughter, it was true, but still it surprised Bruno—he'd been serious. All week, he'd been tearing up the solar system as if he owned the place, grappling to anything handy regardless of consequence, helping mainly his own friends . . . But even Hugo, strapped as ever to the cabin's floor, made mewling noises that were quite a good imitation of amusement.

"I'm sure we could all use a rest," he grumbled, and everyone laughed at that, too.

"You're planning to melt through solid rock?" Shiao asked. "He could be buried quite deep, couldn't he?"

"Unlikely," Deliah said. "For the same reasons already cited. His equipment needs to be on the surface—or to stick up *through* the surface, at any rate—and he'll want to be close to it. It's the same reason your eyes and ears are up next to your brain—so the signals don't have far to travel."

"So how deep should we expect to burrow?"

She shrugged. "Less than fifty meters, at a guess. Of course, at the rate this ship tunnels that could still take a pretty long time."

"Three minutes to touchdown," the ship noted.

"There'll be a-a-access ports at the surface," Muddy said, finally climbing onto his acceleration couch. His hands and voice were shaking, Bruno saw. He was going in to face his personal Satan. Was there ever a better reason to be terrified? "He never uses his ports, but they're always there. I've seen his secret f-facilities elsewhere in the solar system, and I doubt he'd deviate much from pattern. We should be armed, by the way; we can expect a stiff resistance from robot guards. Captain Shiao?"

"Yes, sir?"

"Can you recommend some hand weapons to our fax machine, please?"

"Certainly." From his folding couch, Shiao rattled off a series of model numbers, technical specifications, magazine sizes and battery capacities, piezoelectric coefficients and physical dimensions. Beside him, the fax hummed and glowed.

"Acknowledged, sir," *Sabadell-Andorra* replied a few moments later. "Weapons are ready."

With shaking hands, Muddy snapped his couch harness in place. "Right. Well, everyone should pick one up on the way out. I don't suppose we have sufficient mass in the reservoir to make s-spacesuits?"

"Only two complete ones," the ship replied apologetically. "We are low on certain key elements, notably oxygen."

"We could send two of us ahead in full armor," Cheng Shiao suggested. "I will, naturally, volunteer."

It took Bruno a moment to realize the suggestion was aimed solely at him. He *was* the commander of this expedition, in every conceivable sense. Such a decision *was* clearly his. He considered it. Would dividing their forces leave them vulnerable? Would the ship be safer with people aboard to guard her? Did it matter, two people, or four, or six? He wanted no more deaths on his conscience, but wasn't at all sure how to accomplish this under the circumstances.

He did know, in a low, cold-blooded way, that Shiao was the one person here—other than himself—that he'd be most willing to sacrifice, if such sacrifice could not be helped. Shiao was the person most willing to sacrifice *himself*, and also the one most qualified—far more qualified than Bruno— to break into the fortress of a mad genius.

The sun moved out of the bow window, which turned clear again, showing stars and a few wispy tendrils of solar corona. Their little ship could be anywhere, really; looking up there gave no impression that they were about to land on a planet.

"All right," Bruno said finally, "Shiao and I will don space suits and attempt to seize control of Marlon's study, wherever it may be. I'm not sure whether we can reverse the damage he's done, but if so that will be the likeliest place from which to accomplish it. The rest of you stay with the ship."

"I object," Vivian said immediately, from her little couch

beside Shiao's own. "I *am* a Commandant-Inspector of the Royal Constabulary."

"Also a sixteen-year-old girl," Bruno and Shiao said together.

"I didn't have any heroics in mind, thank you," she said, with a cool stiffness that belied her age. "I'm thinking of Declarant Sykes' household control systems. There must be an interface somewhere, and if I can find it I may be able to issue law-enforcement overrides to the resident intelligence. If not, I may at least be able to sabotage it in some way."

Bruno thought about this. In no way did he wish to further endanger Vivian's life. There was danger enough, without sending her off to the mercies of armed robots and other household security systems.

"None of us have backup patterns we can rely on," he reminded her. "Our actions here carry the sting of permanence. If you die, you'll *die*."

"I'm aware of that, Declarant."

"Hmm. Yes. Well, I leave it up to Shiao. He seems quite protective of you."

"I—" Shiao began, but was immediately interrupted.

"I order you to agree," Vivian said.

Shiao reddened; his protective instincts were suddenly frustrated, bottled in. He didn't like that one bit.

"Cheng," she warned, her copper eyes flashing angrily, "this won't look good on my report. Physically, I'm sure you could prevent me, but you *do not* want to refuse a direct order. Nor would you want, in any way, to endanger this mission. Would you like to be the cause of our failure?"

"I . . . would not," he said, with visible effort.

"I'll take every precaution," she said, softening. "I have no desire to upset you."

He slumped back into his couch. "I'll agree, Commandant-Inspector, on the sole condition that you not go alone."

"I'll go with her," Deliah said. "I've dealt with some balky intelligences in my time."

Hugo, strapped right where it had been for the past several

days, started up an urgent mewling. "Me! Me! Me!" it seemed almost to be saying.

"Steady, old thing," Bruno said in his best tone of reassurance.

"Thirty seconds to touchdown," the ship informed them.

Muddy, eyes on his sensors, worried at the hypercomputer interfaces with badly shaking hands. "We appear to be d-directly over the central complex, with several access ports nearby. The habitable area consists of four main chambers plus assorted closets and conduits, eighteen meters below ground. Optimal landing site . . . identified."

Suddenly, the space above them was alive with brief, intense, moon-sized flashes of light. They were taking fire again.

"He's detected us," Shiao said unnecessarily.

"Centroid of detonations is eighty kilometers above us," said Muddy. "We're close to the source—he may not be physically able to aim any lower than that. Ship, probability of a hit?"

"Twenty percent, each second."

"Time to touchdown?"

"Three seconds. Two. One. Zero."

The deck thumped beneath them, gently. Paradoxically, the sense of gravity lessened immediately, as if they'd been parked and stationary all along, and now the ground had dropped out from under them. Above, the view still gave no impression of a planetary environment; on Mercury, outer space started a millimeter above the soil. And the blasts of the zero-point field inversion weapon started eighty kilometers above that!

"He won't hit us on the ground," Deliah said hopefully. "He might hurt his own equipment."

"It looks like taking off again will be a bit of trouble, though," Tusité observed quietly. Her eyes had begun to take on a kind of refugee stare, an unwillingness to be further surprised or intimidated.

Bruno was out of his harness and up within four seconds

of touchdown; Shiao was even faster. At the hatchway, the familiar sizzling sounds had begun as *Sabadell-Andorra* melted its way into one of Muddy's promised 'access ports.'

"Time to penetration?" Muddy called out anxiously.

"Ninety-two seconds," the ship replied.

"Spacesuits," Shiao said. "Quickly." He picked up a bundle from beside the fax machine, tossed it to Bruno, then picked up another bundle for himself. Bruno struggled into the garment as best he could, and the suit itself did its best to help him. Still, he'd only worn one of these things once before in his life, and at that time he'd had palace servants to help him into it. It took him well over a minute to get dressed. Shiao—finished in a quarter the time—passed out weapons and then, for nearly a full thirty seconds, tapped a ringing, armorclad toe on the deck.

"All right," Bruno said when he was finally ready.

Hugo, to his astonishment, stood up alongside him. Had the battered old robot somehow struggled free of its restraining straps? They lay on the floor, neatly piled a meter away from the iron rings they'd been strung through. Good Lord, had Hugo actually *unfastened* all the hasps, with his clumsy golden fingers? It seemed inconceivable.

"Mewl," the blank metal face said, with what sounded for all the worlds like satisfaction.

Bother it, there was no time for this. "You stay here, Hugo. Guard the ship, with Muddy."

"Pick a weapon, sir," Cheng Shiao suggested urgently, pointing at a pile of clutter beside the fax. "His defenses may still be coming on-line. For everyone's safety, we should be moving along as quickly as possible."

"Hmm. Indeed," Bruno said, peering down at the weapons pile through the clear dome of his space helmet. Should he select one of the pistols? The rifle? The vibrating impervium sword? At the very bottom of the pile was a simple wellstone rod, a meter and a half in length and as big around as a stairway banister. Bruno reached for it, pulled it up from the clutter, felt the heft of it in his hand. It was very light, like a toy made of foam. But it was wellstone; currently it emulated a black polymer surface, but it could become almost anything in his hands. Less a weapon than a humble *tool*, like an oversized hammer, but he took it nonetheless.

Shiao saw this, and nodded. He himself had taken up a pistol in one hand and a sword in the other, and waited now by the door with grim impatience.

The sizzling noises stopped.

"Safe to open hatch," *Sabadell-Andorra* said.

"I'm scared," Tusité said, as if unable to help herself.

"We'll b-be scared together," Muddy reassured her, in a voice at least as shaky. He threw a trembling arm around her.

Meanwhile, Shiao threw the latches and pulled the door open. On the other side was a simple pressure vessel, a metal cylinder with a door of its own facing off to one side. In that door was a little circular window of some heavily tinted, glassine material, through which a gray-white moonscape was visible. There were two more cylinders nearby outside, their hulls reflecting mirror-bright in the harsh sunlight, and beyond them were some other, smaller glittery things less easily identified.

And farther away still, where the ground started rising up into low, rounded hills, Bruno saw the inky blackness of superabsorbers. Solar energy conversion, nearly 100% efficient. He thought of his own little sun, imprisoned in converters and finally murdered outright, and he winced inwardly. Marlon had thought things through much better than Bruno ever had; he would not want for energy in this place.

The floor of the cylinder opened into a spiral staircase leading down into darkness.

"Come," Shiao said without delay, leaping for the staircase and beckoning Bruno to follow. The gravity was light here— probably no more than half a gee. Shiao seemed to glide down the stairs like a man-shaped balloon, his feet only occasionally touching down. In moments, the shadows had swallowed him whole. Gulping, Bruno started after him, probably with a good deal less grace.

Had Bruno been a claustrophobic or acrophobic sort, these stairs would be a nightmare—each one just barely wide enough for his foot, the spiral itself just barely wide enough for his suited body, and without any sort of banister. As the first turn completed, the stairs above him closed over in a tight, low ceiling that was barely high enough to accommodate his helmet dome. His suit headlamps switched on; they were the only source of illumination, although far below it seemed he could see the dull reflections of Shiao's lights. He clanked downward, metal toes on metal stairs, for what seemed like a long time: four turns, five, six . . .

Finally, at the eighth turn of the spiral, the stairs opened out into a chamber that Shiao's headlamps—and now Bruno's own—showed to be roughly the size of a di-clad worker's platform. Ahead, the chamber was lined wall to wall with glossy black robots. They were short, long armed, long fingered. Some of them carried glossy black pistols of strange design; others were empty handed, but reached out those empty hands and made popping, blue-white electrical arcs across the spaces between them. There were twenty of the robots lined up across the room, and in fact, Bruno saw that in places they were two rows deep, and behind them all was a fax machine that, every few seconds, glowed and hummed and spat out a new comrade to join them. Rarely had Bruno—or anyone, really—seen a sight so menacing.

"Freeze! Royal Constabulary!" Shiao said in quick but officious tones. "This facility is a suspected crime scene. All autronic and telerobotic mechanical entities are ordered to shut down forthwith."

Ignoring him, the robots, moving as a single entity, took a giant, clanking step forward.

That was all the encouragement Shiao needed—he raised his sword and pistol, uttered an uncharacteristically wild exclamation, and leaped directly at them. Pistols coughed—not only Shiao's own but those of the robots as well. Shiao staggered. Bruno himself was knocked back by a series of impacts across his chest and arms. Bullets exploded in yellow-white pops, snapping miniature shrapnel into walls and floor and ceiling.

Shiao cried out again, not in pain but in a sort of battle mania. In one motion he straightened his body, aimed, and fired his pistol point-blank into the skull of the nearest robot. The robot, alas, neither staggered nor fell.

Breathing hard, too hard, Bruno realized he himself was essentially unhurt—these space suits were tough, bullet-proof. His helmet dome was slightly chipped in two places, and the white outer fabric of the suit itself was discolored here and there. Unfortunately, the gleaming hulls of the robot guards appeared to be tougher still.

Undaunted, Shiao hefted his sword against the same attacker. That worked much better—the impervium blade, vibrating so rapidly its edges were a fog, sliced through the robot's neck, decapitating it cleanly. But still the robot did not fall; still it reached for Shiao with long, bright-sparking hands. A dozen robots pressed around Shiao, clawing silently, mere moments from zapping him or crushing him or lifting him off the floor and doing Heaven knows what. Another six of the things were advancing on Bruno—*clank, clank, clank.* And he realized he had never—not once in his life—struck a blow in anger. He had never learned how.

The situation was, in a word, desperate.

But there *was* a rod of wellstone in Bruno's hands, gripped tightly, held out before him at chest level, and with a few whispered commands he caused its surface—in the middle and on the ends, well away from his hands— to seethe with all manner of exotic fields and substances, all manner of EM radiation and software pathogens and electrochemical reactions. He had no idea what these enemies were made of, which of the thousands of improbably durable materials had been woven together to form these gleaming hulls, but he figured surely *something* would hurt them. Ditto their sensory and computational systems—no matter how rugged the design, in the end they had to be made of something, controlled by something, *vulnerable to something* in the wellstone's vast library.

The robots advanced, and advanced some more. In another moment they'd be upon him . . .

"Back, you!" Bruno shouted at them. With more conviction than skill, he lashed out with the rod before the robots quite had a chance to lash out at him.

The results are, of course, known to all, as the blitterstaff has been a standard antiautomata weapon for hundreds of years. But recall that de Towaji had no history to fall back on; he invented the thing right there and then, with little time for a careful consideration of its properties. Try to imagine, then, his sense of stunned relief and triumph, when the advancing robots *screamed* and *bled* and *melted* at his touch! Six of them toppled immediately: masses of twitching, disorganized, heterogeneous matter that ruined the floor wherever they fell, warping and buckling it with blitter scars.

Six more robots advanced over the smoldering carcasses of their brethren. Six more fell. Some few of the victims retained, at least approximately, the shapes their creator had given them, but as for *function,* not one of them remained conscious or coherent for longer than a few milliseconds.

Cheng Shiao had meanwhile given a good account of himself, having completely dismembered three of the robots through a series of carefully aimed strikes. Their severed arms and legs, littering the deck around him, naturally fought on, but mindlessly, their distant heads and torsos unable to advise them.

But Shiao was sorely pressed, his spacesuit a mess of burns and gouges, his helmet dome spiderwebbed with cracks. Angry robots surrounded him three rings deep, and their bludgeoning claws struck at him again and again, with telling blows. He staggered, lurched, fought as madly and yet also as *carefully* as his skills and training permitted. But it wasn't enough. His doom was certain.

Bruno, realizing the power of this thing he carried in his hands, had become a bit giddy with it all. He advanced on the robots, screaming and laughing in a voice that none would recognize, and dashed them one by one to oil-smeared flinders.

"Away! Away!" he shouted, and while robots are incapable of fear, their controlling software does have some inkling of caution. Walking directly into a weapon, or holding still while one is wielded against them, is *inefficient* compared to a duck-and-roll attack or even a simple outflanking maneuver. So Shiao's attackers, becoming aware of the blitterstaff in their midst, began to shrink back from it as though afraid. They would have dived for Bruno's knees, surely, or ducked aside to get behind him, if he weren't whirling the thing around him with such crazy abandon.

One by one, they slipped into its range and were destroyed, and with each fallen comrade, the panic of the others seemed to increase. Soon they were ignoring Shiao entirely, stumbling over each other in their press to escape. Bruno shouted his laughter over and over, all the bottled rage finding its outlet at last. Even Shiao cringed before him.

But the fight wasn't over yet. The fax machine had begun to spit out new designs: tentacled robots capable of leaving a damaged limb behind, and soon afterward, toylike robots too small and fast and numerous to hold at bay. The surviving longarms had got their act together as well, falling back to a position along the far wall, from which they hurled a staggering stream of explosive bullets while slowly fanning out along the walls. Bruno's rage began to cool; he sensed the danger all around him. These were not tenpins, after all, but vicious, remorseless killing machines that would take the first opening he provided them.

He had to get to that *fax*, had to shut it down. It was the source of all these enemies, and who knew what it might spew out next?

"To the fax!" he said to Shiao.

Wobbling slightly on his bullet-scarred feet, Shiao finally came up alongside Bruno. The two began to advance, but resistance ahead was stiff, the new robots less and less willing to give ground, and harder and harder to score with a clean kill. Multijointed impervium tentacles, blitter-struck and writhing madly, piled up in drifts on the floor ahead of them, while the robots who'd lost them fought on with grim, fear-less determination.

It could have gone on like that for a long time, inch by bloody, oily inch, had a new factor not entered the fray. "Mewl!" a battered-looking robot of tin and gold cried, wading into the carnage to stomp and stomp and *stomp* the little toy soldiers. "My! My! Mewl!"

"Hugo!" Bruno cried, alarmed for his friend. "Go back. Go back to the ship!"

"Mewl!" Hugo replied sternly, looking Bruno full in the face while stomping flat yet another little robot.

The enemy robots seemed perplexed for a moment, unsure what to make of this development. It didn't take them long to figure it out, though—within seconds Hugo was swarmed, covered head to toe in angry little robots, and a tentacled monstrosity was advancing, flailing about with all manner of evil weapons.

But Shiao saw that moment of confusion, the distraction of the toy soldiers, and struck hard, slicing half the tentacles off another monstrosity and driving a sharp thrust directly into the heart of a third. They fought on, of course, but soon Bruno was there beside him, laying about with the blitter-staff, and finally the tentacled robots—there were five of them now—began to fall.

And then, all at once, the two men were right there at the fax orifice, a simple frame of wellstone surrounding a fog-shrouded vertical plate. Shiao looked at Bruno, who tapped the rim of the thing with his varicolored staff. That was all it took—the fax machine groaned, expelled a cubic meter of white plastic beads, and promptly expired in a mess of oil and smoke.

After that, it was simply a cleanup operation. Bruno ran to a beleaguered Hugo, kicking toy soldiers off him one by one. Hugo had fallen to his knees, and one of his arms had come off and was dangling by a single wire. But there weren't *that* many toy soldiers, now that their supply was finite. The tide had clearly turned against them. A few tried to leap onto Bruno's left arm, apparently aiming for the environmental controls there, and a few others tried—somewhat pathetically—to retreat toward the protection of the remaining longarms. Bruno finished them all off, though, while Shiao hacked the longarms apart with his sword. The last enemy they killed together, Shiao lopping the head off and Bruno going after the body, reducing it with one blow to a pile of steaming shards, like a dropped soup bowl.

Then the two men fell against each other, weeping and laughing with relief.

"I thought I was doomed!" Shiao expanded, spreading his arms wide. "Well fought, sir! Well fought! What on Earth did you *do* to those poor bastards?"

"Dropped a library on them," Bruno panted, and laughed at his own joke. He turned to Hugo. "*You* came at just the right time, old thing. And fought well! You're smarter than I credit, aren't you?"

Hugo, more battered than ever, said nothing, but stared at the arm dangling from its scarred, scorched shoulder.

"We'll fix you," Bruno promised. "You've done your part. More than your part. Are you able to make it back to the ship?"

Hugo seemed to consider for a moment, before slowly shaking its head. The neck joints squeaked alarmingly. Indeed, Hugo did look much the worse for wear, unlikely to rise at all, much less climb eight turns of stairs. Presently, it fell from its knees to its metal buttocks, landing with a dull clank.

"Er," Bruno said, "damn, will you survive at all?"

Hugo considered that as well, and finally—squeakily—nodded. With its remaining hand, it gestured for Bruno and Shiao to go on without it.

"Very well, friend," Bruno said, still fighting his surprise. "God willing, we'll return for you shortly."

Then he marched toward the far wall—which was featureless—and said, "Door."

Not surprisingly, nothing happened—Marlon's stronghold

was programmed to *kill* invaders, not to obey them. But Shiao, in a move no doubt routine among the Royal Constabulary, took up the impervium sword again, knocked twice on the wall as politely as you please, then carved a perfect rectangular door of his own.

"I shall lead this time," Bruno said, stepping forward.

But Shiao, whose body blocked the new doorway, turned and gave him a hard look. "No, sir, you shall not. You, at least, must reach Sykes' study alive." Then he was stepping through, into another darkened chamber.

He screamed almost at once. Bruno hurried through to see what was the matter.

On the other side was a chamber much like the one they'd just left, with another fax machine in precisely the same place. There were no *robots* this time, for which Bruno was grateful, but instead a viscid, blue-green substance, seemingly halfway between a slimy fluid and a vapor, floated from the rectangular orifice. Indeed, the room was full of it already, tendrils lapping around at knee level, like ground fog.

"What is it?" Bruno demanded. "What's wrong?"

"This substance is corrosive!" Shiao warned at once, backing away, forcing Bruno back through the doorway again. "It's eating through the armor of my boots!"

"Is it?" Bruno asked, alarmed. He bent to look. Indeed, Shiao's boots—in none too good a shape to begin with—were bubbling and smoking at their surface, as the blue-green substance ate its way in. Curiously, though, where any reasonable chemical corrosion would have slowed down as it progressed, as its reagents were slowly consumed in the reaction, this one seemed to be holding steady, chewing its way through the armor with an almost mechanical efficiency.

Almost mechanical, indeed.

"That's a disassembler fog," Bruno said. "Nonreplicating, by the look of it. Hold still, please! It's a spatially discontinuous cellular automaton, each microscopic unit technically independent, but owing to power and mass distribution issues it's effective only in clusters of a milliliter or more. Actually, I think I've seen this exact strain before! I think this is the stuff the Tongans used to use in the garbage dumps at Ha'atafu!"

"Can you neutralize it?" Shiao asked, with quite remarkable calm.

"I expect so," Bruno agreed. "It really is more of a tool than a weapon. Quite tractable, generally." Whispering to the wellstone rod, he caused its surface, on one end, to form a layer of Bondril, a substance far stickier than natural atoms could ever produce. Then he touched this end to Shiao's left boot, and *rolled* it up and down. The tiny disassembler automata were plucked up by the trillions of trillions, until finally there were none left on the boot at all. Or at least, not enough to get any organized activity together. With the rod's other end, Bruno repeated the procedure on Shiao's right boot, until it was clear as well.

"Now they're simply eating your staff," Shiao complained, though he did sound relieved.

Bruno couldn't shrug inside his spacesuit, but he did say "Piffle." The disassemblers *were* disassembling his staff, dropping out a fine silicon dust beneath them, but a few more whispered commands caused the affected areas to *sizzle* with pulsed electrical currents at frequencies designed specifically to kill disassemblers. In moments, the bubbling and smoldering had ceased. Then he simply commanded the wellstone's outermost layer to slough off, leaving him with a good-as-new staff only slightly thinner than the one he'd started with.

"What *would* the Queendom do without you?" Shiao wanted to know.

Bruno declined to comment, saying simply, "We still have the fog in the room to contend with. Come."

"Will your library trick work this time?" Shiao pressed, again blocking Bruno's passage through the doorway.

"Let's find out," Bruno said, and nudged him through.

Interestingly, there didn't seem to be any more fog in the

room than there had been when they stepped out. A quick look at the fax revealed that it was off, not functioning any longer.

"Perhaps Vivian has had some success," Shiao said hopefully.

"Indeed. Or else the fog has simply attacked the fax that produced it. An inelegant design, if so. If you'll excuse me, please?"

"Mmm." Reluctantly, Shiao stepped aside to let Bruno have access to the edge of the blue-green fog bank. The staff was returned to blitter mode and dipped lightly into the fog.

The result was instantaneous: the fog—really just a suspension of electromagnetic fields generated by the individual disassemblers—vanished at once, and in its place a much sparser cloud of gray-white dust settled harmlessly to the floor.

"Very good," Shiao said approvingly. "Very good indeed. We've only one or two more rooms to get through, eh?"

"Mmm. Time will tell, my friend. It doesn't pay to underestimate Marlon Sykes."

Again, Shiao cut a hole through the far wall. Again, he preceded Bruno through it. Again, he screamed.

"What now?" Bruno asked, hurrying through behind him. "Oh. Oh. My goodness."

He'd been struggling, actually, to remain afraid rather than angry, to maintain the edge of caution and improvisation that fear encouraged so readily. Now, there'd be no need to force it. The third chamber was much like the first and second had been: large, dark, empty of furnishings . . . It even had a fax in the same exact location, although it, too, appeared to be powered down or broken, its status lights off, its wellstone housing inactivated.

What was different this time was that the room—virtually the *entire* room—was occupied by an enormous, soft-skinned, pinkish brown spider.

Well, perhaps "spider" was the wrong term, since it had six legs instead of eight, and since each leg terminated in a perfect little human hand, and since its meat-colored body carried a swollen, bulbous caricature of Wenders Rodenbeck's face in place of a ten-eyed spider head. Its two eyes glowed a malevolent red in the darkness.

Bruno quickly decided he'd never seen anything so horrific in all his years, and he couldn't help echoing Shiao's heartfelt scream.

He could be more horrified, though; he discovered this when the spider turned its red eyes upon him, opened its fanged mouth wide, and spoke in a rasping parody of Wenders Rodenbeck's actual voice.

"Ah, de Towaji. Welcome."

"My God!" was all Bruno could think to say in return. He hefted his staff like the weapon it was, pointing one end up at that hideous face. "My God, man! My *God*."

"He told me you might be coming," the spider said, around a quite incredible mouthful of dripping fangs. "I'm pleased that you have. I never disliked you, you know, even when He commanded that I should."

"Wenders," Bruno said, "what has he *done* to you?"

"Made a hideous monster of me, obviously," the spider quipped. Then the eyes narrowed, and the legs and body lurched, and suddenly that swollen face was two meters closer to Bruno's own. A leg raised; a finger shook, tsk tsk. "Do I finally frighten you, Declarant? Actually, this form was my own idea. Well, His idea, but I agreed to it. Rather than the alternatives, of which I was offered several. Unpleasant. But I'm the man himself inside—playwright, lawyer, defender of planets, same as ever. Same as he made me, anyway. You do realize I'm to murder you?"

"I've little doubt of it," Bruno agreed, afraid to move, afraid to do anything. The sheer *size* of this creature implied there was nothing Bruno or Shiao could do to stop it. Mortally wounded, it could nonetheless murder them both a dozen times over, simply with its death throes.

"You've been grievously mistreated, sir," Shiao offered up to the thing.

The spider, swiveling its head toward Shiao, looked surprised. "Have I? How, exactly? Do I know you, sir?"

"Actually," Shiao said, craning his neck to look the thing in the eye, "you and I just spent three weeks together on a derelict platform, about ten million kilometers sunward of here."

"Really!" The spider was instantly intrigued, its monstrous eyebrows shooting up, its many knees—or perhaps elbows—bending until its leathery bulk plopped heavily onto the floor. "A guy can't help but be intrigued by *that*. Where am I now? Not with you any longer?"

"No, sir," Shiao agreed. "You were killed about twenty minutes ago. By Declarant Sykes."

"Ah. Well, I can't say I'm surprised. I'm always tying Him up in court and such, without realizing just how badly that upsets Him. I'd probably kill *myself*, if I met me. Bastard. But how did I die? Was I dramatic? Was I brave?"

"Yes, sir. Very brave. You were on a spaceship blasting for Mercury, on a mission to save the Queendom, and you ran afoul of some stray collapsium."

"Extraordinary!" the spider said. "I always *told* people I'd die that way, sooner or later. Not saving the Queendom, I mean—running afoul of collapsium. Nasty stuff, that. Meaning no offense to you, Declarant."

"Er, none taken," Bruno said quickly.

"I'm to kill you," the spider said again. "Have I mentioned? I'm conditioned for it, though obviously I've never had the actual opportunity. Any idea what that's like?"

"Why haven't you killed Declarant Sykes?" Shiao suggested.

The spider responded with a deep, awful rumbling noise that Bruno eventually identified as laughter. "Kill him? Kill *him*, what a thought! Oh, I could never do that. My ordeal here has brought the two of us very close together. I'm written into his script, and vice versa. You probably wouldn't understand that, but take my word: It's a tangible connection."

"I *do* understand it," Shiao insisted. "You and *I* became very close, during our time on the platform. I was very sorry to see you die. And I'm very *happy*, if a bit dumfounded, to discover that a copy of you still exists in . . . some form."

"Really." Again, the spider seemed almost dreamily intrigued.

"You mustn't do it," Bruno said, suddenly finding his voice, and with it his anger. "You mustn't do Marlon's bidding. He has a way of breaking people, of conscripting their minds as well as their bodies. Perhaps you can't see what a joke he's made of you, what a shadow of your former self, but I tell you, *the very same thing has happened to me*. And do you know where *I* am? I'm guarding the spaceship that brought us all here. I'm *determined* to overcome the damage Marlon has done, to me and to everyone else. You must let us pass, sir. We'll carve a hole in that wall, there, and pass through it into Marlon's study, and if we survive our business there, we *will* return to help you!"

Again, the spider laughed. "You need to understand, sir, I'm conditioned to resist those sort of appeals. You're not dealing with amateur security here; we've been optimizing for years and years."

Bruno's anger flared. "All right then, you, why haven't you killed us already? Why talk to us at all?"

Shiao sighed angrily, looking as if he'd just realized something important. "Declarant, perhaps his purpose is simply to *delay* us. A familiar face, an encouragement to stand around persuading him . . . We haven't the time, sir."

Perhaps the spider had been conditioned to react to *that* phrase with violence, to delay the fight as long as possible and then commit to it wholeheartedly, with intent to win. Perhaps it was angered for some reason, or had simply heard enough. In any case, it leaped for Shiao with surprising nimbleness, snatching him up in its oversized jaws and driving its dripping, mirror-bright fangs *hard* against the fabric of his space suit. Over the suit radios, Bruno heard Shiao gasp, heard the breath squeezed out of his body as it had so recently been squeezed out of Rodenbeck's, inside the Ring Collapsiter fragment.

All thought fled from Bruno's mind. He had let Rodenbeck

die, had *carelessly* let him slip too close to the collapsium and be crushed to death. He simply would not repeat that mistake.

Throwing down his staff, he dodged between two pink-brown spider legs to retrieve the impervium sword where Shiao had dropped it. At his touch, the thing came alive, its blade vibrating all in a blur, its handle acoustically isolated and quite firm and steady in his grip. Then, with a patience and precision that would have astonished him a minute earlier, he stepped forward and lopped off the spider's swollen Rodenbeck head.

He fully expected the thing to die badly, messily, and in this he was not disappointed; the spider thrashed violently as its head was parting company with the rest of it, and as a result the head *flew* across the room—with Shiao still inside it—and crashed hard against the wall. The body's spasms did not end there. Quite the reverse: its legs, with surprising coordination, carried the body forward to crash hard against another wall, and another, and another one still. The hands flailed madly, grabbing at anything. The body rolled. Bruno was lifted, dashed, trampled, and for one dizzy moment, crushed up hard against the ceiling. The wind was knocked out of him immediately, and his limbs were twisted all the wrong ways, and his skull suffered a number of sharp blows against the dome of his helmet, which *should* have been too far from his head to make contact, if his neck had been holding onto it properly. Those were the hard parts of the ordeal; he waited patiently through the rest of it, willing himself limp, knowing he had nothing to gain by struggling against this agonizing tumbling and buffeting.

Finally, what seemed like hours later, the spider gave a final shudder and lay still.

Bruno tried to breathe, waited a few seconds, tried again. Now, finally, he could hold off panic no longer. He managed a little, gasping inhalation, but it only seemed to make things worse. He tried again, and again. Finally, when he didn't black out, he realized he must actually be getting enough oxygen to survive, regardless of how it *felt*. He willed himself to be patient one final time, and partially succeeded.

A minute later, or maybe just a few seconds, he managed a fairly deep, fairly refreshing breath. A few more followed, more easily, and after another minute he gritted his teeth and forced himself to sit up.

Shiao was nearby, still trapped inside the spider's head. His helmet dome had shattered, and his suit's tough outer layer hung around him in scorched tatters, revealing the tubes and hoses of the midlayer underneath. His headlamps had shattered and gone out, and of course, like everything else in the room, he was covered in sticky red blood. It was only the faint, purposeful movement of Shiao's arm casting moving shadows on the wall behind him that let Bruno know he was alive at all.

"Shiao?" He called out.

No reply.

Gathering his breath and wits, Bruno managed to flip over onto his hands and knees, and crawl—slowly and painfully—to the enormous fallen head.

"Shiao?"

This time, he was answered with a groan. Bruno completed the journey, then threw himself back over into a sitting position. It took another several seconds to get his breath again. "Shiao?" He touched the man's arm, felt it move beneath his fingers. Shiao's head stirred. His eyes opened.

"Tight," he whispered.

Tight? Belatedly, Bruno realized the spider's jaw, in death, continued to clamp down on Shiao's body. Not as hard as before, probably, but hard enough to keep him from breathing properly. Mustering his strength, Bruno got to his knees, then his feet. He grabbed an edge of jaw and tugged on it. He'd half feared that the thing wouldn't budge, that he'd have to search under the spider's bus-sized carcass somehow, to find the sword again, to cut Shiao free. But no, the jaw wasn't clamped, it was just *heavy*. With effort, he lifted it a few centimeters. With greater effort, he lifted it farther, and with the last of his strength lifted it a bit farther still, then gently kicked Shiao's body out from between the fangs.

Shiao gasped, exhaled, gasped again. He was breathing. Not normally, perhaps. Not easily. But breathing nonetheless. Now fully exhausted, Bruno sat down beside his fallen comrade with no thought at all for what should happen next.

Perhaps fortunately, this decision was made for him: in the far wall of the chamber, a door opened up. And there in the doorway, framed with light, stood Declarant-Philander Marlon Fineas Jimson Sykes.

"Good Lord, Bruno," he said wonderingly, in the clear, strong voice so familiar from days gone by. "You really *are* my peer."

in which lives are pledged and traded

Incredibly, Cheng Shiao lifted his blood-streaked head up into the light and spoke. "Declarant-Philander Marlon Fineas Jimson Sykes, it is my . . . duty as a Captain of the Royal Constabulary to place you under immediate arrest, for suspicion . . . of the crimes of murder, high treason, and regicide in the first degree."

The voice was weak, bubbling wetly, but the words themselves were clear enough. Shadows danced in Bruno's headlight beams as Shiao continued. "You have the right to an attorney. You have the right . . . to be interrogated by disposable copies. You have the right to commit suicide without entering a plea. Do you . . . understand these rights?"

For a moment, no one moved or spoke. Then, finally, Marlon's silhouette said, "Cheng Shiao, right? I remember you. We once investigated a murder case together."

"A murder for which you . . . are now prime suspect," Shiao agreed.

"Hmm," Marlon shifted slightly in the doorway, and Bruno's sound pickups clearly transmitted the rubbing and creaking of fabrics. Marlon actually seemed to consider the offer for a moment, but finally he shook his head. "It seems a shame to kill you both; it really does. I admire nothing so much as tenacity. There will be a new society after I'm finished here, and perhaps there's a place for both of you in it somewhere. Oh, I'm sure you can't conceive of that right now, but I do pride myself on being a fair man. Come. I'll show you around, and then place you both in fax storage. That's humane, isn't it?"

Neither Bruno nor Shiao answered.

Sighing, Marlon reached into a little pocket in his gray-blue waistcoat and withdrew a complex little pistol of some sort, which he proceeded to aim at Cheng Shiao's head.

"Really, Bruno, you *know* I'm capable of violence. Now, shall I shoot your friend, or save him? The choice is up to you."

"Stop!" Bruno said at once, raising both hands to the level of his shoulders. "Lower the weapon. Show us what you wish to show us, but you will not harm this man. I won't allow it."

"Won't you?" Marlon said, amused. "All right then. Come."

With effort, Bruno got his armored feet down under his armored body and slowly hauled himself erect. Every part of him throbbed with hurt; he could only imagine what Shiao must be going through.

"Forgive me, friend," he said then, extending a hand downward for Shiao to grasp. Shiao's fingers, all but exposed in the tatters of glove, gripped weakly, and with a tentative quality that suggested great pain. But grip they did, and soon Bruno was helping him up.

"I owe you everything, sir," Shiao said quietly as he wobbled to a standing position. "I'd follow you anywhere. I mean this in the literal sense."

"You're a fool, then," Bruno said back, in the same low tones, carried externally through the speaker beneath his chin. "I don't see how I can possibly get us out of this."

"Nevertheless," Shiao said, straightening.

Together, using one another for support, the two of them

hobbled toward that backlit doorway, toward the gun Marlon was pointing at them.

"That's it," Marlon said gently. "That's fine, both of you. The fighting's all done now—no one could possibly say you haven't tried. I'll see that history *does* mark your deeds, if only as a footnote to my own."

Then he was sidling back, making room for the two of them to step, side by side, through the doorway. The apartment on the other side of it was surprisingly small, surprisingly modest—a rumpled cot on one side, a fax, a toilet, and on the other side a wellstone desk much like the one Bruno had always used.

Bruno noted that the fax was dark, apparently lifeless. Ditto the desk, which was *bare* wellstone at the moment—a translucent gray matrix that emulated nothing.

"My winter quarters," Marlon apologized, catching Bruno's look. "It isn't much, but then it doesn't really need to be, does it?"

"Your systems are down," Bruno said.

Marlon's smile was sheepish. "Well, yes, there is that. Not entirely down, mind you—not yet, anyway. But the most *critical* systems—the ones on which the Queendom's fate depends—are inaccessible. I was hoping perhaps you could help me with that."

"I?" Bruno asked innocently.

Marlon's smile vanished. "I don't know what you've done, Bruno, but you'll kindly undo it. Immediately! The project has reached a critical juncture, and if I'm not at the controls in the next few hours there will *be* no *arc de fin*. The sun will still collapse, mind you, but there'll be no purpose to it, no benefit to anyone. *Senseless* death and destruction is something we all wish to avoid, I'd think."

"Hence your magnanimity," Bruno said.

"Oh, tch tch, Bruno. After all these years, you still doubt the special bond between us? Come, help me out of this jam. If you reflect a moment, you'll realize you have no actual choice about it."

Wobbling against Shiao's weight, Bruno sighed. "Marlon, can't you just stop this? I *believe* you. You've discovered the *arc de fin,* where I have not. Isn't that enough? History will mark your triumph either way. But if you end this villainy now, if you're willing to leave bad enough alone, you'll at least be remembered with some measure of approval. A would-be monster who, in the end, didn't have the heart for it. The *sun,* Marlon. Was there ever a more fundamental symbol of nurture, of comfort, of *life itself*?"

"I expect not," Marlon agreed, amicably enough. "I've come too far, though, Bruno. I wouldn't stop this if I could, and at this point I don't see that it's even possible. Now, that's an *honest* response. I could just as easily have agreed to your demand, let you reactivate my systems, and then killed you. That's what a *monster* would do. But I have more respect than that."

"And if *I* agree to *your* demand," Bruno countered, "and your systems are reactivated, you could still kill us both."

"I could," Marlon conceded. "But I give you my word that you and all your friends will be stored safely."

"Safely?" Shiao snorted. "Surely this place . . . will be among the first destroyed, and there *is* no Iscog to carry our patterns away from here."

Marlon shrugged. "Whether this camp will survive I'm not sure—it'll be on the nightside during the worst conflagrations, vulnerable only to neutrinos passing all the way through the planet. But the question is moot—I have a spaceship to escape in."

"Ah," Shiao said. "Of course you do."

"No insolence, please," Marlon said wearily. "I've already given you your lives, what more do you expect?"

There was no right answer to that question. No answer was attempted.

Finally, Marlon rolled his eyes, sighed heavily, and pointed the gun again at Shiao's head. It was a strange little thing, four tubes emerging from the rim of a parabolic dish, not parallel but *converged* on the geometric center of Shiao's skull. The whole thing was translucent and blue and quite fragile looking, like a funny toy designed to mock the concept of "gun." But Bruno had never seen anything like it, and that was reason enough to be afraid.

"Fifteen seconds, gentlemen. You've presumed on my patience long enough."

"Give him nothing," Shiao said calmly.

But Bruno held up a placating hand. "Marlon, please. This isn't easy for us."

"The others with you," Marlon said. "They'll die as well. Slowly, badly, if I have any say in the matter. Five seconds."

"I surrender," Bruno said quickly. "Please, harm none of them."

Marlon relaxed. "You're no fool, de Towaji. You understand: Your lives can end *along* with several billion others, or they can continue while those billions die anyway. Those are the only choices available. The equation is simple."

"Indeed," Bruno said, his heart quailing. He still hoped for some miracle, some way to bring this horrific matter to a less-than-horrific conclusion. But to achieve that miracle, even to *hope* for it, he must live at least a little while longer . . . "Can you access some sort of intercom or public address system? I'll need to speak with my friends."

"That can be arranged," Marlon said, stepping toward the live wellstone wall in which the doorway had appeared. He looked somewhat less than trusting as he tapped out a series of commands on the wellstone's surface.

A pickup and wall speaker appeared beside Bruno, at the same level as the speaker beneath his chin.

"Er, hello?" he tried. "Vivian, are you there?"

"Bruno!" Deliah van Skettering's voice called back immediately. "We were worried; you've been gone so long!"

"You may remain worried," Bruno said. Then, finally, he knew what he must do: He must order Deliah and Vivian and Tusité and Muddy away from this place. Could he not save the Queendom? Was it arrogance to think he ever could? Well, then at least he would save *something*, and not in the foul clutches of Marlon Sykes. He would order them away, and Marlon, with his systems down, would have no choice but to let them escape. Meanwhile, he would vent his anger on the available targets: Shiao first, naturally, but Shiao had just got done placing his fate in Bruno's hands. And Shiao's death, his inevitable death, might conceivably give Bruno enough time to throw himself hands-first at Marlon's throat—

But Vivian Rajmon's high, teenaged voice called out before he could quite get the words formed. "Cheng? R.C. Captain Cheng Shiao, are you all right?"

"I'm here, Commandant-Inspector," Shiao said, suddenly attentive. "I . . . would have you know that my heart was lost the moment I met you, Commandant-Inspector. It would have been yours, if you'd have had it—yours for a million years. But my *life* belongs to de Towaji, and to the Queendom. Forgive me."

And with those words, Bruno's hoped-for miracle occurred: Shiao's body, crippled and broken and bloodied though it was, somehow found the strength to *leap* four meters across the room at Marlon Sykes. Marlon had been suspicious, waiting for trouble of some sort, but Cheng Shiao was a hard man to stop. The gun went off with a little popping sound, but a moment later Shiao swept it from Marlon's hand, knocking it across the room so that it spun along the floor and came to rest beneath the rumpled cot. He knocked *Marlon* down as well, in the same clean motion.

"Good night!" Bruno couldn't help exclaiming.

Then Vivian's voice came again. "Cheng! Cheng!"

And Muddy's voice. "What's happening, sir? Can we help?"

Shiao wrestled Marlon facedown onto the floor, and then from somewhere, some pocket or recess in the tattered space-suit, produced a ball of handcuff putty and slapped it down on the small of Marlon's back. Rattlesnake-quick, it lashed out to encircle wrists and ankles, leaving Marlon neatly trussed and screaming. "Dealbreakers! Dealbreakers! Rotten, stinking, dishonest . . ."

But there was no look of triumph or even relief on Shiao's face. Only pain. He rolled away, falling onto his back, and Bruno could see the wound Marlon's gun had made in Shiao's abdominal cavity. Not a bullet hole, or a laser burn, but a *void*—a six-centimeter absence where armor and flesh should be. Transported? Vanished? The dream of matter, somehow undreamt? It hardly mattered; Shiao would not survive the injury. Already it was filling with blood. Cheng Shiao would be dead in sixty seconds, if that.

"Cheng!" Vivian called out again.

"He's injured," Bruno said back to her. "You must turn the faxes back on. Quickly!"

"I can't," she said. "I can't do it; *you* have to. We replaced part of the domestic software with your own household AI."

"You what?"

"It was in the ship's library. Never mind! Help Cheng!"

Bruno frowned, and for some reason he looked up at the ceiling. "House? Hello, are you here?"

"Good day, sir," that old, familiar voice said. "I'm detecting numerous diagnostic errors, and I seem to be under some sort of direct software assault from a native AI, but I await your instructions nonetheless. It's good to be working with you again, sir."

"Turn the faxes on!" Bruno cried, leveling a finger at Shiao's struggling, bleeding, *dying* body. "Help me get him into the fax! Quickly! Quickly!"

"Working," the house replied easily. "Fax machine activated."

Sure enough, the orifice hummed to life, flashed briefly, and extruded a humanoid robot of gold and tin, faceless and graceful, precisely like the servants Bruno had employed for so very many years. The space between fax and victim was several meters, but the robot danced across it in an instant, swept Shiao's body off the floor in a bloody arc, and hurled it directly into the orifice. The body vanished at once, and an instant later the robot had leaped through as well, vanished as well. The whole affair had taken three seconds.

Marlon still struggled on the floor, rolling and flopping, trying to face Bruno and only partially succeeding. "Nobody wins," he said urgently. "I know what you're thinking, Bruno, but you can't possibly grapple all that collapsium up away from the sun. Not in time, not at *all*. You can have your *arc de fin*; you can see the very lights and darknesses of uncreation. This year! This month! I give it to you, sir, my gift. All the credit, all the glory, if you'll only let me at the controls. Let me at them!"

"No," Bruno said flatly.

"No? Think hard, Bruno. I tell you, *you cannot save the sun*. Will you at least see that its death has meaning?"

"No. Indeed, I stand here wondering . . ." The hairs prickled up on the back of Bruno's neck. He felt awake, really *awake*, for perhaps the first time in his life. "I stand here wondering what I was thinking all that time. An *arc de fin*? What use is that? If we're to live forever, won't we see the end of time with our own two eyes? All too soon, I fear! We'll look back and say 'Already? Already the world is ending, the stars winking out? Why, we'd only just begun!' And if that end is *spoiled* by de Towaji, a trillion years before the fact, why . . . one wonders why we've bothered to live at all."

"You're mad," Marlon said, his voice edging on panic. Straining against the putty, he managed to lift his head enough to look Bruno in the eye. "It's my own fault; I've *driven* you mad. I've killed your Queen!"

"Indeed," Bruno agreed, nodding slowly. "Perhaps that's it. Perhaps that's all it is. The work of decades falls away like ashes, leaving nothing, no sense of purpose or desire. There is no Tamra for me to hide from, no Tamra for me to return to when at long last I'm finished. To live forever without her? Even to contemplate it? I suppose I *am* mad."

Marlon's eyes were sharp, his tone urgent. "Listen to me, Bruno. Ask a question with me. Where do people go when they die? Nowhere? Where exactly *is* nowhere?"

Ah, but Bruno was awake—he saw the trick in that question. He was encouraged to conclude that "nowhere," since it didn't exist, was of zero size, and by corollary that everything that no longer existed—being also of zero size and therefore located "nowhere"—could be found there, instantly, without effort. With zero movement, zero searching, zero time. Ah, but by that logic, everything that *never* existed could be found there as well. So could everything that existed now, but someday wouldn't. At the end of time, *everything* would be nowhere, including time itself, and so Bruno declined to fall for the trick. The size of nowhere was surely infinite, in time as well as space, else he and Marlon and everyone else would be there already.

He raised a finger in Marlon's direction, and waggled it. "House, remove this body as well."

"No, Bruno! No! Believe me, you can't stop this. It's pointless to try!"

The robot appeared, danced across the floor to where Marlon lay, and scooped him up.

"It's never pointless to *try*," Bruno mused.

And then the fax machine hummed, and there was no one else in the room there with him.

"Bruno?" Vivian's voice quietly, sadly, said from the speaker, treading with utmost tenderness. "Bruno, is Cheng all right?"

"He's stored, dear," Bruno replied wearily. "He's safe for the moment. But the sun, alas, is not."

It seemed to take a long time to hobble over to Marlon's little wellstone desk. "House," he said along the way, "activate that. Thank you."

He sat down at the wellwood chair, taking the load off his feet, off his back, off his pain. The old grapple controls were there, the old holographic displays, as if Marlon had cribbed them from Bruno's own designs. Tortured them, probably, from Muddy's own pained and screaming lips. How *tired* Muddy must have been, after years of torment! How extraordinary, that he'd managed to accomplish so much in spite of it.

Bruno pulled up an interface and quietly immersed himself.

Here was the sun, here the dotted line where the Ring Collapsiter had once stood. And beneath it, in a hundred spinning fragments, were the Ring Collapsiter's children, and he saw at once that there were simply too many of them, that they were simply too large, that most were simply too close to the sun to retrieve. They were mere *hours* from penetration, from the beginning of Sol's slow and painful death. Still, he grabbed the nearest one with Marlon's EM grapples, which were of a fine and strong design. He tugged, he twisted, he prodded and nudged. None of it, of course, worked. The best he could accomplish, really, would be to tear it apart, to break it, to let it collapse into a *real* black hole that he'd have even less hope of manipulating.

"Ah, well," he whispered, "she was a good star while she lasted."

And then he remembered the ring. The ring! The wellstone ring he'd plucked from his own hypercomputer, minutes before he'd destroyed it and the planet it stood on! That ring contained the program, the dance card, the recipe by which collapsium was converted to hypercollapsite vacuogel.

Perhaps all was *not* lost.

He stood, quickly, knocking over the chair behind him. The ring was on his finger, but his *finger* was inside this blasted spacesuit! "Off," he said to it. "Off, you!" And he struggled with it as the hasps unfastened, as the seams parted, as the blood-smeared helmet dome fell away and rang against the floor like a bell. Finally an arm was free, and he used that to free the other one, and he was about to peel his legs out of it as well when he decided that *bah*, it didn't matter. He pulled the chair up under him and stuffed the suit underneath it, trailing from the tops of his armored boots.

He plucked the blue-jeweled wellgold ring from his finger then, and plinked it down on the wellwood desktop. Little tendrils of blue light fanned out around it for an instant, symbolic of the enormous volume of data he'd just dumped into the system. He thrust his fingers once more into the grapple controls, but *this* time the collapsium shrank and vanished at his touch, all thousand kilometers of it contracting—within minutes!—into an all-but-invisible, all-but-intangible hyper-collapsite cap, not unlike the one crowning *Sabadell-Andorra's* bow. Last time, it had taken him a day, but all his careful steps were encoded here, sure as any music reel on Enzo's faux-antique player piano. And they could be played at high speed.

The rest was easy: he charged the thing up with a stream of protons and repelled it electrically. Inertia meant little to its hypercollapsite structure; in an instant it was moving, to the solar north, up out of the plane of the ecliptic where the planets all orbited and the people all lived. In another instant, it was moving *fast*, and in the instant beyond *that* it had exceeded solar escape velocity and was no longer Bruno's problem. Perhaps, in hundreds or thousands of years, civilization would expand enough to find such litter annoying—even hazardous—but at this point that was a risk Bruno was quite willing to take.

Settling in, he converted another collapsium fragment, and another, and another, and soon he was automating the process, overseeing it rather than controlling it directly with his fingers. He moved the system's attention here, and there, and especially *there*, where the collapsiter's children were already playing in the plasma loops of the upper chromopause.

He became aware of other people, standing around him while he worked. He listened to their breathing, to the rustle and ripple of their clothes as they shifted slowly from foot to foot, but really they were very quiet: they didn't cough or clear their throats, didn't ask questions, didn't disturb him in the slightest. Only when he realized theirs was an *awed* silence did he begin to get annoyed.

"Haven't you seen anyone clean up a mess before?" he asked gruffly.

But nobody answered him. Nobody dared. He continued with his work: twenty, fifty, *eighty* fragments cleared. It was slow going after that, the fragments more distant, the light-lag stretching his response times out to two minutes and more. But still, he persisted. Only when he'd cleared eighty-five fragments did he begin to fret. Only when he'd cleared ninety did he begin, truly, to doubt. Only when he'd cleared ninety-five did he know for certain, and only when he'd cleared ninety-eight did he admit defeat.

But admit it he did, pushing the chair back, standing up, turning around awkwardly with the spacesuit bunched up around his ankles. All his friends were there, waiting for him, keeping him company while he worked. Sad-faced Muddy with his jester's hair; little Vivian looking *almost* like the girl she used to be; Hugo, with his arm reattached and a band of shiny new metal around its socket; Deliah van Skettering staring rapt at Bruno's activities, interested as much in the mechanics as in the actual result. And Tusité, yes, the closest thing here to an innocent, uninvolved civilian. They had waited here like this for *hours*. Their faces—even Hugo's—were expectant, almost exultant; he hated to disappoint them. But disappoint them he must.

"There are, ah, two fragments," he began slowly, "that lie on the far side of the sun, inaccessible to grapples operating from the surface of Mercury. Now, I've dealt with several of these already—their orbits are relatively fast, and even here the sun is only a few degrees wide, not really *so* huge. So it's largely a matter of waiting a few hours for the fragments to come 'round where we can see them. The trouble is, these two aren't *going* to emerge—their trajectories intersect the photosphere long before they'll be visible or accessible to us."

Faces fell at the news, but otherwise no one replied to it, or reacted in any way. *They* were tired as well, Bruno saw: tired of hoping, tired of being afraid. Too tired, in the end, to react at all.

"I'm sorry," he told them sincerely. "The fault is entirely mine; if I'd juggled the priorities differently, if I'd handled these two fragments a few hours ago, this problem would not have occurred. And so, I have failed Tamra's Queendom a final time."

"So close," Deliah said. There was no reproach in her voice, though, no regret. In fact, she sounded almost proud. "So *close,* Bruno. You've done . . . The situation was *hopeless* two weeks ago—maybe it was hopeless way before that, and we just didn't know it. So if it's hopeless now, you're hardly to blame."

Then Muddy stepped forward, his arms outstretched, and for a moment Bruno thought he was going to be hugged. But instead, Muddy reached past him, plucked the little wellgold ring off the desktop, and pranced away.

"Hopeless?" he sang, his body twisting, twirling on one foot, so that Bruno believed, all at once, that he really *had* been a jester at some foul court of Marlon's. "Hopeless? There's never zero hope, as long as some dope has a life to throw away. Okay?" And with those words he was off, running for the door.

"Muddy?" Bruno said. "Muddy!"

He tried to give chase, but the spacesuit tripped him up, and he was obliged—with Tusité's help—to peel his feet out of it one by one. By this time, Muddy had a substantial lead. Bruno chased him on the blood-sticky floor of the spider room; the gritty, dusty floor of the fog room; the oily, carcass-strewn floor of the robot room; and up the spiral stairs themselves. The lights were on, at least—the place looked not so much *menacing* now as sadly defeated. But Muddy reached the hatch of *Sabadell-Andorra* fully ten seconds ahead of him, and by the time Bruno got there, there was only a smooth, seamless impervium surface to pound on.

A speaker emerged.

"Bruno, stand back, please. I'm going to melt the access cylinder's hull back into place."

Indeed, the ship's hull gleamed through a rough opening, metal and wellstone melted and folded and wrinkled away from what had, until moments ago, been the hatch. Now the edges of that hole began to sizzle and pop, and slowly the pulled-back ridges of material began to smooth inward again, covering up the impervium hull, pushing it back and away into the vacuum of Mercury's surface.

"Muddy!" Bruno shouted. "You open this hatch immediately! What do you think you're doing?"

"Making amends," Muddy answered cryptically.

"Open the hatch, Muddy! You can't make off with this ship; it isn't *right*."

"Make off?" Muddy sounded hurt. "I'm taking her into the photosphere, Bruno. I'm going after those fragments."

Bruno's skin went cold. "You're what? Muddy, they'll be *inside the sun* by the time you get to them."

The loudspeaker was not a face; Bruno could read no emotion there. "Grapples can reach inside the sun, yes?" Muddy said. "At close range? I'll convert the fragments to hypercollapsites and simply pull them out."

"By pulling yourself in," Bruno said, finally understanding. His voice was soft, disbelieving, probably not easy to hear over the sizzling of wellstone reactions. "You'll be killed. I don't see how you could possibly survive."

"Nor I," Muddy agreed, and Bruno thought his voice sounded, if not exactly *happy*, then at least vindicated. "I was created for one purpose, Bruno: to prove that you could be broken, that you could be cowardly and contemptible and weak. I carried the proof of myself right to you, like the craven that I was. But now, Bruno, I'm spent, and therefore free to define a new purpose. Let me show you that you can also be *brave*."

"Muddy, my God. At least leave a *copy* behind."

There was a pause, and then Muddy's voice said, "I have, sir. It's you."

Before Bruno could reply, before he could *conceive* of a reply, the crackling edges of the wellstone reaction closed in over the loudspeaker, first a ring around it and then a circular wave splashing in across it and finally a smooth, blank cylinder wall. The sizzling stopped.

A rocket would have made some sound, even in vacuum,

as its hot exhaust gases expanded and flowed across the landscape, impinging on the surface of the access port. But a grappleship made no sound at all. Through the little window in the airlock, Bruno could see a shadow pass briefly over the landscape, and that was all.

He stood there a long time, with his nose pressed up against the hot glass.

chapter twenty-four

in which an historic
tally is counted

They watched on the sensors of Marlon's desk as *Sabadell-Andorra* raced to the scene of the collapsium's photopause penetration. As promised, the fragments shrank and vanished from view, and even Bruno had a hard time identifying their gravitational signatures as the tug of *Sabadell-Andorra's* grapples flung them away from solar space. And then there was the gravitational signature of the ship itself, of the ertial shield crowning her bow; they watched this plunge headlong into the photosphere's dense plasma, where even impervium could expect a lifetime measured in fractions of a second.

Once the ship was burned away, of course, there *was* no mass for the ertial shield to drag around behind it. Weightless, massless, all but inertialess, it caught a whiff of the solar convections, the outward currents in the plasma that, higher up in the photosphere, gave rise to the solar wind. It caught this breeze, yes, right at the very source, and was flicked at once toward eternity.

Bruno lost interest after that. There were a lot of tearful thanks, a lot of hugs and shoulder thumps, a lot of shaken hands. Cheng Shiao came back from the dead to congratulate Bruno on his excellent work and to offer up his deepest thanks for saving all of their lives, in so many ways. But Bruno could barely pay attention to the words, and in time his friends withdrew, realizing how deep his grief must be. The loss of his home, his ship, his brother, were as nothing to the loss of his Queen. *They* felt that loss—that yawning, hollow emptiness—and they had far less to lose of her than Bruno did.

They left him alone there in the study, alone not only with his grief but with his *guilt,* because he knew—as Muddy must surely have known—that the Queendom itself barely existed for him, except as an interest and possession of Tamra's. He'd have let it fall, let the sun explode and the Earth run with fire, let the Iscog scatter to the far corners of the galaxy, if only he could have saved her.

Brave? He was the worst sort of coward, the worst sort of villain, because he was willing to hide behind a mask of heroism. Were all heroes that way, inside their secret selves? What an empty thought.

Time passed; he slept on the cot, awoke, ate from the fax and then slept again. In time, Deliah came to him and announced that they'd gotten Marlon's spaceship working and were ready to go. Back to Earth, she said, and only looked puzzled when he told her he didn't deserve to set foot there.

An argument ensued; they tried, both one by one and as a gang, to persuade him to board the ship with them. But he refused to be persuaded, and refused to be persuaded, and finally they concluded his grief had consumed all else within him—which was certainly true. They wondered aloud whether he could be trusted to remain here alone without harming himself. They extracted a promise from him regarding this, and in the end they simply had to trust him with it. He *did* have some experience in living alone, after all.

And so they departed, and Bruno remained behind. History does not record what he did there, as Mercury's long day collapsed slowly into afternoon, as the sun set and darkness fell and the ground gave up its heat. Mercury's night is among the coldest in the solar system; perhaps it matched his mood. Perhaps he donned a spacesuit and spent long hours walking under the stars' cold light. Perhaps he remained indoors, and meditated, or slept.

Did his heart begin to turn, when the sun reached its nadir at midnight? Did it turn before dawn, when the night had reached its coldest and the sun's stealthy advance upon the horizon had begun, finally, to heat the ground again?

This much is known: that ten weeks after the Solar Rescue, when The Honorable Helen Beckart, Regent of the Crown and Judge Adjudicator of the House of Parliament, arrived at Mercury with her entourage and bodyguards, they found a de Towaji more at peace than the one Vivian Rajmon had tearfully described to them.

"Declarant-Philander," Beckart said to him upon their meeting, inclining her head deeply. She wore a black cassock and frock, a black tricorned hat, black stockings and shoes. Fortunately, her skin was pale, or she'd have disappeared entirely.

"Judge Adjudicator," Bruno returned, rising from his cot to bow. "I trust your landing was pleasant."

"It was," she said. "Your house's instructions were most helpful."

Bruno *had* come to somewhat better terms with the universe, in his time alone here. His shame and guilt were a burden not so easily dispelled, but he was slowly forgiving himself for them, and for the events that had caused them. He forgave Tamra, too, for editing herself out of the equation like that. She'd had no way of knowing help was on the way; even Bruno hadn't known that for sure. To err was human, yes?

Bruno had suffered from impure thoughts, from callousness, from introversion, and though his behavior might appear irreproachable, still he knew the difference. *Tamra's* sin was to think and feel too purely, and to act in haste. Did the two sins balance out? Who could say? They were all just children, after all, the whole of humanity, exploring only the very earliest beginnings of their long, long lives.

Still, at the sight of Helen Beckart he felt a distinct knot of unease start tying itself up in his belly. Bruno was wearing black as well, in a band around his right biceps, but Beckart's was the black of her official uniform, not of grieving. She stood there in the doorway of Marlon's study like a legal document, waiting for Bruno to break her seal.

He cleared his throat and spoke more gruffly than he'd intended. "It isn't another medal, I hope."

Her smile was polite, devoid of any true joy. And who could blame her? "No, Declarant, I'm afraid it's more serious than that."

"Hmm? Yes? Well, do come in. Can I offer you refreshment?"

"No, thank you." She strode into the room, followed by two gray-robed pages, a pair of faceless silver robots, and a sedately hovering squadron of courtroom cameras. He saw that she carried something in her hands, a black velvet bag or wrapping of some sort.

"Is that for me?"

She nodded once. "It is. Forgive me, Declarant; I'm only doing my job."

In spite of everything, his heart quailed a bit at those words. Had he done something? Said something? But when Beckart opened the bag, what she withdrew was simply Tamra's crown of monocrystalline diamond. A souvenir? An object willed to Bruno by the instruments of Tamra's estate?

"I . . . don't understand," he said, shrugging.

Beckart reddened. "An election has been held, Declarant. Its results were as near unanimity as any election has ever been. I'm afraid . . . Sir, I'm afraid you're the new monarch of Sol."

Bruno blinked, unable to process that statement. "I beg your pardon?"

"As I say, sir. You are the new monarch."

"Is this a joke?"

"It is not," Beckart told him seriously. "I've spared you the formal ceremony, at least, but these cameras *are* recording for posterity. Kneel, please, that I might place this crown atop your head."

Bruno gaped, then snorted. "Why, I refuse. I refuse! I, the monarch of Sol? A king? *Me?* It's the silliest thing I've ever heard."

"It isn't," Beckart said to him, her eyes apologetic but certain. "I voted for you myself. It's a cruel fate to practice upon you but . . . we *are* human, sir, we citizens of the Queendom. Our needs are valid."

"I refuse," Bruno said again, in a sterner voice.

But Beckart shook her head. "You're a figurehead, sir. You haven't the authority to refuse. Now I ask you, please, to kneel, else these bailiffs will be forced to *make* you do it."

"You can't be serious!" he protested.

But she was: the bailiff robots stepped forward, gripped him firmly and without pity, and pressed him to the ground, knees first. Some Latin and Tongan words were recited from a document, and twenty seconds later the crown was encircling his brow. The Queendom had its King at last.

Every child knows of the Winter Palace that de Towaji commanded to be built in high orbit around Earth. Every child knows of the year he spent there, shunning attention, appearing only for the wedding of Vivian and Cheng Shiao, and the funerals of the thousands upon thousands of True Dead the destruction of the Iscog and Ring Collapsiter had left behind.

Not that de Towaji was idle during the time of his seclusion; far from it. Following the trial and confession of Marlon Sykes—who had steadfastly refused treatment for megalomania and homocidia—Bruno's first decree was that a *cage de fin* should be constructed, inside which time would not pass.

Sykes—hunted by every search engine in the Queendom and meticulously reconverged to a single copy—would be placed within it.

"There you will see the lights and darknesses of uncreation," de Towaji is known to have said, "for the span of the universe will pass for you in a single instant."

"Thank you, Sire," Sykes is known to have replied. And together the two of them designed the thing, and built it, and it is rumored that they spent a final evening together, drinking alcohol and smoking from weed pipes, singing and dancing and weeping together, their enmity in brief abeyance. Despite all Marlon's villainy and Bruno's long reticence, the two did after all have more in common with one another than with any other person, living or dead. Perhaps this is the origin of the nursery rhyme:

> *A cigarette, a mandolin, a glass of wine,*
> *A trip to see the devil at the end of time.*

In any case, the recordings clearly show both men dry eyed and somber at the execution, as Bruno closed his old friend and nemesis inside the *cage de fin* and fired him on an inertialess trajectory out of the solar system, at very nearly the speed of light.

When this was done, and a sigh of relieved closure was heaved by all and sundry, de Towaji commenced to brood and agonize over the decision to restore the Iscog. The last words of Wenders Rodenbeck—in his nonspider form, at least— weren't lost on Bruno at all. Collapsium *was* dangerous stuff to have around. In the end, though, he was swayed by the ruling opinion of the Queendom's citizens themselves. The collapsium's dangers meant little to them, it seemed, in comparison to its benefits.

"*Fire* is dangerous, Your Highness," they insisted, in billions upon billions of respectfully snitty letters. "Shall we ban that as well?"

It seemed to be a kind of slogan. Still, it *was* Bruno's money they were talking about spending, and of course, in retrospect the old Iscog could be seen to suffer from all manner of unfortunate design errors and oversights. The Ring Collapsiter, for all its grievous faults, did indeed point the way to a new and better paradigm in material telecommunications. So Bruno began the slow, hard work of designing a new Iscog— a *Nescog*—from the neubles up.

But every child knows that he had barely begun this effort, barely scratched the surface of the new design, on the morning when his most famous visitor arrived.

There was a polite but rather urgent-sounding knock on his study wall, and he rose from his desk and walked over there and said, "Door." And a door opened up, and he *gasped*, and some say he nearly fainted when he saw who it was.

"You," he managed to say as he staggered back.

"Me," the visitor agreed. She stepped inside, pursing her lips, surveying the room with a critical eye. She took in the desk, the chair, the chandelier and clutter-strewn floor. The hugeness of the place, the emptiness, the decoration all in crystal and alabaster and silver. Finally, she nodded. "About what one would expect, yes. This really is a hideous building, Bruno."

Still reeling, he said, "My Taj Mahal. The tomb of my undying love."

She laughed. "You're not supposed to *live* in the tomb of your undying love."

He came forward and touched her shoulder gently, lightly, afraid to confirm her solidity. "Am I dreaming? Are you real?"

She laughed again, but there were tears in her eyes. "I *feel* real. They tell me I am. I'm out of date, though—*years* out of date."

He gasped, backing away a step. "You're not *Marlon's* copy, surely?"

But she just shook her head. "It seems the Royal Registry finally earned its keep. They've been closed for years, I guess, but the way I hear it, there was this disc at the bottom of a closet . . ." Her eyes clouded. "Bruno, is it true, all these things I hear? Did I really cut my throat? Are you really the King?"

"No more," he said at once, snatching the diamond crown off his head and placing it on hers.

She laughed, and the tears spilled down her face. "You can't abdicate, Bruno; I've tried it. Lord, how I've tried it. They won't even let you *die* . . ."

Suddenly, it occurred to him that this was really happening. He grabbed her by the shoulders, crushed her to him. "Tamra! My Queen!" And he was crying, too, and laughing, and trying to tell her so many things at once that no words came out at all. They stood like that for a long time.

"Strange," he mused later, as they rocked back and forth with her brown hair tickling his nose. "I'm the King, and you're the Queen, and here we've never even been married."

"I accept," she murmured, then giggled a little and kissed him lightly on the neck.

And the rest, as they say, is history.

in which an appendix
is provided

collapsium

Perhaps it was novel, to imagine black holes not as highly compressed stars but as very heavy elementary particles— mega-particles, like protons massing a billion tons, their surfaces able to devour light, to bend time and space, to tear energies loose from the zero-point field of the "empty" vacuum itself . . .

An enterprise worth pursuing!

Einstein may have changed the world with his famous equation linking mass and energy, but when you ask the more fundamental question—just what *is* mass?—you soon find yourself scribbling:

$$E = mc2$$
$$m = E/c^2$$
$$E/c^2 = E/c^2$$
$$E = E$$

Mass is like energy because energy is like itself, just an electromagnetic vibration of the zero-point vacuum. Soon the quantum-age profusion of particles and forces falls away like a bad dream, leaving only charge, electromagnetism, and the vacuum. There is nothing else, no other force or substance required to construct the universe. And you wonder why you ever thought there was.

It all comes down to *zitterbewegung* vibrations—the "trembling motion" of charged particles buffeted by the very real energies of the zero-point field. Even the neutron is composed of quarks, charged $+2/3$, $-1/3$, and $-1/3$ proton equivalents, and the secondary fields emitted by these trembling particles give rise to a net force that is always attractive, always infinite in range, always difficult to block or channel or deflect. Call it gravity—Newton did. The experiment had been performed dozens of times before Bruno de Towaji came along: isolate a proton, subject it to oscillating electric fields at frequencies comparable to those of gravitation, and measure the increase in its mass. The Haisch effect. Bruno's "genius" was simply to dump in a neuble's worth of mass-energy, upping the frequency and amplitude of the oscillation, upping the illusory mass until the neuble was gone and the proton weighed a billion tons—enough to collapse it into a miniature black hole.

The rest had seemed obvious enough: *two* black holes, not only vibrating but vibrating *each other,* their interactions exactly 180 degrees out of phase with their *zitterbewegung* motions, gravities therefore canceling out. That turned out to be statically rather than dynamically stable, but *eight* holes arranged in a cube *just so,* at excruciatingly precise distances, would hold their positions indefinitely, for billions of years, for as long as the Hawking-bled holes themselves would last. A stiff cage, a "collapson," the elementary building block of a wholly new material: crystalline collapsium.

Obvious.

And once you did this, once you began bricking the collapsons together into three-dimensional structures, you were well on your way to the control of physical reality at its most fundamental levels.

wellstone

Consider the humble semiconductor, which is an insulating substance that can nonetheless conduct electrons within a certain range or "band" of energies. The most common of these is silicon, whose native oxide is the main crustal component of every terrestrial moon and planet. Silicon's electrical properties are fixed by immutable physics, but through "doping," the carefully controlled introduction of impurities, its crystals can be tuned so that, for example, room-temperature electrons have a good chance of jumping up into the conduction band when a voltage is applied.

Now, by layering these doped silica in particular ways, we can trap conduction electrons in a membrane so thin that from one face to the other, their behavior as tiny quantum wave packets takes precedence over their behavior as particles. This is called a "quantum well." From there, confining the electrons along a second dimension produces a "quantum wire," and finally, with three dimensions, a "quantum dot."

The important thing about a quantum dot is that if it's the right size, the electrons trapped in it will arrange themselves as though they were part of an atom, even though there's no atomic nucleus for them to surround. Which atom they emulate depends on the number of electrons and the exact geometry of the wells confining them, and in fact where a normal atom is spherical, such "designer atoms" can be fashioned into cubes or tetrahedrons or any other shape, and filled not only with electrons but with positrons, muons, tau leptons, and other exotica to produce "atoms" with properties that simply don't occur in nature.

Lastly, the quantum dots needn't reside within the physical structure of our semiconductor; they can be maintained just above it through a careful balancing of electrical charges. In fact, this is the preferred method, since it permits the dots' characteristics to be adjusted without any physical modification of the substrate.

So picture this: a diffuse lattice of crystalline silicon, superfine threads much thinner than a human hair crisscrossing to form a translucent structure with roughly the density of balsa wood, a structure which, like balsa wood, is mostly empty space. Except that with the application of electrical currents, that space can be filled with "atoms" of any desired species, producing a virtual substance with the *mass* of diffuse silicon, but the chemical, physical, and electrical properties of some new, hybrid material.

Being half composed of silicon, wellstone iron is less strong than its natural cousin, less conductive and ferromagnetic, basically less ironlike, and if you bash it over and over with a golf club it will gradually lose *any* resemblance, reverting to shattered silicon and empty space. On the other hand, it's feather-light, wholly rustproof, and changeable at the flick of a bit into zinc, rubidium, or even imaginary substances like unobtanium, impossibilium, and rainbow kryptonite.

Well, half-kryptonite anyway; the rest is still silicon. However, since the theoretical properties of the "pure" substance will never occur outside a quantum well, the distinction is largely moot. The copyrighted element Bunkerlite, for example, is a million times stronger than the wellstone matrix that supports it. Together, they're merely *half* a million times stronger.

Wellstone can also form compounds, amalgams, admixtures, sinters, and even whole solid-state devices; a thin square of it can be a hypercomputer if you like, or a clear glass window, or a stunningly accurate painting of your sister.

So it's handy stuff to have around, particularly in conjunction with nanoassemblers and other semiadvanced technologies of the third millennium. The thing you need to remember is that by Bruno de Towaji's time it was also dirt-common, its infinite potential mainly in the hands of bored or inept programmers who'd rather be looking at counterfeit naked pictures of the Queen.

semisafe black holes

A neuble-mass black hole—precisely the size of a proton—can absorb exactly two excess electrons before electrostatic repulsion overcomes gravitational attraction. By that time the hole's mass—and therefore its Schwarzchild radius—has become $9.1E-31$ percent larger. This infinitesimal widening is sufficient that the hole *can* consume an unlucky proton that strikes it just right—a statistical rarity but, given prolonged contact, an eventual certainty.

That second widening slightly increases the chance that another proton will fall in, which in turn increases the chances of still another, and a few billion iterations later the invading protons are free to crowd around the event horizon and spiral in, forming an ever-widening hole whose mass can eventually grow to disrupt—and finally crush—the collapsium lattice around it.

feigenbaum's number

When a system is in transition from a laminar (or "smooth") to a turbulent (or "messy") state, it passes through a condition known as "chaotic frequency doubling," in which cyclic events come more and more frequently, until finally they smear into a jumble we resignedly call "random." Examine the trail of smoke rising up from a burning ember or weed pipe in the absence of wind and you can see this phenomenon directly: near the source, the smoke is a thin, clean line, like a length of ribbon. Higher up, it's a rising and unpredictable snarl of overlapping vortex rolls and curls. In between lies the chaotic transition zone, where single vortices break into double vortices break into quadruple vortices, and so on. This zone leaps up and down as you watch, its position and dimensions malleable in the face of quite small perturbations, but understand that if all the variables were constant— the air perfectly still, the embers' combustion perfectly uniform—the transition zone would hang exactly *so*, its frequency doublings happening over and over at the same exact positions, as if rows of invisible knives hung there, cleaving the vortices in twain as they rose, doubling their number with each successive row.

Here's the kicker: the spacing of these invisible knives is known in advance, regardless of the nature or conditions of the experiment. The interval between the first and second row is larger than the interval between the second and third by a ratio of exactly 4.6692016090. The same ratio, always, for smoke curls or ocean waves or ripples through an electromagnetic field. Feigenbaum's number: one of the many mysterious constants that underlie our universe.

true vacuum

Normal "empty" space is nothing of the kind, is in fact a catchpool of invisible energies at every possible wavelength, and it's only when these wavelengths are excluded—by closely spaced conducting plates, by fierce applications of charge and vibration, or, best of all, by sheets or shells of static collapsium—that anything like "emptiness" can actually be achieved. The physicist Hendrick Casimir had proved as much even before the age of space flight, and the Queendom's communication and transportation networks relied on the principle for their daily operation.

But still Bruno had brooded: this Casimir supervacuum wasn't really blank, empty, or null. Not completely, not in any fundamental sense. A particle placed within it didn't freeze in place, locked down by absolute zero, and Bruno had wondered just *how much* energy could be pulled from the vacuum before it finally did. An infinite amount for every possible wavelength? Unlikely. So he'd concocted a simple experiment: a spherical shell of collapsium, a kind of piñata of bright pinpoint holes slowly bleeding their mass-energy off as blue-white light. Then he'd measured the difference in vacuum energy between the inside and outside of the sphere. Then he'd put another collapsium shell outside the first—spaced carefully, so the gravitic frequencies would cancel and the two wouldn't fall in on each other—and measured the energies again.

And then, somehow, even though these steps were fantastically difficult and expensive and demanding of his deepest attention, he'd repeated them eleven times more.

And for what? To learn what? That the vacuum increased with every Onion layer? That the energy difference between layers shrank progressively as one moved inward? That the rate of this shrinkage was neither exponential nor logarithmic nor asymptotic, but spaced—precisely!—according to Feigenbaum's number? Pi he could maybe have accepted. With greater difficulty, "e" or "i" or, just possibly, "gnu." But 4.6692016090? What could such a thing imply? That the universe was chaotic straight through to its core? That all of physics was mad?

How absurd.

electromagnetic grapple

Electrons, like fluids, resist acceleration but resist compression even more. "Press" on them with voltages, and they flow through the conduits laid out before them, spill down waterfall diodes, choke through bottleneck resistors . . . Fluid pressure can also power reciprocating devices that slosh the flow back and forth through "alternating current" conduits.

Unlike fluids, though, electrons give rise to electromagnetic fields when accelerated and give rise to *oscillating* fields when sloshed back and forth. These oscillations can, in turn, affect the motion of charged particles, such as the quarks of which protons and neutrons are made. So imagine an ultrahigh frequency EM field of infinite range, a field whose tugging vibrations universally attract matter of all types. Newton's phantom "gravitation," inexplicable for centuries and misunderstood for centuries more.

Lumps of matter emit such fields naturally, in spherically symmetric echoes of the invisible "vacuum" energy storming around them, but even before the Queendom's rise it was possible—even trivial—to generate tightly focused beams of this "gravity" for industrial or agricultural or sexual purposes. The scene suddenly fell into place around Bruno; here were the power generators, slowly bleeding the dream of matter off into the much more pliable dreams of AC voltage and amperage. Here were the inductors, the accumulators, the LRC loops, exactly as they might appear in any of Bruno's own EM grapples. And down there at the far end of the station were the hazy forms of the revpic chambers themselves. But where Bruno's equipment was designed to move individual collapsons, or small collections of them—hence his helplessness in the face of the careening Onion—here around him was a device for holding up *millions* of black holes against the pull of solar gravity.

Holding what on the other end? What kept the grapple station itself from falling? He tried to imagine the station's complement beam anchored to Jupiter, and almost laughed out loud at the idea of that giant planet being reeled in like a fish. No, the beam was probably anchored to some huge, distant star, was probably *dragging* that star sunward, and dragging the entire Queendom of Sol out toward it, altering the paths and positions of the two stars in their slow galactic orbits. Two boats joined by even a very long elastic cord were doomed, eventually, to collide, yes? In a million years, perhaps, if the cords weren't cut before then.

They *would* be cut if the collapsiter was ever finished—if the Queendom managed to survive its construction.

muon contamination

"Muons are short-lived," Bruno noted, perhaps too gruffly. "Time dilation has extended their life spans?"

"Indeed," Marlon said. "They're quite close to the event horizons, and moving at very nearly the speed of light. Plays hell with the collapsium, I'm afraid—relativistic mass increase is enough to disturb the gravitational balance. For a while, I was seriously thinking the whole region might deconstitute and become a single, massive black hole."

"Hmm. You've since ruled this out?"

Marlon shrugged uneasily. "There are a lot of variables. What equilibrium the system has found is *chaotic* equilibrium—the collapson nodes wander in and out of phase at irregular intervals. So far, they haven't wandered far enough to lose gravitational rigidity, but the margin is slim, about twenty percent. It seems to be holding—that's about all I can say."

"You've considered beaming antimuons in to annihilate the contamination?" Bruno inquired.

"Of course," Marlon replied. "Simulations indicated that the resultant gamma radiation would destabilize the lattice almost as rapidly as gravitic radiation. Our one limited experiment matched the predictions perfectly, so I saw little point in pursuing the matter further."

"What's the half-life of the particles?"

"Half-life? Most of them are gone already; they'd've decayed almost immediately. It's only the ones that fell into orbits around the collapson nodes that lingered, and most of *those* are gone as well. It's only the ones that fell in *close* that remain, all swollen with relativistic mass. So the half-life was probably about a second, although I don't think that's what you're really asking. What you want to know is when the remaining muons will be decayed and gone, or close enough to gone that the Ring Collapsiter's lattice structure regains stability."

"You see through the murk of my thoughts," Bruno agreed.

"Well, unfortunately, I don't have an answer. Again, there are too many variables to construct an accurate prediction. I can *guess* intelligently: the maximum stable orbit for a particle around a neuble-mass black hole is around a third of the way to the next node in the lattice, a little over one centimeter. Any further than that and the particle will simply be ejected, or else captured by a neighboring hole. The *minimum* stable orbit is around 1.14 proton radii, and that's where the long-lived particles mostly are. That would put the orbital velocity within, let's see . . ."

He tapped some calculations into his slate; they appeared, solved, on Bruno's own. "That puts them at about seventy percent of light speed," Marlon said, "which would mean only minor time dilation if they weren't sitting in this tremendous gravity field. The *gravitational* time dilation factor would be . . . three times ten to the thirteenth. At that rate, a muon's lifetime would be—" He tapped some more numbers in. "—three times ten to the seventh seconds. Very approximately, of course."

defeating inertia

He began with the basics: a standard collapsium lattice with its cube-shaped nodes spaced a little more than two centimeters apart. Denser and looser arrangements were possible; all manner of crystalline symmetries, hexagonal and gyroidal and orthorhombic, with stability islands occurring like spectral lines, seemingly random, at a number of different scales. But that one was the "standard" composition, the one he'd selected for the Iscog's first primitive collapsiters. By chance? By intuition? Many other crystals had been tried over the years, but that one still yielded the greatest blending of stability and mechanical/industrial usefulness.

This zpf-damping foam, though, would need to be a thousand times denser. Were there stability islands anywhere in the proper range for the foam to work? He crafted a series of simulations to confirm it, then backed them up with a rigorous mathematical proof. But the foam's structure was another major problem—not a simple lattice at all, but something more akin to a quasicrystal of supercooled fluid packets, spiderwebbed in four dimensions. A vacuogel hypercollapsite? More math was needed to prove *that* wasn't a ridiculous idea. He fretted through the whole process, gnawing absently on the end of his thumb, but one by one the answers all came back affirmative: the material was physically possible.

Relieved, he called for a toilet, some coffee, a weed pipe,

and a tray of bagels, then indulged in a few minutes of stretching and smoking and refueling his body before diving back in to tackle the issues of construction. Were there valid intermediate states the collapsium could pass through to reach the hypercollapsite state? A proof confirmed that there ought to be, but he needed a whole chain of them—stepping stones from the large and simple to the tiny and intricate—and his initial searches turned up only a single state on anything like the proper pathway.

He grumbled and fretted for a while, converting greater and greater swaths of his study walls into hypercomputer blocks. Finally, when the entire room—right down to the floor beneath his feet—was one giant computing device, he hit on a prime-number sorting algorithm that enabled the wellstone to spit out the whole series for him in the space of an hour. It even pointed to some alternate reaction paths and a handful of quite interesting dead-ends that he resolved to investigate further when time permitted.

The robots sneaked in with more food and drink, which he paused once more to consume, and then fell—most unwillingly—asleep.

glossary

Antiautomata (adj) Describes any weapon intended for use against robots.

Arc de fin (n) A hypothetical device for diverting photons from the fourth-dimensional extremum of spacetime. Attributed to Bruno de Towaji.

Archimedes (prop. n) Greek physicist from the Classical era.

AU (n) Astronomical Unit; the mean distance from the center of Sol to the center of Earth. Equal to 149,604,970 kilometers, or 499.028 light-seconds.

Autronic (adj) Capable of self-directed activity. Commonly used to differentiate robots from teleoperated or "waldo" devices.

Blitterstaff (n) An antiautomata weapon employing a library of rapidly shifting wellstone compositions. Attributed to Bruno de Towaji.

Bondril (n) Copyrighted wellstone substance employed as a glue. Much stronger than atomic glues.

Bunkerlite (n) Copyrighted, superreflective wellstone substance employed as protective cloth or armor. Attributed to Marlon Sykes.

Casimir, Hendrick (prop. n) Dutch physicist of the Old Modern era.

Casimir effect (n) The exclusion of vacuum wavelengths by closely spaced, uncharged, conducting plates, causing the plates to be pressed together. Earliest evidence of the zero-point field.

Catalonia (prop. n) Former Mediterranean nation at the northeast of the Iberian peninsula, historically a part of Spain.

Centroid (n) The geometric center of an object or figure.

Cerenkov, Pavel (prop. n) Russian physicist-laureate of the Old Modern era.

Cerenkov blue (n) Characteristic spectrum of electron-emitted Cerenkov radiation.

Cerenkov radiation (n) Electromagnetic radiation emitted by particles temporarily exceeding the local speed of light, e.g., upon exit from a collapsium lattice.

Chromopause (n) The outer surface of a stellar chromosphere.

Chromosphere (n) A transparent layer, usually several thousand kilometers deep, between the photosphere and corona of a star, i.e., the star's "middle atmosphere." Temperature is typically several thousand kelvins, with roughly the pressure of Earth's atmosphere in low Earth orbit.

Cislunar (adj) Within the gravitational sphere of influence of the Earth/Moon system.

Collapsiter (n) A high-bandwidth packet switching transceiver composed exclusively of collapsium. Attributed to Bruno de Towaji.

Collapsium (n) A rhombohedral crystalline material composed of neuble-mass black holes. Since the black holes absorb and exclude a broad range of vacuum wavelengths, the interior of the lattice is a Casimir supervacuum. See Appendix A: Collapsium, pg. 361. Attributed to Bruno de Towaji.

Collapson (n) A cubic structure of eight neuble-mass black holes in sympathetic pseudo-*zitterbewegung* vibration. The most stable collapsons measure 2.3865791101 centimeters edge to edge.

Collapson node (n) A neuble-mass black hole that is part of a collapson.

Componeer (n) Any person bearing royal certification in gravitic engineering. Descended from late U.S. Army Corps of Engineers training standards.

Converge (also **Reconverge**) (v) To combine two separate entities, or two copies of the same entity, using a fax machine. In practice, rarely applied except to humans.

Copy-hour (n) One hour's labor from a single instantiation of an individual. A standard human resource measure during the Queendom era.

Corona (n) The deep, sparse, superhot "upper atmosphere" of a star, responsible for most X-ray emissions. Variable in size with the solar "seasons," the corona of Sol extends 5 to 10 light-seconds above the chromopause, at near-vacuum densities.

Datavore (n) Any rogue autonomous software capable of inhabiting telecommunications networks. Several distinct phyla are known to have existed in the Iscog prior to its demise.

Declarant (n) The highest title accorded by the Queendom of Sol; descended from the Tongan award of Nopélé, or knighthood. Only twenty-nine declarancies were ever issued.

Desaturation (n) In sailing, the firing of rocket thrusters to balance cumulative attitude errors absorbed by reaction momentum wheels.

Di-clad (adj) Sheathed in an outer layer of monocrystalline diamond.

Disassembler fog (n) A suspension of microscopic deconstruction mechanisms, sometimes employed in the recycling of objects too large to fax.

Downsystem (adv) Toward the sun.

Electrogravitic (adj) Synonym for electromagnetic.

Electromagnetic grapple See **Grapple, electromagnetic.**

Ertial (adj) Antonym of inertial, applied to inertially shielded devices. Attributed to Bruno de Towaji.

Fax (n) Abbreviated form of "facsimile." A device for reproducing physical objects from stored or transmitted data patterns. By the time of the Restoration, faxing of human beings had become possible, and with the advent of collapsiter-based telecommunications soon afterward, the reliable transmission of human patterns quickly became routine.

Faxware (n) Anything produced by a fax machine. Colloquially, the control systems and filters employed by the Iscog.

Feigenbaum, Mitchell (prop. n) American physicist-laureate of the Late Modern era.

Feigenbaum's number (n) Physical constant with the dimensionless value 4.6692016090, representing the rational spacing of frequency doublings along any relevant axis of a system in chaotic transition. See Appendix A: Feigenbaum's number, pg. 367

Fibe-op (n, adj) Abbreviated form of "fiber optic." Any thin, flexible conduit for the transmission of visible light.

Fibrediamond (n) Composite material of whiskered crystalline carbon in a resin matrix. Unless sheathed in a superreflective coating, fibrediamond is notably flammable.

Flatspace Society, the (prop. n) Queendom-era lobbying organization dedicated to the prohibition of collapsium.

Ghost (n) Any electromagnetic trace preserved in rock. Colloquially, a visual image of past events, especially involving deceased persons.

Ghosting (n) The process by which a ghost is formed.

Girona (prop. n) A minor city in the El Gironès comarque of Catalonia, situated at the confluence of the Ter, Güell, Galligants, and Onyar rivers, some 80 kilometers from the nation's former capital at Barcelona.

Grapple, electromagnetic (n) An industrial gravity projector specifically intended to anchor or manipulate massive objects.

Grappleship (n) A vehicle propelled by means of electromagnetic grapples. Use of grappleships was considered impractical in the Queendom until the advent of ertial shielding, though high-powered inertial devices were capable of attaining enormous accclerations.

Gravity laser (n) A gravity projector whose emissions are coherent, i.e., monochromatic and phase-locked. Attributed to Bruno de Towaji.

Gravity projector (n) A revpic-driven device for simulating the secondary fields emitted by charged particles under *zitterbewegung* vibration. Attributed to Boyle Schmenton.

Haisch, Bernhard (prop. n) American physicist-laureate of the Old Modern era.

Haisch effect (n) The increase in "mass" experienced by an object—usually a subatomic particle—under vibration at gravitic frequencies.

Hawking, Stephen (prop. n) British physicist-laureate of the Old Modern era.

Hawking radiation (n) Photon and particle emissions of a hypermassive object, resulting from Heisenberg tunneling across the event horizon.

Holie (n) Abbreviated form of "hologram." Any three-dimensional image. Colloquially, a projected, dynamic three-dimensional image, or device for producing same.

Hypercollapsite (n) A quasicrystalline material composed of neuble-mass black holes. Usually organized as a vacuogel.

Hypercomputer (n) Any computing device capable of altering its internal layout. Colloquially, a computing device made of wellstone.

Hypercondensed (adj) Condensed to the point of gravitational collapse, i.e., until a black hole or "hypermass" is formed. Colloquially, condensed to any level the speaker finds impressive. Also "hypercompressed."

Hypermass (n) A mass that has been hypercompressed; a black hole.

Immorbid (adj) Not subject to life-threatening disease or deterioration.

Impervium (n) Public-domain wellstone substance; the hardest superreflector known. Attributed to Marlon Sykes.

Instantiate (v) To produce a single instance of a person or object; to fax from a stored or received pattern.

Iscog (n) An acronym for the Inner-System Collapsiter Grid. The first broadband interplanetary telecom network capable of transmitting live human patterns. Attributed to Bruno de Towaji.

Isotropic (adj) Exactly the same in all directions. A theoretical construct which may not occur in nature, although the zero-point field is often regarded as isotropic.

Kataki ha'u o' kai Traditional Tongan encouragement to begin a meal. Literally translated as, "Please come and eat."

Kuiper Belt (n) A ring-shaped region in the ecliptic plane of any solar system, in which gravitational perturbations have amplified the concentration of large, icy bodies or "comets." Sol's Kuiper Belt extends from 40 AU at its lower boundary to 1,000 AU at its upper and has an overall density approximately one-fourth that of its much smaller Asteroid Belt.

Laminar (adj) Completely predictable by closed-form equations. A theoretical construct that does not occur in nature but is extremely useful as an approximation. Most dynamic systems are considered to have a laminar range. (Literally: "layered.")

Laureate (n) An honor bestowed by the Queendom for extraordinary service. Descended from the Nobel citation of Swedish monarchy in the Old Modern era.

Lepton (n) A member of the class of low-rest-mass, spin ½ "elementary particles" or charge-zpf resonance states that include the neutrino, electron, muon, and tau. Leptons are not subject to the hypothetical "strong nuclear force" of quantum-age physics.

Light-hour (n) The distance traveled by light through a standard vacuum in one hour. Equal to 3,600 light-seconds, or 1,079,252,848,8 kilometers.

Light-second (n) The distance traveled by light through a standard vacuum in one second: 299,792.46 kilometers.

Lithosphere (n) The rocky outer crust of a terrestrial planet, composed primarily of silicon dioxide.

Lorentz-invariant (adj) Exactly the same at all velocities. The zero-point field is thought to be Lorentz-invariant.

Malo e lelei Traditional Tongan greeting, widely used within the Queendom. Literally translated as, "Thank you, hello."

Meson (n) member of the class of high-rest-mass, integer-spin particles that include the pion, kaon, rho, omega, eta, psi, B, and D. Mesons are composed of a quark-antiquark pair, and are subject to the hypothetical "strong nuclear force" of quantum-age physics.

Milligee (n) One one-thousandth of the acceleration experienced by a body at rest on either pole of Earth's reference ellipsoid (i.e., $\frac{1}{1000}$ of one gee); 0.0098202 meters per second squared.

Monocrystalline (adj) Composed of a single crystal, without seams and, ideally, without flaws. Sometimes used colloquially as a term of admiration.

Morbidity filter (n) One of dozens of software filters applied to human patterns in the Iscog, intended to eliminate mortality by disease and age-related deterioration. Attributed to Ernst Krogh.

Muon (n) An unstable lepton possessing charge +1 and mass $\frac{1}{9}$ that of a proton, with a half-life of 10^{-6} seconds.

Nanoassembler (n) Any device capable of assembling objects at the atomic level. Most nanoassemblers (e.g., the standard fax machine) are of macroscopic size.

Nasen (n or adj) An acronym for "neutrino amplification through stimulated emission." A coherent neutrino beam sometimes employed for interplanetary communication thanks to its extremely small divergence angle. However, the difficulty of generating such a beam, plus its ready interactions with matter, limit its usefulness.

Nescog (n) Successor to the Iscog; a high-bandwidth telecommunications network employing numerous supraluminal signal shunts.

Neuble (n) A di-clad neutronium sphere, explosively formed, usually incorporating one or more layers of wellstone for added strength and versatility. A standard industrial neuble masses one billion metric tons, with a radius of 2.67 centimeters.

Neutronium (n) Matter that has been supercondensed, crushing nuclear protons and orbital electron shells together into a mass of neutrons. Unstable except at very high pressures. Any quantity of neutronium may be considered a single atomic nucleus; however, under most conditions the substance will behave as a fluid.

Piezoelectric (adj) Describes a substance, often crystalline, that produces a voltage when pressure is applied to it, or which experiences mechanical deformation in response to a voltage.

Perihelion (n) The point of an orbit that lies closest to the sun.

Petajoule (n) 10^{15} joules or watt-seconds. A measure of energy equivalent to the vaporization of 2.985 million tons of liquid water at boiling point.

Philander (n) A title granted to formal consorts of the Queen of All Things. Only four Philanders were ever named.

Photopause (n) The irregular, granulated "surface" of a star.

Photosphere (n) The hot, opaque, convectively stable plasma layer of a star beginning at the photopause, responsible for most thermal and visible emissions. Usually less than 1000 kilometers deep, with temperatures of several thousand kelvins and the approximate pressure of Earth's stratosphere. The photosphere floats atop the deep hydrogen convection zones of the stellar interior.

Picosecond (n) 10^{-12} seconds; a measure of time roughly equivalent to the vacuum travel of light across a gap of 0.3 millimeters.

Pion (n) An unstable, spin-zero meson possessing $\frac{1}{9}$ the mass and $+1$, 0, or -1 times the charge of a proton, and a half-life of 2.6×10^{-8} seconds.

Plibble (n) Fruit of the plibble tree. Origin unknown.

Pseudoatom (n) The organization of electrons into Schrödinger orbitals and pseudo-orbitals, made possible with great precision in a designer quantum dot. The properties of pseudoatoms do not necessarily mimic those of natural atoms.

Pseudochemistry (n) Electron shell interactions taking place among pseudoatoms, or between pseudoatoms and natural atomic matter.

Quantum well (n) A semiconductor designed to trap electrons in a two-dimensional layer thin enough for wave behavior to overwhelm particle behavior. The equivalent one-dimensional structure is a quantum wire. The nanoscopic, zero-dimensional equivalent is a quantum dot, capable of trapping electrons in pseudoatomic orbitals.

Quod erat demonstrandum Latin: "which was to be proved."

Random (adj) Aperiodic and nondeterministic; a condition in which any point, state, or member of a system, group, or set has an equal probability of being sampled. Colloquially, any system, group, or set whose forward characteristics are difficult to compute. Randomness is a hypothetical construct that does not occur in nature.

Reportant (n) A person or mechanism gathering information for public distribution.

Restoration, the (n) Interglobal election that established the Queendom of Sol under Tamra I. The term derives from the presumption that monarchy is the "natural" state of human beings, owing to a genetic predisposition.

Revpic (n) An acronym for "relativistically vibrating, para-infinite, Charged." The word "plate" is generally presumed, and indicates a thin, rigid sheet of wellstone that serves as the primary component of a gravity projector.

Ring Collapsiter (prop. n) The first supraluminal signal shunt, intended to be part of the Iscog. Attributed to Marlon Sykes.

Sol (prop. n) Formal name for the Earth's sun, derived from the Latin. The Greek *Helios* was considered archaic for most Queendom uses.

Superabsorber (n) Any material capable of absorbing 100% of incident light in a given wavelength band. The only known universal superabsorber (i.e., functioning at all wavelengths) is the event horizon of a hypermass. (Approximations of 100% absorption are generally referred to as "black.")

Supercondensed (adj) Condensed to the point of proton-electron recombination, i.e., until neutronium is formed. Colloquially, condensed to any point the speaker finds impressive.

Superconductor (n) Any material capable of passing electron pairs with zero resistance. (Approximations of zero resistance are generally referred to as "conductors.")

Supercooled (n) Cooled below the point of an expected phase transition, typically the freezing point of a liquid. Colloquially, cooled to any point the speaker finds impressive.

Superreflector (n) Any material capable of reflecting 100% of incident light in a given wavelength band. No universal superreflectors are known. (Approximations of 100% reflectance are generally referred to as "mirrors.")

Supervacuum (n) A state of vacuum in which some wavelengths of the zero-point field have been suppressed or excluded. Since the speed of light is a function of vacuum energy, supervacuum is useful for the transmission of matter and information at supraluminal velocities.

Supraluminal (adj) Exceeding the standard vacuum speed of light.

Telegravitic (adj) Involving gravity projectors.

Telerobotic (adj) Controlled from afar. Rarely applied except to machines.

Terraform ash (n) A wellstone substance of shifting composition, intended to provoke pseudochemical reactions in a planetary atmosphere. Also known as "wellstone flake."

Tonga (n) Former Polynesian kingdom consisting of the Tongatapu, Ha'apai, and Vava'u archipelagos, and scattered islands occasionally including parts of Fiji. Tonga was the only Polynesian nation never to be conquered or colonized by a foreign power, and was the last human monarchy prior to establishment of the Queendom of Sol.

Tongatapu (n) The largest and most populous island of Tonga; home to its traditional capital at Nuku'alofa.

True Vacuum (n) A hypothetical state of vacuum in which *all* zpf wavelenths are excluded or suppressed.

Turbulent (adj) The mathematical state between laminar and hypothetical "random" activity. Any condition in which the motion of a point varies rapidly.

Upsystem (adv) Away from the sun.

Vacougel (n) Any fibrous or spongy substance consisting mostly of empty space.

Vacuum (n, adj) The default state of spacetime in the absence of charge. On stochastic average, half the available photon states of a standard vacuum are filled.

Wellstone (n) A substance consisting of fine, semiconductive fibers alternating with quantum dots, capable of emulating a broad range of natural, artificial, and hypothetical materials. See Appendix A: Wellstone, pg. 363.

Wellwood (n) An emulation of lignous cellulose (wood), often employed as the default state of wellstone devices.

Zero-point field (zpf) (n) Technical name for the isotropic, Lorentz-invariant energy field of the vacuum's half-filled photon states. When interacting with point charges, the zero-point field gives rise to fourth-dimensional spacetime curvature which creates the illusion of mass, gravity, and inertia in the three-dimensional universe.

Zitterbewegung (n) The "trembling motion" of charged particles interacting with the zero-point field. *Zitterbewegung* creates the secondary fields or spacetime curvatures associated with gravity and inertia.

technical notes

Many readers will be unfamiliar with the physical/cosmological theories on which this story is based, and may find the apparent contradictions jarring. Research into zero-point fields and forces has produced a growing and quite impressive body of literature that, as of this writing, has received little attention outside the astrophysics community. The situation vis-à-vis "quantum-dot" technology is somewhat better, though the implications may still sound a bit magical to some.

The gravitational theories that gave birth to this book are some of the most fascinating and cutting-edge science being performed today. As far as I know, "collapsium" is my own invention, although I've since encountered the word in different context in a couple of places. For helping deduce and refine the mechanism by which collapsium could actually work, I'm deeply indebted to Drs. Richard M. Powers, the Right Reverend Gary E. Snyder, Bjorn Ostman, Boris Gudiken, Arthur C. Clarke, and especially Bernhard Haisch of the Lockheed Martin Solar and Astrophysics Laboratory in Palo Alto.

For those wanting to learn more about this body of work, three of Haisch's papers on the subject, coauthored with Drs. A. Rueda and H. E. Puthoff, include "Physics of the Zero-Point Field: Implications for Inertia, Gravitation and Mass"

Speculations in Science and Technology, 1996), "Inertia as a Zero-Point Lorentz Force" (*Phys. Review A*, Feb 1994), and the wonderfully for-dummies "Beyond E=mc²" (*The Sciences,* Nov/Dec 1994), which is available on-line at http://www.jse.com/haisch/sciences.html).

In discussions of charge-derived gravitation, the most common question is usually, "Why do neutrons have mass?" The answer is simply that neutrons are composed of quarks whose charges cancel out. The quarks themselves *are* charged, and therefore exhibit the *zitterbewegung* motions that give rise to gravity and inertia. The neutron's "mass" is therefore a derived, rather than fundamental, property.

A more difficult question to answer is, "Why does gravity affect photons and neutrinos?" Current theory has a hard time explaining this, but I believe the short answer is probably "because charge warps spacetime." For a detailed explanation of this concept, I'll refer you to Steven C. Bell of Lockheed Martin Astronautics, whose "On Quantized Electronic Schwarzschild and Kerr Relativistic Models for the Spherical Orbitals of Hydrogen" can be found online at http://www.mindspring.com/~sb635/pap4.htm.

A formal unification of these theories has yet to be completed; while Bell makes a compelling case for charge as a general-relativistic influence on spacetime curvature, no one has yet approached it as the *only* such influence. Still, I think at least one road is clearly leading in that direction.

As for collapsium itself, the "Haisch effect" of Appendix A has never been tested in the laboratory. I doubt the necessary technology will exist for at least the next several decades. Nonetheless, assuming the effect is real, it should be possible to collapse a proton into a black hole by increasing its apparent mass. Collapse occurs when the Schwarzschild radius of the increased mass equals or exceeds the proton's radius:

$$R_s \approx 1.5E\text{-}15 \text{ m}$$
$$R_s = 2\mu/C^2 = (2)(6.672E\text{-}11)(M)/(3.0E\text{+}08)^2$$
$$\therefore M = 8.768E11 \text{ kg}$$

Hence the mass of one billion metric tons for the "neubles" that feed the process.

Gravitational effects of such a tiny hypermass are indicated by the following equations:

Gravity at 6 cm Range:
$$g_R = \mu/R^2 = (66.72)(0.06)^2 = 18533.3 \text{ m/sec}^2$$
(approximately 1900 times Earth surface gravity, g_e)

Gravity Gradient:
$$\delta g_R/\delta R = -2\mu/R^3 = (-2)(66.72)/(0.06)^3 =$$
$$-6.18E\text{+}05 \text{ sec}^{-2}$$
or, $\delta g_R/\delta R = -6.3E\text{+}04 \; g_e/m$
(changes by 630 Earth gravities in first centimeter)
Meanwhile, only four meters away . . .

Gravity at 4.06 m Range:
$$g_R = \mu/R^2 = (66.72)/(0.06+4.0)^2 = 4.23 \text{ m/sec}^2$$
(approximately 0.4 times Earth surface gravity, g_e)

Gravity Gradient:
$$\delta g_R/\delta R = -2\mu/R^3 = (-2)(66.72)/(0.06+4.0)^3 =$$
$$-1.99 \text{ sec}^{-2}$$
or, $\delta_R/\delta R = -0.203 \; g_e/m$
(changes by 0.2 Earth gravities in first meter)

So it's certainly nothing you'd want to be standing very close to. For anyone who's read my 1995 novel *Flies from the Amber* or who is otherwise familiar with the spacetime effects of a hypermass, the question of gravitational time dilation naturally occurs. Sorry, the math will disappoint you:

$$\gamma = 1 - 2\mu/(RC^2) = 1 - (2)(66.72)/(0.06)(3.0E\text{+}08)^2$$
$$\gamma = 2.47E\text{-}14$$

In other words, even at the lethal 6 cm range, time passes only 0.0000000000025% more slowly than in the outside universe. So for human beings, collapsium does not constitute a forward-only time machine unless, like Marlon's *cage de fin*, it's moving at relativistic velocity. *C'est la vie*.

As for the obvious, "Why don't the collapsium's black holes fall into each other?" the answer lies in sympathetic vibrations. This is the same principle that lets "stealth" helicopters fly silently: the sounds produced by the engine and blades are measured, and a "negative" of the wave pattern—a set of equivalent sound waves 180 degrees out of phase—is produced to cancel it. If gravity is truly the result of vibration, an equivalent damping mechanism is quite plausible.

The terms "supervacuum" and "True Vacuum" are my own; however, information on the well-studied Casimir effect and its influence on vacuum energy can be found in Phillip Gibbs' online physics FAQ at http://www.aal.co.nz/~duckett/casimir. html, or in Dr. Robert L. Forward's *Future Magic* (Avon Books, 1988), or any of countless other sources.

Given the existence of neubles, building small planets around them is a natural—albeit hideously expensive—idea. Bruno's world contains 1500 neubles, at the core of a soil-and-rock sphere 636 meters across, yielding a surface gravity of

$$g = \mu/R^2 = (6.672E-11) (1.5E16) / (636/2)^2 = 9.9 \text{m/sec}^2$$

almost exactly one gee.

For information about the theory and practice of quantum wells, wires, and dots, the best reference I've found is Richard Turton's *The Quantum Dot* (Oxford University Press, 1995), although for the past several years *Science News* magazine has run occasional short articles on the subject that have also been important in shaping my speculations. The term "wellstone" was supplied by Gary Snyder of Pioneer Astronautics.

$$\bullet \quad \bullet \quad \bullet$$

There are, of course, innumerable technical details in this book, both major and minor, only a handful of which are directly (and sketchily) addressed in this appendix. However, readers with additional questions are encouraged to pursue them. The answers may well enrich us all.

marlon

When Tamra was an eight-year-old princess and all but innu-
merate, her parents had sought an overqualified tutor, using
the carrot of housing and stipend, plus full scholarship to any
University in the solar system once the job was complete.
Marlon, who'd been among the top mathematics students in
North America's preparatory schools, had answered the ad
while summering in Tonga, and to his considerable surprise
had been accepted for the job. His higher education plans
had been indefinite anyway—many offers, none of them sat-
isfactory—so it had been easy enough to put them on hold for
two more years of sun and fun.

He hadn't counted on the princess herself, though—her
rages and giggles and thick-headed retrenchments, her mer-
ciless taunts, her utter lack of interest or respect or mathematical insight—and once his contract was up he'd been only
too happy to light out for the Mexico City School of Physical
Sciences to enjoy his eight-year free ride at the expense of
Their Majesties Longo and Piatra Lutui.

He was as surprised as anyone when Piatra died, and
Longo drank himself after her, and drowned, and Tamra was
groomed to be not only queen of Tonga, but Queen of All
Things. He was even more surprised to note, in her increasingly high-profile network appearances, that his shrill, malicious little girl had become a wry and arch and frightfully

alluring young lady, unfazed by crowds and cameras, unhindered by any appearance of self-consciousness or doubt. So when her post-coronation dick hunt was announced, he'd answered *that* ad and, to his even greater surprise, had been accepted for that job as well.

It hadn't lasted long: just six months of fighting, of constant maneuvering, of discovering she hadn't changed so much after all. And yet, *that* time Marlon hadn't been so eager to leave; he'd had to be thrown bodily from the palace by a pair of dainty robots before he'd realized he could not, in fact, smooth things over this time. And oh, how he wanted to smooth things over! In exchange for her virginity, she'd apparently taken something from him, some essential ability to be satisfied without her.

At first he'd tried to ignore it—his status as deposed First Philander of Sol made him popular enough with the ladies—but as time wore on . . . In her search for the next Philander, Tamra seemed much more selective, appearing in public on the arms of many gentlemen but taking—it was rumored—few or possibly even none of them to her bed. Marlon couldn't help but take heart from this, to approve of his being so difficult to replace. Where, after all, could a better man be found? So, cautiously and with utmost attention to his dignity and self-respect, he began once more to court her: to drop short messages into her queue, to send inexpensive but thoughtful gifts, to arrange to be "caught" by tabloid reporters in the company of this or that desirable creature at this or that noble gathering. Not so much to make her jealous as to provide the opportunity for her to reflect on his various merits.

It was working, too; Queen Tamra began replying to his messages, and over time there grew a wistful, vaguely flirtatious overtone in their conversations which he was careful to respond to only with rue and good-natured regret. *If only it were that simple, my dear* . . . Another year or two and he'd have been straddling her again, possessing the possessor of the human race, taking his pleasure from her as once he'd taken her girlhood. And filling, yes, that awful hole she'd left in his existence on the day the robots threw him out.

But then that bastard de Towaji had showed up, with his collapsides and his boyish, hat-in-hands charm and his rapidly mushrooming fortune. Also orphaned at the age of fifteen! He'd had more years to get over it, of course, and maybe *that,* finally, was what really drew Tamra to him. Either way, Marlon had found himself facedown once more on the greasy boardwalk of love. Bruno had moved in quickly, establishing his territorial claims with an ease that seemed calculated to infuriate. And he *stayed,* first six months and then twelve, and then twenty-four, forty-eight, then months without number, Tamra snuggling in the arms of her little pet genius. *Declarant*-Philander, well well.

It was hard to be sure just how big a role spite had played in Marlon's discovery of superreflectance. Not zero, certainly, and he'd approached his Declarancy with grim smugness, a sense that vindication was at last on its way. But that bastard de Towaji had been right there for the ceremony, a step below and behind his lady love, and Tamra's eyes had shown Marlon a sort of polite recognition and nothing more.

That was the day he knew he hated her, hated them both, hated everyone who'd ever lived. Marlon's evils were many decades after that in coming, but it was *that night,* bitterly humping some socialite or other, that he'd officially crossed Humanity off his list of things to bother worrying about.

Like most of history's monsters, Marlon Fineas Jimson Sykes leaves us all to wonder how things might have turned out, if this or that chance detail of his life had chanced the other way. But looking back on it, most in the Queendom would probably change nothing, even if they could. There *is* broad agreement: it has all ended well enough.

about the author

Wil McCarthy, after ten years of rocket science with Lockheed Martin, traded the hectic limelight of the space program for the peace and quiet (ha!) of commercial robotics at Omnitech, where he works as a research and development hack.

He writes a monthly column for the SciFi Channel's news magazine (www.scifi.com/sfw), and his less truthful writings have appeared in *Aboriginal SF, Analog, Interzone, Asimov's Science Fiction, Science Fiction Age,* and various anthologies. His most recent novel, *Bloom,* was selected as a *New York Times* Notable Book. Further biographical and bibliographic information is available at:

www.sff.net/people/wmccarth

IF YOU LOVED *THE COLLAPSIUM*,
BE SURE NOT TO MISS

WIL MCCARTHY'S

THE
WELLSTONE

Set in the same richly innovative future,
this novel explores the ramifications of living in
a society of immortals. . . .

Available from Bantam Spectra in March of 2003

Here is a special preview:

One man in a sphere of brass.

One man alone in the vacuum of space.

One man hurtling toward solid rock at forty meters per second—fast enough to kill him, to end his mission here and now, to cap a damnfool end on a long and decidedly damnfool life. To leave his children defenseless.

In the porthole ahead is the planette Varna, his destination, swathed in white clouds and shining seas, in grasslands, in forests whose vertical dimension is already apparent against the dinner-bowl curve of horizon. Not planet: planette. It looks small because it *is* small, barely twelve hundred meters across. Condensed matter core, fifteen hundred neubles—very nice. The surface workmanship is exquisite; he sees continents, islands, majestic little mountain ranges jutting up above the trees. Telescopes, he realizes, don't do justice to this remotest of Lune's satellites.

The man's name is Radmer, or Conrad Mursk if you're old enough. Very few people are old enough. Radmer's own age would be difficult to guess—his hair is still partly blond, his weathered skin not really all that wrinkled. He still has his teeth, although they're worn down, and a few of them are cracked or broken. But even in zero gravity, as he kicks and kicks the potter's wheel that winds the gyroscopes which keep the sphere from tumbling, there's a kind of weight or weariness to his movements that might make you wonder. Older?

To be fair, the air inside the three-meter sphere isn't very good. Cold and damp, it smells of carbon dioxide, wet brass, and the chloride tang of spent oxygen candles. Old breath and new—the only way to refresh the air is to dump it overboard, but after two and a half days he's out of candles and out of time, and there's a healthy fear stealing upon him as the moment of truth approaches. Opening the purge valve would be a highly risky stunt right now.

Giving the winding mechanism a final kick, he ratchets his chair back a few notches and unfolds the sextant. This takes several seconds—it's a complicated instrument with a great

...ny appendages. When it's locked into the appropriate ...ckets on the arms of his chair, and then properly sighted in, ...e takes a series of readings spaced five clock-ticks apart, and adjusts a pair of dials until the little brass arrow stops moving. Then, sighing worriedly, he folds the thing up again, stows it carefully in its rack, and clicks the chair forward again to kick the potter's wheel a few more times. Course correction needs a stable platform, you bet.

When he's satisfied the gyros are fully wound, he takes up the course correction chains, winces in anticipation, and jerks out the sequence the sextant has indicated. *Wham! Wham!* The sphere is kicked—hard—by explosive charges on its hull. Caps, caps, fore, starboard, starboard . . . It's quite a pummeling, like throwing himself under a team of horses, but before his head has even stopped ringing he's setting the sextant up again and retaking those critical measurements.

The planette's atmosphere is as miniature as the rest of it, and there's the problem: from wispy stratosphere to stony lithosphere is less than half a second's travel, if he comes straight in. That's not long enough for the parachute to inflate, even if his timing is perfect. To survive the impact, he has to graze the planette's edge, to cut through the atmosphere horizontally. Shooting an apple is easy; shooting its skin off cleanly is rather more difficult, especially when *you're* the bullet.

Could he have sent a message in a bottle? A dozen messages in a dozen bottles, to shower every planette from here to murdered Earth? That *would* be an empty gesture, albeit an easier one. God knows he's needed elsewhere, has been *demanded* in a dozen different elsewheres as the world of Lune comes slowly unraveled. But somehow this dubious errand has captured his imagination. No, more than that: his *hope*. Can a man live without hope? Can a world?

Alas, the sextant's news is less than ideal: he's overcorrected on two of three axes. Sighing again more heavily, he stows the thing and gets set up for the next course correction, gathering the chains up from their moorings. When he jerks

on the first one, though, no team of horses runs him ov
Nothing happens at all.

With a stab of alarm, he realizes he's been squandering
correction charges, not thinking about it, not thinking to save
a few kicks on each axis for terminal approach. Can he re-
cover? By reorienting the ship, which he needs to do for landing anyway? Yes, certainly, unless he's been *really* unlucky and
run out of charges simultaneously on all six of the sphere's or-
dinal faces.

Outside the forward porthole, there is nothing but Varna:
individual trees beneath a swirl of cloud, growing visibly.
There is, to put it mildly, little time to waste.

Attitude control is strictly manual; Radmer throws off his
safety harness and hurls himself at a set of handles mounted
on the hull's interior. They're cold, barely above freezing, and
damp enough that his fingers will slip if he doesn't grip with
all his might, which, fortunately, he does.

There's a metallic screech and groan, brass against brass,
as the outer hull begins to roll against the bearings connecting it to the inner cage, where his feet are braced. The potter's wheel and gyros hold a fixed orientation in space while
the three-meter sphere, complete with chair and storage
racks, is rotated around them. Sunlight flashes briefly through
one porthole; through the other, the green-white face of Lune,
from whence he came.

Like most men his age, Radmer is a good deal stronger
than he looks. Still, the hull's rotation is as difficult to stop as
it is to start. It's his own strength he's fighting, the momentum he himself has imparted. Despite the cold, the effort
makes him sweat inside his coat and leathers.

He'd like to move the hull so his chair is facing backward,
to serve as a crash couch. Because yes, even the *best* landing
is going to be rough. But with the starboard charges expended, that would still leave him with one uncorrectable
axis. Instead, he points the chair in the "caps" direction,
ninety degrees from where he wants it, fires two charges in
perpendicular directions, then points the chair forward again

quickly straps in, so he can take another sextant reading
the planette.

Perfect? Close enough? No, he's off again, drifting somehow from an ideal ballistic trajectory. He starts dialing for another correction, realizes he's out of time, and hurriedly stows
the sextant instead, to keep it from becoming a projectile in
its own right.

He's about to unstrap again, to face the chair aft for impact, but he's *really* out of time, the hull already singing with
atmospheric contact. So he grabs an armrest with one hand
and the parachute's ripcord with the other, and prepares to be
thrown hard against the straps.

There are prayers he could utter right now, battle hymns
he could sing, but perhaps thinking of them is enough.
Quicker, anyway; he runs through several in the blink of an
eye. And then the sphere slaps into denser air—more gently
than he's expecting. Which could be bad, which could mean
he's cut too high, his angle too shallow. Will he skip off the
planette's atmosphere to tumble back Luneward in disgrace?

Air is squealing all around him, and for a moment, he sees
Varna through three separate portholes, and hazy blue-black
sky through a fourth. He sees individual blades of grass, no
fooling, and then the ground is retreating again and it's time,
slightly *past* time, to pop the chute. The sudden weight of his
arm seems to help as he yanks the lanyard; he's looking "down"
across the sphere, decelerating hard. He hears the chute de-
ploy with a clanging of brass doors, and suddenly he *is* facing
the right way as air drag pulls it around behind the vehicle
and jerks its lines taut.

And then disaster strikes, in the form of a treetop's spreading arms. He doesn't hit them hard, but for an instant there
are actual acacia leaves snapping across the porthole glass,
and the contact is enough to set the sphere rolling around its
inner cage. Which is bad, because the chute, which hasn't
fully opened, is fouling—he can see it behind him, an orange-
and-white streamer, its hemp lines twirling together in an in-
extricable mess.

And then the blue of atmosphere is fading to black ag.
and after three long seconds of deceleration he's back, su.
denly, in zero gee. Having missed the planette. Having *actu.
ally missed the damn planette*. Through the portholes, the
slowly tumbling view is clear enough: Varna shrinking away
behind him.

Varna moving laterally?

Varna approaching again? More slowly, yes, but definitely
approaching. Because he's cut through a swath of thick atmosphere, because he's hit a tree, because he's deployed a
streamer chute that, while it couldn't quite stop him, could at
least slow him down below the planette's escape velocity.

The air doesn't whistle this time, barely puffs, barely makes
a sound at all as he falls back through it. What *does* create
sound and sensation is the water beneath the air, which he
slaps into hard, and the solid surface a couple of meters beneath that. He crashes against it and rolls; through the portholes he sees foam, blue water, blue sky, brown sand or silt
kicking off the bottom in his wake.

The sphere tumbles around the screeching gyro platform
for a few moments, but the platform is overwhelmed and
starts to tumble along as well, its bearings frozen against the
spinning hull. His chair goes with it, tumbling, and he loses
his sense of direction almost immediately. Then, with a jerk,
all movement stops. He's looking upward: sky only.

He has landed on the planette. His mad scheme has become, retroactively, a perfectly reasonable idea.

To his sides he sees fish and waving grasses, sunlight filtering down in rays through the shallow water. One side of
the sphere is higher, its porthole only half-submerged. The
shores are hidden behind the knife-edge of water against the
glass, but he does see treetops in the distance, perhaps the
very ones he struck. The porthole between his legs shows a
sandy bottom, a few crushed reeds.

He takes a few moments to gather himself—it *was* a rough
landing, and he remains quite reasonably terrified—but time
is short, and his business urgent. He finds the buckles of his

harness: damp brass, warmed by his body. He's unbuck-
it a hundred times today; the action is as automatic as
oughing.

Being a sphere, his carriage-sized spaceship was expected
to roll a bit on landing, coming to rest in an unknown orientation. For this reason, the sphere has two exit hatches, one
presently underwater, the other above it, pointing skyward at
a cockeyed angle. He climbs to this one, using the potter's
wheel and gyro assembly for a staircase.

He moves carefully; it's a small world, yes, but thanks to
the planette's superdense neutronium core, gravity here is
"gee," or about the same as at the surface of Lune. Or, reaching back a ways into the mists of time, Earth. With one hand
he grasps a slick handle on the hull; with the other, the lock-
ing wheel on the hatch itself. It spins easily—no screeching
or sticking—and he's abstractly relieved by this.

Like many wise men, Radmer worries a lot, and this errand has given his imagination more than the usual to work
with. But while the sphere was built in a hurry, he has to give
a nod to the smiths and armorers and watchmakers of
Highrock, who clearly knew their business well enough.

Having landed in one piece, this craft has every chance of
taking him home again. Compared to this planette, Lune is a
huge target, virtually impossible to miss; so as long as the mo-
tors ignite and the parachute opens cleanly, he should be
back in the war by next Friday at the latest.

Back in the death, the misery, the collapse of nations. The
people of Lune are not Radmer's children per se, although a
great many of them are, in one way or another, his descen-
dants. And the world itself is his, or was long ago. How gladly
he would die to protect it!

His hatch flips inward, clanks against the hull, then hangs
down, swinging back and forth, while Radmer works out his
handholds on the outer hull and, finally, lifts himself through.

It's like climbing up into a pleasant dream. It's warm out
here, and the bright sky and brighter sun cast brilliant reflections on the lapping waters of the sea, which, spanning eighty

meters at its widest, stretches nearly from horizon to hor.
The shoreline is a few meters of pristine beach, fading b.
into palm trees and elephant grass. The breeze smells sweet
pungent, like ice cream and salt somehow. Like fresh bee.
and flowers.

Farther back, behind the planette's round edge, rise a pair
of low hills, green with pine and acacia, and on one of these
hills is exactly what Radmer has come here to find, what the
astronomer Rigby has claimed to see from his mountain ob-
servatory on the clearest of nights: a little white cottage of
wellstone marble.

Silently, on some great universal scorecard, Radmer's obsession ticks over from "reasonable" to "downright sensible."
So like any dutiful soldier, he strips off his coat and riding
leathers, then hops in the water and swims for it.

It isn't far. Soon he is dripping on the white sands of the
beach, strolling in his felt johnnysuit beneath the shade of
palms, on a course for the not-so-distant hills. The air is hazy,
perhaps by design; it enhances the illusion of distance, of space.
He loses sight of the cottage as he plunges into the chest-
high wall of grass, then is startled at how quickly it reappears
again, immediately before him.

Overgrown, yes, overshadowed by vegetation. But certainly not a ruin, sitting here in this little glade or clearing on
the hillside. Nor has it been abandoned. Kneeling in the dirt
before it is the figure of a naked man, white hair frizzed and
trailing to his waist.

You know that feeling, when you see something at once
ancient and familiar, when your neck prickles and your stomach flutters and all your little hairs stand at attention? This is
how Radmer feels as he approaches the cottage, as he eye-
balls the naked man kneeling there in front of it.

He considers kneeling himself, but rejects the idea.

"Bruno," he says instead, from ten meters away. "Bruno de
Towaji." A whole string of titles could be appended to the
name, both fore and aft, but applying them to this dismal figure seems inappropriate. Still, there is no question in Radmer's

, or in his mind. There is no mistaking that face. True, the
̶ges of time are apparent; the Olders age in slow but very
̶rticular ways. Hair and beard faded yellow-white, yes, and
̶rown out to a length past which it simply frays and abrades.
The skin smooth, but deeply freckled and tanned with the
weary brown of accumulated melanin, sharply creased in its
various corners and crannies. Teeth worn to chalky nubs in that
slack, hanging jaw.

Radmer himself looks somewhat like this, but with his
shorter hair and longer teeth, and the fact that he's clothed, it
isn't quite so apparent. And though the armies to which he
has formally belonged are all dust and gone, he still carries
himself like a soldier, while the man in the dirt—digging up
yams with his bare hands, Radmer sees now—has the absent,
casual quality of a sleepwalker.

And something more: the eyes flicking slowly from here to
there, taking in the house, the forest, the soft ground beneath
them, the sea. Lingering overlong on the distant brass sphere,
and on Radmer himself—disturbances in this long-familiar
environment. But he's not really seeing them. Not seeing at
all. Or rather: seeing but not processing. Not affected by
what is seen.

The old man rises, clutching two small yams in each hand,
and begins walking—not limping or shuffling—toward the
little house. Radmer follows.

"De Towaji, sir. Sire. I need to speak with you."

The old man pauses, casts a cloudy, troubled glance over
his shoulder, then continues on.

This is a condition Radmer has heard of: neurosensory
dystrophia—pathways worn smooth in the brain through constant, repetitive stimulation. When the nervous system is old
and the daily routine goes on unbroken for years or decades,
its victims can be trapped by it. He's heard of couples and
even whole villages succumbing, but typically it's the people
who live alone—especially in isolated areas—who are most at
risk.

He imagines Bruno de Towaji performing these same ac-

tions day after day, varying little or not at all. Like an anim
fossil. Like a ghost, haunting this place, oblivious to the fa
of his own demise.

The good news is that the symptoms are temporary, subsiding soon after the routine itself is interrupted. The arrival
of a visitor is normally sufficient. But barring strange mira-
cles, de Towaji must have been here on the planette for a long
time indeed—much longer than Radmer cares to think
about. Whole histories come and gone, an unthinkable span
of time.

Radmer follows along into the shade of the overhanging
forest, and then the old man enters the cottage through an
open doorway that looks like it may never have had a door of
any kind, or even a curtain. The windows are the same.
Probably there's no winter here, perhaps no serious weather
of any kind. Rigby could confirm that. Still, there's something
unsavorily primeval about a house fully open on the sides.

The inside is a single room, shockingly clean, dominated
by a water fountain made, like the house and floor, of white
wellstone marble. Here de Towaji kneels again, and patiently
washes the four yams he's retrieved.

Radmer tries again. "I suspect you can hear me, Sire.
Perhaps you'll remember an architect by the name of Mursk?
Conrad Mursk? We worked together once, long ago. Before
that, I was a companion to your son."

When the yams are clean, de Towaji sets them down on
the floor, rises again, and moves to a corner of the house,
where a pile of small stones rests atop a little shelf. Flint? For
starting a cooking fire? Surely raw yams would have busted
the poor man's guts out long ago. He then turns toward the
house's only exit and commences that slow, deliberate walk
again. When Radmer blocks the way, de Towaji literally runs
into him.

Then blinks and looks him over.

"Sire," Radmer says.

Slowly, the old man nods. "Ah. Ah. I . . . know you."

"Yes, Sire."

Mursk."

"Yes, Sire. Very good."

"The architect. You . . . crushed the moon. Squoze it."

Radmer glances behind him at the half-disc of Lune in the sky. The clouds, the continents, the splatters of ocean . . . . But this isn't a map. This is the world itself, seen from a height of fifty thousand kilometers. "We crushed it together, Sire. Long ago."

Gruffly: "You're . . . in my way."

Radmer can't bring himself to bar the doorway any longer. Bowing, he steps back and to the side, allowing de Towaji to pass. At once, the old man's expression eases.

"Forgive me, Sire. I don't know if I'm rescuing you, or desecrating . . . Excuse me! Sire!"

Impatience is a rare emotion among the Olders, but seeing de Towaji prepare to ignore him again, Radmer feels it now, and dares to grab his long-ago master by the arm.

"Bruno! I have little time for this. Rouse yourself and listen to me: a great evil has been loosed upon that squozen moon of ours. Its future is now very much in peril."

The old man frowns, and it is no regal frown meant to convey official displeasure, but a private and unconscious one. A gesture of simple unhappiness.

"Future," the old man muses, or perhaps recites. He continues looking down the path ahead, deeper into the forest. "I remember that word. Where is the future? When will it get here?"

"I fear it will not, Sire."

De Towaji's gaze clears a bit, and a look of pained amusement passes briefly over his features. He speaks very slowly. "Lad, I guarantee it will not. All these . . . futures we thought we were building. Where are they? In the past. This is the past, by the time I finish saying so." He pauses for a long moment to make the point, then adds, "There is no future, only past."

Now Radmer is angry. "I'm not here to debate the semantics of it, Sire. People are dying as we speak, and still others

are being enslaved. Millions more are at risk, and *there's* an[
thing to allow into our past, if it's within our power to prever[
it."

Bruno tries to pull away. "I'm in the past as well, lad. Leave me." Then, more regally: *"Leave me."*

"I won't," Radmer tells him. "Not yet—not until you've heard me out."

Resistance ceases; a kind of bitter calm settles over de Towaji. He is waking up, yes, and he doesn't like it. The look is clear in his eyes: a fear of being needed again, of bearing up under that burden after being free of it for so very long. Radmer understands, suddenly, that the old man's isolation and senility did not come upon him by accident.

His grip tightens, and his voice is almost cruel as he says, "Even if you were *dead* I would make you listen, Sire. Because I fancy you can help us, and I don't much care if it pleases you. Where else have we got to turn? Nowhere. And when I speak the name of our peril, I think you might even *want* to help."

"Unlikely. You have no idea how wearily I washed up on this shore, lad. Not the least beginning of an idea."

Tightly: "I fancy I do, Sire. I've been depended on a time or two myself. And we live on, don't we? Never too old to be bothered, to be mined for blood and sweat, to be dusted off and put to use again in one way or another. Not even a grave to rest in, not for the likes of us. But the alternative—to live on with no purpose at all—is appalling and obscene."

Finally, Bruno de Towaji matches Radmer's anger, and meets his gaze. "You think so, do you? Smug bastard. Speak the name of your peril, then, and begone from my sight."

Radmer does as he's told, and has the grim pleasure of watching the old man's face light up with a terrible mix of wonder and righteous anger and, yes, even fear.

Now de Towaji is fully awake, blinking, looking Radmer up and down. "Lune, you say? The collapsiter grid is gone. Did I dream that? Between the stars we travel no more. How did you get here, lad? And . . . how will you return?"

Radmer feels the corners of his mouth begin to stir. Seeing Bruno again has brought back a lot of memories, a lot of old grief. With the clarity of hindsight, he does feel some understanding of his bonds to this man, but they were formed and broken long ago, in events so huge that from the inside they hadn't looked like anything at all. Joyrides and camp riots, the green virile fires of youth.

But this is too practical a question for a man who wants to be left alone. Radmer senses that a hurdle has been crossed, a new cascade of events set in motion. He will be taking this man, this intellect, this trove of living history back to Lune with him. And in that moment he dares, for the first time in months, to hope.

Come visit

BANTAM SPECTRA

on the INTERNET

Spectra invites you to join us
at our on-line home.

You'll find:

< Interviews with your favorite authors and
excerpts from their latest books
< Bulletin boards that put you in touch with
other science fiction fans, with Spectra
authors, and with the Bantam editors who
bring them to you
< A guide to the best science fiction re-
sources on the Internet

Join us as we catch you up with all of Spectra's finest
authors, featuring monthly listings of upcoming titles
and special previews, as well as contests, interviews,
and more! We'll keep you in touch with the field, both
its past and its future—and everything in between.

Look for the Spectra Spotlight
on the World Wide Web at:

http://www.bantamdell.com.

SF 30 4/02